THE FAR CRY / THE S(

A Fredric Brown Double-Novel

THE
SCREAMING
MIMI

FREDRIC
BROWN

THE
FAR
CRY

Double
Novel

• • • • • • •

Bruin
Books

Designed and edited by Jonathan Eeds.

Cover design by Michelle Policicchio.

Original cover art provided by the Viet Hung Gallery, 90 Nguyen Hue Street, Ho Chi Minh City, VN.

A very special thanks to Barry N. Malzberg for his continued support.

Additional thanks to Mark Terry of Facsimile Dust Jackets LLC for supplying the British first edition dust jacket image of THE FAR CRY, which our artists drew inspiration from for our cover art. Mark's website can be found at www.facsimiledustjackets.com.

This book was crafted in the USA but is printed globally.

ISBN 978-0-9883062-9-5

Published September, 2016
Bruin Books, LLC
Eugene, Oregon, USA

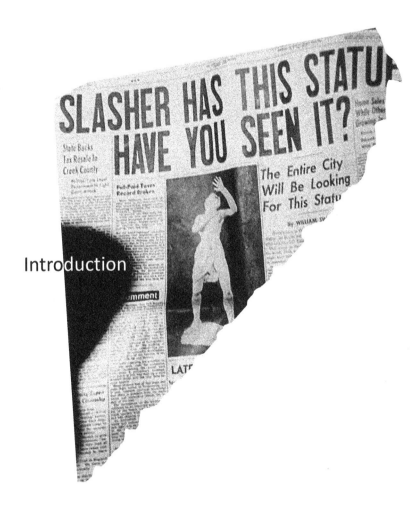

Introduction

Divided Selves, Imprisoned Souls

Barry N. Malzberg

Fred Brown worked as a skip-tracer for a while; he had a number of jobs, notably in linotyping before writing became his sole professional activity, and it must have been this part of his biography which—along with his long experience as a steady consumer of alcohol—had the most profound influence upon his fiction. What skip-tracing taught him was the fluidity of identity, its central deceit, the arbitrary nature of lives and occupation . . . his deadbeats could change residence, occupations, roles, resumes with criminal dispatch. And of course they were criminals, that fluidity was part of the con (as we are learning upon national stages larger than Milwaukee in this Year of our Lord) and it was the propelling aspect of Brown's fiction. Nothing could be trusted, nothing was stable or as it appeared to be and as Brown's protagonists and their equally evasive cops and victims wandered through the rubble of their lives, the central message was stated by the author himself as the last line of his 1949 novelette . . . "Nothing matters." Which is just a variant of course of arguing that everything matters. Brown could have had it both ways: synchronicity was his specialty. He was a small, restless guy addicted to long bus rides. Nothing could keep him in place until emphysema got him. Two wives, two sons, an improvised career.

Brown (1909-1972) carries one distinction which is at

the heart of that fluidity: he was the only writer in the United States in the twentieth century who was equally prominent, equally successful in two genres. His mysteries beginning in 1947 were absolutely distinctive and the first of them, *The Fabulous Clipjoint*, was the first winner of the new Mystery Writers of America Edgar Award for the best first novel of 1947. By that year Brown was already a well-known science fiction story, an important if not particularly prolific constituent of John Campbell and Astounding's Golden Age, who had published one novelette (*Arena*, 1945) which was the basis of a *Star Trek* adaptation decades later, was anthologized in the major Science Fiction Hall of Fame anthology Robert Silverberg edited for the Science Fiction Writers of America in 1970, and Brown had also been a significant contributor to the earliest issues of Horace Gold's innovative Galaxy Magazine in the early 1950's. Brown wrote science fiction at shorter lengths with great originality and force, he wrote short-shorts (stories under 2000 words) with even greater originality and force and published several volumes in that form, all of them collected into the major volume *From These Ashes* by the New England Science Fiction Society in the early 90's. Many of those short-short stories achieved the kind of peculiar fame which can most irritate writers . . . they became utterly detached from the author. Millions knew the plot of those stories but would misascribe them to someone else (often Isaac Asimov) or assume that like limericks and dirty jokes they had some-how like the earliest amoebas or mollusks been generated by the sea. The most famous of these famous detached stories is probably *Answer*, the one about the group of scientists who invent the ultimate computer, the ultimate seer and put to it as the first and great question: "Tell us, is there a God?" A slash of lightning, a brutal roar and then the ex-tinguishing of all lights in the Great Dome. "There is now," says an enormous voice.

Well, that was Fred Brown . . . he was a man who got to the point. The science fiction, more than half a century after his last published story (a weak collaboration in Fantasy &

Science Fiction) is affixed to whatever part of the canon which may survive, fragments to shore amongst all the ruins and *What Mad Universe* (1949), the first of his five science fiction novels remains probably the most vicious, insightful, paradigmatic anatomization of science fiction fandom's grandiosity, madness and solipsism that has ever been published. (I had a try at this subject 23 years later in *Gather In The Hall of the Planets* and Donald Wollheim could think of nothing better to put as a sell-line than "Not since *What Mad Universe* has there been a novel like this". (I had more sex but Brown, a quarter of a century earlier, gave me about three fifths of the insight.) *The Lights In The Sky Are Stars* (1953), about an astronaut who did not quite go to the stars, moody and technologically phobic foreshadows my *Beyond Apollo* by two decades and again if I had more data, he was there all those years earlier with foreshadowing and original insight.

So as a science fiction writer I can revere this guy, quirky and at times as causelessly dismissive as his contempt for the category itself could be. (He warned his friend Phil Klass when *What Mad Universe* was published, "Phil, they are taking over. The fans are taking over. They will occupy everything in twenty years. There won't even be any room left for writers like us.") As a mystery writer he was not quite as innovative, probably because the mystery field as he encountered it in the 1940's was already a good deal more literarily sophisticated than science fiction, but he was considerably more prolific and perhaps in his time more influential in this category. Science fiction in the forties was growing, changing almost monthly, developing from a hundred sources in a thousand directions, the category itself as a self-defined branch of literature was not even twenty years old at the beginning of that decade. (The first specialized science fiction magazine and the first use of "science fiction" as a defining term had been originated by Hugo Gernsback in 1926.) The mystery had a far longer, more embracing history: putting aside Conan Doyle, Chesterton, Milne, the field had found its most important voices and direction in a

hundred outlets (science fiction had no more than five magazines until the 1940's) and by the *Black Mask*. Raymond
Chandler and Cornell Woolrich, emergent in the 1930's, had
attained protocols and narrative attacks of great force and
distinction. A hundred flowers were blooming. One of those
flowers—with his trick plots, desperate cynicism, down-and-
out-in-Milwaukee ambiance was a certain Fred Brown and
the Edgar was proclamation of his impact, but he was in J.T.
McIntosh's three hundred there. In science fiction he was
nonpareil.

The Screaming Mimi and *The Far Cry*, novels both
absolutely typical of his output and—because there is no way
in which Fred Brown could be defined as "typical"—
absolutely distinctive evoke Brown's life, works and attitude
with absolute conviction and in his dragged-out, doll-driven,
doll-mystified characters he can be said to not only refract
down-rent Wisconsin but cast headlight beams on the serial
killer Greatest Hits novels which were to come. Murder
more for fun than profit, all of it taking place on the
backstage, somewhere in the dark and incessant woods
which circled the city and rotted in counterpoint to its
jukeboxes. Anita Ekberg was a victim in the 1958 film
adaptation of *Screaming Mimi* and she is as forgotten now
as Fred Brown's Milwaukee has been forgotten as the
generator of LaFollete and Joseph McCarthy. But I would
suggest that his crazy world lives on and that the light cast
by the headlights of the buses he would ride day and night
while dreaming his plot illumines our own quirky and
terrible time with a harshness we might well misidentify as
knowledge.

New Jersey: August 2016

THE FAR CRY

THE FAR CRY

FREDRIC BROWN

BRUIN CRIMEWORKS

[1]

Sudden terror in her eyes, Jenny backed away from the knife, her hand groping behind her for the knob of the kitchen door. She was too frightened to scream and anyway there was no one to hear, no one but the man who came toward her with the knife and he was mad, he must be mad. Her hand found the knob and turned it; the door swung outward into the night and she whirled through it, running. Death ran after her.

Eight years passed.

Then:

What happened started quite casually, as most things do. It started on the eighteenth of May, a Thursday.

There was a man named George Weaver who had just taken a room at La Fonda, a hotel in Taos, New Mexico. He had just finished shaving; he was wiping the residue of lather from his face with the moistened end of a towel when the phone rang. He hung the towel over the edge of the washbowl and went out to the hotel room to answer the phone. "Hello," he said.

"George Weaver?" The voice was familiar but he couldn't place it. He said, "Yes, this is Weaver."

"This is Luke, George. Luke Ashley."

Weaver's face lighted up. "The hell it is! What are you doing in Taos? How'd you know I was here? Where are you?"

The telephone chuckled. "Which question do I answer first?"

"Where are you?"

"At the hotel desk downstairs."

"Then the other questions can wait. Come on up, Luke."

Weaver cradled the phone, then opened the door of his room and left it ajar while he went back into the bathroom and finished drying his face. A chance to see Luke Ashley was both pleasant and unexpected. He hadn't seen Luke in—it must be over two years now.

Looking at his face in the bathroom mirror, Weaver wondered how much change Luke would see in it. The last few months had been pretty hard on that face; they'd done things to it—and it hadn't been much of a face to begin with. Always a little thin, it looked gaunt now and the eyes had a haunted look.

He heard Ashley come in and met him halfway across the room. "Luke, old boy. How in *hell* did you know I was here? I didn't know I was stopping over here myself until I checked in an hour ago. Intended to drive on through to Santa Fe."

Ashley was tall, thin, balding; he looked a bit like William Gillette as Sherlock Holmes—a very appropriate resemblance, Weaver had often thought, for a writer of true crime stories for the fact detective magazines. And Ashley sometimes humorously capitalized on it. As now, he said:

"Elementary, my dear Weaver. I saw your car parked outside—a green Chevy coupe with a Missouri license." Ashley sprawled himself into an easy chair and threw his long legs over the arm of it. "Put on a shirt, George, and we'll go down and have a drink somewhere."

"But how did you—? That car's only a year old, Luke, and you never saw it. How'd you know what kind of car I had?"

Ashley sighed. "All right, if we must get down to mundane facts. I'm on my way to the coast—L. A.—and I routed myself through Kansas City so I could stop over a few hours to see you. You'd left only a day ahead of me and Vi told me you were heading for Santa Fe and what route you planned to take. She described your car and gave me the license number in case I caught up with you, so I've been watching for it. When I got to Taos just now, I drove once around the plaza and there you were parked in front of the hotel here. So I came in and asked the clerk if they had any George Weavers on hand, and they did."

Weaver nodded, "You must really have been high-balling to catch up to me when I had a full day's start. Well, not too much, maybe; I've been taking my time driving, watching the scenery and not pushing too many hours a day. I've got orders not to be in a hurry about anything. I—I suppose Vi told you about that?"

"A little. I didn't talk to her very long. What are your plans, George?"

Weaver had taken a sport shirt from the suitcase open on the bed and had put it on. Now, buttoning it, he walked over to the window and stood looking out. He said, "Look at those God damned beautiful mountains. I could look at them all summer—and maybe I will. I *was* heading for Santa Fe, but now I don't know if I'll go the last seventy miles or not. Hell, it's five years now since I lived there and I don't know whether I want to see the people I used to know then or not. Haven't kept up correspondence with any of them. Vi keeps up correspondence with Madge Burke there, the girl who used to work in the restaurant with her, but that's about our only contact.

"I like this place, Luke. Partly because I don't know anybody here, partly because it's smaller than Santa Fe and more peaceful. Besides, it's got something; I don't know what. I feel better already, I think. Anyway, I'm going to stay here at least long enough to look around. If I find a place I'd like to live in, at a price that I can afford, I'll stay all summer."

Ashley nodded. "Taos is a good little town. Beautiful summer climate—it's even better than Santa Fe in the summer. Same altitude, seven thousand. Winters are colder than Santa Fe, I'm told, but that isn't a factor if you're not staying that long anyway. And it's an artists' colony, which means there are interesting people to meet if you get tired of being a hermit and want company."

"You sound as though you know the place pretty well, Luke."

"Just from having spent a week or so here three summers ago. I was writing up the Manby murder case. That was a screwy deal if there ever was one. Know anything about it?"

Weaver shook his head.

"You'll probably hear about it if you stay here; it's a local legend. And there was another pretty good murder case here seven—no, eight years ago. Girl named Jenny Ames. I tried to get enough dope to write that one up too while I was working on Manby, but I couldn't get enough solid facts to make a good story out of it. And they never caught the killer anyway, and that's a bad angle for a fact crime story."

Weaver said "I think I remember the name. That would have been while I was living in Santa Fe, and I think I read something about it in the papers. What are you working on now, Luke?"

"Put your shirt tail in and I'll tell you over a drink. Or leave your shirt tail out—nobody in Taos will care.

Weaver put it in. They went down to the plaza and wandered around it and into El Patio; they had cool, tinkling Tom Collinses under a huge sunshade in the open air.

Luke Ashley took a deep breath. "It *is* nice here, George. I'd forgotten what it's like to breathe this air. It's mañana country, and picturesque as hell. Those blanket Indians you see on the plaza, they're not Chamber of Commerce window dressing. There's a thousand-Indian pueblo a couple miles from town and that's the way they really live and dress. And if you get to know any of the Taos Indians, you'll like them; they're real people."

"You haven't told me yet what you're doing, Luke. Why the trip to Los Angeles and what will you be doing there and for how long?"

"Just hadn't got around to telling you; didn't mean to be mysterious about it. Regal Pictures is making a documentary on the big-shot gangsters of the Prohibition era in Chicago, centering around the Valentine Day massacre there. I've done a lot of writing about those days and they hired, me as technical adviser. It's a three-month contract, so I'm driving out in order to have my car to get around in while I'm there. Left Chicago three days ago and I'm due in L. A. in three more. That's all about me.

"Now how about you, George? Vi told me you were coming out here for the summer and that she would join you later, but she—uh—"

"Acted a little funny about it?"

"Well I wouldn't say that— Oh, hell, she *did* act a little funny about it. If you don't mind telling me, what's the score?"

Weaver made wet circles on the table with the bottom of his glass. He saw from the whiteness of his knuckles that his hand was clenched too tightly around the drink and he made his fingers relax.

He said, "A little case of overwork, Luke, that's all. They called it a breakdown. I was in a sanatorium for six weeks. I'd been working too hard and all of a sudden I hit the ceiling and came apart.

"The stay at the san got me over the worst of it but the doc said I'd better get away from work and spend the summer somewhere trying not to think about—" He managed a grin. "—about whatever business it was that I was in back in Kansas City. I'm supposed to forget it completely, so how can I talk about it? If you happen to remember that business I was in, don't mention real estate to me"

"Real estate? You mean that stuff about land and buildings?"

Weaver pretended to shudder. "Maybe that was it. Anyway, I'm ordered to paint pictures or write poetry or something, for the summer. To get away from everything and into something else. Three months at least, maybe longer. To do anything that interests me—doesn't matter much what—as long as I don't make any money at it."

"Listen, George, with this legal contract, I'm pretty solvent. If I can lend you some dough—"

"Thanks a lot, Luke. But I think I'll get by. I had some pretty stiff losses back in Kansas City—worrying about them and trying to make up for them is part of what started my breakdown—but I cashed out a few thousand bucks, enough to get by on for the summer, even for the fall if I stay that long, and still have a few bucks left to start myself in business again when I've got myself completely straightened out. I sold out my business so I wouldn't have to think about, it, but it won't take much capital to get started again. That's one good thing about real estate—if you know the game and know the town you're operating in, and I know Kansas City inside out, all you need to start out is enough dough to rent an office and finance yourself a little while. You get listings and take a cut on selling property that doesn't belong to you."

Ashley nodded. "Well, if you run short I can spare some. How long is Vi staying in K. C., before she comes out to join you?"

"She's coming in two or three weeks. We're sending the girls to a summer camp back in the Ozarks—the same one Ellen went to last year, and this year Betty is old enough to go too. But the camp doesn't open until the first of June so Vi is sticking it out back there till she can get the girls into the camp. She'll join me after that."

"How old are your girls now, George?"

"Ellen's six and a half. Betty'll be five in two weeks—just the minimum age the camp will take. They're good kids. Drive me crazy when I'm around them, but I miss them already."

"Do you good to be away from them, though. If peace and quiet is what the doctor ordered—"

"It is. Peace and quiet and anything non-commercial I can get myself interested in. And the girls won't mind being in camp. Anyway, Ellen won't—she was crazy about the place last summer, and I guess Betty'll like it too. And they'll be better off in camp than—"

He broke off, realizing what he'd been about to say. You don't tell even your closest friend that your children might be better off getting away from their mother for a while—and it was probably an exaggeration anyway; Vi wasn't that bad.

If Ashley guessed, he didn't ask. He said, "Something's happened to our drinks. Mice, maybe?"

"Could be. Should we have another?"

Ashley looked at his watch. "Maybe we should eat. It's only noon, but I've been driving since six-thirty on a light breakfast. Are you hungry?"

"No—but my appetite's been off. I didn't have any breakfast but coffee this morning, so I should probably try to put something down."

"Let's go, then. There used to be a place here—up the street toward the post office—called La Doña Luz. Wonderful grub. Duncan Hines rating. Run by a guy called Frenchy. If it's still here—"

It was still there. They ate mountain trout and Weaver found he had an appetite after all. It was the best meal he'd eaten in a long time.

La Doña Luz had a bar but they walked back to El Patio so they could have their after-lunch drink in the open air again. It was that kind of weather.

They talked about old times together—pleasant, casual conversation. Nothing sinister, nothing sinister at all. Just times they'd gone fishing together, poker games they'd played in, a couple of hunting trips they'd shared—all over two leisurely drinks in the leisurely sunshine.

After a little while Weaver said, "Let's take a drive a-round. I want a closer look at those mountains. I'll do the driving if you're tired. And, by the way, I'm getting more and more sure that I want to stay here for the summer if I can find a place."

"Okay, let's go. And I'm rested up now, so I'll drive. Let's take my buggy; it's a convertible and I've got the top down."

Ashley drove. Through Arroyo Seco and toward the mountains, along a road that got rougher the farther they went. After a while Ashley waved a hand toward an adobe house set back about twenty yards from the road the first house they'd seen in about an eighth of a mile. He said, "That's where Jenny Ames got it."

"Who?"

"Jenny Ames. I mentioned her before. Victim in the mur-der case I couldn't get enough data on. Wasted two days be-fore I saw I wasn't getting anywhere and gave up. But I got a good price for the Manby story so my stay here paid off."

They were past the house by then. Weaver had looked at it back over his shoulder until a turn in the road cut off his view.

"Nice place for a murder," he said. "Plenty isolated."

"Yes, plenty. It's the last house back on this road, nothing between it and the mountains. The road peters out from here; we won't be able to go much farther." He slowed down and pointed to his left. "The girl ran away from the house, back that way toward the foothills; took the murderer—what the hell was his name?—almost a quarter of a mile to catch her."

The road got worse. Ashley decided they'd better turn around and did so at the first wide place he came to.

Weaver asked, "Anybody living there now?"

"Where? Oh, you mean the murder place? It looked deserted when we passed it just now. Nobody was living there three years ago when I tried to write up the story. Up to that time nobody'd lived there since the murder."

"Supposed to be haunted or something?"

"Not that I heard of. Don't know why it would be since the murder itself happened so far away from the building. No, I think the main reason is that it's a little too far from town for most people. And it wouldn't be much good for year-round living because the road gets pretty bad. And there are mostly Spanish people living out this way, and they wouldn't be interested because the land's no good and they want places they can farm, or at least have a garden. Land around there's just sand and sagebrush."

"But there must be a hell of a view from that place. How far is it from Taos?"

"Ummm—we came through Arroyo Seco and that's eight miles from Taos. I'd guess that house is another mile and a half or so. Say nine or ten miles from Taos. Why? You're not thinking of buying the place, are you?"

"No, not buying it. But if I could rent it for the summer, why not? There ought to be peace and quiet enough to last me the rest of my life, way out here. Know anything wrong with the idea?"

They were back at the place again and Ashley stopped the car. He looked dubiously across the creek at the house beyond. "Pretty primitive, pal. No plumbing: you'd have to carry water from the creek here—although that's only a few yards and the water's probably purer than you'd get out of a faucet. But there's electricity. And God knows there's isolation if that's what you want. Shall we go up and look at it closer?"

"Sure."

Ashley drove the convertible across the little wooden bridge that spanned the creek between the road and the house.

It was a three-room flat-roofed adobe building. Behind it, ten yards back, stood a rickety wooden outhouse and ten yards beyond that along the same path was a wooden shed. They walked around the house; its windows were boarded and both of the doors were locked.

"Good solid construction," Ashley said. "Cost a little to fix up, but not much. Labor's cheap here." He peered through a knothole in one of the boards across a window. "The furniture's still in there. Looks like the same stuff that was there when I was inside the place three years ago which means it's the stuff Nelson left."

Weaver was staring up at the mountains. He asked, "Who's Nelson?"

"I remembered the name. The guy who killed Jenny Ames. Want to hear about it?"

"Not especially. Let's get back into town and find out who owns the place. If I could get it cheap enough— My God, look at that view, I could look at it all summer."

"All right, maybe you will. Come on."

They drove back to town and stopped at the Taos Inn, just before they would have reached the plaza. There was a patio there, too, and Ashley led Weaver to one of the tables. "Order yourself a drink," he said. "I'll go find out about that place for you. I'm going to see a guy called Doughbelly Price."

"You're kidding."

"I'm not. That's his name and he either handles or has a line on most of the property that's for sale or rent around here. And, at least three years ago, he had the handling of the Nelson place."

"But why should you do it, Luke? At least, why shouldn't I come along?"

"And talk about a forbidden subject? Nix, my friend, remember that you don't know what real estate is. Relax and wrap yourself around a cold drink while I find out the facts."

Weaver wrapped himself around a cold drink. In half an hour Ashley was back, grinning. "You got yourself a house," he said. "For free."

"What do you mean, for free?"

"Well, the next thing to it, anyway. Wait a second, I'll get us some coffee; I don't want another drink because I want to do some more driving. Or would you rather have another Tom?"

"Coffee sounds good."

Ashley went into the bar and then came back and sat down across from Weaver. "Coffee coming up. Okay, here's the deal on the house. Price says he's been trying to sell the place and that the house and four acres are listed with him at two thousand bucks—but it's been marked that for eight years and no takers. Furniture—he says it's not anything fancy, but that it's usable—goes with it. That's if you want to buy it, and I told him you didn't."

"Right," Weaver said. "Now get to the for free business you were talking about."

"Price wants somebody to live there for a while to break the jinx, as he puts it. He'll let you have it for the summer if you'll fix it up and live there. He says he thinks the few repairs the house itself will need shouldn't run over about fifty bucks to get the place fixed up livably. That sounds pretty cheap but you can get labor out there for three bucks or so a day.

"He guesses it'll cost you another fifty to get the furniture fixed up, and that you'll probably want to add a few pieces if two of you will be living there and that'll run you another fifty or a hundred bucks—unless you want to get fancy about it. But he says if you improve the place that much you can live there this summer—or as late into the fall as you want to—for free. He says he probably wouldn't rent or sell it this summer anyway so he's got nothing to lose and with that improvement to the place, plus the fact that the jinx has been broken by somebody's living there, he'll have a better chance of selling or renting it next year.

The coffee came. Weaver sipped his, looking up at the bright blue sky over the rim of his cup.

Ashley said, "I told him you'd let him know by tomorrow."

"We can let him know today," Weaver said. "Maybe this Doughbelly Price—*is* there such a character, by the way, or are you kidding me?"

"It could happen only in Taos," Ashley said, "but there is such a character. And if you strain like that at a gnat, he has his office next to that of Jimmy Valentine, who is a public accountant. No, I'm not kidding you."

"All right, I'll believe you. What I started to say was that maybe this Doughbelly Price is crazy, but I'm not. I'm taking him up on that deal. As soon as we're through with this coffee."

"Good. I'll go around with you, and after that I'll have to push on. I want to get to L. A. as soon as I can and if I can put another couple of hundred miles behind me before I hole-in for the night, I'll be that much closer."

Doughbelly Price was a little man in a big Stetson. He shook hands with Weaver and said, "Maybe I'm nuts for making you a deal like that, but I've been stuck with that joint for eight years. Maybe you can take the curse off of it."

Weaver grinned at him. "What do I sign?"

"What do you want to sign anything for? I couldn't read it anyway. Here's the keys. Go on out and fix it up and live there."

Weaver had himself a house.

He tried to talk Price into having a drink to seal the bargain, but Price said he had another appointment. He said, "Listen, Weaver, if you don't know nobody around here, you'll get yourself cheated less if you just get a contractor to do that fixing. Ellis DeLong, maybe. Unless you're a contractor yourself and know the local angles you ain't going to save yourself no money by hiring your own labor."

After they left Doughbelly Price's office Weaver had a little trouble persuading Luke Ashley to have one final drink for a stirrup cup before he left, but he finally prevailed. "All right, Luke said finally, "but better watch it yourself, George, in this altitude. Yes, you lived this high in Santa Fe, but not recently; you're used to Kansas City."

They had the final drink together in the little bar of La Doña Luz.

Ashley said, "Listen, George, I've got an idea. Living right there where the Jenny Ames murder happened, you might get a chance to dig in on it—and you might find it interesting to do the digging. If you do, and can round up enough facts to let me write the case up—after my three months in Holly-wood—I'll cut you in on the deal. My by-line, of course, be-cause that'll make it sell quicker, but I'll give you a cut of the check, half or more, depending on how much of the work is yours and how much is mine. And the true detectives are pay-ing good rates right now. You might get enough out of it to cover what fixing that house up is going to cost you—and that would make your rent for the summer really for free."

"Nuts to Jenny Ames." Weaver said. "I'm out here to rest up, not to play detective on an eight-year-old murder case.

"All right, but sooner or later you'll get bored resting up —and the idea might sound better to you. If you change your mind before the summer's over, the deal stands. You might find it more interesting than you think. It was a Lonely Heart murder."

"What's a Lonely Heart murder?"

"That's one of the things you'll find out when you start digging in. Well, George, I've really got to go. It was swell see-ing you again."

"Thanks for everything, Luke. And that was a good tag line you used just now; I *will* have to dig in enough to find out what the hell a Lonely Heart murder is. But no farther. I'm going to get myself some water colors and do some splashing around, and that's as hard as I intend to work.

When Ashley had left, Weaver found Ellis De Long in the phone book and talked to him on the phone. He learned that DeLong's place was only half a block off the plaza and walked there.

He explained the deal he'd just made with Price.
"I know the house." DeLong said. "How much do you want done to it?"

"Whatever it needs—in reason. Mr. Price says fifty dollars ought to make it livable-in, outside of furniture. I'll double that if I have to, but I'd just as soon not. How soon can you get at it?"

"Tomorrow, I think. Work is slack right now. I'll send two men on the job and I doubt if it takes them more than a couple of days."

"That's fine." Weaver said. "Until I can get in the place I'm staying at La Fonda—you can get in touch with me there if anything comes up."

He went back to his room at the hotel and wrote a letter to Vi. Not a long letter, nor an affectionate one. They'd passed that stage long ago, shortly after the birth of Betty, almost five years ago. It was for the sake of Ellen and Betty—

He wrote:

Dear Vi,
I've taken a place in Taos, a bit out of town but not too far; it's about twenty minutes' drive. It's a little primitive and isolated, but the scenery is marvelous—and it's a wonderful bargain for the summer. I hope you'll like it. (She probably wouldn't, he thought; but then again he wished she weren't coming.) You can reach me General Delivery in Taos to let me know when you'll arrive. The train doesn't come here so buy your ticket to Santa Fe and I'll drive down there—it's seventy miles—and pick you up to save you the bus ride. Give my love to Ellen and Betty and tell them that their daddy . . .

He walked up to the post office to mail the letter and them back to the hotel. He didn't want another drink just yet; he wasn't hungry enough to eat; he didn't want to go back up to his room. Nor did he want to look for someone to talk to;

he didn't quite know what he did want.

The sun was going down and the air was getting cool now.

He'd have to find something to do for the evening. There was only one movie in town, almost next door to his hotel, and only a Western was playing there. Occasionally, back home, he'd sit through a Western because Ellen was crazy a-bout them (he sometimes called her Hopalong Weaver) but he certainly wasn't going to sit through one in any lesser cause.

Maybe reading would be the answer. He walked across the plaza to the drugstore and picked out a pocket book to read, a mystery.

He sat in the hotel lobby and tried to get interested in it but it bored him. When he found that he'd read the same paragraph three times and still had got no meaning out of it, he put the book in his pocket and went out to walk. Maybe he could work up an appetite so he could eat and get eating over with; then he could go up to his room and stay there. Maybe, in pajamas and removed from the temptation to go out again, he could get interested in the book.

What, he wondered, was a Lonely Heart murder? Isn't every heart lonely, always?

Forget it. He walked.

After a while he found himself striding savagely across the evening. He forced himself to slow down.

The stars came out, and a bright moon, and a cool wind.

[2]

In the morning it was raining hard. From his window Weaver could scarcely see across the plaza, let alone the distant moun-tains that had been so incredibly beautiful in sunlight. He closed the window and got back into bed, cursing himself for having got drunk the night before. Stinking drunk and on a solitary jag, sitting alone at a bar staring at his reflection in a blue-tinted backbar mirror, repelling with curt monosyllables the few who had turned to talk to him.

Why?

There was a bad taste in his mouth and he felt a great need for cold water. He went to the bathroom and drank two glasses of it. His hands were shaking so badly that he didn't care to risk shaving.

He knew he wouldn't be able to go back to sleep so he dressed, a bit fumblingly, and went downstairs to the coffee shop. The thought of food was abhorrent to him but he forced himself to eat some buttered toast with the two cups of coffee that he drank.

He felt a little better then, although his hand still trembled when he held it out and looked at it. (Making sure first, of course, that no one was watching him.) He'd either have to quit drinking so much or learn how to use an electric razor, much as he disliked one.

He solved the problem for the moment by getting shaved in the barbershop a few doors away. It was still raining moderately hard but portals made a porch-like roof over the sidewalks almost all the way around the plaza, so he didn't get wet.

The rain was a mere drizzle by the time he'd had his shave. He was able to walk to where he'd parked his car on a street off the plaza. He drove out the Denver road and turned off at the side road to Arroyo Seco. His Chevy skidded dangerously and he saw that the road ahead was a sea of mud. He fought the skid and stopped the car slowly and carefully. He wondered if he should try to go on and remembered how much worse parts of the dirt road past Seco were than this section of it; surely they were impassable. Cautiously he backed out onto the asphalt main road and drove back to Taos. Living out there on a dirt road had been a mad idea. He'd go to DeLong and cancel the deal for fixing up the house, then give the keys back to Price. He hadn't as yet any investment—unless it was half a day's time—in the place.

DeLong was glad to see him. "A bit wet this morning," he said. "But I've got three men working on your place; they went out there early."

"You mean they made it over that road—or wasn't it so bad then?"

"Oh, it may be a little worse by now than it was earlier but this is the first rain we've had in two weeks so it can't be so bad. You'll get used to a little mud once in a while and it doesn't happen often."

"But—"

"I'm free now. Want to go out there with me and see how things are coming along? We can talk over any doubtful points—things we might not be sure whether you'd want done or not."

Weaver nodded. If things weren't too far along, if his investment wasn't too big, he could still cancel it. The rain had stopped.

DeLong's station wagon had no special tires but he made the road easily. He said, "We'll still have a few rains, but not many. Possibly for the next month there'll be about a day a week when the road will be a bit slippery and you'll have to drive slowly, but you can make it. There's a knack to driving in mud. And we'll have nine-tenths good weather from here on in; there's nothing to worry about."

The three men—one an Anglo, the other two Spanish-Americans—had knocked off for lunch when they got there. DeLong and the Anglo carpenter went over the place with Weaver, discussing what had been done and what should still be done. DeLong told Weaver, "Doughbelly's guess of fifty dollars wasn't bad. Not much material needed—a few new boards and nails, two panes of glass, some plaster patch. I think they can finish today and that about forty or forty-five dollars will cover it. Unless you want a fancy job."

"No, I don't want a fancy job," Weaver said.

The next day the sun was out and the road, although badly rutted, was almost dry.

The workmen had finished. Weaver looked over his domain and found it good—but greatly in need of cleaning. He drove the mile and a half back to Arroyo Seco in search of help. He inquired at the general store and was directed to a

Spanish couple named Sanchez who were willing, for five dollars, to spend the afternoon cleaning. He drove them out to the house and left them there, after inventorying the furniture and other contents to decide what things he'd need right away. He drove into Taos and spent the afternoon picking up a few pieces of used furniture, some dishes and cooking implements and some bedding. He got back at five o'clock with all the smaller items in his car—two heavier pieces would be sent out by truck the next day.

The Sanchezes were just finishing. They'd done a good job and the place looked livable-in.

"I'll drive you back," he told them, "soon as I bring in the rest of the stuff from the car."

Sanchez gave him a hand with the carrying. He asked, "You buy this place, Mister Weaver? Or you just rent, huh?'"

"Just renting. That is, I'm paying rent for the summer by getting the place fixed up."

"You live here alone, huh?"

Weaver explained that his wife would be joining him soon.

"Good." Sanchez nodded emphatically. "After what happened it would be bad to live alone here, Mister Weaver. My boy Pepe, he saw it, he saw the start of it"

"Saw—you mean he saw the murder?"

"Pepe, he saw him go for her, Mister Weaver, with the knife. Through that window Pepe saw it. He had been fishing up the arroyo—"

Weaver said, "Well, that's all the stuff out of the car. Come on; I'll take you home."

As the car crossed the little bridge and turned onto the road, Sanchez pointed back. "Right from here Pepe saw it, in that window, Pepe saw her back away to the door and the other after her with the knife, the man who lived here, Nelson. Then she got through the door and ran and Pepe could not see any more."

"He didn't try to help her, or get help?"

"Help her, Mister Weaver? Pepe he was only ten, only a boy. He came home and told me. I go to the store and talked

on the telephone for the sheriff in Taos and he came but I
don't think he believed my Pepe. He went out to the house
and he look around but find nobody home and no signs
anything happen. He told Pepe that he see things. It was only
when they find her body two months after back in the hills
they know what Pepe told them was true."

After he'd taken the Sanchezes home, Weaver hesitated
briefly deciding whether to return to Taos for the night or
whether to pick up some groceries at the little store in Arroyo
Seco and take them back to the house. Then he remembered
that his clothes and toilet articles were still at the hotel and
that, anyway, he was past check-out time at the hotel and
wouldn't save any money by not staying there for the night.
Besides, he had nothing to read, nothing to do at the house.

He moved the next day and laid in a supply of food. Not
that he intended to do any great amount of cooking for
himself; until Vi got there he'd have one meal a day in Taos,
but he'd manage to make himself coffee in the morning and
to fix himself some kind of a lunch. He laid in a stock of
magazines and pocket books. He wanted to buy paints and
paper but it was Sunday and he couldn't find any place open
that sold artists' supplies.

The next day was beautiful again. Right after a late breakfast he drove into Taos and found a place called the Kiva
where he could buy water colors and suitable paper. He intended to take literally the doctor's suggestion that he try painting; he'd never seriously tried it before but he had a knack for
drawing and thought that with a little practice at handling
colors he might not do too horribly.

He tried painting as soon as he got home and found that
he enjoyed it, although it began to bore him after an hour or
so. He read some, and he looked at the mountains. He even
walked back toward them perhaps a quarter of a mile, and
that made him think of Jenny Ames, one night eight years
ago. This was how far from the house her body had been
found—after a quarter-mile run through the night with a killer
at her heels.

The night that followed was cool and, again, he couldn't

seem to concentrate on reading. He drove into Seco and tried the tavern there. He was the only Anglo in the place and all the conversation was in Spanish. He was used to the sound of Spanish—he'd lived a long time in Santa Fe but he'd never learned to speak it or understand it. That didn't matter tonight because he hadn't wanted to talk to anybody anyway. But there was something wrong with the atmosphere—or was he imagining a vague hostility that wasn't there? And he kept wondering whether they were talking about him—not that he cared if they did, but he couldn't help wondering.

After a while he bought a bottle from the backbar and drove home with it. He drank himself into a sullen stupor and went to bed, well before midnight.

In the morning he woke early and couldn't get back to sleep, although he felt lousy, too lousy even to make breakfast for himself. Was this what he'd come to Taos for? The doctor back home had made no objection to moderate and occasional drinking, but this made two nights out of five that he'd gone to bed drunk and that couldn't be good for him, physically or mentally. The doctor had told him that the heavy drinking that had preceded his breakdown had been a symptom and not a cause, but if he kept on—

He dressed and drove in to Taos—Seco is too small to have a restaurant—and the drive gave him enough appetite to enable him to eat a good breakfast and feel better.

At the post office there was a letter waiting from Vi:

> Dear Georgie—*(He hated being called Georgie and had managed to break Vi of the habit of doing it verbally, but she still wrote to him that way whenever they were apart.)*
> Im glad you found a place you like and hope your feeling good by now, I wish it had been Santa Fe because we both lived there and liked it once and had friends there, I guess it was mostly your friends but if Taos is what you want its all right by me, I dont know just yet what day I will come but it will be about a week yet and Ill write again and let you know in a few days, meanwhile the girls are fine . . .

She always wrote that way, one running sentence to a letter no matter how many subjects she covered, and she always left out the apostrophes in her contractions. Weaver had often thought that possibly they'd never have been married if they'd corresponded before the ceremony. Errors in grammar and spelling and punctuation always irritated him more than they really should; he knew that it amounted almost to a phobia with him, but he just couldn't help it. Vi hadn't had much education and she'd been working as a waitress when he'd met and married her and there'd been nothing he could do about it. He'd tried at first to talk her into taking some classes at night school, but during the first year of their marriage it hadn't bothered him too much—there'd been passion as against grammar—and after the birth of Ellen he'd given up. Vi would always be ignorant and a little stupid—and basically, he'd decided, it was the stupidity that annoyed him more than the ignorance. Many poorly educated people have keen minds; some have that rarer quality, good taste. Vi had neither, and no amount of education would have given them to her.

He sighed, as he put the letter in his pocket, and wished again that she wasn't coming. But providing separate maintenance for the two of them for all summer, in addition to the cost of keeping the girls in camp, would be much more than he dared risk spending; he had to hang onto enough capital to finance a fresh start for himself in business in the fall. Now that he had acquired a place big enough for them both to live in—and had, in effect, paid his rent in advance for the summer, there wasn't any choice in the matter. Besides, they had already, before he'd left Kansas City, given notice on their flat for the first of June and had made arrangements to store the furniture. If Vi didn't come here, she'd have to stay at a hotel or rooming house; he'd have a hell of a time talking her into doing that, especially now that he'd already told her that he had a three-room place paid for, for the summer.

No, there wasn't any out, now.

The weather stayed bright and warm, except for the

evenings, and the mountains stayed beautiful. No rainy, or even cloudy, days. Weaver painted, and the results weren't too bad, although his further efforts didn't seem to get any better than his first ones had been, and occasionally they were worse.

He read and walked and ate and slept and drank. Sometimes there was lonesomeness, but against it a strong basic urge to be alone that kept him from trying to make friends.

He didn't do too badly; he was drinking too much he knew, but at least he learned to avoid, for a while, doing any drinking till after dark. And he rationed his days to keep him going until then; after that there seemed nothing to do but try to read—sometimes he could concentrate enough to enjoy reading and sometimes he couldn't—and to drink until he got tired enough to enable him to sleep.

Whisky was getting to be a bit expensive, though, and he switched to wine, at least for the drinking he did at home. Prices of most things, he was learning, were higher in Taos or Seco than they'd been at home in Kansas City. Rent and clothes were all one could save on—clothes not because they cost less but because there was no need of wearing good ones; denim trousers and wool shirts were almost costume. He'd been wondering whether to write to Vi again while he was waiting to hear from her, and finally decided to do so mostly to tell her to bring more of his old clothes along so he could save by wearing them out during the summer. And he told her not to spend too much for additions to her own wardrobe; she'd need cool things for the daytime and warm ones for the evenings, but they needn't be new or expensive things.

He found a practical use, finally, for the water colors; he composed a long letter to the girls that was only half writing, which Vi would read to them, and the other half little pictures in bright colors, of mountains and adobe houses and animals and Indians. They weren't good pictures, especially, but Ellen and Betty would get a big kick out of them and would think their father was a real artist.

The next day was a Sunday, and the post office wasn't open, nor were the taverns and liquor stores. It was a bad day;

he slept till noon after having drunk too much once more and after having stared too much at the blackness through the windows until some small, and unremembered, hour of the night. He awoke needing a drink, and there was nothing left. He drove into Taos to get himself a drink to pick him up before he remembered the Sunday closing law. He drank a lot of coffee and it helped a little but not much.

The sun was bright and beautiful as he drove back home but he saw the mountains and the scenery with a weary eye; he thought, *the hell with it, what is scenery? It's like a book, possibly wonderful and magic the first time you read it, but can you keep on reading and rereading it indefinitely?*

He tried to paint; he tried to read. Finally the day passed, and the evening, and he was able to go to sleep by midnight.

Monday was better. He woke without a hangover and at eight o'clock. He got his breakfast and wandered out into the bright morning, and things were good again.

But not too good. Sometime late this week or early next week Vi would be coming, and there are worse things than being bored or a little lonesome occasionally. The constant and unavoidable presence of someone who grates upon you is worse than solitude can ever be.

And aren't we all lonely, always? What the hell had Luke Ashley meant by a Lonely Heart murder?

He drove into Taos early in the afternoon because it was time for him to pick out and send a birthday present to Betty. He found a truly beautiful Indian doll that he knew she'd love; it cost about twice what he'd intended to spend, but he bought it and arranged to have it sent.

At the post office there were two letters for him, neither from Kansas City. One was from a friend in Santa Fe whom Luke Ashley also knew; Luke had given him Weaver's address. It suggested that he drive down for a weekend there, even if he intended to spend the summer in Taos. Will Fulton. Weaver remembered Fulton too vaguely to want to spend a week end with him or even to drive seventy miles to see him.

The other letter was from Luke Ashley, on stationery of the Biltmore in Los Angeles. He stepped into the bar at La

Doña Luz and ordered himself a drink before he opened it. He glanced again, first, at the letter from Will Fulton.

"It'd be hell, George, to have you so near and not get a chance to see you at all. Some of us might drive up but. Luke didn't know just where you'd be living, so . . ."

Mentally, Weaver thanked Luke for that; Luke had recognized that he might not want to see anyone from Santa Fe. "All the old gang will be glad . . ."

To hell with the old gang, he thought. He hadn't seen any of them for six years and he didn't want to now. He crumpled the Santa Fe letter and tossed it into the open fireplace. His drink came and he took a sip of it and then opened Luke's letter:

Hope you're not yet bored in your lonely retreat. I told a few people in Santa Fe—I stopped over there that night after I left you—that they could reach you through the Taos post office, but didn't tell them where you'd be living, so they wouldn't bother you in case you didn't want company. Or are you getting bored by now?

If you are, why not take my suggestion and do a little digging in on the Jenny Ames murder? There's even more reason for it now. I just got a letter from my best market telling me that they're starting a series of Lonely Heart murder cases—there have been quite a few of them—and the Jenny Ames deal would fit in beautifully.

If you can dig up enough data to let me do five thousand words on it, it'll pay three hundred bucks extra for photographs, and you can at least take pictures of the place where it happened—and if you do all the leg work and I do all the writing I'll split even with you. Don't sneeze at a hundred and fifty bucks if it's something you can pick up in your spare time. And I know you're not supposed to work, so if this turns out to be work, drop it. You just might get interested in doing it and find out that it's fun instead. It wouldn't be for me, but then this is my racket and it's not yours and playing the other man's game turns out to be fun, while it's new, surprisingly often. Whenever you feel up to it, give it a whirl and see how it goes. If you can get enough dope at all, you should be able to do it in your spare time in a week. Don't forget the pictures—if you get enough good ones, that'll run your take up maybe another fifty bucks, which will be all yours. Picture of the house, one of the place where the girl was buried, maybe a picture of the boy who saw the start of the crime—those you can take yourself. Maybe you can dig up a picture of whoever was sheriff at that time and worked on the case . . .

Weaver had another drink and thought it over.

Why not? he wondered. After all, a hundred and fifty bucks was nothing to be sneezed at if he could get it just for asking questions of a few people and forwarding the data to Luke. And he had a camera that was good enough to take the pictures that might run his share up to two hundred dollars; he'd forgotten to bring it with him to New Mexico but he could write Vi to bring it with her luggage. And he could tell her to bring his portable typewriter, too.

When he'd finished his drink he went back to the post office and bought two airmail postcards. He used the desk there to address and write them, one to Vi telling her to bring the camera and the typewriter, one to Luke, "Okay, will do." He mailed them.

He felt more cheerful than he'd felt for several days. Investigating a murder—even an eight-year-old one—would give him something to do and might be interesting. And earning a hundred and fifty or two hundred dollars would definitely be a good idea, especially at something so far from his usual occupation that it could hardly be classed as work.

He celebrated his decision by having a good dinner in Taos.

It was getting dark when he got back into his car and drove toward Arroyo Seco.

Darker than he dreamed.

[3]

He wasn't in any great hurry to get home, and, as he neared the little town, it came to him that there was no time like the present for starting what he'd decided to do. He stopped at the house of Mr. Sanchez.

Sanchez answered his knock at the door. When he saw who it was he smiled broadly and gestured with his hand.

"Come in, Mister Weaver, come in, please."

Weaver went in. The place was smaller than his own but there were about a dozen children of all ages playing on the floor, doing homework at a table, three of them helping Mrs. Sanchez, who was washing dishes in a huge dishpan. But the room was amazingly quiet.

Twenty-four eyes, all of them dark, focused on Weaver, who stood uncomfortably, his hat in his hand, just inside the door.

Sanchez said, "Please to come this way, Mister Weaver." He led Weaver through a doorway to the right and into a small parlor, furnished with a splendor far beyond the room through which they had just passed. Weaver looked about him, torn between admiration and amusement. The room was spotless, but side by side with a beautiful example of native blanket weaving was a hideously gaudy pillow, "Souvenir from Denver." Next to a hand-carved santo that might have been a hundred or two hundred years in age sat a ceramic Donald Duck. Half of the furniture was locally handmade— the heavy, sturdy Spanish-American style that is so beautiful in its functional simplicity—and the other half was an assort- ment of cheap and flimsy mail-order stuff; from its placement there could be little doubt of which half the Sanchezes were most proud.

Weaver was motioned courteously to a fancy but uncomfortable-looking chair that was obviously in the mail-order category. "Please to sit down, Mister Weaver."

"Thanks." Weaver sat down a bit stiffly, wondering how to begin to explain his errand. None of the others had followed them into the parlor; he decided that the room must be a sanctum sanctorum, and probably for men only. But the door had been left open and, sanctum or not, wide eyes in the other room sought vantage points for staring in at him.

But none of the children in the other room, he had already decided, could be Pepe. Pepe, if he'd been ten years old eight years ago, would be eighteen now, and there had been no boy older than fourteen or fifteen.

Looking at the doorway, which he was facing, Weaver smiled at one little girl and she smiled back shyly. He felt more comfortable and less out of place after that. He nodded toward her and said, "I've got a little girl just about her age, and another a year and a half older."

"They come here with your wife, Mister Weaver?"

"Not this summer. They'll be at a girls' camp back—East." It seemed strange to refer to Kansas as the East but that's how Sanchez would think of it."

Sanchez nodded and said, "Yes, Mister Weaver," and then there was a moment's silence; Weaver realized that it was up to him to broach the object of his visit. No matter how long he waited, Sanchez would be too polite to ask. He cleared his throat and wondered where to start and then realized that the simple truth was the best approach. He told Sanchez that a writer friend of his had asked him to get details about the murder of Jenny Ames so he could write a story about it.

Sanchez nodded politely again. "You want to talk to Pepe then, huh? My boy who saw them? Pepe is at the dance. I will send Luis for him, Mister Weaver." He looked toward the doorway and spoke into the silence beyond it. "Luis, you will bring Pepe home. Quick."

The boy who looked to be about fourteen started toward the outer door.

Weaver said, "Wait, please." and as the boy paused, he tuned to Sanchez. "Please don't pull your son away from a dance, Mr. Sanchez. There's no hurry about this. I can talk to him tomorrow, any time."

Sanchez gestured deprecatingly. "It's not matter, Mister Weaver. The dance it is not for an hour yet. Pepe he left early. He watches the others play pool or maybe Pepe he plays himself. It will not hurt him to come. The poolroom and dance hall are very near. Five minutes it will take to come. Go now, Luis."

It was so definite that Weaver didn't protest further.

While they waited, Weaver said, "Of course I'd like to hear from your son just what he saw that night. But, even besides that, I'm really starting from the beginning. I don't even know yet who or what Jenny Ames was. Or anything about the man who killed her—except that his name was Nelson—or why he killed her. I'm sorry, but I'm afraid I wasn't interested at the time you started to tell me about it. Would it be too much to ask for you to give me the background before Pepe comes?"

"What I know, Mister Weaver, it is little. Nobody knows much. Besides my Pepe, one woman in Taos, she saw Miss Ames while she is alive. She is the only one. Mister Nelson he lived there one month only. He stay alone. Nobody know much about him but he paint pictures. A few times I saw him in the store in town, in Seco. That is all."

"Why did he kill her?"

Sanchez shrugged broadly. "Some say he was crazy, some say he kill her for money she bring when she come to him. She come on the bus from Santa Fe the day he kill her."

"From Santa Fe?" Weaver echoed. It gave him a little turn to remember that, since this had happened eight years ago, he'd been in Santa Fe then. He'd spent five years there, up to six years ago when he and Vi had moved to Kansas City.

"Not from Santa Fe she started. They—how do you say?— trail her back to Albuquerque, she stay at hotel there the night before. Before that—?" He shrugged. "Here comes Pepe now, I think."

Weaver hadn't heard anything, but the door opened and

Luis came back in, after him a tall, dark and very handsome young Spanish-American. He looked queryingly through the door into the parlor and Sanchez said, "Come in, Pepe. This is Mister Weaver, who has taken the house where Mister Nelson lived. He wants to ask you about what you saw that night. He will write the story about it."

Pepe Sanchez came into the room and Weaver stood and put out his hand; he thought there was a momentary hesitation before Pepe took it.

"What do you want to know?" The young man's voice was faintly sullen.

"Well—just what it was that you saw, Pepe. But, unless you're in a hurry to get back to the dance, may I ask you to come out with me to the place where it happened? That way you can show me just where you were standing and tell me what you saw, right from where you saw it. My car's right outside; it'll take only a few minutes to get there and I'll drive you back, of course." He looked at Sanchez. "And if you'd care to come along, Mr. Sanchez, I'd like to offer you both a drink while we're at my place."

Sanchez smiled and bobbed his head. "Thank you. We will be glad."

He seemed to take Pepe's consent for granted and, after a momentary hesitation, so did Weaver. They went through the crowded room and Sanchez opened the door and held it politely.

Weaver, not to be outdone, went to the wrong side of his coupe and ceremoniously held the door open for Sanchez and Pepe before he went around to the other side and got in under the wheel.

He drove the mile and a half to his house, used the little bridge to drive onto and back away from so he could park the car facing back toward Arroyo Seco. They got out.

"Now, Pepe." Sanchez said. "Tell to Mister Weaver."

"I was standing here." Pepe said. He'd moved a few steps from the parked car. He pointed. "Through that window I saw into the house. That is the kitchen."

"About what time was this?" Weaver interrupted. He'd

have to know the day and the date, too, of course, but he could always find that out from newspapers or court records and he wanted to concentrate now on the eyewitness account he was about to hear.

"About like now. About eight o'clock. I was fishing in the arroyo and was coming home. I was late. I was walking past this house and I was about here—"

"The leg, Pepe." Sanchez prompted.

"I had hurt my ankle, twisted it. That is why I was late. I was limping and could not walk fast. The light was on in the kitchen. I could see through the window—"

"Wait." Weaver said. "I'm sorry to keep on interrupting, but let me go inside and turn on the kitchen light, so it will be just like it was then. That was the only light on?"

"Yes, I think."

Weaver went into the house and turned on the kitchen light. He came out and stood beside Pepe again. "All right," he said.

"Yes, this is where I stood, because I could see the back door like now. The young lady was standing against the door, maybe two steps from it with her back toward it. She was backing slow like she was afraid if she moved fast he would move fast, too, before she could got there. She was very afraid. She had one hand behind her like she was reaching for the doorknob and the other hand was out in front like to hold off the knife."

"And you could see the man, too, Nelson?"

"Yes." Pepe said. "His shoulder, the back of his head. His arm raised with the knife in his hand. It looked like a kitchen knife and he held it wrong, not like you hold a knife for fighting. He held it for stabbing down and that is the wrong way."

"You didn't see his face, then. You're sure it was Nelson?"

"Yes, from the shape of his head I could tell, and from his hair. It was light, like straw, and he wore it very short, straight up."

"A crew cut?"

"I think that's what they call it. And later when he went through the door, the kitchen door, after her I saw some of the side of his face when he turned a little bit. I am sure it was Mr. Nelson."

"But you'd never seen the girl before?"

"No. I did not know there was a woman in the house. Mr. Nelson lived there alone. That was why I first stopped to look when I saw her through the window."

Weaver said, "All right, go on. What happened?"

"She got the door opened and got out before he got to her. And he ran out after her. That was all I saw."

"You didn't see either of them after they went through the door?"

"The house was in between. She ran straight back and it was dark. I heard her scream out once when she was far. That was all. I got home as fast as I could, limping, to tell my father. That is all I know. They did not take me back with them."

Weaver nodded. He wanted to ask the elder Sanchez what had happened after that, but he could ask that while they were inside having the drinks he had suggested. He invited them in and poured three generous glasses from the jug of muscatel. They thanked him as he handed glasses to each of them.

Weaver asked Sanchez, "You came back with the sheriff?"

"Yes. The door was not locked and the lights were not on. He knocked first and called and then he went inside and turned on all the lights. Nothing, he said. We came away."

Weaver sipped his wine and looked at Pepe. "What did Jenny Ames look like?"

"Pretty, I think. Her hair was black but her face was very white. Maybe because she was so afraid. Just a few seconds I saw her. That is all I remember."

"How was she dressed?"

"A green dress, I think."

"Blue, Pepe," Sanchez said. "A blue dress she was found in."

Pepe shrugged. "A blue dress, maybe."

"And can you describe Nelson—outside of his hair? You already told me about that."

"He was tall. Taller than you, and heavier. He was very

good-looking, I think. But he was not friendly with people."

"Did anyone see him after that?" Weaver turned to San-chez again.

"Yes. The sheriff, he did not believe Pepe but he come back next day to talk to Mister Nelson. Mister Nelson said he was driving his car the evening before. He said he never had a woman in his place, that Pepe make mistake. And the sheriff looked around house, inside, outside again by day and he find nothing, nothing to show a woman was there. So the sheriff he left. A day, two days after that Mister Nelson left the house and this country. And two months more is found the body of the woman."

Weaver nodded. There were a lot more questions, but he had his full eyewitness account and he could probably find a better source of other information.

He said, "Uh—Pepe. We took you away from a dance, and I want to get you back. But is there time for another drink?"

"Thank you, Mr. Weaver." It was Sanchez who answered, not Pepe. "The dance, it will last late. There is no hurry."

Weaver poured another drink. But he could see from the sullen expression on the boy's face that he didn't enjoy stay-ing, so he set a fast pace in finishing the drink and didn't suggest a third.

He drove them back to Arroyo Seco, dropping Sanchez off at the house and insisting on driving Pepe on to the dance hall, although it was only a few hundred yards further on.

He drove faster going home through the night that sud-denly seemed—for no reason he could name—to press about him.

And, when he got there, it seemed to press about the little adobe house, to press against the panes of the windows once he was inside it.

He poured himself another drink, a stiff one, this time from part of a bottle of whisky that was in the cupboard.

He looked at the kitchen door and shivered a little, almost seeing the girl standing there, terror in her white face under black hair, as she groped behind her for the knob.

Might as well finish the whisky, he decided. He poured

himself another but before he started on it he got paper and
pencil. He'd better get down notes on Pepe Sanchez's eye witness story while it was fresh in his mind, while he was sober,
and before he might forget any details.

He got it down on paper and the whisky was gone so he
poured himself another glass of the wine. It tasted good and
he wondered why he'd bothered changing to the whisky first;
he'd been acquiring a taste for sweet wine. He'd never really
liked the taste of whisky anyway and wine made you just as
drunk but with fewer unpleasant aftereffects.

He sat and thought and drank. He looked at his watch
and it was a few minutes after eleven and after a long while
he looked at his watch again and it was still the same time. So
he'd forgotten to wind his watch that morning and now he
didn't know what time it was. And he didn't care.

He was drunk and he didn't care about that either. But
his bladder did. He went outside and walked to the little
bridge along the creek between the house and the road and
stood for a minute or two, swaying a bit, at the edge of the
bridge. The wind, a cool night wind, blew against him and he
wetted his trouser legs very slightly. Who was it had cau-
tioned against pissing against the wind? Oh yes, Rabelais,
good old Rabelais. He'd have to get a copy of *Gargantua and
Pantagruel* and read it again. Great stuff. The goose's neck
and the ring of Hans Carvel and all that.

He was drunk. He looked back at the house, with the
kitchen window lighted because he'd been sitting in that
room, and then he went on across the bridge and a few steps
along the edge of the road.

This was where Pepe Sanchez had stood.

The window, and through it the back door that led out
into the dark night and violent death after a far cry. Beyond a
murderer's shoulder and an upraised knife, a frightened,
pretty girl with black hair.

Forget it.

Stumble back into the house and sit again at the table.
Stare at the door again and picture the girl backed against it.
Put yourself into her mind—a madman coming toward her,

light glinting from the upraised knife, murder in his face. Pepe had not seen his face, but Jenny had. The door, and night and death beyond.

Funny, Weaver thought, murder really happens. He'd never had direct contact with it before; it was just something you read about and you don't disbelieve it but you don't realize it either.

Somehow, he was realizing this one.

He poured himself another drink and then, when he had drunk part of it, the room was going in circling, dizzying swoops that put a feeling in his genitals like the feeling you get in a dropping elevator.

And then it was gray early morning and he lifted his head from the table. There was the sickly smell of vomit somewhere and there was an awful taste in his mouth and yellow fog in his mind.

He wanted water, lots of cold water. Inside him first, then outside. He drank three dippers of it from the bucket he had carried from the stream. He went outside, then, into the cool freshness of the dawn. He stripped off his clothes and walked into the cold shallow stream. He knelt in it and splashed icy water over his body, gasping with the shock of it, but feeling as though he was washing his follies away and that there'd never be another night as foolish as that one.

Cleansed and shivering, he went back into the house. He dried himself off and put on pajamas. He thought, I don't want to wake to *this*, so he cleaned up the vomit and put away the bottle and the jug and the glasses; he made a bundle of the clothes he had stripped off so he could take them in to the cleaner's without having to look at them again. The day was bright by then although the sun has not yet above the mountains; he turned off the light which was still burning a sickly yellow in the bright daylight.

He got under blankets on the bed and he thought: *Why did I do that? I must never do it again.* And then he slept.

When he wakened the position of the sun told him it was almost noon. He got up and, dressed, feeling a bit shaky but almost human. There was, while he was dressing, the almost-remembrance of a dream, but he couldn't grasp it; it faded even as his mind, reached for it. It didn't matter, he told himself; dreams are random, meaningless things.

He didn't feel up to making coffee for himself so he drove into Taos as soon as he dressed. He had breakfast at the coffee shop at La Fonda and set and wound his watch; it was a quarter of twelve.

He went to the post office and there was no mail for him.

Maybe, he decided, he should go around to the local newspaper—a weekly called *El Crepúsculo*—and get as many of the rest of the facts about the Jenny Ames murder as he could. The sooner he got that off his mind, the better he was going to feel. After last night, he was almost sorry he'd started it. Or would he have got drunk anyway?

It was lunch hour now, just the wrong time to go around. But breakfast had made him feel better and now that he'd eaten, a pickup drink would do him more good than harm, if he held it to one.

He killed time by driving out to Sagebrush Inn, a couple of miles from town in the direction of Santa Fe, for his drink. He held it to two drinks and then it was one-thirty and time for him to try the newspaper office.

The editor, whose desk was just inside the door, was a short, stocky man with sandy hair in a crew cut-like Nelson's, Weaver thought. He introduced himself.

The editor put out a hand. "My name's Callahan, Mr. Weaver. What can I do for you?"

Weaver told him. ". . . so if you've got back files—that is, if your paper goes back eight years—I should have asked that first, I guess."

Callahan grinned. "We go back more, than eight years. This is the oldest paper in the Southwest; it was founded in 1835. I'm afraid you'll have to study what you want here, though; we can't let our bound volumes go out."

"That'll be fine," Weaver said.

Callahan left the outer room and came back with a big volume of bound newspapers which he put down on the counter. "This is the year. As I recall it, Jenny Ames' body was found in July—or it could have been August. You'd better start looking in July."

Weaver thanked him and leafed through to the first July issue; there wasn't any headline that sounded likely so he turned on; nothing for the second issue in July. But there was a headline in the third:

BODY OF UNIDENTIFIED WOMAN FOUND NEAR SECO

Callahan had stepped back to the counter beside him. He said, "Yes, I remember now. That story broke on a Wednesday, just before we went to press. You'll find nothing there but the finding of the body. In the next issue you'll get the details—about all of them that were ever known. Would you like paper and pencil?"

"Paper, if I may have some. I have a pencil."

Weaver read the story of the finding of the body. It had been found by one Ramon Camillo, a resident of Arroyo Seco, while out hunting. It had been buried in a very shallow grave in sandy soil, apparently scooped out by hand and hastily covered. A dog or a coyote had dug a hole down to the body, which was under only six or eight inches of dirt, and Camillo had found the grave because of the odor coming from the hole. He had looked down and seen what looked like black human hair and he had moved enough of the sand to be sure that what was buried there really was a human body. He had returned to Seco and had phoned the sheriff in Taos. The sheriff had brought the coroner and a deputy with him and the body had been exhumed. It was considerably decomposed but appeared—according to the coroner, a Dr. Gomez—to be the body of a young woman, dead for about two to two and a half months. The coroner would perform an autopsy and an inquest would be held.

Weaver glanced at Callahan, who was still standing beside him. "Didn't they connect it up, right away, with the story Pepe Sanchez had told them about seeing Nelson chasing a woman with a knife?"

"Freeman—that's the sheriff who was in office then—says

he did, but that he was saving that angle until the inquest and until he had a chance to see if he could trace Nelson before the alarm went out. I didn't make the connection myself because I didn't know about the Sanchez boy's story until Freeman told me about it afterwards. At the time we went to press with that first story I didn't even know that it I was obvious from first glance that the girl had died of knife wounds—Freeman held that out on me too."

Weaver made a note of the date the body had been found and of the three names that appeared in the story—Ramon Camillo, Sheriff Will Freeman, Dr. Alberto Gomez, the coroner. The rest of it he could remember.

He turned over to the front page of the next week's paper.

The story rated a banner head this time and two and a half columns of the front page. The inquest had been held the previous Tuesday.

Weaver read the story closely and attentively, making notes again of names and dates and relying on his memory for other details. Callahan had gone back to his desk, so there wasn't any hurry. And there ought to be almost enough right here, he thought, to make a story for Luke Ashley. Or maybe not—Luke must have read this too if he'd spent a few days on the case, and he must have decided something was missing.

The inquest had opened with Ramon Camillo's story of his fining of the body—the same story, with a few added but unimportant details, as had been told in the previous issue.

Then Pepe Sanchez had been put on the stand and had told his story of two months previous. It was substantially the story Pepe had told Weaver the evening before—although it had been more vivid and real there in the dark with Pepe pointing at the lighted window and telling what he had seen from the very spot from which he had seen it.

The sheriff himself had then taken the stand and had told his share of the events of that night. How he'd had the call from Sanchez and had taken a deputy with him to Seco; how they'd gone to Nelson's place but had failed to find anything to substantiate the boy's story and had returned to Taos. How he'd gone out again the next day and had talked to Nelson and had—with Nelson's permission made an even more thorough investigation and had found nothing suspicious or nothing to contradict Nelson's story that he had never had a woman guest—let alone chased one out into the night with a knife.

Freeman testified that Nelson's reputation had backed up his statement that he had never had a woman guest. Nelson had done occasional moderate drinking at local public places and he had made a few casual acquaintances, but none of them had been women. As far as was known, he had never either visited anyone or been visited. He claimed to be an artist—and had various canvases and painting equipment at his house when the sheriff had searched it but he had never exhibited locally. Nor, to the knowledge of anyone in Taos, had he ever sold a painting.

The next few witnesses were people who, as the result of slight and casual contacts with Nelson, confirmed—but added little to—what Freeman had already told about Nelson's local reputation and local lack of knowledge concerning him.

The next witness was, next to Pepe, the star of the proceedings; it was she who was able to identify the victim, at least by description and the circumstance of dates, as the girl who, two months before, had ridden up from Santa Fe with her on the bus on the afternoon of the murder—and to supply her name, Jenny Ames.

The witness was Carlotta Evers; she was clerk and bookkeeper at a Taos clothing store.

Miss Evers testified that on the day in question she had been returning from a vacation in Santa Fe and had boarded the afternoon bus for Taos just before it left the bus station at one o'clock. The only seat left vacant was one next to a pretty, dark-haired girl; she had taken that seat and had fallen into conversation, during the several-hour trip, with the girl, who had seemed very eager to talk, especially after she learned that Miss Evers lived in Taos.

She introduced herself as Jenny Ames and said that she was coming to Taos to live, and to marry a man who was then living there. She asked Miss Evers if she knew an artist named Charles Nelson. Miss Evers had not known him. But she answered innumerable eager questions about Taos itself and the country around it—Jenny Ames had told her that Nelson lived about ten miles out of Taos, past a place called Arroyo Seco—and she said that Jenny Ames had been "starry-eyed" in her eagerness to get there.

The conversation had been casual and two months before and Miss Evers could not remember whether Jenny Ames had mentioned where she came from or not; if even the general section of the country had been mentioned she could not remember it. She did have the impression that it wasn't New Mexico, possibly from the number of questions Jenny Ames had asked about the Spanish-American people who made up the bulk of the population of that state. She couldn't describe Jenny Ames any more accurately than Pepe Sanchez had, except for details of clothing—but the descriptions coincided as far as they went.

Miss Evers testified further that Jenny Ames had told her that her fiancé was meeting her at the bus station in Taos and that she wanted Miss Evers to meet him when they got there. He had written her that he had arranged to reserve a room for her in a hotel in Taos; that he was taking her first to see his own place, where they'd live after they were married, then that he would bring her back to Taos for the night, as the marriage ceremony was arranged for the following day.

Jenny Ames had told her further that she had got to know Charles Nelson through a Lonely Hearts Club that advertised in a magazine, that they had corresponded for a while and then Nelson had come to visit her and had stayed a week in the city—or town—in which she lived, and that during that time they had fallen in love and become engaged, that he couldn't stay there because he was teaching in a Taos art school and was on brief vacation, that he had to return to his job, and that they had subsequently made the arrangement, by correspondence, for her to join him in Taos and marry him there—tomorrow.

When the bus had pulled in, Jenny Ames had introduced Miss Evers to Charles Nelson, who was waiting to greet her. But the couple had seemed—quite understandably—anxious

to be alone together and Miss Evers had left them immediately after the introduction. She had already given Jenny
Ames her Taos address and had asked her to use it after she
was married and settled down. She had seen them get into
Nelson's car and drive away.

She was sure of the date because it had been a Sunday,
the last day of her vacation, and the dates of her vacation were
on record at the clothing store.

Dr. Alberto Gomez, the coroner, had next taken the
stand. He testified that he had examined the body and that it
was the body of a girl of about twenty—within two years one
way or the other—about five feet four inches tall, weighing (at
time of death) probably about a hundred and ten pounds, fair
complexion and black hair. It had been buried at least two
months. Cause of death had been several knife wounds in the
body, almost anyone of which could have been fatal. They had
been struck with a broad, single-edged knife at least eight
inches long. Yes, a kitchen knife—if it was a moderately sharp
one—could have been the weapon used.

No, neither Pepe Sanchez nor Carlotta Evers had been
called upon to view the body; in its present state of decom-
position neither could have been expected to make an identification from having seen the deceased once—and for seconds
only, in Pepe's case—two months before. Positive identification would come only from dental records; even fingerprints
were unobtainable at this stage. In answer to a question from
a member of the jury—yes, the body had been fully clothed
and there was no evidence of rape.

Sheriff Freeman was called again to the stand. He testified that he had made a note of the date of his call to Arroyo
Seco to investigate the Sanchez boy's story and that it was the
same date that Miss Evers had given for her meeting of Jenny
Ames and of Charles Nelson, May 17th. He testified that he
had checked all hotels, rooming houses and tourist courts in
or near Taos and that Charles Nelson had not—as Miss Evers
had testified that Jenny Ames had told her—reserved a room
for Jenny Ames for that night. Also that no application had
been made by Nelson for a marriage license nor had he made

arrangements with any local clergyman or civil official to have a marriage performed.

He stated that he had sent out descriptions of Charles Nelson to law-enforcement agencies all over the country and had been attempting to trace his movements after leaving the house beyond Seco, but thus far without success. It had not yet been possible to determine even the exact date of his departure, although it had probably been within a day or two, a few days at the outside, after the murder; he had found no one either in Taos or Seco who had seen Nelson after he, Freeman, had seen him the morning after the murder. Perhaps it had been that interview—although Nelson had come through it without arousing suspicion—that had frightened him into leaving. Until then, Nelson would not have known that the Sanchez boy had seen—what he had seen.

Freeman testified further that he had had no greater success in tracing any of Nelson's movements before he had come to Taos, about six weeks before the murder. He had paid his rent for the house beyond Seco in cash and in advance and had given no references. If he had ever mentioned anything concerning his past to anyone in Taos, that person had not yet come forward—and the sheriff wished that he would.

Nor had Freeman been able to find where Jenny Ames had come from or any facts about her except what she had told Carlotta Evers. Inquiries were still being made—and the nationwide publicity being given the case should bring reports from somewhere, soon.

The coroner's jury had been out twelve minutes and had brought in a verdict of willful murder.

Weaver made his final notation and then turned to the front page of the following issue. The only story was a statement by the sheriff that the inquiry into the murder of Jenny Ames was being continued and that a lead to the whereabouts of Charles Nelson had been obtained.

In the next issue there was nothing.

He left the volume open on the counter and turned around to Callahan's desk, waited till the editor looked up.

"Anything further after that one issue?"

"Not a thing, Mr. Weaver. The story died on its feet after the inquest. They never did find out where Jenny Ames came from nor where Nelson came from or went to."

"What was the lead on Nelson the sheriff thought he had the following week?"

"Damn if I even remember. Whatever it was, it petered out."

Weaver closed the bound volume and stood looking at it a moment. He stood there long enough to light a cigarette and then turned back to the editor's desk.

"Thanks a lot," he said. "I'd like to buy you a drink; can you knock off long enough?"

Callahan glanced at his watch. "Shouldn't. But I will." They went around the corner to El Patio and found a table and ordered drinks. Callahan turned to watch the Spanish-American girl who had taken their order go back indoors toward the bar. "Jail-bait," he said. "When those Spanish gals look eighteen, they're probably fourteen." He sighed. "Well, it's fun to window-shop. Say, I hear someone has taken the place Nelson lived in. Is it you? Is that part of your interest in the case?"

"I'm the one who took it. But I wouldn't be interested just for that reason; I told you the truth about why I'm looking it up. By the way, didn't the girl have any luggage?"

"Yes, she got off the bus with two suitcases and Nelson put them in his car. But they weren't found; he must have taken them with him when he left."

Weaver frowned. "A funny case. Especially in that they never traced the girl back farther than they did. Of course it was a pretty cold trail by that time, but even so—"

He broke off as their drinks came. Callahan's eyes followed the girl back to the door again, and then he turned back. "That part of it was strange, all right. The case got fairly wide publicity and you'd think someone who knew the girl would have read about the murder—or that she'd have been reported missing wherever she came from." The editor shrugged. "But she may have come from some one-horse town where nobody happened to read about it. That's what most of us figured."

Weaver suggested, "Or possibly the woman who talked to her on the bus got the name wrong. I mean, it might have been Jenny Haines or Jenny James or something like that."

"No, it was Ames all right. She signed it— Oh, that's one thing that did come up later, after what you read. They did trace her as far as Albuquerque; she stayed at a hotel there the night before the murder. She registered there as Jenny Ames."

"They never found the Lonely Hearts agency through which Nelson got into correspondence with her?"

Callahan shook his head. "That angle was tried—and Uncle Sammy's boys did the asking because the U. S. mails would have been involved. But no dice; those outfits don't keep records of individual correspondents, once they've turned them over to other correspondents and collected their fee. I suppose they'd have to have warehouses full of files if they did. Well, I'm afraid I'd better push back to the office— still have some work to do for today."

"Sure you won't have another drink?"

"I'll take a rain check. Thanks." Callahan pushed back his chair and stood.

Weaver said, "Wait a minute. I just had a thought that's so ridiculously simple someone else *must* have had it eight years ago, but I don't see the catch in it. You say she signed the register in an Albuquerque hotel. There's always a blank where you put down where you came from; didn't Jenny Ames fill it out?"

"She filled it out, but she put down 'Taos, N. M.' She planned to marry here and stay here so she must have figured this was her real address." Callahan smiled grimly. "Well— she stayed here all right."

[4]

Night again, pressing against the windowpanes. Silence except for the far wild yapping of the coyotes.

And Weaver, sober tonight—although he was sipping a little wine as he tried to read—found the night and the silence, for the first time, just a bit frightening.

You see, other evenings here he'd been alone. Tonight—not quite. Jenny Ames was there, somehow. Today, when he had learned the little about her that there was to be known, she'd come alive for him. Yesterday she'd been a name.

Tonight her presence was in the room, in his mind. She was the more vivid to him because he knew so little about her. A photograph, had one existed, would have spoiled the illusion—but there was no photograph, only vague description with which his imagination could do as it willed. A pretty girl, young, with black hair, who had loved—or thought she loved—a monster and who had come to marry him.

Out of mystery she had come. And into deeper mystery, the ultimate mystery, she had gone. And she had been in this very room, perhaps sat in this very chair, during the few hours that had elapsed between her arrival here and her leaving—into the final darkness.

Never to return. Never to answer the questions left behind her.

Where did you come from, Jenny? Why did no one trace you here? Did no one love you, care about you, in the place from which you came? What had life and people done to you, Jenny, that had made you so desperate as to write to a Lonely Hearts Club, to meet and love a murderer?

What made you love him, Jenny? What wiles did he use on you, that time he visited the town you lived in? How did he make you love him so?

So many questions left behind you.

Why did he kill you, Jenny? Because he was mad and for that reason only? Or was there gain for him somehow, and method in his madness? And did you know, before you died, why you died?

Did you have time to think, in those awful minutes after you saw the knife and before you felt it, time to wonder, time to realize that he had planned it all?

And he had planned it, Jenny. No room had been taken for you, no arrangements for a wedding made. He brought you here to kill you. But why?

Those damned coyotes, he thought. No, they weren't new to him. In the years he'd lived in Santa Fe he'd heard them often—never, of course, from his quarters in town, but whenever he'd driven out of town and into wild country. Often at night he'd stopped his car along a road and shut off the engine and the lights to sit there listening, enjoying—or was it enjoying?—the wild loneliness of that sound, the primitive unanswerable yearning in it.

Tonight it was getting on his nerves.

Did you ever hear that sound, Jenny? Possibly not, for it was soon after darkness fell that you died, and perhaps they had not yet started their nightly lament against the wailing wall of the sky. Or had they started, back there in the hills? Did you run toward that sound as toward a lesser evil?

He poured himself more wine and thought nuts; he'd be going crazy himself if he let himself keep thinking like that. He'd found out, now, all there was to be found out about Jenny Ames and he'd better write it up from his notes and send it to Luke so it would be off his mind. Should he rent a typewriter in Taos tomorrow instead of waiting till Vi came with his portable?

But something told him he wouldn't get it off his mind that easily.

Was it just because he lived here where it had happened? Well, that was part of it, but it was more than that. This interest in Jenny Ames—was it because, when he'd started this, he'd been interested in nothing and therefore what might have otherwise been a normal interest had become a compelling one? Yes, that could be it.

But it was more than that.

Why? Was it something within himself? An aftermath of his breakdown, his—face it—his teetering on the brink of madness those weeks in the san, that now was going to give him an obsession with an eight-year-old crime, a girl eight years dead? Was his interest psychopathic, abnormal?

Or was it, after all, just a normal interest, accentuated a bit perhaps by his lack of interest in other things? Wasn't the mystery of the crime—and of its victim and its motive sufficient to interest anyone? The fact that Jenny hadn't been traced, that almost nothing was known about her, where she had come from and what she had been—why hadn't those simple things come to light?

Nelson—that was different; it's understandable why a killer's past and his movements after he has successfully committed a crime are going to be hard to learn. Especially the latter, when he has a two months' start before the fact that he has killed is known. And if, as seemed probable, he had planned to kill even before he came here, obviously the name he gave was false and he would have said nothing, left no clue, through which his true identity and his antecedents could be learned.

But Jenny.

Did you have a secret, Jenny?

He swore at himself and tried to stop thinking about it.

He tried again to read and he couldn't concentrate on the book at all. And it was only nine o'clock; he couldn't possibly go to sleep after having slept so late that morning.

He'd *have* to get himself something to do or try to do evenings besides reading. God, even a deck of cards to play solitaire. Or maybe he should try to write; he'd wanted to write a novel once, but that had been a long time ago and the vague idea he'd had seemed silly now. God, no wonder; that had been in his late teens, twenty years ago.

No, he'd never write that novel now, or any other. But

shorter things, perhaps? He wished again that he'd brought his typewriter. Maybe factual things would be easy to write. He wondered if a job like Luke's—digging up facts on past or recent crimes—would be interesting. Well, he was having a chance to find out if he could do writing like that, if he wanted to try his hand at it. Maybe he should write the article about Jenny Ames himself. Not try to sell it himself, of course; that wouldn't be fair to Luke because the whole thing had been Luke's idea. But possibly instead of sending Luke merely notes to work from he should surprise him by sending him the story ready written. His style and approach might be way off the beam—at least unless he studied some fact detective magazines first to familiarize himself with them—but that wouldn't matter; Luke could rewrite it. But even if Luke submitted it as originally written, he'd rather have Luke use his own by-line and they could split even on the deal, because it would be Luke's by-line that would sell the story and make it get Luke's rates instead of beginner's rates. Or should he—? No, real estate was his racket, not writing. This one story and never tackle another.

He tried to read again and found, after a while, that again he'd been reading the same paragraph over and over and still didn't know what it said.

He put down the book and took another sip of wine. It was sweet wine and he'd found it particularly good for solitary drinking such as this. He could go through all the motions of drinking and feel the effect, eventually even get a bit drunk, but not with the devastating completeness of whisky. And *never* whisky and wine both; that's what had got him last night. Wine alone made him merely mellow and fuzzy around the edges, and it was sometimes nice to be fuzzy around the edges.

But, whisky or wine, he had been drinking a lot since he'd come here.

All right, damn it, he thought; you've been bored stiff most of the time and you might as well admit it. The mountains are God damn beautiful but you can't look at mountains all the time; the air is wonderful, but breathing isn't enough.

And you can't read and you can't paint and—

He was staring at the door and tried, suddenly, to wrench his mind away from the thing it was trying to picture there. And then he thought, *why? Why should I?*

So the doctor told you to get interested in something, and you've found something that interests you and you keep fighting to keep your mind away from it. Anything except making money, the doctor said, and this makes money only slightly and incidentally; you've already got enough data to send Luke, if that's as far as your interest went.

So maybe your interest verges on the psychopathic, but if you don't get interested in something, you'll go crazy anyway, so—

He felt better, lots better.

He looked at the kitchen door and let himself think. He remembered the angle of vision he'd had from the outside, when he'd stood where Pepe Sanchez had stood, and tried to visualize and place the figures as they'd stood when Pepe had first seen them. Let's see—the table had been moved—but when he'd first seen the place, it had been about three feet farther from the door. He moved it back and—yes, that was better. Nelson would have been standing beside the table when Pepe first saw him, probably just having taken the knife from its drawer. And Jenny there, in line between the window and the back door, moving backwards toward the door.

Weaver went to the back door and opened it, staring out into the moonless dark. For the moment, the coyotes were silent; the whole night was completely silent, utterly without sound.

From somewhere back there in the distant dark his mind seemed to hear the eight-year-old echo of a far cry, the one scream Jenny Ames had screamed. Had it been when she first knew that the killer was going to catch her?

Had there been a moon that night? Stars? He hadn't thought to ask Pepe, he hadn't thought that it mattered, and it hadn't then. But it mattered now; it mattered because he was interested, because he wanted to know what that night had been like, just as he wanted to know what Jenny had been like—and even Nelson.

There was no moon tonight, just a faint glimmer of star-light. But he could see easily now that his eyes had accus-tomed themselves to the lack of light. He could make out the outline of the outhouse and, beyond it, the shed. And beyond them the ground was level, sandy, sloping slightly upward toward the foothills of the mountains.

He walked out, leaving the kitchen door open behind him—as it would have been left open that night long ago and found that he could see the clumps of chamiso, the line of cot-tonwoods in the distance to the left, pale white like skeletons in the starlight.

A girl, running.

He stood there for what seemed like a very long time. Then there was the sound of a car coming along the road to-ward the house, from Seco. Unless someone was lost—on a road that petered out to nothing less than half a mile beyond this house, the last one—then the car was coming here.

He walked around the outside of the house in time to see the oncoming headlights slow down and stop directly in front.

"Hi, Weaver. Up and about? Want to talk awhile?"

It was Callahan's voice. Weaver called, "Sure, come on in," and the lights of the car went off. Callahan got out and walked across the bridge from the car. "Bit late for a call," he said, "but I thought I'd see if your lights were on."

"It isn't late," Weaver said. He glanced at his wrist watch and saw that it was only half-past nine; he'd thought it was considerably later than that. "Glad to have some company for a change."

He wondered if he was lying about that; he was glad to see Callahan, but maybe it was because he could pump him, now that he was here, for more details about Jenny Ames. Several questions had occurred to him that the editor might be able to answer.

Inside, Callahan said, "Got it fixed up pretty good. Did I tell you that I live on this road too? Third house back, about a quarter of a mile. Out in this country that makes me one your neighbors."

"Glad you live so near," Weaver told him. "Let's go in the kitchen—that's my sitting room. And can I offer you some muscatel? Sorry, but it's all I've got on hand."

"Well—one. My wife's in Santa Fe, went down there for a duplicate bridge tournament and she's staying overnight with friends. I got a little restless and thought I'd drive down this way and see if your lights were on. If they hadn't been, I'd have gone back; it's a little late for a call."

"Don't sound so damn formal," Weaver said. "So drop in at three in the morning if you feel like it and my lights are on." He poured wine into a glass and handed it to Callahan, then refilled his own glass. "What time do people go to bed around here anyway?"

"The Spanish people—and that's most of them out this way—about nine o'clock. They think we Anglos are crazy—and maybe they're right."

"Maybe they are at that," Weaver said. "Which reminds me. Do they like us?"

"Well—no. Not particularly."

"I thought so. I'm not new to Spanish-Americans, not after living five years in Santa Fe. I even know enough to call them that and not Mexicans. But I've noticed a difference in Arroyo Seco. They're polite as hell, but—"

"*Salud,*" Callahan said. "They're polite as hell but—That's just about it."

There was a sloppiness to Callahan's enunciation that made Weaver look at him more closely and he saw now that the editor was already a bit drunk; his face was slightly flushed and his eyes were beginning to be glassy. Obviously he'd been drinking before he came here, possibly alone at home.

Weaver said, "But why? I mean, why more than in Santa Fe or other towns where Spanish-Americans and Anglos live together? Why especially in Taos?"

"Oh, not Taos. Just Arroyo Seco—this is one of the last strongholds of the old-line Spanish-Americans that hate Anglo ways and everything about Anglos. Especially ones like us who try to live out here among them—taking over their land, buying it when they have to sell—and then fixing it so they can never get it back."

"How do you mean, fixing it so they can't get it back?"

"Fixing it up too well. Take this place, just for an example. The people who lived here before Nelson did bought it for five hundred dollars—the Spanish-American family who lived here, at least a dozen of them, had a bad year and deaths in the family and doctor bills. It was a two-room place then, falling apart. So five hundred was a fair price. But what do the Robinsons—that was their name—do? They fix it up. They add a room; they fix the floors and the woodwork; they put in two oil burners instead of one wood stove. They have electricity run from the last house a quarter-mile back. They put up a new outhouse and add a shed. So—now the property's worth a couple of thousand instead of five hundred and none of the natives out here can ever buy it back; it's fancy, it's only for *ricos*, rich people. The average cash income for those people is only a couple of hundred dollars a year. A place like this is a palace to most of them."

"Well, *I* didn't fix it up. I see what you mean, though. I felt it in Seco, when I stopped at the tavern one night."

"I don't. Stop there, I mean. I speak enough Spanish to catch phrases I'm not supposed—or am I?—to overhear. But even if you didn't speak Spanish you could feel the antagonism. Not that I blame them; we're changing this country, their way of life. We're interlopers. They've lived here practically since Coronado. But don't let it worry you, Weaver."

"Worry me how?"

"I mean they're not going to come here some night to assassinate you or anything like that. Just don't tangle with them, outside of business. Let them alone and they'll let you alone. But do your drinking in Taos and you'll like it better. Just be polite to them as they are to you, but don't think you can make friends. There's a barrier."

Callahan took another sip of his wine. "And it's probably good for us. Gives us the wrong side of race prejudice. We damn Anglos are prejudiced against any minority group we live with; does us good to *be* a minority group and get the dir-

ty end of the stick for once. Sure, the reasons aren't completely logical or justified—but are the reasons we're prejudiced
against Jews or Negroes or Chinamen any better? It's good
for our immortal souls, if any, to be hated a bit. Do you realize, Weaver, that almost every other country in the world—
even those that are on 'our side'—hates us more or less because of what we are? So let's have a sample of it right here at
home; maybe it'll teach us we're not completely God's chosen
people."

"Ummm," Weaver said. "Maybe you've got something
there."

"Yeah, good for us. You know, I had something I wanted
to tell you, but damned if I can remember what it was"

"Something about Jenny Ames?"

"I think it was, but I can't remember it right now. Well,
I'll think of it some other time. How are you and Jenny getting
along?"

Weaver felt himself bristle a little, and then wondered
why he had.

"Got about all I need." he said. "I've got Pepe Sanchez's
eyewitness account and the newspaper story. That's really
enough but I'd still like to talk to a few people who remember
it, if they're still around. Who is?"

"Well, Freeman's not still around; he died a couple of
years ago. Doc Gomez, who was coroner then is still alive but
he's living up in Colorado somewhere. Alamosa, I think. Let's
see—who else was there?"

"The woman who rode up on the bus with her. Evers?"

"Sure, Carlotta Evers. She's still in Taos. Works at the
supermarket on the west side of the plaza. But be careful—or
are you married?"

"I'm married," Weaver said. "Who else might be around?
Let's see—there was the man who found the body. Ramon Camillo, I think his name was."

"I don't know. He was from Seco, maybe he still lives
there. I didn't know him, aside from seeing him at the inquest."

"The people who knew Nelson, who'd talked to him. Who

were they?"

"Don't know, offhand. I guess I knew him as well as any-body else, which means I'd talked to him three or four times. Once his car broke down in front of my place and he couldn't get it started. I wandered out to see if I could help and he said sure if I had a phone he'd like to use it to have a repairman come out from Taos. So I phoned the A-1 and they sent out a man and got his car going. I forget what was wrong with it, but it wasn't anything serious; the mechanic had it running ten minutes after he got there."

"Did Nelson wait inside your place?"

"Sure, when I insisted. I gave him a drink, even, but he wouldn't take a second one. Which reminds me, I will, if I may."

Weaver poured it.

"Didn't Nelson tell you anything at all about himself?"

"Sure. A pack of lies. I remembered most of it when they were looking for him but when it got checked back on, none of it was true. Said he'd come here from a little town in California, Gersonville. Turned out there isn't any town in California by that name. That he'd lived in Woodstock, New York—that's another artists' colony like Taos is—but they couldn't find anyone in Woodstock that knew him, either by name or description. But he really was an artist, or tried to be one. I'm no judge, but Will Freeman says the place out here was littered with canvases."

"What happened to them? Did he take them all along with him?"

"Guess so, I don't know. I never heard anything to the contrary."

Weaver looked at him thoughtfully. "You say you're no judge. That sounds as though you'd seen some of his paint-ings. Did you?"

"Some of his water colors, that time his car broke down. He'd been out painting somewhere and was on his way back and while we were talking he showed me what he'd just done. I was polite about it, sure, but it made nuts to me. It was sup-posed to be mountains, but what mountains I couldn't guess

—and I've seen all the scenery for lots of miles around here. Oh sure, I know there's such a thing as abstract art and that some of it is supposed to be good, but if this was—well, as I said, I'm no judge."

"You never saw any of his oil paintings?"

"No, and the only person I know of who did see them was Freeman—the two times he was in Nelson's place looking around, the night of the murder and the day after. He wasn't any judge of painting either, but he said they looked like crap to him. As I told you, I think, Nelson never had any guests out here. The only two people known to have been inside the place while he lived here were Jenny Ames and the sheriff. Those water colors, though, they looked to me like something an insane man might do."

"About that day he was inside your place talking to you," Weaver said. "You say what he told you was malarkey, but what—well, what impression did he make on you? What did he seem to be?"

"Well, I think he was queer. And I don't mean strange, I mean homosexual. My guess is that Jenny Ames was pretty safe with him those few hours after she got there and before he killed her. And I'm not alone, incidentally, in thinking, Nelson was probably queer—that's the impression he gave other people around Taos—and Taos is pretty good at judging. It gets a lot of them. I guess any artists' colony does. Lezzies, too."

Callahan sipped his wine. "Freeman had the same idea that Nelson was as queer as a bedbug. One reason why he doubted Pepe's story—he didn't see what Nelson would be doing with a girl out there to begin with."

Weaver was interested. "You're fairly sure of that? I mean that he was straight homo—not even ambivalent?"

"Ninety-nine percent sure, and I'm pretty good at guessing. For instance, *you're* not homo."

"Thanks," Weaver said. "But let's stick to Nelson. Anything else about him you can remember?"

"Well, I wouldn't be surprised if he was a lunger. T. b. He looked big and husky, but that's the kind that often gets it.

And he had one coughing spell in my house that sounded like it to me—and I noticed that he coughed carefully into his handkerchief. Besides, he had slight flushed spots in his cheeks—unless they were make-up, and he wasn't that queer; he didn't swish. You know it's a funny thing about homos— the masculine-looking kind, not the out-and-out pansies— how girls will fall for them. And fall hard. Girls who haven't been around enough, that is, to spot them as competition instead of prospects. And most of them can be charming as hell when they want to turn on the charm. Nelson didn't, around here, but he probably could have. And he was handsome enough to make women fall for him."

"You're doing fine," Weaver said. "Any other impressions about him?"

"Not that I can remember. Damn, what was it I was going to tell you? With that pumping you've been doing, I've been telling you everything else but. Well, it couldn't have been too important or I'd have remembered it. If I think of it in time I'll let you know. Guess I'd better push along."

"Why? It's still early, not much after ten."

"Sure, but tomorrow's Wednesday, our big day. The day before we go to press. I'll have to get down early—and bright. Thanks for the drinks."

Weaver walked with Callahan to the car and stood on the bridge until the car went out of sight along the curving road. He decided that he rather liked Callahan—and certainly Callahan had been helpful in filling out his picture of, Nelson. But—didn't that picture make the motive of the crime even more murky than it had been? Or did it? A homosexual perhaps fighting his homosexuality, trying to make himself respond to a woman who loved him, suddenly going berserk with hatred and revulsion when he couldn't?

It seemed possible. Only, of course, if Nelson had been psychopathic—aside from or in addition to his homosexuality to begin with.

But the tuberculosis—if Callahan was right about it— where did it fit into the picture? Perhaps it didn't; perhaps it was incidental.

Weaver turned around and found himself staring into the window of the still lighted kitchen. And again trying to picture what Pepe Sanchez had seen there.

He shook himself a little.

Nuts, he told himself, *I'm letting this get me.*

Back in the foothills the coyotes were yapping again, their nightly chorus of the damned yearning for the unattainable.

Weaver leaned against the wall and stared up at the stars. A long distance away he could still hear the faint sound of Callahan's car.

The stars, the silly, far, twinkling stars. Somewhere he'd read that the nearest one was eight light-years away. That meant that the light he was seeing from it now, tonight, had left it eight years ago, perhaps on the very night— He shook himself a little. It was all right to let himself get interested in— this—but he couldn't let it get him like that.

He went back into the house and decided that for once he was going to bed early and reasonably sober. He did.

[5]

He woke, the next morning, in time to see the sun come up over the mountains. It was beautiful; the cool morning air was good to breathe. Life was suddenly good until he remembered the date.

It was Wednesday, the 31st of May. Tomorrow was the first day of June, the day the girls would go to camp, and Vi world be coming. Strange that she hadn't written already, telling him when to meet her in Santa Fe.

Well, if she didn't write in time, that was her grief and she could take the bus, much as she hated riding buses. Not that he blamed her for that—although there were plenty of things he did blame her for. Indirectly, he knew damned well, the animosity between them (which they kept so carefully submerged for the, sake of the girls) had been the cause of the breakdown he'd had. The direct reason, of course, had been that he'd worked too hard, far too hard. But if he analyzed the reasons why he'd worked too hard there were two of them, simple and obvious. First, in order to spend less time in an intolerable home. Second, in order to try (vainly) to earn enough money so he could provide separate maintenance for them, enable them to live apart without the necessity of a divorce—and all the things that a divorce would do to girls the ages of Ellen and Betty.

But the money part hadn't worked out; instead he'd toiled himself into a breakdown that had set him back to scratch again, now with no possibility of a separation in the foreseeable future. Not even the possibility of their living apart this summer while he was recovering.

Another part of it had been his own fault, the drinking. Drinking too much makes any problem worse.

And Vi drank too much, too. That really put the lid on it.

He made coffee for himself and fried two eggs, and then managed to kill a little time washing the few dishes and glasses that were dirty and straightening up and dusting the house.

If he had his typewriter—

The hell with a typewriter; he'd better make at least some notes in longhand before he forgot some of the things he'd learned. All he had on paper were names and dates and all the other details—especially things like those Callahan had told him last night—were still in his head.

He found writing paper and worked for about an hour. When he'd finished, it was still only nine o'clock, far too early to go into Taos for mail. He felt a little better now than he had a few days ago when he'd tried painting last; maybe he should try it again now.

But that reminded him of something else. All those canvases of Nelson's that the sheriff had seen around the house when he'd called here after the murder. Was it possible that some of them, or even some sketches, had been left behind? Possibly somewhere inside the house where he hadn't looked, possibly in the wooden shed twenty yards behind the house? He'd looked in that shed just once to date; he'd decided that he wouldn't need it for anything so he'd merely glanced in and noticed that it seemed to contain only junk, some odds and ends of broken furniture, some rusty bedsprings, an empty oil drum. He'd scarcely stepped inside and hadn't bothered to inventory the contents. There might be some pictures there.

There were. He went through the house systematically first and didn't find so much as a pencil sketch, but in the shed were three unframed canvases tilted with their faces against the wall. They were very dirty, but the shed had been dry and they were intact. He took them out into the sunlight and then got a rag from the house to wipe them off. He put them in a neat row, face out this time, against the side of the shed and stepped back to study them.

They weren't bad.

They were considerably better, anyway, than anything he himself could ever hope to do. They weren't really good, however; he knew enough about art to feel sure of that. But there was deep sincerity in them; the man who'd painted them had considered himself to be a serious artist and had done his best.

They were all pictures of mountains, but they were mountains in such shapes and colors as mountains have never been. They were mountains that writhed in dark agony against spectral skies. They were mountains of another dimension, on another world under an alien sun.

Weaver said "Jesus Christ" softly, and not irreverently, to himself as he studied then.

The pictures weren't signed, but they didn't have to be. He knew that they were Nelson's—and he knew that they meant two things; that Nelson was a little mad and that he had had at least a touch of genius to have expressed that madness so perfectly in paint on canvas.

He took them inside the house and propped them up on the table, one after another, to study them in light that was not so glaring.

He'd lost all inclination to get out his own water colors.

He drove into Taos and it was ten-thirty, still far too early to find mail at the post office. He drove past Doughbelly Price's office and saw through the window that Price was seated at his desk, still wearing the big hat. Weaver parked his Chevy and went in. Doughbelly looked up. "Hi, Weaver. You and the house getting along all right together out there?"

"We're doing fine," Weaver said. "Listen, out in the shed behind the house I found three paintings. Not signed but I think they're by Nelson. Who owns them?"

"I guess I do. Nelson hadn't paid his second month's rent yet and so I was told that any stuff he left behind him was mine, which wasn't much. But I didn't notice no paintings. Where were they?"

"In the shed, against the wall."

"Hell, I remember now, I did see them when I looked through the joint after Nelson had high-tailed. I looked at 'em, and they looked to me like the rest of the junk in the shed. Why? They ain't worth anything. Sit down."

Weaver sat down. "I rather like them," he said. "Whether they're worth anything or not I don't know, but I'd like to have them."

Doughbelly Price's eyes twinkled under the brim of the Stetson. "You're going to be gypped if you offer me anything for them. I asked a friend of mine, ran a gallery here then, whether Nelson's stuff had any commercial value. He said no. Said Nelson had wanted to exhibit there and had shown him a few things and they weren't worth nothing."

"That's good," Weaver said, "because I couldn't offer you much anyway."

"Tell you what, Weaver, how's this for a deal? It wouldn't hurt the value of the place out there none to have a few pictures hanged on the walls, no matter how lousy the pictures are. So how about this? You get all three of the things framed —there's lots of places around here does framing—and hang 'em. When you leave here take one of 'em, to cover getting the three framed—anyone you want—and leave the other two. Or if you still want all three, we'll dicker then."

"Done," Weaver said.

He left his car parked where it was and walked to and around the plaza, looking into windows, killing time until he could get his mail. There'd surely be a letter from Vi today telling him when to meet her.

Somebody said, "Hi, Weaver," and he turned. It was Callahan.

Weaver said, "Hi. How'd you go for a drink?" He'd figured it was too early to have a drink alone, but having one with someone would take the curse off it.

The editor shook his head regretfully. "My busy day, remember? Just ducked out for a cup of coffee. Can I buy you one?"

Weaver decided he might as well have a cup of coffee. At least it would kill time. They went to the coffee shop at La Fonda and sat at the counter.

Callahan shoveled two teaspoons of sugar into his. "Guess I was a little tight when I drove over to your place last night. Sorry I barged in on you so late."

"Don't be foolish. You got there early and left early, and it did me good to have someone to talk to. I've been spending too much time alone since I've been here."

"Your wife's coming soon?"

"Yes."

"Be glad to meet her. Say, I remembered, as soon as I got home, what it was I'd been wanting to tell you about the Nelson business. I remembered about the one report they got on him after he left here. Amarillo."

"In the Texas Panhandle?"

"Yes. When they circulated reports on him after the body had been found, a report came in from there. Two months before—a day or two after he left Taos, it must have been—he stayed one night at an Amarillo hotel."

"Under what name?"

"His own. I mean, Charles Nelson. And he registered from Taos. He must have felt sure there was no pursuit after him yet, that the body hadn't been found."

Weaver said, "He must have been heading east then. Anyone there remember anything about him?"

"Not worth mentioning. The name clicked with the hotel clerk when he read about the murder here in Taos and he checked back on the register and found it. But he remembered Nelson himself only well enough to verify the descripttion. He told the police there and they checked around and found the garage where he'd left his car overnight—piled high with luggage and canvases and stuff. And the attendant there thought he remembered—he wasn't too sure—that Nelson had asked about the roads down to El Paso."

"El Paso? Hell, if he was going to El Paso, he'd not have gone by way of Amarillo from Taos. That's two legs of a triangle—it'd be at least a couple hundred miles out of his way."

"More than that, I think. It could have been that he had business in Amarillo, of course. But, more likely, he was heading on east and asked about roads to the south just to throw off anybody that might be trying to trace him later."

"But why, in that case, register under the name they'd be looking for him under?"

"Easy answer to that. He cashed some traveler's checks. Had three twenty-dollar checks left in a book of them, in the name of Nelson and cashed them at the hotel he stayed at. He must not have figured it was much of a risk, but he might have taken the extra precaution—it didn't cost anything—to ask about roads in the wrong direction, just in case."

Weaver said, "About the traveler's checks . . . Couldn't they—?"

"They did," Callahan interrupted. "Sure, they traced the ones he'd cashed there, and found they'd been bought in Denver three months before; he'd bought a book of ten of them at a bank there. The other seven turned out to have been cashed in Taos during the time he was living here. He must have realized, after he lammed out, that he still had three uncashed twenty-dollar traveler's checks and took the slight chance of registering under his own name—if Nelson was his own name—one night so he could get his sixty bucks out of them. It was a minor and calculated risk; the chance was remote that the body would have been found so soon—if, in fact, it ever was found. Way back there in the hills, he probably figured it was safe forever."

"Did they do any checking in Denver, where he bought the traveler's checks?"

"Oh, sure, but he must have been just passing through. He bought them for cash at a bank where he was a stranger and no other lead to him turned up there at all. Well, I'd better get back to the office."

Callahan insisted on paying the check for the coffees and Weaver let him; the amount wasn't enough to argue about.

They went out to the plaza and started around it; at the corner Weaver pointed. "Is that the supermarket Carlotta Evers works at?"

"Yes. Want to meet her?"

"I'd like to, if you're not in too much of a hurry—"

"Not so much I can't spare another two minutes. Come on."

Business wasn't rushing, at that hour, in the supermarket. Callahan led Weaver to one of the cash-out registers where a dark-haired woman of about thirty or thirty-five—she looked as though she might be half Spanish, half Anglo—quite pretty, was ringing up an order of groceries. There was no one in line behind the customer and as soon as he'd carried his bag of groceries away, Callahan introduced Weaver and explained his interest in Jenny Ames.

Weaver said, "I'd like to talk to you about it, Miss Evers. May I take you to dinner tonight?"

Her smile showed a gold tooth that made her look slightly less attractive. "Thanks. I'd be glad to."

"Where and when shall I meet you?"

"Well—would six be too early? I get off at five and that would give me time to dress. I live right near here, just past the Harwood."

Weaver said that six would he fine and absorbed complicated directions—all directions in Taos are complicated—about how to find the right door.

Another customer approached the register then, and Weaver took his leave and walked back to the newspaper office with Callahan. From there to the post office; it was time now for the first mail to be in.

There was a letter from Vi:

"Dear Georgie—"

His skin crawled a bit at the grammar, spelling and punctuation that followed (no matter how ridiculous he knew it was that he should feel that way), but its purport was simple. She would take the girls to camp Friday; she herself would leave Kansas City late Saturday afternoon; her train would reach Santa Fe at six o'clock Sunday morning. She was glad that he was going to meet her. The girls sent their love.

He wondered irritably why she couldn't have chosen a train that arrived at a reasonable hour; there were several every day and there was no reason why she had to choose one that got in at such an ungodly time. He'd have to get up at about three o'clock in the morning to meet that train; either that or drive to Santa Fe on Saturday and stay at a hotel there. Probably that would be the lesser of the evils.

Besides, the information was incomplete; the train didn't get into Santa Fe at six o'clock or any other time. The nearest passenger stop for Santa Fe is Lamy, eighteen miles away, and the trains connect there with a bus that carries passengers the final lap into Santa Fe. From her letter he couldn't tell whether the train got into Lamy at six o' clock or whether that was the time the connecting bus reached Santa Fe.

He'd been intending to drive to Lamy to meet the train itself, but since she was so inconsiderate about the time of her arrival, let her take the bus, he decided, into Santa Fe and he'd meet her there. He bought an airmail postcard at the window and wrote and addressed it at the post office desk; he told her to buy her ticket through to Santa Fe, which would make it include the eighteen-mile bus trip from Lamy, and that he'd meet her at the terminal in Santa Fe. He postscripted a reminder about the typewriter and the camera.

That about filled the postcard, but he remembered something else and bought another one; he told Vi that if she'd either bring or ship ahead of her a few blankets and a few assorted dishes, silverware and cooking utensils, it would save them from having to buy more to supplement the few he had already bought, and would save them some money. He was getting a bit worried about money.

Partly on account of money he decided against having lunch in Taos and drove back to the house to cook something for himself; he'd be feeding Carlotta Evers at a restaurant tonight and that would be enough eating expense for one day.

He cooked himself some ham and eggs. It wasn't too good, but it wasn't too bad either—at least as good as Vi could have cooked it; she was incorrigibly careless in her cooking and sloppy in her housework. Neither praise nor censure could induce her to take the little extra trouble that made the difference between a good meal and a poor one. And she had an aversion to trying any new dishes; she cooked the same things over and over again in the same mediocre way—

Well, he had plenty of faults of his own, he thought; and food was not too important a part of his life. Neither, for that matter, was sex, these last few years; he'd done without it most of the time and could keep on doing without it. But if Vi could only talk intelligently, or even listen intelligently, if only she'd read something besides trashy love story and confession magazines—if she could only be a companion, even in the slightest degree—

Don't be an ass, he told himself; *that isn't Vi's fault. It's yours.*

It was his own fault for having married suddenly and on the basis of a purely physical attraction—and nothing in common besides that—which had been all too brief for both of them. And with physical attraction gone and sex life almost nonexistent, there was nothing left between them at all— nothing except the children who tied them almost irrevocably together. *Almost* irrevocably—if only he could earn enough money—

If only they hadn't had children— And yet, of course, he wouldn't put Ellen and Betty back where they'd come from— even if that were possible—now that he had them and loved them.

But damn, damn. Vi, he had seen within two years of marrying her, was incurably stupid, almost aggressively stu-

pid and dull. Nothing, almost literally nothing, could penetrate the carapace of her indifference to everything worthwhile in literature, art, music, living. Nothing above the level
of sheer unendurable trash. Love pulps, soap operas, cloying
popular ballads—she chewed them all contentedly a cow
chews a cud. She needed, wanted, nothing more; these things
were her life, these things and drinking and the eternal eating
of candy—box after box of it—that had put forty pounds of
weight on her since their marriage, forty flabby pounds that
made her body, once slender and desirable, almost as gross
and bovine as her mind.

He tried to forget about her and the fact that within four
days now she'd be out here with him. He washed the dishes
and utensils he had used, put them away, straightened the
house again. He liked neatness, orderliness, simplicity, and
for a few days more he could have them.

He studied again the three pictures Nelson had left
behind him, envying the conception and the execution of each
of them. Probably only someone slightly off the beam, like
himself, would appreciate them. But he'd give a lot to be able
to do a fraction as well.

He decided he might as well take them in today, when he
drove in to Taos later for his dinner date, and leave them at a
framer's. It would be better if he had them back, already
hung, when Vi came. She'd probably never even notice them
if they were already on the wall. Otherwise he'd have to
explain, and even so she'd think he was crazy to have paid for
the framing of such horrible things. He looked about, wondering where they should be hung, and suddenly an idea
came to him.

The shed where he'd found them—why couldn't the junk
in it be carted away and the place itself cleaned up? Then he
could convert it into a studio for himself, a place where he
could spend time by himself. The three small rooms of the
house—without even a door between two of them—offered
almost no privacy at all.

But why couldn't the shed be made into a den, a retreat,
a studio, a sanctum? He could keep his paints there, and his

books and magazines, and wine—and he could be alone there as much as he wanted. Vi wouldn't understand completely but she would make no objection. And there'd be enough wall space to hang all three of the Nelson canvases; he could have them all to himself.

The thought cheered him tremendously; it was an inspiration that made the summer ahead look infinitely less bleak and boring.

He went out to the shed immediately and looked it over. Yes, it was plenty big enough, about twelve by fourteen. There was a window—with the glass broken—and it was on the side away from the house. The roof didn't seem to leak and the walls were sound except for a knothole or two it would be easy to plug or cover. No electricity, but it wouldn't cost much to run a pair of wires from the house twenty yards away. A small oil burner—he could probably, especially at this season of the year, pick up a used one for a few dollars—would keep it warm on cool evenings. The whole setup would cost him only a few dollars and would be worth hundreds. He could keep his typewriter here, too—

The more he thought of it the more enthusiastic he became; it was the answer to most of the problems that had worried him—particularly the problem of Vi's radio. Vi wouldn't be happy without one, and the interminable programs of soap opera and cheap music would drive him mad if he had to listen to them twelve hours or so a day. Those radio programs had been one of the causes—and not an unimportant cause—of what had happened to him; they'd driven him out of the house, evening after evening, to work or to drink. He simply couldn't stand them, and yet he hated to be brutal with Vi about them because they were such a ridiculously important part of her life.

Would the shed be too dark? No, not if he got himself some flat paint—or maybe even whitewash would do—and painted the walls a light color. And among the junk, that table, if painted and the wobbly leg braced, would do for his typewriter. He could spare one comfortable chair from the house—

Yes, by all means—and before Vi came.

He checked over the items of junk again and found nothing worth salvaging except the table. He measured the window so he could tell Ellis DeLong what size pane to bring. He checked the lock on the door and found that it worked, although it needed oiling.

He drove in to Taos feeling more contented than he'd felt for a long time. He left the three canvases at a frame shop, with orders to frame them as inexpensively as possible, and then went to see Ellis DeLong.

The sunlight was bright and warm and the world was a good place. His thoughts were a long way from murder, murder past or murder yet to come. He didn't think once of Jenny Ames.

But he remembered his date with Carlotta Evers; after he'd made arrangements with DeLong to do the few things the shed required, and as soon as possible, he killed time over a bottle of ale at the Taos Inn until time to pick her up at her apartment near the Harwood.

[6]

They ate Wiener Schnitzel, a specialty of the house, at La Doña Luz. Carlotta was loquacious, but her conversation tended to wander; he had to keep gently leading her back to the topic of Jenny Ames.

"It was so long ago." she almost wailed. "Six or seven years. How can I remember—"

"Eight years, Miss Evers." Weaver turned on his, most charming smile. "Yes, a long time, I'll admit. But can't you remember any more than that?"

"I could have, I guess—if I'd known at the time, or even right after, that it was anything worth remembering. But it wasn't until months after that ride on the bus that I knew it was important—I mean that her body was found and I remembered that the girl I'd talked to had been going to meet Mr. Nelson and so she must be the one I talked to. That sounds mixed up, I guess, but you know what I mean. And after two months I couldn't remember *everything* she said, because I wasn't paying an awful lot of attention at the time. You know how it is when you talk to somebody on a bus; it goes in one ear and out the other, except interesting things like that she was coming to Taos to get married and everything."

"But she promised to look you up, you said, after she was married. Didn't you wonder when you didn't hear from her?"

"After seeing her just that once? Of course not. People always promise things like that and how often do they really do them? And then a week or two later I happened to hear that Mr. Nelson had left and I thought they'd just decided to move away and live somewhere else. But then when they found her body, that was different. I tried then to remember everything I could, and the sheriff helped me. He kept asking me questions for hours. And now you're—" The gold tooth flashed. "Well, I guess this dinner is worth it. Go ahead."

"Attagirl." Weaver said. "Then let's start over again— forgive me—at the beginning. You hadn't seen her in the bus station in Santa Fe before you boarded the bus?"

"No, I was almost late for the bus; it was ten minutes after the time it was supposed to leave when I got there, but you know how buses are, always a little late pulling out, so I made it, just barely. I got on just before it started and all the seats were taken except one so I sat down there, and it happened to be the one next to *her*."

"Do you remember what your first impression of her was?"

"I'm afraid I don't, Mr. Weaver. I remember what my impression of her was after the trip, but not what I thought when I first saw her. Probably just that she was pretty, nice looking, something like that."

"Which of you spoke first?"

"I probably asked her if the seat was taken. You generally do before you sit down beside somebody on a bus." She paused and considered. "I think it was the third or fourth seat back, on the driver's side. And then, just naturally, we got to talking. Probably one of us said it was a beautiful day—it really was—or something like that; that's the way most conversations start. Pretty soon, it couldn't have been more than a minute or two, she asked me how far I was going on the bus—it goes all the way through to Denver, you know, not just to Taos—and I said Taos, and that's when she got really interested. She said she was going to Taos too and that she'd never been there before and would I tell her something about it.

"So I did and she kept asking questions and I guess I was telling her about Taos all the way to Española before I asked her anything about herself; I finally asked her if she was going there on vacation or to take a job or what, and she told me she was going there to marry Charles Nelson and did I know him."

"And did you?"

"I knew who he was, by sight. In a place like this, and eight years ago it wasn't even as big as it is now, you get to know who almost everybody is, even if you don't know them."

"How much did you know about Nelson?"

"Only that he was supposed to be an artist and lived out near Seco, and that he wasn't very sociable and hadn't made any friends here. That's about all."

"According to the newspaper account I read, Jenny Ames thought that Nelson taught at one of the art schools here. Did you tell her she was wrong about that?"

"No, because I wasn't sure he didn't. I mean, from the little I knew about him, I didn't think he worked for anybody but I wasn't positive about it."

Weaver nodded. They'd finished dinner by then and were drinking their coffee. "Just think back, Miss Evers. Try to remember if she said anything at all that would give you even a slight clue to where she came from or give what she'd been doing."

"Well—that's what the sheriff kept asking me, but if she said anything about that, I don't remember—I couldn't remember when he was asking me then, so how could I now? I don't think she said anything at all about herself—her past or where she came from, I mean. She was so interested and excited about where she was going and what she was going to do that the other just didn't come up at all."

"But little things, if you can remember them, may have been clues. Did she, for instance, seem familiar with Spanish-Americans or was she curious about them and what they were like?"

"I don't remember her asking about them. But I don't think she was from New Mexico anywhere. No, don't ask me what it was she said that made me think that—I just remember that I thought it, but I don't know why. And she didn't have any special accent, if you know what I mean. I mean like an Eastern accent or a Texas accent—those I can always tell. Nor Southern. She talked just like most people."

"And what did she tell you about how she met Nelson?"

"That she'd started corresponding with him through a Lonely Hearts Club in some magazine—she didn't say what magazine, I'm sure, or the exact name of the club. That the letters he wrote were wonderful and that after they'd both written awhile, he came for a vacation to the town she lived in and—"

"Did she say *town?* Are you sure of that?"

"I think so, yes. She said that he was there a week and they'd fallen in love with one another but that he had to go back to Taos on account of his job there and they'd arranged for her to follow him as soon as she could get ready, and they were going to get married here. She thought he was awfully handsome and wonderful—I guess any girl thinks that about a man she's going to marry."

It wasn't pay dirt, Weaver was beginning to realize. Except for irrelevant little things such as the sequence of conversation, he hadn't learned anything he hadn't already known.

He tried a different tack. "Can you describe her?"

"Well—no better than I did for the sheriff. She had on a light summer coat, tan, I think. And a hat, but I don't remember what kind. Maybe it was a tam. She was—oh, medium height and weight, kind of a nice figure as far as you could tell with her wearing a coat—and a kind of a pretty face, some

make-up but not too much. Dark hair, I didn't remember
whether it was black or dark brown, but it turned out that it
was black. And—well, that's about all, except that she seemed
awfully eager and excited. But she thought she was coming
here to get married, so you can't blame her for that."

Weaver didn't blame her for that.

He blamed Carlotta Evers for not remembering the name
of the town Jenny Ames had probably mentioned, and for being so vague about everything else—but, he told himself, eight
years was eight years and he probably wouldn't do any better
himself. He wondered why he'd expected to get anything out
of Carlotta now that the sheriff hadn't been able to get out of
her only two months after the murder.

He tried a few more times, from a few other angles and
with the help of a few post-dinner drinks, and then gave up.
He took Carlotta Evers home to her apartment, and made no
passes.

He felt that he didn't want to drink wine after the several
highballs he'd had after dinner with Carlotta so he picked up
a bottle of whisky at a liquor store which was still open on the
plaza and took it home with him.

He made himself a drink, a fairly stiff one, and sat in the
kitchen sipping it and thinking back over his conversation
with Carlotta, wondering if he could deduce from anything
she had said any fact, however slight, that he hadn't already
known about Jenny Ames.

No, nothing—unless that she seemed more real, more
vivid, now that he'd actually talked to someone who had
talked to her. But still no clue to where she'd come from, what
she'd been.

*Why weren't you missed, Jenny? Why did no word
come from whoever knew you after your name was in the
papers all over the country? Did you come from Mars or
Venus? No, Nelson couldn't have written you there; the mail
service is too poor. But why didn't somebody miss you,
somewhere? You were lonely, yes, or you'd never have written to a Lonely Hearts Club, but you must have had relatives
or at least acquaintances who should have recognized your*

name.

Somehow, he thought, it made her seem more pathetic—what happened to her more tragic—that no one knew her. That no one besides the murderer, who had made his getaway, knew whence she came or what she had been. That, besides the murderer, only two people remembered having seen her at all, and one of those two had seen her only for seconds, through a window and from a distance.

You were cheated out of your life, Jenny, before you had a chance to live it. Quite probably you were a virgin, inexperienced in love. Other men had made advances—they must have if you were pretty, as Pepe and Carlotta say you were—but no one you liked had asked you to marry him and that was what you were waiting for, and you were lonely. So lonely that you wrote to a correspondence club.

And hit the jackpot—you thought. A man who corresponded with you and then came to your town to see you. And he was handsome and said he loved you and you loved him, and he said he wanted to marry you. You must have been awfully happy, Jenny, on that bus ride to Taos.

But why, Jenny, did he kill you?

Was he mad, or was there another reason? Was he Bluebeard, and did you open his closet, perhaps, and see the murdered bodies of his other wives? Then turn, to see him picking up the knife?

Damn him, Weaver thought; mad or sane I'd like to find him and kill him with my own hands.

He went to the back door and opened it, stood there staring out into the darkness, listening to the far yapping of the coyotes. He told himself: *this happened eight years ago. It doesn't matter now.*

The next day, seventy degrees at ten o'clock, humidity negligible, sunshine perfect.

A man of DeLong's came out with a truck; he cleared the junk out of the shed, fixed the broken pane, ran wiring from the meter back of the house and rigged a light in the shed. "I brought the paint, Mr. Weaver." he said. "But Ellis said maybe you wanted to do the painting yourself. That right?"

"That's right. Bring brushes?"

"A three-inch brush, yes. And enough paint to do inside and outside—or did you just want to do the inside?"

Weaver decided that since the paint was here, he might as well paint the outside too.

It was the best day he'd had yet. Something to do, something constructive that would give him the privacy he'd want after Vi's arrival. He got buckets of water from the creek and washed the wooden floor of the shed first, then painted the ceiling and the walls while the floor dried. He painted the floor then and was about to start on the outside when he realized it was mid-afternoon and he was hungry; he hadn't eaten anything since an early breakfast.

He drove in to Taos to eat so he could pick up the framed pictures if they were ready for him; they were. He ate quickly and hurried back; he got almost half of the outside painted before darkness stopped him.

He slept well that night, dead tired. He finished painting the outside the next morning; the inside was almost dry by then and he decided it would serve without a second coat. He drove in to Taos and found a small used oil heater, some boards for shelving, an army cot. He bought a few tools and some nails to go with the shelving. He'd want a drape of some kind for the window, but that could wait until Vi got here; that was a woman's job.

He checked the post office for mail—there wasn't any—but didn't stop in Taos to eat or to have a drink. He hurried back to finish and furnish his sanctuary. He finished it before dark, and it was good.

Again he got to bed early and slept well. He awoke at dawn and it was Saturday and he lay in bed trying to decide whether he should go to Santa Fe today and spend the night at a hotel there, or whether he should stay here until three or four o' clock in the morning, time to drive down there and pick up Vi. He damned her again for taking such a train when others were available; she wouldn't be leaving Kansas City until this afternoon, maybe he could still send her a telegram telling her to take the bus at Santa Fe and that he'd meet her in Taos. But no, he should have done that right away instead of promising to meet her and then reneging at the last minute.

If he was going to drive down in the early morning, he realized, he'd have to buy an alarm clock today. It was that thought that decided him; an alarm clock would cost as much as a night in a hotel and he certainly had no other use for one, here in Taos. Yes, he'd drive to Santa Fe today and stay there overnight. A call left at the desk would get him waked in time to meet Vi. Also, in Santa Fe it would be easier to find out whether six o'clock was the time the train pulled into Lamy or the time its connecting bus reached Santa Fe.

While he made and drank coffee he found himself wondering what he could do today; no point in driving to Santa Fe until late afternoon or early evening. Maybe there was some loose end to the Jenny Ames story that he could wind up, and then, as soon as he got his typewriter tomorrow, he could get the thing off to Luke.

But what angle was left that he hadn't tried? Well, there was the hotel in Albuquerque where Jenny had stayed overnight, the night before her fatal trip to Taos. Why not check there? Albuquerque is only sixty-odd miles past Santa Fe; if he left by noon he could drive there today, do his checking, and get back to Santa Fe in the evening. But the paper hadn't mentioned the name of the hotel. Would Callahan remember it, or be able to find out for him?

He killed part of the morning straightening up the house so it would be in perfect order when Vi got there—not that it would stay that way long unless he wanted to keep on doing the work himself—and putting a few finishing touches on the shed. Then he drove to Taos and went to the office of *El Crepúsculo*.

Callahan's desk—an ancient roll-top—was closed and the girl behind the counter said, "Mr. Callahan doesn't come in on Saturdays, sir. But he happens to be in town; he was in here for a minute just a few minutes ago. If you walk around the plaza you'll probably find him somewhere."

Weaver walked around the plaza, looking in at likely places; he found Callahan having a cup of coffee at the counter in the Rio Grande Drugstore. Callahan said, "Hi, Weaver. Cup of coffee? Jeanette! Bring another cup of coffee."

While they drank their coffee, Callahan said, "How goes it with Jenny, Weaver? Get anything from Carlotta?"

"Not much. Guess I've got about all there is to get. There's one angle I might still try, though, if you can help me. I'm driving down to Santa Fe today anyway; I might go on to Albuquerque while I'm at it and see if I can get anything at the hotel she stayed at there. Do you remember the name of it?"

"Ummm, no. Wasn't it in the news story?"

"Pretty positive it wasn't. I made notes of all names and dates and if the hotel had been there, I'd have noted it down."

"Let me think awhile. It may come to me. You're not in a hurry to leave, are you?"

"No."

"Not that I think you'll get anything important there. You know, the more you think about that case—and you've got me thinking about at lately—the funnier it gets. No beginning and no end—nothing except what happened here. We don't know where Nelson came from—unless the Colorado license plates on his car meant he came from there and I doubt it—nor where he went, outside of that one stop in Amarillo. We don't know where the Ames girl came from, beyond that one night in Albuquerque. We don't know—we don't know much of anything."

"Did they trace the license number on Nelson's car?"

"Would have if anybody had noticed it or remembered it. But nobody did. Like your car—I've seen it and noticed that it's a Missouri license, but I don't remember the number."

"Not sure I remember it myself. I see what you mean. Listen, you say Sheriff Freeman's dead, but what about any deputies of his who may have worked on the case? Would any of them be around?"

"Afraid not. Freeman had only two deputies. One of them went into the army shortly after that; I don't know what happened to him except that he never came back to Taos. The other—let's see—he got a job with the state police a couple of years ago, but the last I heard he was working in the southern part of the state, around Lordsburg, hell of a ways from here. You might find him, but I doubt if it would be worth the trouble. Joe Sandoval his name is; he did some leg work on the case, but he's no mental heavyweight. Hey, I just thought how you can get the name of that Albuquerque hotel."

"How?"

"At the *Albuquerque Tribune*; they'll have it in their files. They covered the case—even had a reporter up here for the inquest. And to them the fact that she'd spent the night before she was killed at a hotel there is a local angle; their stories would be sure to play it up—probably with an interview with the desk clerk who'd registered her, if he remembered her at all."

"Thanks. Silly of me not to have thought of that myself."

Callahan laughed. "Sillier of me—as a newspaperman not to have thought of it sooner. Well, I'd better push along; got some errands to do yet and want to get home by noon. Have a good trip."

It was a good trip. The road from Taos to Santa Fe and thence to Albuquerque goes through some spectacular and breathtaking country, and it is at its best in early June.

Weaver thought it strange, but not too strange, that as he drove through the narrow, tortuous streets of Santa Fe—streets laid out for burro traffic rather than for automobiles—he had no desire to look up any of the people he knew there. Had known, rather. Why, now, try to renew contacts that meant nothing to him any longer? The past was gone—like Jenny Ames was gone. White bones by now, crumbling. Where? He'd never thought to ask. Unless for a photograph to accompany the story, what did it matter? No, he didn't want to see Jenny's grave. He'd always hated the thought of graves and cemeteries; he'd never gone to visit the graves of his own parents. Not because he was above sentiment, or below it, but because it had seemed such a useless, even a ridiculous gesture. As though the dead knew whether you came to visit their graves or not.

The way to visit the dead is the approach of one's mind

to their memory, not the approach of one's body to their graves.

It was hot in Albuquerque when he arrived there in midafternoon, enough to make him appreciate the mountain mildness of Taos summer. And Albuquerque had grown greatly in size since he'd last seen it. There'd been only a slight difference in Santa Fe, but Albuquerque seemed almost twice the size it had been when he'd last seen it five years before. It had been a large town then; it was a small city now.

He found a place to park near the *Albuquerque Tribune* office. He went in and explained what he wanted to a young man who came to the desk. A few minutes later he was looking through a bound volume of papers eight years old. He started with July 15th, the day the body had been found; the story hadn't reached Albuquerque in time to make the paper that day.

The next issue had a full column—and Callahan had been right; the local angle was played up. A fair portion of the story—and the rest of it included nothing that hadn't been in the Taos paper—was devoted to the fact that Jenny Ames had spent the night before her death, the night of May 16th, at the Colfax Hotel in Albuquerque, that she had undoubtedly taken the eleven o'clock bus the following morning for Santa Fe.

There was an interview with the clerk at the Colfax Hotel, Ward Haver by name, but little was brought out except the fact that he remembered the girl but vaguely; that she had checked in, according to the records, at four o' clock in the afternoon and had checked out at ten-thirty the following morning. She'd stayed in Room 36.

Weaver read the rest of the story and skimmed through the papers following; nothing further that was new to him. He closed the bound volume; the young man who had brought it to him came back to the desk and Weaver asked him, "Your current editor—did he hold the job eight years ago?"

"Mr. Carson? I'm not sure; I know he's been with the paper quite a while, but I've been here only two years myself. Shall I ask him?"

"Well—I'd like to see him in any case. If he wasn't here

then, he'll probably know who to refer me to. My name's Weaver, George Weaver."

"Just a moment, Mr. Weaver."

Then he was being shown through a door into a private office and a man with thinning gray hair said, "Yes. Mr. Weaver? I'm Carson."

"Were you editor here at the time of the Jenny Ames murder near Taos, eight years ago?"

"I wasn't editor then, but I worked here. Worked on the case, in fact."

"You were the man who was sent to Taos to cover the inquest?"

"No, that was Tommy Mainwarren; he isn't here anymore. But I covered the local angle, the hotel and the depots and whatnot."

"Good, that's what I'm interested in right now." Weaver explained briefly why he was interested. "Do you have a few minutes to spare?"

"A few, yes. Just what do you want to know?"

"Well, this occurred to me while I was reading your story just now, in the outer office. How was it learned so quickly that Jenny Ames had stayed here at the Colfax Hotel? I assumed that the clerk had probably read a news story and had remembered the name—but the hotel angle was in the first story you ran, so it couldn't have been that."

"Let's see—we first learned about the story when our regular Taos correspondent, whoever it may have been then—I don't remember, phoned us a tip on the story. It looked like a big story so Tommy Mainwarren was sent up there right away to cover it. When he phoned in the story I took it down. That happened to be several hours before press time and I got to thinking about the fact that she'd taken the one o'clock bus out of Santa Fe. That bus leaves Albuquerque around eleven and she might have come from here. I asked Henderson—he was the editor then—if I could check that angle and he told me to go ahead.

"I trotted down to the bus depot and tried to get something—but I couldn't. Nobody remembered after two months

—and you can't blame them for that with only a pretty general description—anything about the girl. Be funny, for that matter, if anybody had. You don't have to give your name to buy a bus ticket and unless you do something unusual—like spitting in the ticket seller's eye or breaking a window in the bus while you're riding it—nobody's going to remember you after two months. None of the ticket sellers who'd been working that day remembered her, nor did the driver who'd had that run—I was lucky enough to catch him at the station."

The editor struck a match under his desk and pulled fire into an ancient pipe. "But the local angle was still worth trying for and it hit me that she might have stayed over in a hotel here if she had come through this way, so I phoned hotels and asked them to check their registrations for the name Jenny Ames on—whatever night it would have been. Hit pay dirt at the Colfax."

Weaver nodded. "That was good work. And—well, I just read the story you wrote so I guess I know what you found out. The clerk remembered her, but not very well."

"He was barely sure that he remembered her at all. If we'd had a picture of her to refresh his memory we might have got more. But the records showed when she checked in and when she checked out—just in time to get that eleven o'clock bus to Santa Fe, so there's no doubt she was on it even if they don't remember her. And the clerk thinks he remembers she had two suitcases. I guess the story contained the fact that she put Taos as her address on the registration card?"

"Yes."

"Logical enough," Carson said, "although too bad she figured it that way. She must have thought that was going to be her permanent address and she might as well start using it instead of an obsolete address she didn't intend to return to. Anything else?" He stared at the ceiling a few seconds. "Oh, yes, I tried to see how she came into Albuquerque the day before. She checked in at the hotel sometime late in the afternoon—"

"Four o'clock, according to the story."

"That's right, four o'clock. I checked arrival times of

trains and buses; no train came in for several hours before then. But there was a bus arrival at three-thirty. And anyway, since she stayed at the Colfax, it's more likely she came in by bus. The Colfax was just across the street from the bus terminal and half a block down; you see the sign as you come out of the door and it's a natural thing, if you're a stranger in town, to head for the nearest hotel if there's one in sight.

"I checked some more at the bus terminal and couldn't get any proof that she had really come in on that bus, but it seems likely. Especially when I found it had been twenty minutes late that day; got in at ten minutes of four. Allowing ten minutes for her to get her bags if she'd checked them through and to cross the street and walk half a block, that'd make the four o'clock check-in time at the Colfax just right."

Weaver nodded. "You used the past tense about the Colfax Hotel," he said. "Isn't it there anymore?"

"No, it was razed several years ago to make room for a big office building. It was a small hotel—only three stories."

"And the clerk, Ward Haver?"

"Haven't an idea. I didn't know him, outside of that one talk with him."

"The three-thirty bus that she probably came in on. What was its route?"

"Los Angeles-Phoenix-Globe-Socorro. That run. The police tried to trace her back along it to find her starting point, but they didn't get anywhere. Be a miracle, I suppose, if they had, after that length of time. Well, Mr. Weaver, I'm afraid that's all I can tell you."

Weaver thanked him and left.

He looked in an Albuquerque phone book—on the off-chance—for the name of Ward Haver, and it wasn't there. It didn't really matter; the clerk could scarcely have told him anything he hadn't told Carson. And it would be futile for him to try any checking at the bus terminal; that had been tried eight years ago, and by the police as well as by a reporter, and it hadn't paid off then.

There was nothing further for him in Albuquerque. He drove back to Santa Fe and got there by dinner time.

[7]

Vi gave him a perfunctory smile and then her pasty face went quickly sullen again. "It was an *awful* trip, George. I couldn't sleep a wink all night long. I'm so tired. And hungry, too, simply starving. They hadn't opened the dining car yet."

Weaver said, "Come on, we'll find you somewhere to eat. I could use a cup of coffee myself."

"But the *baggage,* George. There's all that stuff you told me to bring, typewriter, bedding, dishes—"

He grinned at her. "They didn't make you carry it, did they? Let's have some breakfast first. We can pick up the luggage afterwards."

Over breakfast—and Vi packed away a big one—Weaver studied her. She managed to pout, to look sullen, even when she was eating. Her eyes seemed even duller. And she'd gained weight, he was sure, in the few weeks since he'd left Kansas City. He could picture her alone in the apartment there, tippling all afternoon and alternating sips of whisky with chocolate creams while she read confession magazines and listened to interminable radio programs. Probably she hadn't been outdoors once since he left, unless it was to go to a movie in the evening. Spots of rouge on her cheeks were the only color in her face.

What had made her that way, he wondered for possibly the ten thousandth time since their marriage. Had it been his fault?

He didn't see how, basically. In a few little things, yes. He hadn't been perfect by any means. But back in the early days of their marriage, when they'd loved one another, at least physically, he'd tried his best to help her get interested in—well, in worthwhile things. He hadn't nagged her about it; he'd simply, for example, exposed her to good music by taking her places where she could hear it, by buying good records and playing them once in a while. By seeing that there were good books and magazines around the house as well as the ones she bought for herself. Not highbrow stuff either; he tried to settle for educating her up to *Collier's* or the *Post* instead of *Dream Romances* and *Movie Confessions*. And, although he liked symphonies and quartets himself, he'd have settled if she'd liked Crosby or Goodman instead of Texas Slim.

No, her taste had been unchangeable, no matter how hard or how subtly he tried to improve it. All that had changed about her was that, once she'd got herself a man, she'd let herself go, cared little about her appearance and less about her figure. She'd vegetated, sunk into a morass of mushy reading and listening, steady drinking, even steadier eating.

About the only thing he could say for her was that she hadn't been unfaithful to him—or did he know even that? She flirted with other men sometimes, was coy with them, but he'd simply assumed she didn't have the incentive to go farther than that. Maybe he was wrong—but it didn't matter. He might have cared once, but he didn't now. Except for the girls' sake, of course.

How on earth was it that the two girls, born of Vi, had good minds? So keen that even now, at their ages, they must know that their mother was a dipsomaniac. They'd know soon enough if she was or became as sloppy morally as she was in every other way. Maybe after all it would be better to make a clean break—

He shook his head to clear it. No, it simply couldn't be done. Right now, especially, when he wasn't earning a cent, it was utterly ridiculous even to think of such a thing.

He said, "There's egg on your chin, dear."

She wiped it off, absently. "Why didn't you take a place in Santa Fe, George?" She frowned at him. "We don't know *anybody* in Taos."

He grinned. "That's why I picked the place, maybe. You know the doctor's orders, Vi. Peace and seclusion. If it was just a matter of not working, we could have stayed in Kansas

City. But wait till you see—"

She was eating again, not listening. And why go on with what he'd started to say? He knew suddenly—and wondered why he hadn't thought of it before—that she wouldn't appreciate mountains and sunshine and beauty. She hadn't liked even Santa Fe, really; it had been at her urging that he'd gone to a bigger city when he'd decided to go in business for himself—choosing Kansas City because he already had a few connections there.

No, Vi wasn't going to like Taos. She was going to like living ten miles outside of Tao, in the last house on a road, even less.

She finished eating and there was egg on her chin again, but he didn't bother telling her about it. This time, though, she took a compact from her purse and looked into the mirror of it; she wiped the egg off before she dabbed her face with the powder puff and then put lipstick—too much of it, of course—on her over-full, petulant lips. She took a comb from her purse.

He said, "Please, Vi."

"Oh, that's right; you don't like it when I use a comb at the table. All right, I'll wait."

She got a cigarette out and he held his lighter for her.

"What time is it, George?"

"A few minutes after seven." He stared past her through the coffee-shop window at the brightening day outside. He wished she'd hurry so they could get going on the drive to Taos. But he'd have to sit here a long time; Vi would want a second cup of coffee and probably a third, and she'd take her time over each of them while a pile of lipstick-smeared cigarette butts grew in the ash tray.

"Do you guess a bar would be open this early, George? I mean, by the time I've had another cup of coffee, I know it seems awful to have a drink this early, but I couldn't *sleep* on the train and I'm so tired that if I had a drink or two I could maybe nap on the way up."

"It's Sunday, Vi. No bars or liquor stores open." He saw her face fall and relented. "But I've got a bottle in the car. You can have a nip as soon as we start."

At least that got her started sooner; she had only a second cup of coffee instead of her usual three.

He got the car from the garage where he'd left it overnight and drove to the railroad office; Vi waited in the car, combing her mousy colored hair with the aid of the rear-vision mirror, while he got the luggage and loaded it into the back of the car.

He waited until they were outside of town and then took the bottle from the glove compartment and handed it to Vi. He didn't want a drink himself, this early.

But he'd long ago given up worrying about Vi's drinking or trying to get her to cut down on it. Once, five years ago, when she'd first shown a tendency toward dipsomania—before then she'd drunk moderately—he'd gone on the wagon for almost a year himself. But Vi's drinking had increased anyway.

She had several nips from the bottle and then, after a while, she dozed, her head falling against his shoulder. Weaver drove carefully to avoid waking her. Thus far she'd asked almost nothing about the place she'd be living in, and he'd told her little in his letters; she wasn't going to like it, he knew. But let her see it first and get the argument all over with at once instead of having to talk about it now and spoil the drive.

They reached Taos by ten o'clock and the house ten miles beyond it twenty minutes later.

Vi didn't like the place. She hated it.

"It gives me the *creeps*, George. Way out here in *nowhere*. No people at all!"

"It's only ten miles to Taos, Vi. Fifteen or twenty minutes in the car. You can make all the friends there that you want. And you can use the car all you wish."

He hoped that she would, even though he worried whenever she drove the car. She wasn't a good driver.

"But, George, it's *awful* after our apartment in Kansas City. It's a dump, that's what it is. A mud hut. And I'm afraid. It gives me the creeps to be way out here. At night—"

"I won't leave you alone here at night. Not that there's anything to be afraid of."

"George, I *won't stay*. An outside toilet! And I *will* be afraid—"

She was almost crying.

Weaver listened patiently. He didn't argue back; he let her get it out of her system. He got her inside and started bringing stuff in from the car. Her radio first—and he plugged it in, turned it on. Let her realize that she'd at least have this— which, anyway, was her main anodyne, more important to her than whisky.

She was sitting sobbing—but listening to the radio— while he brought in the other things. He went out into the kitchen and made them drinks—one for himself this time. He gave her one and sat down with his own.

"Listen, Vi, I'm sorry you dislike it—this much. But it's just for three months. For you, anyway; maybe I'll be staying a little longer but you'll have to go back in three months anyway to get the girls out of camp and into school. And the sublet of the apartment will be over then and you'll have it back. Now be a good sport for that long, huh?"

"But, George—"

"It won't be too bad, Vi. We won't get in one another's hair, even if the place is small. I'm going to be writing and painting and I made that little shed—see it out the back window?—into a studio and workshop for myself. You can play the radio all you want, you can read all the damn magazines you want—and that's what you'd he doing if you were back home, so what's the difference where you do it? And the climate here—well, you're getting a sample right now, and it's like this all summer.

"And besides, I've already got this place paid for, so we can't afford to live anywhere else now."

"All right, all right, all *right*."

The worst was over. He made them each another drink.

She was tired and still sleepy after she drank it and she went into the bedroom to lie down and sleep awhile. After a few minutes George heard her deep breathing and took a deep breath of relief himself.

He walked to the bedroom doorway and stood watching her closely for a minute or two. Strangely, he felt more tenderness, just then, than any other emotion.

Poor Vi; it wasn't really her fault that she was what she was. Their unhappiness was his fault much more than hers. His fault for leaping before he looked, for not having known her long enough, before he suggested marriage, to have realized the complete incompatibility between them.

Poor Vi; she was caught in a trap, even as he. Like him, she acquiesced in a marriage without love because fundamentally she was decent enough to think of the children first. She was weak, silly—but not vicious. Her selfishness was all in little things.

And in one way at least this must be worse for her than for him; she was the more romantic one of the two of them. Love stories, love songs, every form of sentimental mush and gush, were her very life.

He looked down at her closed eyes, her puffy face, her dishwater-colored hair that managed to be stringy despite frequent, and misnamed, permanents. Her skin was getting blotchy from too much drinking and too much candy—he often wondered which was the worse for her. Still under thirty but with her body getting grosser every year, her breasts beginning to be flabby and to sag, striation marks from a difficult delivery marring her thighs, the ugly mole—

Dreaming now, no doubt, of some Prince Charming of a radio program or a magazine story—who, for Vi, would never come. She was stuck with him, George Weaver and, just for a moment, he saw himself through her eyes.

Let her sleep, for as long as she could.

He took his typewriter out to the shed and put it on the table there, stacked paper next to it.

He sat down in front of it and fed a piece of white paper into the machine, then sat staring at it, wondering how he could begin to write the story of Jenny Ames. Then wondering if he could write it at all.

He'd found out all he could—had talked to everybody

who knew anything about her at all, and still he knew absolutely nothing that was not in the newspaper account.

Did it make a story? No, there were too many missing factors. An algebraic equation full of unknowns, and the biggest unknown was Jenny herself.

Picture her, picture her in the horrible moment that Pepe Sanchez had seen. Could he start the story there?

Sudden terror in her eyes, Jenny backed away from the knife, her hand groping behind her for the knob of the kitchen door. She was too frightened to scream and anyway there was no one to hear, no one but the man who came toward her with the knife—and he was mad, he must be mad. Her hand found the knob and turned it; the door swung outward into the night and she whirled through it, running. Death ran after her.

But the words wouldn't come. The picture, but not the words.

Damn, he thought; why was he trying this at all? He wasn't a writer. Why didn't he simply send the facts he had, meager or not, to Luke and tell him that was everything available and then let Luke do the rest? Why didn't he simply get it off his mind, the easy way?

After a while he heard the radio from the house; Vi must be awake again. And it was a talking program but not loud enough for him to understand the voices so that was all right. As long as he couldn't make out the words, the sound itself was almost soothing.

Damn it, he ought to write to Luke anyway. And there was paper in the machine; why not now? He put a date line on the paper and then:

Dear Luke:
I'm afraid I'm being frustrated by the job you gave me. I've been digging in, or trying to—but there just aren't any facts I can find out besides those in the newspaper account of the murder. And you must have read that, and decided it was insufficient, when you made your own investi-

gation of the case. In fact, if you took notes at that time and still have them, I don't know how I can help you at all.

There's still that damnable puzzle of the *motive*. Was it purely a psychopathic crime or was there gain for Nelson? If only Jenny Ames could be traced back beyond Albuquerque, maybe we could get somewhere. But if she couldn't be traced then, how can she be traced now, after eight years?

The odd thing is how deeply I've found myself interested, almost obsessed, in thinking about the missing pieces of the puzzle—and how curious I've become.

It occurs to me—just now, in fact—that Nelson *might* have been traced, at the time, through his painting style. He wasn't just pretending to be an artist; maybe he wasn't too good a painter, but he took himself seriously. Wherever he went from here, he kept on painting. I've got three pictures of his—they were in the shed back of the house—that I've had framed because I like them.

His style is quite individual: I think if I ever saw another painting of his—at least one painted at about the same period—I'd recognize it at sight. It's too late now, probably, but if somebody had thought, then, to hang those three pictures somewhere in Taos, say in the lobby of a hotel where tourists would see them, and put a placard by them explaining that a wanted killer had painted them, sooner or later someone would have said, "Why, I know who painted those—"

I also have a hunch, incidentally, that Nelson stayed in the Southwest. It seems probable that he had t.b., although since he wasn't treated by a doctor here nobody knows how badly he had it. But it's probable that he'd want to stay in the warm dry climate of New Mexico or Arizona—probably that's why he came here in the first place. And if he intended to cut back westward again and wanted to throw pursuit off the trail, that would account for why he registered under the name of Nelson in Amarillo, east of here. (There's also sixty dollars worth of reason in the form of cashed traveler's checks.) But I think he might have gone as far east as Amarillo deliberately and established himself there, as it were, on purpose to make the police think he was heading east or south (he left a red herring query about the roads to El Paso) so he could double back to, say, Arizona and not be traced there. The police should have concentrated their search there—particularly in artists' colonies and tuberculosis sanatoriums. Or maybe they did, for all I know; maybe I'm second guessing. But they *did* miss that angle of reproducing his pictures.

I wish I could think of some equivalently good way of trying to trace Jenny Ames backward to wherever she came from.

Well, if you want me to send you what dope I have, let me know and I'll do it. But I don't think it's really enough—and I'm just cussed enough and *interested* enough to keep on trying—if I can think of any more angles to try. Also it gives me something to do and something to be interested in—and God knows I need both.

Vi is here now; got in this morning.

Do you still want me to go ahead and take some pictures to go with the article? Or, unless I get something more on the story itself, should we forget the whole thing? I can take a picture or two of the house—will probably do that anyway—and maybe an interior shot of the kitchen, showing the doorway Pepe Sanchez saw her run through. And if you think it's worth it, maybe I can find the man who found the body and have him show me the exact spot so I can take a picture of that . . .

He finished the letter and got it ready to mail; then he went back to the house. Vi was eating candy and listening to the radio. The radio voices weren't soothing, now that he could hear them clearly.

"Time for lunch, Vi. Let's celebrate your arrival by eating in Taos this noon. And it'll give you a chance for a look at the town; I drove right through it on the way here. Besides, I've got a letter I want to mail."

"All right, George. But when this program is over. *Shhhhh.*"

Weaver waited.

[8]

Time, a week of it, passed slowly. To Weaver, it seemed like a month.

He worried about money, for one thing. Money is something to worry about when none is coming in and plenty—more than he'd anticipated—going out. There was going to be less left in the fall than he'd hoped. He worried about how difficult it might be for him to get into the swing of things; and if there was no backlog left, he'd be starting cold, from scratch.

The money was going out faster than he'd thought it would go. Vi's drinking—and she disliked wine, so her drinking cost more than his—didn't help. And almost every night she wanted to go, insisted on going, to one of the bars in Taos. And when you go to a bar you buy drinks for others and it runs you at least ten dollars before the evening is over, as against less than half that much if you stay home and do your drinking there. Oh, he enjoyed it—or parts of it—in a way, but there was the money going. Free rent, sure, but they were spending overall as much as if they'd kept their apartment in Kansas City. And, on top of it, the money that it was taking to keep the two girls in camp. Not that he begrudged that.

So he worried. Sometimes he had dreams, almost night-mares, of the kind that had started his breakdown and had sent him to the sanatorium back home.

He told himself, you damned fool, you're here so you won't worry. Forget it. A month or two without worrying at all is better than a whole goddam summer spent in worrying how much you're spending. Forget money.

Sure, but try to forget money when it's going out and not coming in, and when the bottom of your bank account is in sight and you don't know how soon you'll be working again or how much money you'll be able to make when you are. Try to forget money under circumstances like that.

Well, there's one way. Concentrate away from it. Think about something else.

He concentrated on Jenny Ames just for something to concentrate on. He'd tried to paint and it hadn't helped. He'd tried to write, and he couldn't. Neither fact surprised him; he knew that he was neither a painter nor a writer. He was just a—*what* was he? Just a guy who'd learned a little about the real estate business and didn't know enough to do anything else, and had been forbidden to do the only thing he did know. Not that that worried him—he didn't really *like* real estate—except for the fact that no money was coming in.

He found himself thinking a lot about Jenny Ames.

Of an evening, he'd be sitting in the kitchen having a drink with Vi, while it was early dark, still too early for them to drive into Taos if they were going that night, and he'd catch himself staring at the kitchen door that led out into the night, the illimitable dark into which—

Sometimes he'd sit there again after they'd come home, a little drunk, Vi already in bed (she was always ready to turn in when they returned; Weaver seldom was) and—well, he'd almost see Jenny standing there. A girl with a white face and black hair, a green dress, her hand groping behind her for the door.

Once, when he was drunk enough, he talked to her. But she didn't answer.

It was the day after that when he began to find himself

hating the three Nelson paintings hanging in his shack. Oh, he still liked them, but now he hated them too. And that happened to be the day he got a letter from Luke about the paintings. It read:

Dear George:
 You idiot, you. You write and ask me whether it's worthwhile carrying on writing a story about the Jenny Ames murder and you almost convince me, for the first umpteen paragraphs, that it isn't, and then you come up with an idea that's worth its weight in printer's ink.

 There probably ought to be a special law in artists' colonies like Taos that sheriffs and other law officers ought to have a working knowledge of art. Then the sheriff who worked on the Nelson case wouldn't have overlooked, while it was hot, the idea of circularizing the country to find Nelson through his painting style.

 Now after eight years, it's pretty much of an off-chance that he can be found that way. *But,* you idiot, don't you see that whether it works or not isn't the important thing. The important thing is that now you've got a really good story angle, so good that selling the story is a lead-pipe cinch. And you ask if pictures of the paintings should be taken!

 That's your lead. The fact that now, through this article, an eight-year old murder may be solved through an angle that was overlooked at the time of the original investigation. "Does any reader of this article know an artist who paints, or who painted eight years ago, in the style of the three pictures shown here?"

 It's a dilly, George. That's the peg on which you hang the whole thing. Guard those pictures, and that idea, with your life. See that nobody beats you to the punch on it.

I still don't see why somebody didn't think of it at the time—unless the sheriff was the only one who knew about them. That could have been; I didn't learn about them in the course of the brief investigation I made of the case, and I probably would have if their existence had been general knowledge.

But those pictures are a real find, and they make the story money in the bank for you if you handle it right. It makes it so damn good that I hate to cut in on it. Why don't you write it yourself, George?

There are two good reasons why you should. One is that I've got an extension of my contract here; I've been hired to work on two more crime documentaries after this one. I'm making more money than I've ever made before and—hold thumbs for me—if the pictures I'm working on go over, I might never have to go back to magazine writing at all. The other reason is that the idea and the discovery of the paintings is strictly yours and I've got no business to chisel in, even if I needed dough, which I don't.

So let's change my original suggestion to this: You write the article and take the photographs, including really good ones of the paintings, and send them to me. If the article turns out to be salable as written I'll forward it to my agent in New York to peddle for you and won't cut in at all. Counting the price you'll get for the photographs, and counting out the agent's fee of ten percent, you should get at least three hundred, maybe four hundred bucks.

If your story needs rewriting—and it shouldn't if you read a couple of fact detective magazines to get the general style and slant—I'll rewrite it for you. If all the data is there, no matter how you've written it, it shouldn't be more than a

couple of hours work for me, and the charge will
be one bottle of whisky, payable after you've made
the sale and whenever we'll have a chance to drink
it together. It's got to be good whisky—I'm
acquiring expensive habits out here in Hollywood
—but it won't make too big a hole in your profits
on the deal.

Glad to learn that Vi is now with you and . . .

Three or four hundred bucks, Weaver thought. That
much money was worth shooting for. And he'd been thinking
of trying to write the story himself anyway.

"Vi, did you bring my camera?"

"Camera? Oh, George, I *forgot* about it. I remember now
your writing me to bring it, same time you told me to bring
the typewriter, but the camera was put away in the trunk I'd
already sent to storage, the things we didn't want to leave in
the apartment while it was sublet, and I was going to go down
to the storage company and get it and then at the last minute
there were so many things to do and . . ."

"That's all right, Vi. I want to take a few pictures while
we're here, but I can rent or borrow a camera for a few days.
Want to ride in with me now? You can have a drink while I'm
hunting one up. There's a photographer's place near the Taos
Inn; I can probably get one there."

"Sure, George. But I can't go dressed *this way*—"

They left half an hour later, Vi dressed another way, and
drove to Taos. He left Vi at the Taos Inn sipping a martini—
her favorite drink in bars, although it was too much trouble
for her to make them for herself when she drank at home—
while he made arrangements to rent a camera for a few days
and bought several rolls of film to go with it.

He'd get right at taking the pictures, he decided, and he'd
start work right away on the story. Three or four hundred
bucks would make a hell of a lot of difference in his budget.
He knew that he was taking advantage of Luke's generosity to
take him up on the proposition, especially if it turned out that

Luke would really have to rewrite the story, but maybe he could make it up to Luke some time, some way.

Let's see, was there anything else he wanted before starting the story?

Before he went into the bar of the Taos Inn to get Vi, he went to the phone in the lobby and called Callahan.

"Weaver." he said. "Callahan, do you know whether the Seco man who found the body is still around? If I remember the name right, it's Ramon Camillo."

"That's the name, but I don't know if he's still around or not. Ask them at the Arroyo Seco post office; they'll be able to tell you—and to tell you where he lives, if he's still there."

"Thanks, I'll do that."

"Find out what you wanted to find out in Albuquerque?"

"More or less. The hotel's gone, but I talked to the editor of the *Tribune* and got a few little extra details that'll help the story."

"Good. Say, Weaver, I understand your wife's with you now. Why don't you drop around at the house with her some time? Do you play bridge?"

"I do, but the missus doesn't. Sorry."

"Well, bridge isn't the only thing in the world. Drop around anyway—any evening; if our lights are on, we're home."

Weaver promised that they would.

He wondered whether he meant it or not. He liked Callahan all right, but he'd rather meet Mrs. Callahan first before he brought Vi around. Vi was—well, Vi could be embarrassing when she drank too much, and she'd probably drink too much if drinks were served. And if Callahan's wife was the dignified, reserved type of woman, she'd be embarrassed by Vi. Vi seldom got bitchy from drinking—although even that could happen—but four or five drinks could make her pretty sloppy, and that was almost as bad.

Bridge. He wished that they could play bridge. He'd liked it a lot, once. And he'd tried his best to teach Vi to play, but she just—didn't have the brains to learn, or sufficient ability to concentrate. After a year of trying, her bidding and playing were so random and haphazard that—for the sake of the people they'd tried to play with—he'd given up the game completely.

He got Vi out of the bar and drove toward home, stopping at the little post office in Arroyo Seco en route. He asked the postmaster about Ramon Camillo.

"Ramon, he still lives here winters. But summers up in Colorado, Montana, the sheep."

Weaver started to ask whether anybody in Seco besides Camillo would know the exact spot where Jenny Ames' body had been found and then he realized Sanchez would be able to tell him that—and that if he asked Sanchez he wouldn't have to go through the rigmarole of explaining all over again what his interest was.

He thanked the postmaster and drove on to Sanchez's house.

Sanchez opened the door and smiled; he stepped back. "Please to come in, Mr. Weaver?"

"Thanks, no. My wife is waiting in the car and I just want to ask you one question. Is there someone in Seco who knows the exact place where Jenny Ames' body was found and who could take me there and show me?"

"You not need somebody to show you, Mister Weaver. I tell you how you find yourself the place. From your house a quarter mile straight north is cottonwood, big cottonwood, bigger than any tree near. By it, you can see the place. You find easy."

Weaver thanked him and drove on home. It was still only mid-afternoon and a quarter of a mile wasn't far to walk. He loaded the camera and started out, walking straight north. Just beyond the shed he turned back a moment, thinking that he should have asked Vi if she wanted to go along for a walk. Then he decided against it; he didn't want her along because he didn't want to explain what he was doing. He hadn't discussed the Jenny Ames case with her—and was reluctant to do so.

He didn't know exactly why he felt almost revolted at even the thought of mentioning Jenny Ames' name to Vi, but he did feel that way. And anyway there was a very practical reason for keeping his own counsel—the money. If Vi knew of the very excellent chance of three or four hundred dollars coming in, she'd be even more careless of money for the rest of the summer than she'd be otherwise.

So let Vi think he was walking back just to photograph the mountains. For that matter, he might as well take some shots of them too. He had plenty of film and, in any case, he'd have to take some pictures he could show Vi later to account for his having rented the camera. Pictures he took of the house itself could do double duty in that respect and he could take them any time, whether Vi was around or not. He'd have to wait until sometime when she was away from the house to take his shots of the paintings.

He started to pace off the distance roughly; at a yard to a stride a quarter of a mile would be about four hundred and forty paces. He counted up to three hundred and then, as he topped a rise, he knew he could quit counting; the cotton-wood tree ahead of him, halfway up the next slope, was the one. There was no mistaking it; it was the biggest tree any-where in sight and the distance and direction were just about what Sanchez had told him. He headed for it with certainty.

Had Jenny Ames, he wondered, actually run that far before the killer had caught up to her? Or had he caught her sooner and then carried her body farther away from the house before he buried it?

Yes, this was the tree. For there, just under and beyond it, was the depression that had once been a shallow grave. Now weathered to a depth of only about six inches, it was still unmistakably discernible.

He photographed it from several angles, not knowing from which side it would show up best in a photograph. He took a few shots of the mountains, too.

The sun was still warm and bright as he walked back to the house. Might as well photograph it now too, and finish one roll of film.

He backed his car out to the road so it wouldn't be in the picture and then took three shots of the house from three different distances and angles. One of them from the exact spot where Pepe Sanchez had stood. That, no doubt, would be the one they'd use, but it didn't hurt to have other pictures for them to choose among.

The interior shot—and he'd have to make several tries on that, with different time exposures on each so one of them would come out—would have to wait until Vi was away. Too difficult to explain, otherwise.

But come to think of it, he had a perfectly logical excuse for taking pictures of the paintings, if Vi should notice what he was doing and become curious. He could tell her he was just experimenting on how to photograph pictures because; later, he'd want to photograph some of his own water colors, and if he knew the right distance and exposure, he wouldn't have any misses when he tried that.

That made sense as an explanation. Enough for Vi anyway.

He took the pictures from the shed and stood them against the west wall so the afternoon sun would be squarely on them. He shortened the tripod so the camera would be about on center of the pictures and then moved it back and forth until he had the distance just right so the picture would fill the field, set his focus and took the shots. Just one of each of the three pictures; if they didn't come out well the first time he'd try again after he knew whether he'd over—or underexposed.

Vi came out while he was taking the final shot.

"George do you *like* those horrible things? I can't see how you can *stand* them hanging in that shed of yours. And you spend so much time in it, too."

He snapped the camera. "Well, they're interesting, Vi. I don't exactly like them, but I wish I could do as well. And the more you look at them, the more you see in them. But—" And he explained that, really, he was just experimenting with the camera, that he'd never tried to take a picture of a picture before.

Weaver took the three pictures back into the shed and hung them again, closing the door so he couldn't hear Vi's radio. He checked the camera and found there was one frame left on the second roll of film. He filled it with a random shot of mountains framed by the window of his shed and then took the film out. He looked at his watch. Just barely time to get them to the photographer's by five o'clock if he left right away.

He went into the house and turned the radio down a little so he could be heard. "Going into town, Vi, to leave these films. Any shopping you want done?"

"Well—you could get some bread and something for sandwiches if it's all right to have that tonight. I'd rather not cook another hot meal."

"Okay."

"And some whisky, George, and some ginger ale. There's only half a bottle left. I was going to remember it when we were in before, and I forgot."

The photograph shop told him the pictures would be finished day after next. He ordered only contact prints, one of each, until he had a chance to see how they'd turn out.

He got the whisky and the ginger ale, some wine for himself, the bread and sandwich meat.

It was dusk when he returned and Vi said she was hungry so they ate right away.

"George, let's go to a movie tonight. I haven't seen a movie since I came here."

He sighed. "I've got a slight headache, Vi. Why don't you take the car and drive in yourself? Anyway, it's a gangster movie; I happened to notice. You like them and I don't."

When she'd left, half an hour later, the house seemed strangely, wonderfully silent. This was one evening he wouldn't have to spend in his sanctum to get away from the sound of the radio.

He didn't even want to drink, especially, although he poured himself a glass of wine to sip. He sat at the kitchen table because the kitchen seemed more comfortable, more homey than either the living room or the bedroom. He sighed and relaxed.

So his idea about the Nelson pictures had been good. Strange that no one had thought of it at the time. Understandable why the sheriff hadn't, but it seemed a bit strange that

Callahan had missed that particular boat. Unless he hadn't known of the pictures. Callahan could have published pictures of the pictures in his *El Crepúsculo* and could have seen that copies went to likely places. It would have been a feather in his cap if his newspaper had helped to locate a murderer.

On sudden impulse he left his drink standing on the table, put on his coat and started to walk to Callahan's. There was a thin sliver of moon and bright stars, between them giving just enough light so he didn't have to use his flash to see the road as soon as his eyes had adjusted themselves to dimness.

He thought, it must have been just about like this the night Jenny was killed. And she ran through it just about as far as I'm going to walk. The distance to Callahan's is the same as the distance to her grave. Had Callahan lived there then? He'd have to ask.

It seemed like quite a long walk.

The lights were on at Callahan's, so he knocked. Callahan came to the door in bedroom slippers, but he looked pleased. "Come in, Weaver." He looked around. "Didn't you bring the missus? Told you to bring her over to meet my wife."

"She went to a movie tonight. I just strolled over on sudden impulse. You're not busy?"

"Hell, no. Come in."

Weaver met Mrs. Callahan. She was tall and slender, no longer young but quite distinguished in appearance, even in a cotton house dress and an apron. Her smile was pleasant but a bit reserved and her voice, when she spoke, was soft and her diction and grammar precise. Weaver sighed mentally; he'd rather hoped that Mrs. Callahan and Vi would be compatible. They were almost antithetical to one another.

After a few minutes Mrs. Callahan excused herself to do some sewing and Weaver and Callahan were left alone.

"You said you wanted to ask me something, Weaver?"

"Yes, but first—and while I think of it—did you live here eight years ago when the murder happened?"

"No, we were renting then, in Taos; it was our first year here. We bought this place four years ago. Let's see—yes, the man we bought it from was living here at that time; he'd built the place ten years before. Artist named Wayne; he's living in New York now."

"Thanks," Weaver said. "Listen, Callahan, I've got an angle on the case I'd like to talk over with you, but it'll have to be with the understanding that you don't print anything about it in your newspaper—not until the magazine article I'm going to write gets published. Otherwise, if you break it first, my idea won't be new anymore."

Callahan looked at him sharply. "You're really going in for this thing, aren't you? I don't see what angle you could get now—after eight years—that would make a new story."

"But you agree not to use it until I tell you you can?"

"Oh, sure. Won't even talk about it, if you don't want me to. What is it?"

Weaver told him about the pictures and how he intended to use them.

Callahan announced solemnly that he would be treated in a unique and unpublishable manner.

Weaver asked, "The idea *is* new? Nobody thought of it at the time?"

"Nobody knew those pictures were *left* there. I mean, no newspaperman knew about it. Hell, Weaver, there were men here from the big press services, good men. If it'd been known about those pictures being left, I flatter myself I'd have thought of using them the way you're going to—and if I hadn't, one of the other boys who covered the inquest would have thought of it. Freeman never told us about it. The stupid bastard. You say there are three of them?"

Weaver nodded. "I had them framed. And one of them's mine now—I haven't decided which one." He told the editor about the deal he'd made with Doughbelly Price to keep one of the pictures in return for frames for the other two.

"So Doughbelly knew about the pictures too." Callahan swore, and then shook his head. "Well, you're right; we missed a bet. Where were the pictures?"

"In the shed back of the house."

"Well, that partly explains it. I looked through the house

and they weren't there then. That was the day before the inquest and I went out with Will Freeman. I remember I asked him if there was anything out in the shed and he said he'd looked through it and there was just junk there. I'd like to see them. Say—if your wife went in to a movie she must have taken the car. Did you walk here?"

"Yes."

"Whenever you're ready to go, then, I can drop you home, save your walking back. And I can take a look at the paintings—I'd like to see them."

"Thanks," Weaver said. But suddenly he found himself wanting to be alone again. Not that he didn't like Callahan, but what the hell; this was one of the few evenings he'd be able to spend alone in the house—in the kitchen—without being driven to the shed by the sound of Vi's radio. Why hadn't he taken advantage of it?

He said, "But—would you mind if I walked home tonight and showed you the pictures some other time? I've got something to think out—that's one reason why I walked over. My question about the paintings could have waited."

"Sure," Callahan said. "Matter of fact, I'm not too crazy about going out tonight anyway. I'll take a rain check on seeing the pictures. But you're sure you don't want a lift?"

Weaver was sure.

He walked home, as soon as he could get away without being impolite about it.

Again a quarter of a mile seemed a long distance for a girl to have run through the night, even with a killer at her heels. Certainly she must have been the better runner of the two of them to have got that far. But then, out of breath at last—

The poor kid.

When he got home he stood at the kitchen door a long time, looking out into the night beyond.

Why, he wondered, hadn't he started work on the article tonight, while Vi was gone? What was he waiting for?

Why, for that matter, didn't he start now? With the shed to work in, he wouldn't have to stop when Vi got home.

He didn't want to; that was the obvious and only answer.

He didn't.

Vi came home at eleven. She was a little drunk—she hadn't been when she left—and he wondered if she'd really gone to the movie. He didn't ask.

[9]

Almost all of the photographs were good. The ones of Nelson's paintings showed up especially well. Of the three shots of the shallow grave under the cottonwood two were good; of those he chose the one that had been shot toward the mountains, that caught their vastness in awful contrast to the pitiful smallness of the grave. He put that one aside on the counter of the photograph shop with the three of the paintings, and then studied the three pictures he'd taken of the house itself.

Two were good. So was the third, as a photograph, but it was spoiled as an illustration for the story because Vi showed in it. It was the shot taken from the spot where Pepe Sanchez had stood; Weaver hadn't noticed, as he'd snapped the shutter, that Vi had stepped to the window to watch him and could be seen, dimly, through it.

Well, that didn't matter. He still had to take that interior shot, the time exposure, the first time Vi left him alone during the day and at the same time he could take another from the point where the boy had stood. That would wash things up and he could return the camera. The pictures of the paintings were excellent—he'd judged the exposure exactly right—and that was the main thing.

Weaver left the negatives of the ones he'd use with the story for five-by-seven glossy enlargements and then took the set of contact prints with him to Callahan's office.

He put down the three photographs of the pictures in front of the editor. "Came out good," he said. "Thought you might like to see them. But that doesn't cancel your rain check to drop around any time and see the originals."

Callahan bent close over the prints, studying them. "I'll be damned," he said. "They look better than I thought judging from those water colors of his I saw. Guess he worked better in oil. Are you sure Nelson painted them? Were they signed?"

"No—but hell's bells, Callahan, don't throw monkey wrenches like that. Who else *would* have painted them, if Nelson left them behind?"

Callahan grinned up at him. "Don't take it so hard. I know how you can find out for sure whether they're his or not. When Nelson first came here he made the rounds of the galleries to see if one of them would put up work for sale. So—let me think a minute."

He stared off into space over Weaver's shoulder. "There were three galleries in town then, outside of private ones. One of the three is still run by the same man, Ellsworth Grant. It's El Pueblito Gallery, out the Santa Fe road just at the edge of town.

"And Ellie Grant's got a memory like an elephant—he's built like one, too, for that matter. If he saw any of Nelson's work he'll be able to tell you whether these pictures are really his. Only if I were you I'd take the originals to show him instead of these reproductions. They tell me color is a factor in style; each artist tends to use certain combinations of color."

"Thanks, Callahan," Weaver said. "You've been a hell of a big help to me on this, down the line. If I ever do sell the story, you've got a bottle of whisky coming."

Weaver drove home quickly and put the three framed canvases in the back of the car. He remembered having seen the sign of El Pueblito Gallery and had no trouble finding it. He went in.

There was no mistaking Ellsworth Grant, from Callahan's description of him. He weighed at least three hundred pounds. Only his eyes were small; they gleamed at Weaver through thick lenses. "May I help you, sir?"

Weaver introduced himself. He said, "Mr. Grant, I've got three canvases in the back of my car. I'd like to have you look at them and tell me if you know who painted them. I'm not trying to sell them. May I bring them in?"

"No need; I'll walk out to the car with you."

When Weaver lifted the door of the luggage compartment, Ellsworth Grant looked a moment at the top picture on the pile, then lifted it and studied the second one.

"The third is like them? By the same man?"

Weaver nodded.

"Then these two are enough; I can tell you who did them. The man who committed the murder out past Seco some years ago. Let's see—Nelson, his name was, Charles Nelson. In fact, I saw these same pictures out at his place. They weren't framed then."

"You were out there?" Weaver was surprised. He'd been told consistently until now that Nelson had never had a guest at his place before Jenny, and, after the murder, the sheriff.

"Yes, a few days after he came here. He brought in several pictures—not including these—and wanted to exhibit here and I— Let's go back in the gallery. No use standing out here to talk."

Weaver followed him back into the gallery. Grant waved Weaver to a chair and then sat down himself with a sigh of relief.

Weaver asked, "Did he just offer them for exhibit, or did he try to sell them to you?"

"To exhibit for sale, of course. Except under special circumstances—very special ones—galleries don't buy pictures. If we accept an artist's work, we show his pictures and try to sell them, taking a commission on whatever sales we make. Each gallery represents a limited number of artists, and those artists agree not to exhibit in any other gallery. Locally, that is; he may have pictures in other galleries elsewhere."

"But you refused to exhibit Nelson's work?"

"Yes. I considered it, at least slightly. It seemed to me that he had something but that his work was immature. Another few years, possibly— The six or seven canvases he brought me were interesting enough to make me want to see the rest of his work before I came to decision. He invited me to come out to his house and see more; I accepted."

"He drove you out in his car?"

"No, he led the way in his car and I followed in mine. He offered to drive me out and back, but I made the excuse that I had another errand out that way and wished to have my own car. Actually—well, I didn't *think* that I was going to accept his work and it would have been embarrassing to have him drive me back after I'd turned him down."

"I see."

"And I was quite right. He turned surly after I'd given him a definite negative. Until then he had been extremely charming in his manner; he seemed quite likable at first. Perhaps—we are all susceptible to charm—that led me to consider his work more seriously than I would have otherwise. At least to give him the break of wanting to see more canvases than he had brought in to show me."

"You really think his work had no commercial value?"

"I wouldn't go quite that far. It had some merit, but it is of a type that is very difficult to sell, and that's something a gallery must take into consideration. Our space is limited. My gallery was particularly crowded that season and I represented—still represent—a goodly number of the most important local artists. I couldn't have afforded to gamble on a newcomer unless I had been very strongly impressed with his work. So despite a personal prejudice in favor of the type of painting Nelson did, I couldn't see any way clear to representing him. May I ask where you obtained these paintings?"

Weaver explained.

"Too bad I didn't know that he'd left any pictures behind him. I would have suggested circularizing art dealers elsewhere with reproductions of them on the chance—since his style is quite distinctive—that it might have led to his capture."

"That's being taken care of now, Mr. Grant. Probably too late, but at least it gives me a good lead for an article I'm writing about the crime, and reproductions of the pictures will appear with the story."

"You are a writer, then?"

"Not exactly." Weaver explained again, briefly.

There was a soft whistling sound from a room opening

off the back of the gallery. Grant said, "My singing teakettle, Mr. Weaver, has come to a boil. I generally brew myself a cup of tea at this time of the afternoon. Would you care to join me?"

Weaver joined him and was surprised to find that the first cup of tea he'd had in years tasted good.

He asked, "Did Nelson tell you anything about himself?"

"He talked only about his work. I asked no personal questions and he volunteered no information about himself—beyond the fact that he'd just come here and that he hoped to stay indefinitely."

"Do you think he really did, at that time? That he hoped to support himself as an artist?"

"I don't really know. He'd have said, in any case, that he intended to remain here; it would be a selling point in that a gallery would much rather handle the work of a permanently resident artist than of one who was more or less transient. But whether or not he intended to remain here, he must have been quite naive if he expected to support himself as an artist. No matter what gallery backed him, he'd have been lucky to make a few hundred dollars a year. Much better artists than he fail to make a living from their work. They teach painting or have some other means of making a livelihood."

Weaver said, "Speaking of teaching reminds me. Jenny Ames told the woman with whom she rode up on the bus from Santa Fe that Nelson was teaching at one of the art schools here. Was that out of whole cloth—a complete lie Nelson had told her—or could there have been a kernel of truth in it?"

"There could have been no truth in it at all. I greatly doubt that Nelson even applied for such a job; he'd have known better than to think there was even the slightest chance of his getting it. In fact, I can say definitely that he didn't apply at either of the two art schools which were operating then. I heard Miss Evers' testimony at the inquest and I recall now that later I asked the two men who conducted the two schools whether Nelson had applied to them. He hadn't approached them, either as prospective instructor or prospective pupil. Will you have more tea?"

"Thank you."

The big man leaned across and poured more tea into Weaver's cup. "Even today." he said, "it would be impossible for a man of Nelson's qualifications—or lack of them to become an instructor in a school. In those days, before the G. I. bill existed, it would have been even more impossible."

"Could he have intended—even hoped—to open a school of his own?"

Grant smiled. "With no reputation, not even gallery representation? He could hardly have thought of it, let alone considered it seriously."

"What was your personal impression of him, Mr. Grant? For example, did it surprise you to learn, later, that he was a murderer?"

"Well—yes. But I did have the impression that he was a sick man, mentally and physically. Which, of course, turns out to have been the case; his crime was not that of a sane man. Also his abrupt volte-face, turning from extreme charm of manner to abrupt sullen rudeness as soon as he learned that he had nothing to gain from me, convinced me that he was definitely asocial."

"You say he was sick, mentally and physically. In what way?" Without asking leading questions, Weaver wondered whether Grant would confirm Callahan's diagnoses of homosexuality and tuberculosis.

"On the physical side," Grant said, "I noticed that he coughed quite a bit; it could have been a tubercular cough, though I wouldn't be sure of that. When I say he was sick mentally, I do not refer to the obvious fact—obvious to anyone familiar with such things—that he was homosexual." The big man smiled. "Here in Taos that is considered a minor deviation. Being asocial to the degree he was is much less normal. But I had neither of these things in mind. I think he probably—and this is guesswork—had a deep *fear* psychosis."

"If he did have tuberculosis," Weaver suggested, "would fear of death be a probable cause of such a psychosis?"

"Quite possibly. I wouldn't go any farther than that on the basis of having spent possibly two hours in his company."

Weaver tried to think of a fresh angle. "This turn-off-able charm of his," he said, "would you say it would make him attracttive to women, despite his homosexuality?"

"Oh, definitely, if he chose to exert it on them. And he was quite handsome, I would say. He could have been charming to any woman, even one sophisticated enough to recognize him for what he was. A naive girl—" He gestured. "And I would judge the girl who came here to marry him to be quite naive, if only from the manner of her becoming acquainted with him—through a—what do they call it? Lonely Hearts Club."

"Do you know, by the way, if Nelson approached both of the other galleries which were operating here then?"

"Yes, he did. I discussed him with Mr. Rollinson and Mr. Stein; they were in charge of the other two galleries at that time. I was quite interested, of course, after the murder. It was the first experience I'd ever had with a murderer and naturally I was interested in comparing impressions with others who had met him.

"Their experiences, and their verdicts, were quite similar to mine—except that I was the only one of the three of us who had been sufficiently interested to accompany him to his house to see more of his work. Each of the others had talked to him, and only briefly, in their galleries and had looked only at the things he had brought to them. Each, incidentally, shared my experience of having him turn suddenly rude when he had been turned down, and each commented on how charming he had been until that point."

Weaver nodded. Even aside from verification of the authorship of the paintings, he was glad he'd come to Ellsworth Grant. The picture of Charles Nelson was beginning to round out.

He asked, "Would you have any idea why he left these three canvases behind him? Are they inferior to the others you saw?"

"The two of your three that I saw, no; they are about average, perhaps. I saw some of his work that I liked better, others that I liked less. I imagine—you said that you found these in the shed back of the house?—that he may have overlooked them inadvertently. It could have happened, especially if he packed up in a hurry, because he was apparently quite a prolific painter. He had stacks of paintings at his place; I don't see how he could have got all of them, and his other possessions, into his car—and of course he had to take with him everything he wanted; he would hardly have made a shipment which could easily have been traced. It's barely possible that he left three canvases behind simply because he didn't have room for them, but I doubt it. He would have burned them—he was certainly sane enough to have thought of the possibility of his being traced through his painting style if he left samples. I'd say that they were left behind accidentally."

"One thing occurs to me," Weaver said. "Wouldn't those paintings, if it had been generally known that they'd been left behind, have been worth something to a gallery while the murder was fresh? I mean, as the work of a murderer—"

Ellsworth Grant pursed his lips. "I imagine they would have had a certain notoriety value, that they could have been sold at that time. It would depend upon the artistic integrity—if you'll pardon the phrase—of a dealer as to whether he would have handled them for that reason. I would not have sold them for that reason myself, but I fear that one of my two then competitors—and I'll not say which one—would gladly have done so, had he known the paintings were available."

Weaver said, "Somebody in your business must have known. Doughbelly Price, who was apparently the only one besides the sheriff who knew the paintings were there—and who was technically owner of them—asked someone, he tells me, whether they were valuable and was told they weren't."

"That was I, Mr. Weaver. Yes, it was shortly after the discovery of the murder. Doughbelly asked me whether Nelson's paintings were worth anything, and I told him they had negligible commercial value. But—damn it—he didn't mention that he actually *had* any of them and I thought he was asking an abstract question so I gave him an abstract answer. If he'd only happened to mention—" Grant shrugged mountainously. "No use thinking about it now. Will you have more tea, Mr. Weaver?"

Weaver thanked him but declined and left. He drove home slowly, thinking. It was too bad neither Grant nor Callahan had known, eight years ago, about those pictures. Quite possibly, then, they would have led to Nelson's apprehension. The chances were slim now.

But what the hell, he thought; he wasn't trying to find Nelson. He was trying to write a magazine article to make himself a few hundred bucks, and it was a break for him that the right people hadn't known about those pictures at the right time.

And what more did he expect to get, anyway? Why didn't he go ahead and write the article and get it over with?

He wrote it that evening and it came easily; he found that he had to refer to his notes hardly at all and that he could write almost as fast as he could type. He did a rough draft on yellow paper; tomorrow he'd retype it on white, polishing it a little and correcting any mistakes he might have made. Then as soon as he got the other two photographs taken—the interior and the retake of the shot from the point where Pepe Sanchez had stood—he'd send the whole thing to Luke Ashley. And forget it.

And then what? Well, maybe he'd try his hand again at some more water colors. And take some long walks back toward, even into, the mountains.

He turned out the light in the shed and stepped outside, into the night. Vi's radio came blaring at him from the house, clearly audible even this far away, although it hadn't bothered him while he was inside the shed with the door shut.

He went in. Vi was sitting there listening to the radio, just listening. He raised his voice to be heard over it. "Vi, I'm going to take a little walk. Won't be gone long."

"George, in the *dark?*"

"I'll take a flashlight; I'm not going far. And leave the lights on so I can't miss the house, to get back to it."

She turned away listlessly. "All right, George." She lost all further interest in him and went back to her own dream world in a radio program.

Weaver tried to close his ears to it while he found the flashlight. At the door he turned back. There was a bottle of whisky on the table beside Vi, an almost full bottle. He hadn't had a drink all day or evening and a straight shot would go good, he thought. He deserved it after the intensive work he'd put in at the typewriter; he must have spent four hours at it, ever since dinner.

"Mind if I take some of this along, Vi? Little cool out, and I might not meet any St. Bernards."

She shook her head. He found an empty half-pint bottle on the sink and filled it from the fifth, put it into his pocket.

The night was cool and clear, a dry coolness that felt good even though he was wearing only a suit coat. Faint moon again, starlight. About as much light as this, he wondered, the night Jenny ran this way? *This* way; he was walking her last quarter-mile again. He knew now that was where he'd intended to go all along, to where Jenny's grave had been, to the big cottonwood.

He turned off the flashlight and after a moment he could see clearly enough to avoid the clumps of chamiso and to find good footing as he walked. There must have been enough light for Jenny to have avoided them too as she ran this way. One stumble, near the house when the killer must have been right at her heels, and she'd never have made that quarter of a mile.

He turned around and looked back at the house, now a hundred yards behind him and shivered a little, not completely from the cold. He took the bottle from his pocket and took a swig from it. The coyotes were howling back in the hills toward which he was heading. But coyotes are more afraid of you than you are of them.

Keep walking. The rise from which he could see the big cottonwood, and he could see it again, white wraith in the darkness, far ahead. *Jenny, how could you have run this far? You were young, you were running from death—with your life before you and death behind you, but a quarter-mile—it must have been a hell of a run, girl.*

Jenny. Jenny Ames—
Down the slope, up the slope, and at the cottonwood,
your grave, or what had been your grave, until a prowling
coyote dug a hole that found you.

He sat down under the cottonwood and took a drink from the bottle. Pour a libation? Or how ridiculous can you get? Wasn't he being silly enough about this whole affair? He'd already done more work on it than would have earned him a few hundred dollars back in his own racket. Not to mention the money he'd spent on photography, dinner for Carlotta, framing pictures, the trip to Albuquerque—

Forget it, he told himself; go back home and forget it except to polish that story tomorrow, take the other photograph or two, and *then—forget* it.

He took another drink, sitting there beside the faint depresssion that had been a shallow grave.

There's nothing for you here, he told himself. Go back. Go back to Vi, to what you have. Go back to the light, to the life that you know, the life that isn't so horrible but that you can face it and continue to live.

This is death, out here in the dark. Jenny Ames is dead, eight years dead, and death is darkness; darkness is death. Go back to the light.

Go back to life and light; no matter what that light shows, it is better than death and darkness.

Is it?

He finished the half pint and then walked back, more slowly than he had come. Behind him the coyote noises and the dark. Before him, once he had topped the rise, the lights of home. Or, rather, the light of home; only the kitchen light still burned. Had Vi gone to bed already?

Vi had gone to bed, and to sleep. He could hear her snoring lightly as he opened the kitchen door.

He went in and sat down at the kitchen table. The quart bottle stood before him, still a quarter full. But he didn't kill it; he had one more drink and one only, and after a while he went to bed. The sound of Vi's snoring kept him awake a long time.

In the morning Vi was already up, getting breakfast, when he woke.

"George, you were gone an awful long time last night. I got worried about you."

Weaver grinned. "So I noticed."

"Well, I *did*. Before I went to sleep. And those coyotes out there—"

"Coyotes aren't dangerous, Vi."

"Just the same, wandering around outdoors late at night. Have you got something on your mind, George?"

"Nothing. Not a thing."

Coffee in silence. He wondered what she'd think if he told her the truth—and then he wondered what the truth really was.

He went out to the shed as soon as he'd finished breakfast and read over the story he'd written the evening before.

It wasn't good. All the facts were there but—they sounded dull. Dull and distantly in the past. There was something missing, and it was the important part of the story, although he couldn't decide just what it was. It was the part that he couldn't put into words, even to himself.

Or could he? *Jenny Ames wasn't there, in the story.* She was a name and a few facts, but not a person. And without her, the story didn't add up.

For a moment he almost tore the manuscript across, and then he remembered that last night, after writing it, he'd torn up his notes; if he didn't keep the manuscript he would no longer have, all his names and dates except those he remembered offhand.

Names and dates! Actually, that's what was wrong. That had been all he'd been able to get, and there was so much more.

Maybe Luke—no, undoubtedly Luke was the better writer of the two of them, but Luke couldn't do it either. Not from the few and naked facts—and there was so much more.

He stared again at one of the three paintings which were now again hanging on the wall. *Nelson, why?*

He was pacing, then, back and forth the five steps each

way the shed allowed him, wishing violently that he'd never undertaken to write up the murder. Why do people like to read about such things? Murder is a horrible word and a horrible thing; murder with a knife is abominable. Murder stories that are fictional are bad enough, but *real* murder; isn't it a perversion for people to want to read—or write—the bloody details of the real killing of a real human being?

It's as bad for you—to want to write—

But he *didn't* want to write about it; that was the whole trouble. That was what was wrong.

If it wasn't for the fact that he needed the money so badly to help pay his expenses for a wasted summer, to help preserve the small and diminishing balance that would be waiting to finance his reentry into business in the fall or winter— If it wasn't for the money he'd already invested in camera rental, films, prints, framing the pictures, the trip to Albuquerque—

Hell, why not quit now before he got in any deeper? The thing was a gamble anyway; maybe Luke couldn't sell the damned story.

But what if the printing of the pictures did find Jenny's murderer—even now, after all this time?

All right then, *do it*. But for God's sake get it over with, no matter what the form of the story you send Luke. And meanwhile, for Christ's sake, quit having to look at those paintings—

He took them down and stacked them, face to the wall, in the corner behind the cot.

Then he went out again into the bright sunshine and stood there, just outside the shed. The radio from the house was an unintelligible murmur.

He wished Vi would go into town so he could take those remaining photos. Maybe he could talk her into going to Taos this afternoon long enough for him to take them. If all the photos were out of the way, off his mind, if only the story was holding him up, then maybe he could make up his mind to send it to Luke as it stood, to let Luke worry about it, or sell it.

He managed to kill the rest of the morning doing nothing.

He made his suggestion as soon as they'd finished a late lunch. He'd worked out a double-barreled reason for it. "Vi, why don't you drive to Taos this afternoon and see a movie? It's Saturday, so there's one playing. Do you good to get away for a change during the day."

"All right, George. But won't you come along? I hate to go alone."

"I've got a headache, Vi. That's one reason I want to get rid of you—so I can lie down in here and sleep it off; that cot out in the shed's not so comfortable as the bed. And if you were here, I'd have to ask you to keep the radio off so I could sleep, and you wouldn't like that."

"All right, George."

"You run along now, then. I'll do the dishes, the few of them there are. And listen, if you want to stay in town to eat after the show, I can fry myself an egg or something. I know you get bored out here all the time. Take the rest of the day, and the evening if you want it, to get away for a change. Here's ten bucks."

Expensive, those last two photographs—and a chance to be alone.

He took them as soon as the sound of the car had died away down the road, and he took several shots of each so there wouldn't be any possibility of a slip-up this time.

He finished off the roll of film with a few shots of scenery in different directions from the house and then got the roll out of the camera ready to take it to Taos. Too damn bad he'd had to give up the car to get rid of Vi, so he couldn't take the films in today. But maybe if he paid extra the shop would develop and dry and print the pictures while he waited or killed time in town tomorrow.

Meanwhile, the story.

He went back to the shed and sat down at the typewriter again, staring at the blank piece of paper in it.

What was the lead sentence he wanted? He got as far as two words of it: "Jenny Ames—"

The third word and the rest of the sentence wouldn't come.

[10]

He jerked the paper out of his machine and crumpled it. The crime of murder is a meaningless thing, a mere statistic, unless the victim of that murder can be presented as a human being with a background and a history. Not as a name and a vague description.

What, really, did he know of the victim of this murder of which he was trying to write? Her name. That she was young, pretty black-haired, that she wore a green dress the night she died. That she had been in love with the man who was to kill her and that she had come to Taos to marry him.

But from where had she come? Why had no one missed her? She must have had friends if not relatives. No one is ever so utterly alone that he can have his name publicized across a continent and have no one come forward.

It must be that Jenny Ames was not her true name; it was the only answer that made sense. Perhaps she had run away from home because her parents would not consent to her marrying Nelson and she'd changed her name so they couldn't trace her so easily.

That almost made sense. Not quite. Unless she was under age—and, according to the coroner's examination of her, she had been about twenty—why should she have feared pursuit? Her parents could not have annulled a marriage. And, anyway, wouldn't they have known Nelson's name if they had refused to let Jenny marry him?

Of course, despite that angle, age *might* have been a factor. Could it be that in New Mexico a girl cannot legally marry under the age of twenty-one without the consent of her parents? It hadn't arisen in his own case; when he and Vi had been married in Santa Fe she'd been twenty-two, and besides her parents had been dead for some years; she didn't even have any relatives living that he knew of. He'd have to ask

Callahan or someone what the New Mexico law was.

He found himself walking, out under the warm sun.

Damn, if only he had the car. Besides taking the films, he could ask Callahan about that law and could ask him too how good a man the coroner had been—whether there was any chance that he had misjudged the girl's age badly enough that she could have been less than eighteen.

He was under a big cottonwood tree, the big cottonwood tree. He hadn't intended to walk there; he hadn't been paying any attention to where his walk was taking him.

He stared down at the depression that had been a shallow grave.

You thought you knew her name and description, he told himself; now you're not even sure you know her name.

He sat down in the tree's shade, leaning back against its rough trunk.

Why did you change your name, Jenny?

Damn it, he couldn't write that article with so little knowledge, so many gaps in the few things he did know. If he forced himself to write it the words would be meaningless things gibbering out of the pages.

Who were you, Jenny?

He walked back to the house. His head was beginning to ache, and that was funny in a way because a headache had been the excuse he'd given for not going with Vi; circumstances were making an honest man out of him. He found aspirins on the shelf back of the kitchen sink and took two of them.

It was comparatively cool inside the house, much cooler than it was out in the wooden shed. Adobe is wonderful stuff for hot weather; it's cool by day but holds what heat it has by night when the temperature drops outside.

He tried to read for a while and couldn't get interested. Damn it, he thought; he'd counted on reading as one of the things that would help the summer pass restfully and painlessly. Until recently he'd always been able to enjoy reading. Now, always, thoughts got between his eyes and the printed page. He threw down the book angrily.

He called himself a damned fool, but that didn't help.

He went out to the shed and got his water colors and a block of paper and brought them into the house. Maybe he could paint. He tried it, doodling idly at first and then finding himself trying to paint the portrait of a beautiful black-haired girl.

But he wasn't that good; a portrait takes much more draftsmanship than a landscape and draftsmanship had always been his weak point. A slight discrepancy in the shape of a mountain doesn't matter but a slight one in the shape of a nose or an eye makes a portrait into a caricature. And water color is a very difficult medium for portraits, in any case.

He tried several times, but each attempt was a little worse than its predecessor and after a while he gave up. But trying had accomplished something—in trying to visualize Jenny, he had built up in his mind a clear picture of her, even though he couldn't get that picture on paper. It probably wasn't the way she really looked, of course, but did that really matter?

He tore up the pieces of paper he'd spoiled—tore them into very small bits so they couldn't possibly be jigsawed together again—and threw them into the wastebasket. He took his water colors back to the shed.

The headache was still there, although it had dulled a bit. He took two more aspirins and then got a bottle of whisky and made himself a drink, a strong one. He sat sipping it.

He thought, I'll go crazy if I can't read anymore, if I can't find anything to *do*.

After a while the drink was gone and he made himself another. Outside, the shadows were getting long. Pretty soon there'd be a beautiful sunset—and nuts to bothering to go outside and look at it. When you've seen one sunset you've seen them all.

If he only had the car. He could go somewhere, go anywhere and do anything. He probably should have gone to Taos with Vi, to the movie. Watching a movie doesn't take the effort of concentration that reading a book takes. Maybe he should—no, he would *not* descend to listening to the radio.

He'd razzed Vi about her radio programs so long that he'd
look silly, even to himself, if he started listening to radio now,
even if he could find the comparatively few programs that
weren't too horrible.

He poured another drink, straight this time; it was the
only thing in the world he could think of to do.

When Vi got home at eleven he was drunk, asleep on the
bed.

The next day was Sunday.

It was a month, to the day, from the time he'd arrived in
Taos—never dreaming, before he drove in, that he might decide to stay there. This morning he wondered why he'd made
that decision.

It was raining, for one thing. Not an honest hard rain but
a slow dull drizzle from a gray sky, not much more than a mist
really, but more unpleasant than a real rain. But the drizzle
matched his mood and his mood grew worse when, shortly
after lunch, Vi made the simultaneous discovery that there
was no liquor in the house except a little wine, which she
didn't care for, and that it was Sunday and no liquor could be
purchased anywhere.

"George, *why* didn't you get some more yesterday, before you drank everything in the house last night?"

He said mildly, "Vi, you had the car. Afternoon and evening. You knew there was less than a bottle left. If you can't
get by a day without it, you should have got some."

"I can, George, you know I can. You talk like I was a lush.
It was *you* got drunk last night, not me. I don't drink any
more than you do, not as much, and you know the doctor told
you to go easy on drinking until you get well again and—"

It went on and after a while he went out to the shed. He
didn't want a drink himself, although probably by evening he
would, but he wished to hell and back there was some whisky
around, just to keep Vi shut up. There wasn't a thing he
wanted to do in the shed, and it was cool and uncomfortable
there, but it was away from Vi's nagging and Vi's radio.

He lay down on the cot and tried to sleep for a while,
although he knew that if he did sleep he wouldn't be able to

sleep that night and that he'd regret taking a nap now. Damn Sundays, he thought, damn blue laws, damn a place where there was nowhere to go, nothing to do on a Sunday. If it weren't for this shed, his sanctuary— It's just like a little boy's playhouse, he thought, out here in the back yard where he can get away from people and think his own thoughts, imagine his own imaginings. But—

What am I? What am I imagining? Why am I here, in a dull drizzle in Taos, earning no money when I need money, when the money I have won't last too much longer? And if I'm not well now, I'm not going to get well; isn't this worry worse than the pressure of business, of working? Why don't I go back to Kansas City and get back to work so I'll have something constructive to think about instead of living like this?

He went to the window and stood staring out into the grayness and watching the thin rain fall onto the arid soil that absorbed it instantly as it struck, leaving no trace of moisture behind it. The ground underfoot, for walking, would be almost as dry as on a sunny day. Dry and unfertile soil, like himself, wasteland, haunted by the futile yearning of hungry coyotes.

Maybe he should go back to the house for a hat and raincoat and take a walk. Better than standing here brooding. Maybe a walk to the cottonwood where Jenny's grave had been.

But why? What was there now?

Nothing.

He went back to the house for his hat and coat and walked through the thin rain to the big tree, and there was nothing, no one, there, nothing but a place where a girl had been buried once for a short time, and that girl was long dead and why did he keep thinking and wondering about her?

But it was dry under the tree and he sat there a while leaning back against the big bole, staring at grayness within and without.

He was living in Santa Fe, he thought, at the time Jenny Ames came through there on her way to be killed. She came through from Albuquerque and there was a wait of at least half an hour between buses. If he had happened to be at the bus station that day he might have met her, talked to her.

He might have—but no, she was in love with the man to whom she was going, nothing that he could have said to her could have mattered. And—even if he had known then what he knew now—what could he possibly have done? Tell her that the man she was going to marry, as she thought, was going to murder her instead? She'd have thought he was crazy. And then? Get a ticket on the bus, follow her, try to protect her? She'd have called the police, of course.

Daydream. Suppose he'd gone on the bus but without speaking to her, without trying to warn her; he could have managed to sit next to her, since that seat had been the last one taken. Carlotta Evers had been the last one on the bus and he could have beaten her to it. He, instead of Carlotta Evers, could have become acquainted with Jenny on her way to Taos. She'd have introduced him to Nelson and he could have pulled Nelson aside and said, "I know your plans; you'd better change them or I'll see that you're caught and go to the chair. If you don't want that, tell Jenny It was all a mistake, her coming here and that you don't love her and can't marry her." He could have seen that she got a room in Taos. He could have—

Weaver laughed out loud at the absurdity of what he was thinking.

You don't get second chances, knowing the future. There aren't any time machines that take you back to a point in time where you can change something that has already happened. You never know the future until it's happened, and then it's the past and it's unalterable.

The drizzle had stopped. It startled him to look at his wrist watch and to see that it was almost four o'clock and that he'd been sitting here almost three hours. Vi would be furious if she'd got a lunch ready and then had tried to find him in the shed.

He walked back rapidly and went into the house by the kitchen door.

"That you, George?"

"Yes, Vi."

"Getting hungry? I was just thinking about making us something."

It was all right, then; she hadn't missed him.

"Guess I can eat something." he said. "Our breakfast was pretty late, but that was still some time ago."

She came out into the kitchen and he went on into the living room and shut off the radio; it wasn't a soap opera, just a variety show, and she probably hadn't been listening and wouldn't miss it. She didn't.

The sound of something frying in a skillet. Vi fried everything; she didn't seem to know that there were other ways of cooking things. Not that Weaver minded fried food, but he would have liked a change from it once in a while. But he'd long ago given up suggesting variety in Vi's cooking. Just as he'd given up worrying about the way she kept house, and tried not to notice. The table beside the chair she'd been sitting in was littered, the ash tray heaping, the open box of candy, magazines lying open, an empty glass—Vi must have decided that wine, after all, was better than nothing—the lipstick on the cigarette butts and the rim of the glass— Why did Vi wear lipstick when only the two of them were here alone? Certainly not for him. Certainly not because—out here miles from nowhere—someone might come. Just habit, it must be; she wore lipstick for the same reason she wore shoes and a dress. Or for the same reason he himself shaved every day—no, that was different; his face got itchy and uncomfortable if he went a day without shaving, even if he didn't intend to leave the place.

Had Jenny Ames worn lipstick? Probably—almost all women do—but not as incessantly and as thickly as Vi. Sometimes even in her sleep if she went to bed too tight to remember to take it off, and then the pillow would be smeared with red in the morning.

Were you sloppy, Jenny? No, I don't think you were; you were young and neat and clean.

The crumpled spread on the sofa, the mussed pillow, the

calendar askew on the wall, the unswept floor. Through the open door of the bedroom one of Vi's suitcases still on the floor, still not completely unpacked; she took things from it as she needed them and she hadn't yet needed them all.

Jenny, you wouldn't have left a suitcase—

Weaver sat up suddenly. Why hadn't he thought of Jenny's suitcases before?

What had happened to them?

Surely they hadn't been found; it would have been mentioned at the inquest, their contents described. Callahan would have mentioned it, and there would have been clues as to who and what Jenny had been. Even though it contains no written word, the contents of any suitcase tell much about its owner.

Or could the sheriff possibly have been as stupid about Jenny's suitcases as he'd been about Nelson's pictures? Could he have found them, looked through them casually and, if he didn't find any names and addresses, fail to tell anyone that he'd found them?

Or had Nelson taken them away, in a car that was already overcrowded with his own possessions—?

"George, lunch's ready."

He sat at the table across from Vi and ate quickly, not even tasting what he ate. He wanted to get eating over with as fast as he could so he could go to Callahan's, ask Callahan—

"George, you're acting funny. Like you're all excited about something."

He managed to slow down a bit. "Guess I was pretty hungry all of a sudden, that's all. This is good—uh—ham, Vi." He'd had to sneak a quick look at his plate to see what he'd been eating.

"Glad you like it, George. You don't often say nice things about what I cook."

"Or bad things either."

"George, I was thinking. Isn't there *any* place in Taos where we could get something to drink on Sunday? And if there isn't, we're not too awfully far from the Colorado border, are we? Is everything closed in Colorado on Sundays, too?"

"I don't know about Colorado. But it's not too near; couple of hours drive, I think. And my guess is I couldn't buy anything there either. Sorry. I could use a drink myself by now."

Vi looked down at her plate. "You know, George, I'd kind of like us to—to drink together, to get a little tight tonight, like we used to once in a while. You know."

He knew. It had been a long time since they'd had even that. At least six or seven months, before his breakdown. For the several years before that the only times they'd been able to want one another—at least at the same time—had been rare occasions when they'd been drinking together at home and each of them had got a little drunk, not too much, just enough. It hadn't happened often, and when it had happened it had been a purely physical thing but perhaps better than complete continence.

Maybe, Weaver thought, it would be a good thing to let happen tonight. There is such a thing as physical need, physical pressure. It wasn't anything mental; he didn't want Vi now, or any woman, at this moment; he hadn't *felt* any need since leaving the san, but perhaps the need was there just the same. Perhaps it was at least part of his present trouble, part of the reason why he hadn't been able to concentrate on reading or painting, why his mind insisted on dwelling on morbid things instead of normal ones.

He felt a sudden tenderness for Vi—it wasn't her fault that she was what she was and that he couldn't love her; and her problems were probably as great to her as his own were to him. The fact that circumstances and children tied them together despite their incompatibility was no more her fault than his own. Less her fault, really; as the more intelligent of the two of them he should have thought to avoid that entanglement.

He said quietly, "I'll try to think of some way to get some liquor, Vi. I'll take a run in to Taos; maybe I'll find someone who can tell me where to buy a bottle."

He drank his coffee slowly, thinking. Yes, Nelson must

have hidden the suitcases, or at least their contents. Was there any chance at all that he would have hidden them indoors? Hardly, but—the outdoors was so big.

He got up and wandered around, looking. He had his story ready for her question.

"What are you doing, George?"

"Thought I might find some liquor here, Vi. Got a vague recollection of having hidden a bottle from myself one night when I was here before you came. Maybe I'm wrong, but it doesn't hurt to look."

That made enough sense to let him do all the looking he wanted.

For what? Signs of floorboards having been taken up and replaced—after eight years? That was silly, and besides if there were any loose floorboards Ellis DeLong's men would have fixed them while they were working on the place. And anyway, why would Nelson have taken up floorboards to bury something indoors when there was practically an infinity of space outside?

He went outdoors.

The shed? Again, why would Nelson have taken up floorboards and nailed them down again? He stood looking around him.

He told himself, "All right, let's pretend you're a murderer. You've just killed a girl; you buried her where you killed her, a quarter-mile back that way. You come back here and you're tired, dead tired, from the long run and from digging and pushing back dirt. And you haven't got too much stamina to begin with because you've got tuberculosis. You're worn out. But you see her suitcases—or, if they're still in the back of your car, you remember them. And just in case there should be any investigation—though you don't see why there should be, unless that woman, damn her, whom Jenny talked to on the bus should start asking questions—well, anyway you'd better get rid of them. You couldn't explain having two suitcases full of a woman's clothes and possessions. You'd better bury them like you buried the girl. But where?"

He looked around him. Sandy soil and chamiso. Distant

clumps of cottonwood, but so very distant. So far to carry two suitcases when you're worn out already.

Where, then? Weaver closed his eyes and thought. It would have been night. And Nelson would need a light to dig a hole—or at least it would be easier if he could use a light. But the light shouldn't be visible from the road—and how about that little hillock a hundred yards to the east? To go behind it would take him far enough from the house and it was the nearest place that would be' completely hidden from the road. Besides, it was a spot on the way to nowhere; nobody would be likely to walk there and notice that a hole had been dug and filled in. It was much nearer than the cottonwood where he'd buried Jenny, and just as safe.

The sky was grayer now and the shadows were getting long with the approach of evening, but there was still enough light for him to look there now, at least a quick look that could be supplemented by a more thorough search tomorrow. He walked around behind the hillock.

He was still in sight of the house, even though he was out of sight of the road. Vi might wonder what he was doing there—but no, he couldn't see her at any of the windows. She'd probably gone back to her chair and wouldn't notice.

A depression, that was what he was looking for. A little bigger than a suitcase, maybe three by four feet, a shallow depression. It would have been leveled off at first, maybe even a slight mound like a fresh grave, but it would have sunk in when the suitcases had collapsed later.

A small, slightly sunken area—

He picked a bigger than average clump of chamiso to use as a center and started walking in a slow spiral about it. He passed it once before he noticed it on the next round. He stood studying it—a shallow area of depression about the right size. Oval-shaped, not rectangular as he'd thought of it— but it would have weathered to ovalness, of course.

And just about the right size—

Suddenly he was on his knees in the sand, trying to dig with his fingers. But the soil, sandy though the surface was, was hard packed and he stopped quickly and stood up, looking at the house.

No, Vi still wasn't at any of the windows and probably hadn't noticed him as yet. But digging would require a shovel or a trowel—or at the very least, a strong knife—and he couldn't possibly do it now without Vi's noticing him eventually. It would have to be tonight, with a flashlight after Vi was asleep.

He was trembling a little with excitement.

He walked back to the house and went in, putting his hands in his pockets so their shaking wouldn't show. Was there, he wondered, any excuse he could use to get Vi to go Into town now so he wouldn't have to wait those long hours until night? A movie? No, not after what she'd suggested.

"George, that whisky–if you're going to try to get some–"

Suddenly he realized how badly he himself wanted a drink. He said, "Sure, Vi. I'll go right away. Come to think of it, I'll try a near neighbor of ours first; I know him slightly. He just might have an extra bottle on hand, or be able to tell me where I can get one."

He went out into the gathering twilight and started the car.

[11]

From the front, Callahan's house looked dark, but Weaver left his car on the road and walked back toward it anyway. A collie came running at him, barking, and he stood still until he'd made friends with it by talking to it and letting it sniff his hand. No one came to investigate the barking and he was pretty sure no one was home, but he went on to the house anyway and knocked, waited a while and then knocked again.

He swore to himself. Callahan had been his best bet; if he hadn't any liquor on hand himself surely he knew the ropes well enough to know where some could be obtained.

He went back to the car and sat there thinking, trying to

decide the next best bet. Sanchez might be able to get him because of the prejudice against Anglos in that town, he hated to ask any favors. Even if he gave Sanchez money and offered to pay double for the whisky besides— But damn it, besides Callahan, he still knew only a few people, all of them much too casually for him to seek them out on a matter like this. Although if he met one of them on the street he could ask casually. Perhaps that was his only chance, to drive to Taos and park, then wander around the plaza hoping to see someone he knew, however slightly. Or perhaps the desk clerk at the hotel where he'd stayed a few nights would advise him.

He had gone back to his car and was just starting the engine when a car came into sight around the next curve heading toward him—and it was Callahan's car. Callahan was alone in it; he waved and motioned as he turned in the drive toward his house, and Weaver walked back toward him.

"Hi," Callahan said. "Glad I didn't miss you. Just took the wife to a hen party and have to pick her up later. Come on in."

Weaver followed Callahan into the house. He remembered the purpose for which Vi had suggested the whisky and knew he'd better have a story ready that would enable him not to ask Callahan home with him. Vi wouldn't like that.

"Drink?" Callahan was asking him.

"Sure, thanks. In fact, that's what I came to ask you about —whether, by any chance, you happened to have a bottle or two to spare. We're caught short—friends of ours are going to drop in on us, driving through on their way from Kansas City, and they should get here about any minute now. I just realized it was Sunday and that I didn't know where to get any."

"Sure, I can spare a couple of bottles—nothing fancy, though, just drinkin' whisky. I brought back a case from Colorado a week or so ago; always bring back some when I drive up there—the state tax is enough lower to make it worth the trouble. That's a tip, in case you ever go up that way. Pick up a few cartons of cigarettes, too; you save even more on them. But you'll have time for a drink with me here, won't you?"

Weaver said he would. Callahan poured drinks for them from an opened bottle and got two unopened ones from a closet.

They sat at the kitchen table to drink. Weaver had decided there wasn't any real hurry now that his liquor problem had been solved, but he looked at his watch and pretended to decide that he could spare a little time but not too much of it. Callahan wouldn't take money for the two bottles. "Don't remember offhand exactly what they cost. Replace them any time—same brand or an equivalent one; I'm not fussy."

"Okay, and thanks to hell and back. This pulls me out of a jam." He took a drink of the whisky-and-water Callahan had mixed for him. "By the way, Callahan, how old does a girl have to be to get married in New Mexico without her parents' consent?"

"Eighteen. Why? Thinking of taking unto yourself another wife? Would your present one let you?"

"One is plenty, thanks. No, I was thinking about Jenny Ames. I've got a hunch she must have come here under a false name—that would account for nobody's having claimed her—but if she did there must have been a reason for it. It occurred to me that she could have been running away from her parents to marry this Nelson. And she could have figured that, if she was under age, they could have had the marriage annulled if they traced her. At least that's one reason why she might have used a false name."

"I don't think so. That idea was thought of at the time—by me, in fact. I asked Doc Gomez, the coroner, whether he was sure she was past eighteen. He said he'd give a hundred to one on it—that if his guess of twenty was wrong he probably erred the other way; she might have been a year or two older but not younger, certainly not two years younger."

"That's that, then. It seemed like a possibility."

"How's the story coming? Actually writing on it yet?"

"Tried one version but I don't like it. No hurry anyway; got some pictures to go with it that I haven't even taken to the photograph shop yet. And I can't send in the story till I take them and get them back."

He tried to look and sound casual. God, if only he didn't have to wait so many hours before he could get Jenny's suitcases! But there were those hours to be faced in any case, whether he spent them all with Vi or a few more minutes with Callahan. So why was he so fidgety about sitting here?

Callahan was saying, "Better not sit on the story *too* long, though. You may find our sheriff—the present one—breathing down your neck."

"Why? Where does he come in? You didn't tell him about those pictures of Nelson's, did you?"

"Nope, promised you I wouldn't, didn't I? But you forgot to swear Ellie Grant to secrecy when you showed them to him. Ellie tells everybody everything—maybe I should have thought to warn you about that, but I didn't. Anyway, he told Tom—that's the present sheriff, Tom Grayson—about the pictures and Tom likes your idea of trying to locate Nelson through them. He likes it so well he's tempted to beat you to the punch and circularize likely areas with reproductions of those pictures and a description of Nelson. Be quite a feather in his cap if he caught Nelson, after his predecessor had missed the boat. But luckily for you he came around to talk to me after Ellie had spilled the beans to him, and I talked him out of going ahead on his own—right away, anyway—at a slight price."

Weaver frowned.

Callahan waved a hand. "oh, I don't mean money. I just mean you're to give him a build-up in your story—as being currently interested in the case whether publication of the pictures in a magazine brings results or not. Give him as much build-up and credit as you reasonably can. That way, win or lose, he'll get publicity on the deal. That magazine should sell like hot cakes in Taos, because of the local story in it. I've been meaning to look you up to tell you to talk to Tom before you sent in the story."

"I'll do that," Weaver said. "And thanks for stalling him off from trying anything on his own. Although, unless I gave him the pictures or photographs of them, I don't see how he could."

"You'd give him the pictures all right. He could get a writ to take them away from you as evidence in a murder case. Old as it is, that case is still open, don't forget. Well, he won't get a writ as long as you play ball with him."

"I will. I'll look him up and talk to him before I do the story."

"Have another drink?"

"Better not. Our company might show up any minute and my wife will be getting worried if I'm not back. Thanks for everything—for the liquor and for holding off the sheriff. What'd you say his name is?"

"Grayson. Tom Grayson. Nice guy, but he's got a temper—and a rough tongue if you get his temper going."

"I'll try not to. So long."

Weaver took the two bottles out to his car and turned it around toward home. It was fully dark by then, almost eight o'clock. He drove back slowly, not so much because the road was narrow and winding as because—the more he thought of it, the less of a hurry he was in to get home. But maybe he could get Vi drunk quickly if he kept giving her drinks, and at a certain stage of drinking she always got sleepy. But he'd have to watch his own drinking, pretend to drink more than he really did, so he'd be sober enough to do his digging after Vi was safely asleep.

He went into the house whistling, holding up the bottles.

"Better start catching up, Vi," he said. "I had to have a few drinks with a guy before I could talk him out of these, so I'm well ahead of you. Shall I make you a husky one?"

He did, and a weaker one for himself. And another and another. After a while he forgot to keep his own drinks weaker than hers, but that didn't matter; he could drink much more than she could and the difference in their first few drinks had more than evened up for the one he'd had with Callahan, so she'd be drunk before he would.

And she was. Luckily without going into the angry tirade that drink often inspired in her. And luckily, too, forgetting her original suggestion as to why they drink. Just incoherently drunk, then suddenly and overwhelmingly sleepy, then asleep in her chair, leaning back, her mouth open.

He'd wait a few minutes until her sleep was really sound,

and then get her to bed. If she slept in the chair she might awaken and miss him. Once in the bed, she was safe for the night.

He walked on tiptoe and with exaggerated caution out into the kitchen, taking the bottle with him. He was still reasonably sober and he made himself another drink. After all, what did it matter if he was just a little drunk when he did his digging? Keep him from catching cold in the cool night.

He sipped his drink and he wasn't in any hurry now, he found. Now that the way was clear it was delicious to wait, to prolong his suspense. He felt ridiculously, dizzily happy; he was sorry and glad that there was no one with whom he could conceivably share that happiness. Deliberately he prolonged his drink, taking it in small and occasional sips, standing at the window staring out into the darkness in the direction in which he would soon be walking. Not that he could see anything; the sky was still overcast and the night utterly black.

The sound of Vi's snoring. Definitely safe now to put her to bed; she wouldn't waken no matter how clumsy he was.

He was just a trifle unsteady on his feet as he went back into the living room. Fortunately he wouldn't have to carry her; he knew from experience that he could get her to her feet and walk her into the bedroom, supporting part of her weight and doing the steering and that she'd walk automatically without awakening.

Even that way, it made him stagger. God, but she was getting hefty.

He got her on the bed, her head on the pillow. It would be smeared with lipstick in the morning, but he didn't worry about that. She was on top of the covers; he should have thought of pulling them back before he started, but it was too late now. He took off her shoes and then her stockings, and the touch of the flesh of her legs as he unfastened the garters wasn't either disgusting or enticing; it was as impersonal as the touch of the cool metal of the foot of the bed as he steadied himself.

It was too cool to leave her uncovered but he solved that by folding the covers from his own side of the bed back over

Vi. He himself could sleep on the cot in the shed—when he was ready to sleep—and there were two blankets out there. Anyway, sleep for him was too far in the future to think about.

He closed the bedroom door quietly behind him—although he could safely have slammed it—and went through the living room back into the kitchen.

A coat; it would be cold out there. The flashlight. Something to dig with. Damn, why hadn't he borrowed a shovel from Callahan? No, it would have been too difficult to explain. And if he found anything, no one was going to see it or know about it, ever. It was going to be *his* secret, and he wasn't going to blab about it, as he had about the pictures. But what if the suitcases weren't—

He didn't dare let himself think that. They had to be there.

A knife would have to do for digging. He opened the drawer of the kitchen table and picked the biggest one he could find; a heavy kitchen knife with an eight-inch blade.

He stood for a moment staring at it. It had been there, with a few other implements, when he'd moved in. Could this have been the murder knife? The sheriff would have seen it, certainly, in his search of the place after the body had been found, but if Nelson had washed and cleaned it well, how would the sheriff have known?

Nobody could know now. But it *could* have been the knife. It had been there, and it was consistent with Pepe Sanchez's description.

To hell with thinking about that. It would serve for digging, or at least for loosening the packed ground. Something to scrape with. He found a small but heavy iron skillet under the sink; he could use it as a scoop too.

He had one more drink, a short one, straight.

It was cold outside, and black. But the flashlight cut the blackness and the whisky in him helped keep out the cold. He walked to the place where he was going to dig. The other shallow grave, but not—this one—empty.

The soil was hard to cut but the knife went in. He worked hard, fast. He found the skillet was worthless as a scoop; it was easier to loosen dirt with the knife and then scoop it up in both hands.

Less than a foot down he came to the top of the suitcase—or what was left of the top of a suitcase; it had been cheap cardboard and there was only enough of it left now to identify what it had been. From there on he worked with the care of an archeologist uncovering brittle bones. He enlarged the hole carefully, his hands shaking a little—either with nervousness or the cold or both—but gentle, very gentle.

It seemed to take him hours. And maybe it really did for after a while it became more and more difficult to see what he was doing and he realized that the batteries of the flashlight lying at the edge of the excavation had weakened and that the bulb glowed dully and then became only a glowing filament that cast no appreciable light.

He swore and stood up on aching legs, then walked back toward the beacon of the lighted kitchen window of the house. His teeth were chattering with cold and his hands were numb. His knees and his back ached.

He poured himself another drink of straight whisky, a long one, and sat at the kitchen table sipping it slowly, letting its warmth penetrate into his body. The ache in his back got worse instead of better, but after a while the coldness and the numbness of his hands went away.

He tried not to think about what he knew he was going to find. He tried not to think at all—because he knew that if he let himself think he'd find his sanity suspect because of the intensity of his anticipation. It wasn't, a part of his mind knew, that important. It wasn't important at all. What matter things you learn about a girl eight years dead? What matters it to touch, to possess, things that she owned, things that she wore?

You're drunk; blame it on that. You're drunk.

Another drink to drive out the rest of the coldness. A shorter drink, and he made himself drink it very slowly.

Then again the night. This time he went to the car first and got the other flashlight, with fresh batteries, that was in the glove compartment. And back to the shallow grave that was the grave not of Jenny but of the things that had been

Jenny's, the things that his cleverness had enabled him to deduce and to find where no one else had ever found them nor ever would have.

He carefully scraped away the remaining dirt from the top of the suitcase and carefully sloped and shaped the banks of earth on all sides of it so that, when he lifted, no dirt would slide down into the hole.

He lifted with infinite care but the top of the suitcase came away, as he had feared it would. All right, he'd have to take the things out one at a time. He took off his coat and spread it on the ground beside the hole and put down on it first the top of the suitcase. Then other things, one at a time. A folded dress that came apart as he tried to lift it—but that taught him to be more careful with other things.

A rusty thing that had been an alarm clock. A moldy thing that had been a case for toilet articles. A soggy thing that had been a box of stationery and envelopes. Other dresses. Dampish little balls that had been rolled up stockings. Wisps of what had been silk or rayon slips and step-ins. A bra. What had been a lace-topped nightgown. Two pairs of shoes that had been wrapped in paper that was now almost completely disintegrated. A woolen skirt that had probably once been white.

One after another he put them reverently on his spread coat beside the shallow excavation until the suitcase was empty. It was enough for one load; he wrapped the coat around its precious burden and carried it like a baby back toward the house. But not into the house. The shed would be his repository. He put them down carefully, first, on the cot. Then he cleared the table of the typewriter and the few other things that had been on it. He opened out the coat and transferred the things he had found carefully to the table top. Save everything, he thought; until it had been thoroughly examined, even the disintegrating top of the suitcase.

He lighted the oil stove so there'd be warmth and dryness in the shed; he locked the door behind him as he went back through the night to the excavation. He carried his coat back for the next load; it never occurred to him that the night was cold and that he might have worn it and brought a blanket for his carrying. He spread the coat again and carefully worked out the rest of the emptied suitcase, trying to tear it as little as possible. Two pieces came out of the sides, but the rest remained intact.

Then, disappointment. The other suitcase wasn't there and for a moment he thought there was nothing there. Then he saw that there was, but that probably nothing of it would be salvageable; the hole had been dug about two and a half feet deep and things had been thrown loose into the bottom of it, then the suitcase put on top. Obviously Nelson had decided that one of the two suitcases had been worthy of his own use and had merely dumped its contents into the bottom of the hole before he'd put the other suitcase—the cheap cardboard one—in.

Completely unprotected, what had been in the other suitcase was, for practical purposes, gone now. He saw the sole of a shoe but when he pulled it up, only a fragment of the upper adhered. There had been clothes, but they came apart at a touch; he couldn't tell their color, their material, or even what garments they had been.

But he went through it slowly, taking out everything that could be taken. The shoe and its mate, a comb, a chunk of what had once been leather and was about the size and shape of a woman's billfold but was now a solid thing—he handled it, nevertheless, with particular care on the chance that it might be steamed apart and disclose identification—a comb, a razor that was rusted solid but recognizable for what it had been. Some costume jewelry, the metal rusted or corroded, but the stones, when he rubbed them, as bright as new. The costume jewelry was all together; possibly it had been in a cardboard box but the box had ceased to exist. Buttons here and there. The rest had been cloth, and the cloth was gone.

Nothing more. He searched thoroughly, painstakingly, but there was nothing more.

You damned fool, he told himself, what more did you expect? Isn't this enough? Don't you know more of Jenny now than anyone else—except those who knew her before she came here? Don't you *have* more of Jenny Ames than anyone else?

He carried his coat, this time lighter than before, back to the shed. The warmth that the stove had spread showed him that he'd been gone a long time. And the pleasant shock of that warmth showed him how cold he'd been. But he disposed of the rest of his find carefully on the table before he put his coat back on. Again he locked the door before he went back to the excavation and began to scoop the dirt back into it.

The dirt didn't fill the hole again, of course, but that didn't matter. Vi never came this way and the odds were thousands to one against anyone else coming here either.

Flashlight—its batteries dimming now too—back in the car. The house again. Remove evidence. Wash and replace knife and skillet and the other flashlight. Mental note to buy batteries for both flashlights before night. Wash hands, brush clothes and particularly knees of trousers as well as possible. He brushed the dirt from his coat too and hung it back up.

His face, in the mirror over the kitchen sink, was blue from cold. He should have had sense enough to carry the things in something besides his coat. He looked around, wondering if he'd left any evidence of what he'd done. The floor was gritty with sand and dirt that had been brushed from his coat and his trousers; he took a broom and swept it out into the night through the kitchen door.

He looked at his watch and saw that it was three o'clock.

But he wasn't going to, bed, at least not for a long time yet. He poured himself another drink, almost half a tumbler of straight whisky this time, and sipping at it warmed and steadied him.

The sound of Vi's snoring from the bedroom showed him that she hadn't awakened, but he went to the door and opened it, looking to be sure that she was still under the covers he'd folded over her from his own side of the bed.

This time he turned the light off as he left the kitchen; he wouldn't be coming back to the house tonight. He'd left the shed light on so he could see his way back there; he carried the bottle and a glass with him.

He sat at the table and poured himself a drink—but with extreme care so that not a drop might spill on the precious objects so near the glass. He put the bottle on the floor, safely out of the way.

He touched this, that, of the things that had been Jenny's. Could there be laundry tags on any of the pathetic shreds of what had been clothing? He searched carefully, reverently, but couldn't find any.

The box of toilet articles. He almost missed the monogram on it because the gilt had come off; there was merely a depression in the leatherette. J. A.

J. A. Jenny Ames. Or, if she had really changed her name, she'd changed it from a name that had the same initials. But then, he'd read somewhere, many people did that; it was natural when you picked a new name to use the same initials. Especially if one had anything that was monogrammed. Probably she'd even kept her right first name.

Jenny Andrews? Jenny Anderson? Jenny Adams?

What did a name matter?

He spread the things carefully so they'd dry in the increasing heat of the shed. The oil heater he'd bought for it had been somewhat too large for so small a place. It had been running full blast now since he'd turned it on and the place was getting to be almost like an oven—but that would dry out Jenny's things more quickly so he left it on, even though he himself was beginning to sweat a little in the heat.

Jar of what looked as though it had been cold cream, although the label was gone and the contents had dried to a gray crust inside it. What had been a tube of toothpaste, a toothbrush with wilted bristles but the yellow plastic handle as bright as though it had been bought yesterday. Nail scissors rusted shut forever. A tortoise-shell comb that was as good as new. A small jar, again with the label gone, possibly it had been deodorant; again only a gray crust left of what had been its contents. A little tin box that had contained aspirins. Those were the contents of the box of toilet articles.

Little things, pathetic things. Are all the souvenirs of the dead so pathetic? This comb that had once gone through raven hair, this wisp of cloth, now falling apart at a touch, that had once been silk or rayon step-ins about soft young hips. These rotting stockings that had once encased slender legs to tender thighs. This bra that had cupped rounded breasts. This frock that had hidden Jenny from a hostile world—how hostile she had never known until that final awful hour.

Spread them carefully in the arid heat. Touch them gently with your sweating fingers, for they have not long to last and when they are gone all of Jenny will be gone; they're all that's left of her now.

He picked up the sodden box of stationery that, aside from the thing that might have been a wallet, was the highest hope. *Did you save letters, Jenny?*

No, the wallet first. He picked it up and studied it carefully. It wasn't in as bad condition as he'd thought at first, now that it had dried a bit he could open it. It stuck together and he had to peel carefully, but it came apart, and it was empty. No money, no cards, nothing behind the cellophane window except leather. He worked with it, looking for something in some compartment, but there was nothing. Either it had been a new wallet that Jenny had not yet started to use, or Nelson had carefully seen that it was emptied before he'd buried the suitcase that had contained it.

He put it down in disappointment and again pulled the box of stationery toward him across the table.

Did you save letters, Jenny? Or, if you did, did your murderer take them out of this box as he may have taken identification out of your billfold?

Craighill Bond; he could read the letters in the embossing on the lid of the box, although the ink of the printing was gone. He slid the box closer to him and this time the bottom of it stuck to the table and the rest slid toward him. Well, he'd study the bottom of it later. He lifted carefully and the lid came up; two sides came with it and the other two fell away.

Two piles of envelopes, stuck together in two solid pulpy masses. The paper underneath, a solid sheaf. This had been in the center of the suitcase, he remembered, or there'd be even less of it left.

One by one he peeled the envelopes apart to make certain that they were all new, unused ones—although from the uniformity of the stacks he felt sure of that already.

The paper too—until he picked up the solid sheaf of it and turned it over. The bottom sheet, although stuck to the others, was a different kind, a very slightly different size and shade, and it was written upon, although the ink of the writing was gone and there were only scratches and grooves to indicate that there had been writing there.

Weaver's hands shook and the palms and backs of them were wet with sweat. He put the sheaf of stuck-together paper down before him on the table, bottom up, and studied the scratch marks. They were clear and definite; whoever had done that writing had used a stub pen and a heavy touch; it looked like a man's writing rather than a woman's.

The final word looked like a signature. It *was* a signature. He made it out.

"Charles."

And the line above it. He bent and caught a reflection of the light in the faint markings. Last word of the line, *"love."* Something *"all my love." "With all my love."*

A letter—and legible—from Nelson to Jenny. And, if he'd gone through the suitcase before he'd buried it, he'd missed this letter because it had been under blank stationery at the bottom of the stationery box!

Weaver stopped a minute. He had to. He poured himself another short drink—although just at that moment he felt soberer than he'd ever felt in his life—and he poured it only after shoving his chair back from the table and being sure that neither glass nor bottle came anywhere near the precious thing he'd just discovered.

Just a short drink; he downed it at a gulp. He sat there a full minute before he pulled his chair back to the table.

How gentle can you be? That's how gentle he was as he picked up the sheaf of paper again and tried from one corner to see whether the bottom piece—the letter—would peel away from the rest without sticking or coming apart.

It would. It did. A fraction of an inch at a time—but his

fingers had suddenly become precision instruments that gauged the strain to a thousandth of an ounce. It peeled away and there was writing and even the ink, enough of it to show faintly, was still there.

"*Beloved Jenny—*"

He could read that much at a glance. No date, no return address. But— "*Beloved Jenny—*"

Infinite care in a little room. A millimeter at a time he peeled, and he kept himself from trying to read more until he had the whole piece loose from the sheaf. And then the sheet was loose, separate. He put it down flat on the table.

Parts of it were more difficult to read than others, but the strokes of the coarse stub pen helped in places where the ink was faint.

Beloved Jenny—

I can hardly believe that you will be with me so soon now, that all of life and happiness lies before us, then and forever, that you will be my wife for all time to come.

Let me know the day, Jenny darling, as soon as you can name it. I only wish that I could come to get you—but you know why it is far wiser that you come here to join me and that you leave.

End of first page.

Still no lead as to where Jenny had come from. Would there be, on one of the two inside pages?

Should he wait till he was sober before he tried to peel it apart? Until the paper was completely dry? No, maybe it would stick worse then; maybe it would stick together completely and irrevocably.

It peeled almost easily. It lay open before him.

no traces behind you. Beloved, it is a wonderful thing that you are doing, no matter what others might think, and don't worry about the others. We'll make it all right as soon as we can, and it doesn't look as though that should take too long. We'll set the world on fire, Jenny darling; with you to help me I can do anything.

You'll love the place we'll live in, and you'll love Taos. It's as different from Barton as Heaven is from Hell. We'll be happier than either of us ever dreamed of being. And I'll be successful. I know the sacrifice you're making for our happiness, and I'll see that it's not in vain.

You'll love it here, Jenny. And I'll love you anywhere, anywhere and for ever—my bride, my love, my life, my own.

Barton! He had the key; it could only be the name of the town Jenny came from! But where was Barton?

Let it ride till you've read the rest of the letter. Only a few words on the last page. Only pen scratchings here, but there are only a few of them.

So hurry, darling. Make the day as soon as you can, and let me know so I'll have the license ready, and a room for you if we can't be married the first day.

That was all, except the ending which he'd read first. *"With all my love, Charles."*

Barton! That was the important word. Where was Barton? He hurried back to the house and looked in the gazetteer section of the dictionary, but it wasn't listed. All towns of over ten thousand population *were* listed, so Barton was smaller than that. All the better; the smaller the town the easier it would be to get the information he wanted.

But damn, oh, damn it, he'd have to wait till he could go to Taos in the morning and have access to a big gazetteer to find out where it was.

But he wanted to leave *now.*

Could he wake Callahan—he'd seen quite a library of books in the editor's place and surely there'd be a gazetteer among them—at three-thirty in the morning?

Yes, he could do just that if he was willing to tell Callahan of his tremendously important discovery. But he wasn't. Besides, if he did know, at this moment, where Barton was, he couldn't just walk out on Vi. He'd have to plot and plan and lie in order to get there at all.

He'd left the whisky back in the shed and he closed up the house again and turned out the lights before he went back there for his next drink.

When he drank it he was drunk, suddenly drunk. Not mentally—his mind was as clear as the cold mountain water that flowed in the stream between his house and the road. Or so he thought. But the walls of the shed were swaying. He was pacing back and forth the length of it and he had to put his hand against a wall to brace himself at almost every turn. And the place was hot as hell by now and sweat was running down him.

How could he go to Barton? What story could he tell Vi?

His mind wanted to keep on working at it but his body rebelled; his body ached with weariness. He compromised with his body by letting it lie down on the cot. He could think lying down as well as . . .

[12]

Knocking on the door awakened him. Bright daylight came through the translucent window drapes and made the ceiling light, still burning, a pale yellow. The room was terrifically hot and he was soaked with sweat.

Knocking, louder. Vi's voice. "George! Are you there? Are you all right?"

He swung his feet from the cot to the floor. His shoes were still on and they hurt his feet. He shook his head to clear it and found that it ached badly and that shaking it made him dizzy. But he had to answer, and quickly.

His voice cracked when he first tried to use it, but it worked on the second try. "Yes, Vi. I'm all right. Be in the house in a minute. Make some coffee, huh?"

"Okay, George." He couldn't hear her footsteps but a moment later he heard the slam of the kitchen screen door of the house.

God, but it was hot. He could hardly approach the oil stove to turn it off; it had been running, turned to its highest heat, for—he looked at his watch and saw that it was ten o'clock—for eight or nine hours now. He used his handkerchief to turn it off so he wouldn't burn his hand. He didn't want to unlock the door and open it right away lest Vi come back for some reason and see the things that were still on the table, but he threw open the window to let some of the heat out.

He wanted to get out of the heat himself, out into the relative coolness of the bright sunshine outdoors, but first he'd have to hide the things on the table. There was a folded piece of canvas in one corner of the shed—why hadn't he used that last night instead of carrying things in his coat?—and it turned out to be big enough to wrap all of his booty. He slid the bundle back under the cot; the blanket hanging over the edge concealed it perfectly. He unlocked the door and went out, locking it again from the outside and stuffing the key in his pocket.

He felt like hell. He was wringing wet and the inside of his mouth felt like the Gobi Desert. He staggered a little on his way to the house, but once through the kitchen door he made himself walk straight. Straight to the bucket of drinking water beside the sink. He drank two full dippers of it before he went to the kitchen table and sat down.

"George, are you sick? You look—" Vi stared at him.

"Just hung over, Vi. 'Fraid I really hung one on—it sneaked up on me. You passed out early."

"But what did you *do?* Your clothes—they're *awful.*"

"Slept in them. And I guess I fell once or twice. I was out in the shed part of the time and in here part of the time. Must have fallen in between."

"But what did you *do?*"

"I told you. Got drunk. And I feel awful, Vi; layoff me, please. How's about some coffee? A cup of that and I may feel human enough to clean myself up."

"It's right in front of you, George." It was. He started to

drink it.

Things were coming back to him. Barton. He had to get to Taos to find out where Barton was. But he couldn't go in looking like this. Or could he? He remembered a barbershop that had a "Baths" sign. And he wanted and needed a long hot bath, not just a sponge bath like he'd have to take here.

"Vi, I'm going in to Taos. I'll sneak in the back way so nobody will see me. I'll take some clean clothes with me and take a bath there and change—and I'll leave this suit to be cleaned. I'm such a mess that's the only way I'll straighten out."

"All right, George. But don't you want something to eat? Some eggs, maybe?"

The thought of eating sickened him and he shook his head. "Go ahead and eat if you want to, Vi. Maybe after I'm cleaned up I'll have a bite of breakfast in town. Anything you want me to bring back?"

"Well, you can take the grocery list."

He finished his coffee and made a bundle of fresh clothes to take with him. He was still a little uncertain on his feet, he found, so he drove carefully and much more slowly than usual. His head contained a dull steady throbbing now and he had to keep blinking his eyes to keep them in focus on the road.

He parked back of the plaza and walked through an alley to the barbershop. The bath should have felt wonderful, but it didn't; his head hurt too much. And he was in a hurry because he had to get to the Harwood Library before it closed from twelve until two o'clock in the afternoon. But there was time after his bath to get a shave in the barbershop and to take his suit to the cleaners. He'd made a bundle of his dirty linen and he threw it into the back of his car and drove the few blocks to the library.

He felt a little better, not much.

He knew where the big atlas was; he'd happened to notice it on a previous stop there. He took it back to one of the tables and looked under Barton in the general index of towns in the United States.

There were two Bartons. One in Wyoming and one in California.

The Wyoming one was out, if Jenny had come directly from here to Taos, as the letter had indicated. From Wyoming she'd have come into Taos from the north, through Denver. There wasn't any way at all that she could have come through Albuquerque, a hundred and thirty miles to the south, if she'd started from any point in Wyoming.

Barton, Calif. Kern Co. Pop. 3500.

He found the map of California and found Kern County. He found the dot that was Barton and it was in the southern part of the state, about twenty-five miles south of Bakersfield. Less than a hundred miles north and slightly west of Los Angeles.

That was it, that had to be it. From there she would definitely have come through Albuquerque and on the bus which had pulled in minutes before the time she'd checked into the hotel.

He looked at the map again. How far from here? He turned to a bigger map of the Southwest that included New Mexico and Arizona as well as southern California. About a thousand miles. A day and a half to drive, if he really pushed, but he'd better figure two days each way. Four days round trip, minimum. But maybe it'd take a little digging—not the kind of digging he'd done last night—to get what he wanted. Have to allow five days, possibly six.

What story could he possibly tell Vi to account for his being gone five or six days? And it wouldn't be fair to her to leave her alone that long, way out there in the house at the end of nowhere. Besides, he'd be taking the car; he couldn't leave her there.

Well, there was Santa Fe. She'd wanted to spend some time there. She had friends; she'd kept up a desultory correspondence with at least two people there and had been wanting to see them again. Sure, he could leave her in Santa Fe and she'd be happier there than she was at the moment here. If her friends didn't offer to put her up, she could stay at a hotel.

But the story, the excuse—what on earth could he tell her

that would explain his own trip and make sense?

He was still sitting there at the table with his finger on the map of California when the librarian came over and told him she was sorry but that it was noon and they were closing until two o'clock.

He apologized and said that he'd already found what he wanted; he put the atlas back on the shelf and left.

His eyes and his head bothered him again on the way home. He was glad when the drive was over and the car parked beside the house. He had to sit down as soon as he was inside.

"Did you leave the groceries in the car, George? Or did you forget them?"

He dropped his head into his hands. "Oh Lord, Vi, I forgot them. I'll go in again, at least as far as Seco, but let me rest awhile first. I've got the grandfather of all headaches."

"George, you look and act like you're really sick. Maybe you caught a cold falling around last night. Did you lay there after you fell?"

"You mean did I lie there. I—maybe I did, Vi, but not very long. I'll be all right. Just let me alone. I want to lie down awhile."

"All right, and I'll drive in to Seco and get what groceries we really need today. Don't worry about them."

"Thanks, Vi." He went into the bedroom. Vi still hadn't made the bed but he straightened out the covers and lay down on top of them.

Vi followed him in and held a hand against his forehead. The hand felt very cool and he knew that meant that his forehead was hot. She said, "George, you've got a fever. Hadn't I better get you a doctor? You might be coming down with pneumonia or something."

"I'll be all right. Just let me alone."

"Did you eat anything in town?"

"I don't want to eat. Vi, this is just hangover; I'll be all right tonight if I can get some sleep."

"All right, George."

He heard her getting ready to go and then heard the

sound of the car driving off. Groaning, he pulled his shoes
back on and got up. He had to check up on a few things while
he had the chance. He'd been in a hell of a shape—and a hell
of a hurry, too—when he'd left the shed this morning. Had he
left any evidence of what he'd been doing?

He went out to the shed and it seemed to be all right. The
temperature was back to normal so he closed the window. The
whisky bottle—still with a few ounces of whisky in it—was on
the floor beside the table. The glass lay near it, broken. He
didn't remember having broken the glass. He picked up the
shards and put them into the wastebasket.

The canvas bundle, that was the main thing. Was there
any chance at all of Vi's coming out here and finding it under
the bed? He didn't know *why* it was so important that Vi—or
anybody else—should never find that bundle or see its contents, but it was important, vitally important. Was there a
better place to hide it than under the cot? He couldn't keep
the door locked all the time; the mere fact that he did so might
make Vi curious enough to search. And even aside from that,
she might decide to change the blankets on the cot and—
There must be a better place.

He found it, finally—against the wall behind the three
framed canvases of Nelson. Tilted just a little more they made
room for the bundle, and Vi would never look there unless she
was making a deliberate search of the place.

He went back to the house, taking the bottle of whisky
with him. Maybe a drink of it, straight, would help. He poured
himself a medium-sized shot in a glass and made himself
down it. It tasted horrible and almost made him retch but it
stayed down and in a few minutes he really did feel a little
better.

He took his shoes off again and lay back down on the bed.
He hadn't yet gone to sleep when he heard the car coming
back. Its door slammed and Vi came in. She tiptoed into the
bedroom and was reaching out to touch his forehead again
when he spoke to her.

"Oh, you're still awake, George? Feeling any better?"

"A little, I guess."

"Are you *sure* you don't want a doctor?"

"I'm sure, Vi. Unless I'm not all right by tomorrow. I had a spot of dog hair while you were gone and I think it helped."

She left him alone and after a while he dozed off. When he woke it was twilight outside and he felt better and he was hungry. He wasn't going to be sick after all—and that was almost a miracle after the silly things he'd done the night before, staying outdoors so long in the cold without his coat and then sleeping in a place that was like an oven and waking drenched with sweat.

Vi was cooking supper; she'd taken the radio into the kitchen with her but she'd had it going softly; he hadn't even heard it in the bedroom with the door closed.

"Feel any better, George?"

"Feeling wonderful." That was exaggerating a little but not much. He knew now that he'd be all right by tomorrow. And—maybe in his sleep—he'd figured out the approach he was going to use on Vi concerning the trip.

He waited until they were drinking coffee at the end of the meal. "Vi, I've been thinking. You'd probably like to see those friends of yours in Santa Fe while you're out here. Be a shame for you to get within seventy miles of them and then go back without seeing them at all."

"I *would* like to see Mabel and the Colbys, George. Maybe we could go down there for a while next week?"

"Why not sooner? What's wrong with tomorrow? But listen, here's the deal; I want to see Luke Ashley, out in Los Angeles. Why can't I leave you in Santa Fe and—"

"*Los Angeles?* Why, that's thousands of miles, George. It'd take you a week, just the driving. And it'd cost—"

"Nothing but the gas. And it's one thousand miles and I can do it in two days each way, easily. I wouldn't want to stay there more than a day, maybe two at the most, just long enough to see Luke and to rest up before I start back. He'd put me up the night or two I'd be there. Now listen, and don't make objections till I finish. We both need a change—and you want to spend some time in Santa Fe and I don't. So you take your change in the form of Santa Fe and I'll take the trip to see Luke. You can stay at a hotel there unless your friends ask you to stay with them, and I'll drop you off there on my way west and pick you up on my way back."

"I *do* want to go to Santa Fe, George, but—why do you want to see Luke so bad? You did see him on his way through here, you told me."

"It's not that I'm crazy about seeing Luke; that isn't it at all. What I really want is a long drive alone, and going to see Luke just gives me a place to head for. You know, Vi, I felt better on the way out here than I have any time since. The way I really should have spent this summer was traveling— but of course that would have cost more than we can afford. But if I take one run out to L. A. and back, right now, to break up the middle of the summer, I'll feel a hell of a lot better when I get back. And we can kill two birds with one stone by letting you have the time in Santa Fe while I'm gone."

"Gee, George—"

It was as easy as that.

The details took some compromising. Weaver wanted to leave early the next morning; he'd have started then and there if he'd dared suggest it. Vi wanted to wait at least another day so she'd have time to get clothes ready, and she wanted Weaver to spend at least a day or two with her in Santa Fe before he went on. They compromised on driving down to Santa Fe the next afternoon, Weaver to spend one evening and night there—she couldn't see why he didn't want to see their old friends at *all*—and he would drive on from Santa Fe early the following morning.

In bed that night, after Vi was asleep, Weaver tried not to think what a hole in his diminishing bank balance that trip was going to make; he'd have to give Vi at least fifty dollars for expenses in Santa Fe—although, if she didn't have to stay at a hotel, she ought to have some left out of it. His own expenses, counting gas, would probably run almost that much no matter how careful he was.

Well, if he sold the article about the murder—

But there was a catch to that. He wasn't ever going to write that article, he knew now. And neither was Luke—at least not with any data Weaver would ever give him.

He wondered how long, now, he'd known—and never quite admitted to himself—that that article would never be written. At least since last night when he'd found the suitcase. Maybe long before that.

[13]

Santa Fe to Albuquerque in the early dawn. Socorro, then the marker that said Arizona, New Mexico. Springerville, Globe. Three hundred miles and it was barely after noon. Ninety more miles to Phoenix. He rested an hour in Phoenix. He pushed on.

(Wonder what Vi would think if she knew he wasn't going to Los Angeles at all, that he was going a thousand miles for a rendezvous with a girl who'd been dead for eight years?)

A hundred and seventy more miles to Blythe on the California border. And it was dark by then and he was utterly weary; he checked in at a hotel that didn't look expensive, but charged him five dollars just the same and slept solidly and dreamlessly for ten hours.

(Vi would think he was insane. And would she be too wrong?)

He drove out of Blythe at seven, and it was a relatively short lap from there. Indio, San Bernardino.

Barton. Pop. 3500.

It was still early afternoon and he wasn't tired; the bulk of his driving had been done the day before and he'd had a good night's sleep.

(Here he was. But why was he here?)

A wide main street, the only important street in the little town. Wider for one block in the middle of town, where all the business places were. Angle parking. He parked and got out of the car.

He went into the corner drugstore first. The phone book

was a ridiculous off-chance, but he tried it. No Ames listed. He had a coke and asked the proprietor if there was anyone in town by the name of Ames.

"No, sir. Don't know anyone named Ames who ever lived here. Not offhand."

"You've been here long?" Weaver asked.

"Born here, fifty years ago."

"And lived here all that time?"

"Except for a few years during the war. The *first* war, I mean."

Weaver drank his coke and didn't ask any more questions. There were other questions to ask, but not in a place where he had already mentioned the name Ames.

He had a sandwich and coffee at the restaurant three doors down. The waitress didn't look like a good bet. Too young; eight years ago she'd have been in the third or fourth grade of school. But it didn't hurt to try.

"You lived here long, Miss?"

"All my life, except for one year, last year. I worked in L. A., but I didn't like it and came back home."

"I was wondering." Weaver said. "I used to know a girl from Barton. First name was Jenny and I can't remember her last name. I think it began with an A. Do you know who I mean?"

"Jenny? I'm afraid not, not if her last name is an A. I know a Jenny Wilson; she was in my class at high school."

"She wouldn't be the one—unless you're a lot older than you look. The Jenny I knew—she'd be close to thirty now."

"No, it wouldn't be Jenny Wilson, then. She's only nineteen, not even as old as I am. You might ask Pop; he knows about everybody that ever lived here."

"Pop?"

(Surely not Pop. 3500?)

"My father. Up by the cash register. You'll meet him when you pay your check."

Weaver finished his sandwich and coffee, left a tip and went to the register. The man behind the counter rang up forty-five cents and gave him change. "Kind of hot out today," he said.

"Sure is. By the way, I'm trying to remember someone I knew once who came from Barton, about eight years ago. Your daughter says you know about everybody who ever lived here." Weaver leaned on the counter casually.

"Well, try me. I know a lot of people."

"A girl named Jenny. I think the last name begins with an A, but I can't remember it. She'd have been around twenty when she left here."

"She was twenty-two. Jenny Albright."

Weaver reached for a cigarette in his pocket and then realized that his hands might tremble when he tried to light it, so he didn't try it.

"That's the name," he said. "Her folks still live here?"

"Her mother does. Her father died, year or so after she went away. Sure, I remember Jenny. Nice girl, although—"

"Although what?"

"Nothing. I just meant I didn't really know her very well."

"I'd rather like to talk to her mother while I'm here. Do you know where she lives?"

"A few blocks from here, on Beech Street. That's the next street north, parallel to this one. I don't know the house number but I guess it's in the phone book. What's Jenny doing now?"

Weaver said, "I don't know. I've lost track of her; I'm trying to find out where she is. Well, thanks a lot."

He went out into the hot sunlight and stood a moment indecisively. Should he look up Jenny's mother next? Or talk to a few other people first, get a few more preliminary facts to make his story better? Maybe he should do that; he could use a drink, for one thing, and bartenders are usually talkative if their customers want them to be. And he hadn't had a drink since night before last, in Santa Fe with Vi and her friends.

He found a tavern a few doors away and it was dim and cool and comfortable inside. He was the only customer and the bartender looked more than old enough to remember eight years back if he'd lived here that long.

Weaver ordered a whisky and soda. "Nice little town,

Barton," he said. "First time I've ever been here but I like the looks of it."

"Yeah."

"You lived here long?"

"All my life in California. I'm a native son, born in Mojave. Lived in Barton fifteen years."

"Sure a nice little town, Weaver said again. Have a drink with me?"

"Sure, thanks."

"Used to know a girl who came from here. Jenny Albright. Remember her?"

"Henry Albright's daughter?"

"If she ever mentioned her father's first name I don't remember it. But she said he died six or seven years ago."

"Yeah. Well, I didn't really know her personally, just by sight, and I'd forgot what her first name was, but that must be the one. If it is, and if she knew her father died, it was funny she didn't come back or write or anything. I remember people wondering about it."

Weaver said, "I think she learned about it quite a while after it happened. What did Henry Albright do?"

"Head teller at the bank. His daughter worked there too, up to the time she left."

"Oh." Weaver said.

"Look, mister, are you a detective or something?" The bartender didn't sound belligerent, just curious.

"Me? Hell, no. Why?"

"Just remembering something about the way the girl left town."

"How was that? And will you make us two more drinks?"

"Sure. I dunno, maybe I shouldn't have said anything. But a lot of people wondered and there was a lot of talk."

"You mean she got in trouble?"

"Well, not the kind of trouble girls usually get in, if that's what you mean. She was a good girl, I guess, that way. From what I heard, her parents were so strict with her she *had* to be. Henry wasn't a customer here—he practically ran the local Baptist Church, and I guess he pretty much ran his family too.

Hard and strict, and his wife too. I don't know as I blame any daughter of his—especially an only child—for taking her walking papers."

"If that was all she took." Weaver said. "I gather that's what you were hinting at."

"Well, that was the talk. Nobody knows for sure, unless people at the bank. And if she didn't take anything from the bank when she left, Henry must've made it up."

"Is there any indication that he did?"

"Well—say, you're sure you're not a detective or anything? Nobody knows, so I don't want to get the girl in trouble or keep her from getting a job or whatever it is."

"Nothing like that." Weaver said. "In fact, Jenny Albright is dead, so you can't get her into any trouble if you tried. And if her father's dead too—well, it can't make any difference. No, I knew Jenny just well enough to be curious about—well, what she was really like."

"You're not kidding me about her being dead?"

"No. Honestly."

"Well, then it doesn't matter. She left suddenly, and some people here thought she might have taken money from the bank with her. There were a couple of things that made it look that way. For one, she never wrote home again, as far as anybody knows. For another, just after she left Henry Albright sold his home—one that he owned outright—and bought a smaller place, with only a down payment on it. Looked like he was raising money."

"Seems funny a girl would do something like that to her own family."

"Yeah, but maybe she didn't figure that her father would make it up out of his own pocket, just thought she was stealing it from the bank. And maybe she never knew that he did make it up. Say—"

"What?"

"Just wondered something. If she really did run off with money from the bank, it's funny she was using her right name when you knew her."

"She wasn't. I happened to find out her right name accidentally—and after she died."

"Oh. Well, like we were saying, it's still funny that a girl brought up like that—no matter how strict her parents were— would suddenly up and embezzle from a bank. My guess is, if she did, there was a man in it somewhere and she was doing it for him. Some women'll do anything for a man if they love him."

"I guess so." Weaver said. "It couldn't have been any of the local swains, could it? I mean, did anyone else disappear about the same time Jenny did?"

"Nope. I guess—I'm remembering more about it now—I guess maybe that was part of the trouble with her, that she never had any local dates to speak of. Her parents were hellers when it came to things like that, wouldn't let a man get within fifty feet of her, even after she was twenty. I remember hearing that a guy she'd been corresponding with came to town once to see her—dunno how she got into correspondence with him—but anyway—"

"Was he an artist?"

"I wouldn't know. Anyway, way I heard it, she got to see him a few times and then her parents learned he was around —she must've managed to keep it secret up to then—and clamped down the lid, wouldn't even let her out of the house. Nope, I don't blame her for running away. Not too much, even if she stole money to take with her. Served the old heller right, way I see it. You can't treat a girl over twenty like she was fourteen and living in a nunnery at that, not without expecting her to bust out one way or another."

Weaver nodded.

He had the picture now, probably as clear as he'd ever have it.

So that was it, Jenny. And you were so starved for romance that you wrote to a Lonely Hearts Club and got into correspondence—you must have used a post-office box or general delivery so your mother wouldn't see the letters— with a man who sounded wonderful and romantic. And he came to see you, and he made love to you and said he wanted to marry you, so you fell head over heels in love with him.

Then your parents learned he was here and kept you away from him. (Why didn't you just tell them off, Jenny? It must have been because, from so many years of submission, you were afraid to or didn't realize that you could.) But back to the prison of your home, losing the man you loved, as you thought.

And then, again, his passionate letters. And he wanted so badly to marry you right away, but it might have to be years because he had to wait until he'd saved up enough money to start his art school in Taos. If he only had five thousand dollars, or ten, or whatever he figured your bank carried in ready cash (Had he pumped you about that, Jenny, while he was here?) he could start his school at once and marry you right away.

And you loved him madly—

"Have another one, mister? On me, this time?"

"Huh?" Weaver was startled. He'd forgotten where he was and to whom he'd been talking. "Oh, sure. Thanks."

"I was just thinking. About Mrs. Albright. If you're *sure* her daughter's dead, she ought to know about it. I don't like her much—she's like her husband, Temperance and trying to get local Prohibition and close us up and stuff like that. But just the same, if you're sure Jenny's dead—"

"I'll tell her." Weaver said. "You're right; she ought to know."

"Or if you haven't got time, Mr.—"

"Weaver. George Weaver."

"Glad to know you; my name's Joe Deaver. Say, that's funny; our names rhyme. Weaver and Deaver. Anyway, I was just going to say if you haven't got time to see the old battle-ax or if you don't find her in or something, I can get word to her for you. My wife's a Baptist, too, goes to the same church. I don't go for that kind of stuff myself."

"Thanks," Weaver said. *(What was your mother like, Jenny?)* I'll look her up, if she's home. If she isn't—well, in that case I'll drop back and let you know. Or maybe I can phone her from here and make sure she'll be home. Mind if I look in your phone book and then use your phone?"

"Help yourself, Mr. Weaver."

"Make us a couple more drinks while I do."

Mrs. Henry Albright was listed in the phone book. Seven-eighteen Beech Street. One-eight-two-R. Weaver found a nickel in his pocket and called the number. A female voice answered.

"Mrs. Albright?"

"Yes."

"You don't know me, Mrs. Albright. My name is Weaver; I'd like to see you for a few minutes, if I may. I called to be sure you'd be home."

"Yes, I'll be home all afternoon. What do you want to see me about?"

"A personal matter, Mrs. Albright, something I'd rather not explain over the phone. But I'm not selling anything, and it *is* both personal and important."

"Very well. I will be here."

He didn't like the sound of her voice; it was cold and hard.

"Thank you, Mrs. Albright. I'll be there within half an hour."

He went back to the bar. He rather wished now that he'd settled for getting word to Jenny's mother through Joe Deaver—but Joe had heard his end of the conversation and he couldn't change his mind now.

He drank his drink and decided that another would help. "Two more for us, Joe."

"Thanks, but I'll skip this one. I've got six hours yet on this shift."

"Okay, but don't skip mine. From the frost on that woman's voice, I'd better be fortified."

The bartender chuckled. "What the hell do you care? You're doing *her* a favor. But, come to think of it, you'd better stay sober or you won't get inside the door."

"Which wouldn't sadden me too much, Joe. But I'll be sober. I'm used to drinking at high altitude where drinks hit you harder. Down here near sea level, I'd have to drink twice as much as usual now before I'd start to feel it."

"Know what you mean. I was in Denver once, and that's only a mile high and I could tell the difference when it came to drinking. How high is wherever you come from?"

"Seven thousand. Taos, New Mexico. It's seventy miles north of Santa Fe."

"Is that where Jenny Albright died?"

"Yes."

"Of what?"

Weaver hesitated. He'd been talking too much. He said, "I don't know, exactly; I learned about it a long time afterwards."

"Oh. Sure hot, isn't it? Wonder why Jenny went to Taos. I had a hunch it was Tucson, Arizona."

"Tucson? Why did you think that?"

"Well—I never mentioned it to anyone because if Jenny *did* run off with money from the bank, I was for her. But it doesn't matter now. About a year after she left here I was driving east and stopped over in Tucson the first night. I saw a guy on the street there that I thought was the guy who'd come here to see Jenny. And if it was him she ran off to go to, I figured maybe she was there too. But it was none of my business; I didn't hunt for her."

Weaver saw that he'd spilled part of his drink. He put down the glass on the bar. "You're sure it was the same man?"

"I thought it was. He was wearing his hair different—longer; he had a crew cut when he was here. And he had a mustache. But I thought it was the same guy. He was in here a few times for drinks during the few days he was in Barton, so I knew him pretty well by sight—but it was afterwards that I learned he'd been here to see Jenny. You know how things get around in a small town."

"Did you speak to him? In Tucson, I mean?"

"Nope. I just passed him on the street and I wasn't *sure*. And besides, if Jenny *was* with him, married or otherwise and she had really swiped money from the bank here—well, it would have scared them to have been spotted. So he didn't notice me and I didn't speak to him."

Tucson. T. b. It fitted; it had to be. He'd already guessed that Nelson had doubled back from Amarillo to get to the hot dry Southwest, and Tucson was right in the center of that. And the change in haircut, the mustache—they made it even more likely that Joe Deaver had seen the right man.

It added up.

But seven years ago—

"Give me one more, Joe. Then I got to get going."

"Sure, Mr. Weaver. Wish you were sticking around Barton awhile longer, though. You're a good customer."

Weaver managed to hide his excitement and wisecrack back, to force himself not to gulp the last drink.

Then the hot sunshine again, and he'd had a bit more to drink than he'd thought. He wasn't drunk, but he wasn't completely sober either. He'd done a hell of a lot of drinking within the space of less than an hour. But what the hell—look at all he'd learned.

He started his car and he was in such a hurry to get to Tucson that he almost decided not to go to the Beech Street address to see Mrs. Albright. But—he'd promised. And what the hell difference could ten or fifteen minutes make? He found the house, he found the door, he found the knocker.

[14]

She was tall and thin and pale and gray. She had lips like rubber bands and eyes like buttons too small for their button-holes.

"Mrs. Albright?"

"Yes, I'm Mrs. Albright."

"My name is Weaver. I just called you on the phone. I'm afraid I have bad news for you. About your—daughter." He couldn't help the hesitation on the last word; he couldn't think of this woman as ever having had a daughter, as ever having undergone the necessary preliminaries to having a daughter.

"Mr. Weaver, you have been drinking. Your breath is offensive."

"My breath is irrelevant, madam. I—" How the hell can you tell a woman who antagonizes you at sight and is antagonized by you, bad news and sound sympathetic about it? "I'm sorry, Mrs. Albright, I'm afraid I must tell you that your daughter is dead."

"When? Where?" She might have been asking a laundryman when the laundry would be delivered—if she didn't like the laundryman.

"A few days after she left home. In New Mexico."

"And your purpose in telling me this?"

"I thought you might be interested. I see that I was wrong." He bowed slightly, not quite losing his balance. He turned and started for the porch steps.

"Mr. Weaver—" Her voice sounded almost human. He turned back. "Mr. Weaver, perhaps I owe you an explanation. I *am* sorry to learn that Jenny is dead."

"Very big of you, madam."

"But no more sorry than to learn of the death of anyone. She was not our daughter as of the time she left us. You did not know that, of course, so your reason for coming here was generous if misguided. Thank you."

"Thank *you*," Weaver said, "for being so kind as to be interested."

The door was closing. Damn the bitch. He wanted to hurt her. If he could. "I thought," he said, "it might even interest you to know the manner of her death." The door stopped closing, a few inches open. He said, "A madman killed her with a knife."

As good an exit line as any. He went back to his car and got in. He glanced back and the door had closed. But he felt sorry and ashamed of himself. He almost opened the door of his car to go back—but what could he possibly say that wouldn't make things worse than they already were? And she *had* asked for it. What the hell kind of mother had she been, not to be interested in what happened to her own daughter? If Jenny's father had been anything like her mother, how had she ever lived at home for twenty-two years—and why hadn't she taken the whole damn bank with her—some sum that her father couldn't possibly have paid back? Oh, yes, they'd paid it back, but out of pride, to save their own name and reputation, not to spare Jenny pursuit and prosecution.

He drove out of Barton fast, turning corners viciously. On the open road he upped the speed to eighty to get away from the place.

Could he make Tucson tonight? He pulled off the road and studied a map he'd picked up at a filling station the day before. Tucson was six hundred miles away and it was after three o'clock in the afternoon now; no, he couldn't possibly make it tonight. But he'd push on as far as he could before he holed in, get an early start in the morning, and try to make Tucson by noon.

San Bernardino, Indio, Blythe. And it was nine o'clock. Up at seven and off at eight. Phoenix at eleven o'clock, Tucson at half-past one.

What now? The police? No, *not* the police. Too much to explain, and everything given away, the whole thing in the newspapers. He'd have to see what he could find out by himself, and then decide what to do about it. Chance in a million, probably, that Nelson would still be here after seven years. Best he'd be likely to get would be a lead to the next place Nelson had gone.

Two lines to work on. Picture galleries—thank God he'd brought his photographs of Nelson's pictures with him on the off-chance that they'd come in handy. Sanatoriums that took t. b. patients, in case Nelson's t. b. had developed to the point of hospitalization during his stay here.

Try the sanatoriums first, he decided.

He put his car in a parking lot in the middle of town to get it off his hands; since he didn't know the town, he'd save time using a taxi.

He went to the Chamber of Commerce first; a woman there gave him a list of sanatoriums that specialized in t. b. cases and, with her help, he crossed off several that had started within the last few years. There weren't as many as he feared; he should be able to cover them in one afternoon.

Telephoning would be useless, of course. Nelson certainly wouldn't have registered under the name he'd used in Taos; in each case he'd have to find someone who'd worked there at least seven years and try to identify Nelson by description. It was going to be tough going, he thought.

It turned out to be easy going, ridiculously easy going. He hit it on the second try. A small gray-haired man with thick glasses and bright eyes looking through them sat behind a desk and said, "Yes, we had a patient of that description. Ah—I can look up the records if it's important to be exact, but offhand I'd say he came to us between six and seven years ago. He was here two years."

Weaver leaned forward, his fingers digging into his knees. "And do you know where he went when he left here? Have you been in touch with him since?"

"He died here. His tuberculosis seemed to be only pulmonary when he first came to us, but it developed into tuberculosis of the bone—of the spine. We tried surgery, spinal fusion, but it did not help. You say he was a murderer? Then his case, I fear, has long since been settled before a higher court."

"I see," Weaver said. He felt strange, somehow. "If you don't mind, doctor, I'd like to make sure, absolutely sure, that we're talking about the same man. You say he was an artist. Did he do any painting while he was here?"

"During the first few months we allowed him to paint a few hours a day. After that, he was unable to continue. But he completed several paintings during that time; one of them is on the wall behind you."

Weaver turned and looked.

Mountains, in colors and shapes such as mountains have never been. Mountains that writhed in dark agony against spectral skies, mountains of another dimension, in another world, under an alien sun. Nelson's work, beyond the remote possibility of a doubt, as individual as his fingerprints would have been. Possibly more individual; in infinity fingerprints might repeat, style never.

Weaver looked at the picture for a long time. The voice of Dr. Grabow came over his shoulder. "Interesting technique. Not many people like it, but I do. Dealers have told me it is worthless—not that I tried to sell it; it happens that several have been here in my office on other business and I asked them out of curiosity. But I like it. There's something—"

Weaver asked, "Was he mad?"

He turned back and looked at the doctor, who was smiling. "What is madness, Mr. Weaver? I am not a psychiatrist, so I do not know. If I were a psychiatrist, I would know even less. Nothing is more confusing than trying to define madness. I don't even know whether I am sane myself. Do you?"

Weaver said, "I want to know. I really want to know. Was he insane?"

"He was a sadist, I believe. Sadism is mental abnormality—whether or not it is insanity, I do not know. The sadism was latent while he was here, but it might easily have become active, given opportunity. He was homosexual, of course—you mentioned that yourself in describing him, and you were quite right. Homosexuality again is an aberration but is not insanity, definitely not. The point at which he nearest approached true insanity—whatever that is—would be his fear psychosis. He feared death. Everyone does, of course, but in his case the degree of fear was probably psychopathic. He killed for money?"

"Yes," Weaver said. "He killed for money."

"Understandable. Desperation, the fear psychosis. If he needed money in order to give himself the treatment that might have saved his life, I do not doubt that he would have gone to any length to get the money he needed."

"How much money did he have?"

"Somewhere around ten thousand dollars, I would say. Enough to pay his way almost—not quite—to the end. Including the surgery he underwent. He wrote checks regularly until the last month or two. By then all surgery had failed and he was a dying man; we knew that he had only weeks to live and he had already paid us so much that—well, we're not a charity institution but we didn't have him transferred to one. We carried him through."

A better break, Jenny, than he gave you. Or was his death worse than yours? He must have seen it coming—longer, much longer.

Weaver stood up. "Thank you very much, Dr. Grabow." His voice sounded strangely flat to him. He looked again, on his way out, at the twisted mountains in the painting on the wall.

The hot sunlight. Fourteen minutes after three o'clock, and it was all over. He knew the whole story now. And there was nothing to do about it.

There's never anything to do about something that happened years ago—or yesterday or a minute ago.

He went back to his car in the parking lot and sat in it to study his road maps. Over five hundred miles back to Santa Fe. And what was in Santa Fe? Vi. No, he couldn't possibly make another five hundred miles today and tonight, not possibly. He felt let down, worn-out, dull, passive. And anyway he was still ahead of schedule; Vi wasn't expecting him before tomorrow evening or the evening after that.

Some problems multiply themselves. He had a drink and he got drunk. It got dark and he got drunker. It wasn't a happy drunk; it was a dull brooding one.

There must have been hallucinations in it because—sometime, somewhere—there was a man, a big man, who said, "Mr. Weaver?" He said, "Yeah? My name's Weaver." Not belligerently, not worriedly, not anything at all. And the big man peeled back a lapel and said, "Police. Like you to drop around to the station. They want to talk to you." And under the lapel was a badge. It was interesting. Weaver said, "Sure, pal. How'd you know my name?" And the big man said, "I asked you and you told me." And that didn't make sense, but he went with the big man and they took him to a room with bars and there was a cot in the room; he lay down on the cot and slept and then somebody shook him and said, "All right, you can go now." "Go where?" "Anywhere. Listen, mister, it's all right; we made a mistake. We're sorry. Now beat it or we'll

change the charge to D and D." "D and D? What the hell is D
and D?" "Drunk and disorderly. Now listen, you're drunk and
you know it and I know it and if you want to sleep it off here,
it's okay by us. But—we're telling you to scram if you want to
scram and if you don't you're being disorderly—and that adds
up to D and D and if you're smart you'll scram because there'll
be a fine tomorrow if we have to book you D and D." A fine
tomorrow. It was all mixed up, however the hell he tried to
interpret it, but what the hell, he wasn't belligerent and he
didn't want trouble with anybody so he scrammed, and afterwards he knew it hadn't really happened because it couldn't
have—not with a cop picking him up by name when nobody
knew his name and he was just on the way through. Yes, here
he was back in a bar—the same or another—and it was a
screwy dream he'd had because it couldn't have happened. It
was just something that he remembered that didn't happen,
and some other things must have happened that he didn't
remember, because he woke up in a hotel room and had no
recollection of having got there; the last thing he remembered
was the man from Chicago who was explaining—what was
it?—in such great detail. Anyway, he awoke in a hotel room,
asleep in his clothes although he'd taken his shoes and coat
and tie off, thank God. And his money—except about twelve
dollars, and he must have spent that—was still in his wallet so
that was all right. His watch had run down and he phoned
down to the desk and learned that it was ten o'clock.

His suitcase wasn't with him; he must have left it in the
car. No use taking a bath until he had clean clothes to put on
afterwards, so he went downstairs, oriented himself and
found the parking lot—only two blocks away, luckily—and
carried his suitcase back to the hotel.

As he bathed and dressed, something puzzled him. What
was that crazy memory he seemed to have about having been
in jail the night before? Arrested without charge and released
without explanation—and the big man who'd turned back his
lapel to show a badge—had all of that been a dream? It must
have been; it didn't make any sense otherwise.

He drove out of Tucson before noon. About five hundred

miles to Santa Fe. Well, he could make it in ten hours if he kept going. He kept going. Not thinking—any more than he could help—just driving. Sometimes through mountains—but on wide, easy roads—sometimes across the open desert where he could make eighty without even feeling that he was going fast.

In spite of a stop to eat in Lordsburg—he didn't know whether it was breakfast or lunch or what—he made Socorro by seven o'clock—and he was tired then but it was only seventy-five miles to Albuquerque and another sixty to Santa Fe; he could make that in not much over two more hours, so he kept going, stopping only for a sandwich and coffee.

Santa Fe, nine-thirty. He stopped at the outskirts of town so he could phone the Colbys, with whom Vi was staying. He hoped she'd be there. If he could talk Vi into it, he'd push on the last seventy miles to Taos—and the ten miles beyond—tonight, to get it over with, to get back home. But there was no answer at the Colbys.

He drank coffee to keep himself awake, realizing now that the driving was over, how utterly tired he was, and how miserable mentally and physically. He didn't even want a drink—after a binge like last night's he seldom felt able to drink again the next day. And he'd been drinking too damned much anyway.

He phoned again at ten and again at ten-thirty. They were still out. And by then he realized that he was too tired to face that last eighty miles of driving even if he did contact Vi—and that he'd rather check into a hotel and get a long night's sleep than reach her now and be talked into coming around and joining the party, whatever they were doing.

He took a room at the Montezuma and fell sound asleep the instant he got into bed. He slept eleven hours; it was ten o'clock in the morning when he awoke. He had breakfast and phoned the Colbys at eleven.

"George, old boy!" Wayne Colby's voice said. "Been hoping to hear from you. Come on around for lunch with us."

"Just had breakfast, thanks. But I'll drop around to pick up Vi. Like to get started back to Taos right away."

"Don't be silly; you're going to give us an afternoon at least. Look, today's Saturday, that's why I'm not working. And what's wrong with going back to Taos tomorrow, Sunday?"

"I—well, I'll drop around and we'll talk about it, Wayne." He didn't have an excuse ready to explain why he couldn't stay over, but the stall would give him time to think one up.

He had one ready by the time he reached the Colbys' apartment, and he didn't push it too far; he said they had to leave Santa Fe in time to get back home by six o'clock, and that gave him several hours to spend with them. Rather boring hours and he was constantly having to say "Pardon?" when somebody asked him a question and he hadn't heard it, but the hours passed.

He pried Vi away at four o'clock. Taos at five-thirty. He'd pleaded a six o'clock appointment to the Colbys as his reason for having to leave at four, but on the way back he explained to Vi that he didn't really have one; he was just tired of traveling and of being away, that he was now in a hurry to get back home.

He wondered if he really was. And, if so, why.

"George, it's Saturday, remember. We'd better lay in some liquor, hadn't we, before we find we can't get any on Sunday?"

"Sure, Vi." He remembered the two fifths he'd borrowed from Callahan and got five bottles so he could return Callahan's two. But Callahan's place was dark when they drove past it, so he didn't stop. He'd take it over to Callahan tomorrow.

Six o'clock when they got home. Weaver parked the car while Vi unlocked the door and went in. She'd turned the kitchen light on and was standing in the middle of the room, looking around, when Weaver joined her.

"George, I think somebody's been *in* here."

"Why, Vi? Anything gone?"

"Well—not that I can see—but things have been *moved.*"

"I'll—just a minute." Weaver went quickly through the rest of the house. No one was there, then, but someone had been there all right. Things on top of the dresser had been moved and the drawer in which he kept his shirts was closed all the way—he always left it an inch or so open because it stuck when closed tightly. After a struggle or two with it, he'd stopped closing it completely; he was sure he hadn't done so when he'd packed for the trip.

He joined Vi in the kitchen. "Nothing gone that I can see, Vi." He didn't want to worry her, so he didn't mention the drawer. "Are you sure things have been moved?"

"Well—*almost* sure, George. But there's nothing gone that I can find."

He grinned. "If anything was gone you of, course couldn't find it." He went to the kitchen door. "Well, I'll look around the rest of the place."

Not to be too obvious in heading quickly for the shed he walked once around the house itself and even opened the door of the outside toilet and looked in before he went to the shed.

Were there scratches on the padlock? Yes, but he couldn't be sure that they hadn't been there before without his having noticed. He went inside and turned on the light.

His portable typewriter was still there, probably the only thing in the shed that could have been stolen for resale. His eyes took that in and then went to the three stacked pictures behind which the canvas bundle was hidden. He could see canvas at the end of the pictures—and he'd hidden it carefully; it hadn't showed before.

He took out the bundle and opened it on the floor, kneeling. The shreds of clothing, the toilet articles and their case, the fragments of the suitcase and the remnants of the box of stationery. All there. All there but one thing. The letter Nelson had written to Jenny was gone.

[15]

Weaver locked the shed, behind him, wondering why he bothered, and walked back to the house thoughtfully. Who in hell would have searched the house and the shed and have stolen only that letter? It didn't make sense.

Jenny dead eight years. Nelson dead four or five. Case closed.

Vi was frying eggs. He said, "Nothing missing, Vi, that I can discover. Nobody around. You must be imagining things."

"Guess so, George. Want to make us a drink before we eat?"

He made drinks. He made them strong—his own because he thought it might get the cobwebs out of his brain and let him think more clearly, Vi's because she was watching and would complain if he made hers weaker than his own.

"Forgot to ask you, George. How's Luke?"

"Huh?" He'd forgotten his story of the original destination of his trip. Then he remembered. "Oh, fine. And L. A.'s just like it always was only more so. How was your stay in Santa Fe?"

"Wonderful, George." There was something about her expression that made him wonder how she meant that. She'd always liked Wayne Colby—and Madge Colby always took sleeping powders when she went to bed. But it didn't really matter; he didn't give a damn. And she was probably assuming that at least part of the purpose of *his* trip had been a bit of straying off the reservation.

Well, hadn't it been? He hadn't thought of Vi once, really, from the time he left her in Santa Fe until the time he got back; he'd thought only of another woman, one eight years dead. And did that make it better or worse?

Jenny. Had the trip laid her ghost? He knew all about her now, who she was and where she'd come from and why she had died and who had killed her and what had happened to him afterwards. He knew the whole thing now; he could start trying to forget it.

But who had stolen that letter—and in God's name, *why?*

He drank his drink and thought about it. Finally he had the answer; he'd last seen that letter the night when he'd found it and had been so terribly drunk. And it had been a find so important to him that he must have hidden it, not put it with the rest of Jenny's things, and then forgot about hiding it. Tomorrow, just to satisfy his curiosity, he'd hunt and find it. That's what *must* have happened. But what about the other evidences of a search—the drawer he himself had noticed, whatever it was Vi had noticed that made her think things had been moved? Well—it could have been that someone had been here but he'd been looking only for money or jewelry, and there hadn't been any money or jewelry around. Sure, that explained everything there was to explain.

He felt better, with that out of the way.

It didn't leave a loose end. He hated loose ends.

Maybe that was why he'd been so interested—almost obsessed—by the case of Jenny; at the first there'd been so *many* loose ends, so much that was unexplained. Maybe, now that he had all the answers, he could even get himself around to the point of view where he could write up the case after all. Hadn't he been rather ridiculous about that?

He finished his drink. Vi was putting fried eggs on the table so he didn't make another one just yet, although the first one had done him good.

They ate and he wiped dishes for her, what few dishes there were, because he wanted something to do. He made them another drink while she put them away.

"Vi—"

"What, George?"

"Nothing. Skip it." What had he been going to say? What *was* there to say? What had there ever been—in the last five years, anyway—to say between them?

"All right, George. Mind if I turn on the radio awhile?"

He shook his head. She went into the living room and he heard the click of the switch. He stepped out of the kitchen door, glass in hand, into the cool evening; it was just getting dark.

He wanted to take a walk—but he didn't want to take a walk, because he knew where he'd walk to, and it was meaningless for him to go there.

He thought, am I going crazy? *Really* crazy, not just a nervous breakdown or its aftermath?

He tried to look at it objectively; if this had happened to another man, and had been told to him coldly, objectively, he'd say that the other man was insane. But, from the inside, it looked different.

But why had it happened?

Because—well, because he'd been wide open for it, for one thing. Nature abhors a vacuum. And maybe, to some extent, contrast of his picture of Jenny with the reality of Vi? That may have been a factor. Poor stupid, uninteresting Vi, with her radio (he could hear it now, indistinguishable but gushing voices), with her need for candy and whisky and getting fat and sloppy physically as she was already fat and sloppy mentally, with her lackadaisical housekeeping and bad cooking and—well, above all perhaps her lack of interest in anything at all that could be a bond between them. She was getting more and more like—go ahead and think it; it's true— like a cow. But it's not a cow's fault that she's a cow, is it? He should remember that, always. And at least it was lucky, for her sake, that she now loved him no more than he loved her.

His glass was empty. He went back into the kitchen. The bottle that he'd opened was gone; Vi must have taken it into the next room with her.

The radio sounded blaring from here. "Where are you from, Mrs. Radzinski?" "Well, from Denver, really, but I've been living in Alamosa. That's where I came here from, I mean." "Alamosa? Beautiful little town, Mrs. Radzinski. To be from, I mean. I'm just kidding you, Mrs. Radzinski. I've never been there—but I'd like to go there some day. Now, Mrs. Radzinski—"

Weaver didn't want to go into the living room for his drink. He opened a new bottle instead and poured himself a big double drink so it would last awhile. He went outside again and the radio must have been turned louder in the meantime for he could hear the words now, not just the voices. He took his drink to the shed.

He got out the canvas from behind the stacked pictures. He unrolled it and looked and reached—and jerked his hand back. God damn it, he told himself; you're not a fetishist. Don't act like one. He rolled the canvas up again and put it back.

Where could he have hidden that letter? And what if he hadn't— He jerked his mind away from that possibility just as he'd jerked his hand away from the contents of the canvas. If the letter had been stolen, then the case wasn't closed because there was an unexplained factor.

But the case *was* closed.

He didn't like the light; he didn't like being in the shed. He turned out the light and went outdoors; he sat down on the step. He finished his drink and started for the kitchen to get another, then remembered he'd brought the new bottle with him and it was in the shed. He went back in and made himself another drink.

You fool, are you going to get drunk again tonight? Wasn't night before last bad enough—so drunk you don't remember checking in at a hotel, so drunk that you remember something that didn't happen at all, that couldn't have happened because it doesn't make sense? But how did you imagine it? Maybe there had really been a big man with a badge behind his lapel and maybe he showed it to you just to shush you up and later your mind manufactured the rest as a dream while you were asleep in the hotel you don't remember going to. But not even a complete dream; you remember going to the cell, but you don't remember leaving it—and that's because your dream stopped there.

He'd better stop drinking now, right now, because he was feeling it. And it was silly enough to get drunk ever, but to get blind and drunk two nights out of three— God, was he becoming an alcoholic?

But back there in the house Vi was probably getting

drunk too.

Maybe he should—

No, he thought; it's purely animal when it's only that. And you're a little more than an animal, you hope. Better to have only dreams than so sordid a reality that two people want one another only when both of them are drunk.

He got up and started to walk.

There was a sliver of moonlight, just enough to see by when his eyes were accustomed to it. It was on a night like this, he thought, that Jenny was killed.

There was the cottonwood.

He couldn't make out the outlines of the shallow grave, not in this dim light, but he sat awhile under the big tree. He found himself dreaming the fantasy dream again—the dream in which he'd happened to stop in the bus depot that day eight years ago in Santa Fe, before he'd even met Vi, and happening to meet Jenny there and—and it was such an absurd fantasy because she wouldn't have paid any attention to him if he had been there, and why should she have?

He walked back to the house.

The radio was roaring. But it seemed to be between two stations, neither of them quite succeeding in drowning out the other, so he looked into the living room and Vi was asleep in the chair, her chin hanging—and showing the start of another chin below it. He looked at the level of the whisky in the bottle on the table beside her; she'd been putting it away even faster than he had. But then he'd walked to the shallow grave and that had taken time. "Bong, *bong, bong,*" said the radio; "This is KJA, your Albuquerque station. The time is nine o'clock. We bring you Wilson Randolph with the news. But first—Sun*shine* Bread! Sun*shine* Bread! Yes, folks, the bread that's *packed* with Vitamins, the bread to ask for the next time you go to your grocer's. Sun*shine*—"

He got it turned off before he would have had to scream. The time announcement had penetrated, but it was so unbelievable that he looked at his wrist watch. The radio had been right; it was really only nine o'clock.

The silence sounded strange.

"Vi," he said, to break it. "Let me help you into bed, huh?"

She didn't answer, but she was partly conscious when he put his hands under her arms and lifted her out of the chair. She walked, staggeringly; he didn't have to carry her. He got her shoes and stockings off and opened the top of her dress. She started snoring the moment he put her on the bed. Weaver covered her up and closed the door so he wouldn't have to listen to her snoring. He went out into the other room and made himself another drink.

Nine o'clock. Oh Christ, only nine o'clock. And he wasn't sleepy. He'd slept late that morning in Santa Fe so he wasn't tired and he wasn't sleepy; it would be hours yet before he could even think about going to bed unless he wanted to lie awake and stare into darkness.

And how long now, already, had he been staring into darkness?

Try to read? God, it had been over a month since he'd been able to concentrate more than a few minutes at a time on reading.

Only nine o'clock.

Silence so deep that he heard the car coming a long way off and when it got near he went to the front window to look; with this the last house on the road it had to be coming here.

The car turned into the driveway. It parked behind his own.

A man got out of it and he switched off the car lights as though he intended to stay for a while. It wasn't Callahan; Weaver didn't recognize him.

Weaver wondered what the hell and then he decided he didn't care what the hell; he went to the door and opened it just as the man got there. He was a short but heavy—set man in a blue serge suit. He looked familiar, at close range; Weaver decided that he'd seen him a few times, probably around Taos.

"Mr. Weaver?"

"Yes. I'm Weaver."

"I'm Tom Grayson. Sheriff. Like to talk to you."

"Come in," Weaver said. He stepped back from the door.

"Let's go out to the kitchen to talk, Sheriff. My wife's asleep in the bedroom and we'll be less likely to wake her if we talk out there."

Grayson knew his way to the kitchen.

"Drink, Sheriff?" Weaver discovered that he still had his own glass in his hand.

"Thanks, no. Not right now. Listen, Mr. Weaver, you got yourself in trouble, do you know that? I got you out. But I've got an explanation coming—and you've got some listening to do."

"Trouble?" Weaver stared at him.

"Day before yesterday. In Tucson."

"My God," Weaver said. It had happened, then—his arrest and release. "Sit down, Sheriff. And tell me what you're talking about. I mean—well, I was drunk in Tucson. I thought I remembered— But *why?* What did I do?"

"Nothing in Tucson. But you sure made an ass of yourself in Barton."

Weaver put his drink down carefully on the table. "Will you give it to me in words of one syllable, Sheriff? I don't get it at all."

"A Mrs. Albright phoned the police in Barton. She said a man who said his name was Weaver and who was driving a car with a Missouri license phoned her and then came to see her; he was drunk and acted—well, more than suspiciously; she thought he was insane. He told her that her daughter had been murdered by a madman with a knife—and that she thought, if his story was true, he must have been the murderer."

"My God," Weaver said. "I had that coming. Go on."

"The Barton police figured he'd maybe been other places, asking questions around, so they phoned a few places where he'd likely have gone. Especially the taverns, because she said he'd been drunk. And he had been at one of the taverns and had asked a lot of questions about Jenny Albright. He'd given the same name there and had said he came from Taos. He'd shown a hell of a lot of interest in a guy who'd dated Jenny and whom the bartender had seen later in Tucson. He'd sounded like maybe he was going to Tucson to look for the guy. Everything beginning to make sense to you now, Mr. Weaver?"

Weaver said, "The mills of the gods grind slowly but they grind exceeding small."

"Huh?"

"Never mind, Sheriff. Go ahead."

"So the Barton police phoned Tucson, gave your description, and said they'd better pick you up for investigation. That was the middle of the evening; they found you in a tavern, drunk."

"They did indeed. Go on, Sheriff. And are you sure you won't have a drink?"

"No drink. I'm leading up to bawling the hell out of you Weaver, and I can't do that if I'm drinking your liquor. Are you sure you're sober enough now to get and remember what I'm saying?"

"I'll never forget it, Sheriff. Go ahead."

"Well, meanwhile, they phoned me in Taos—I mean the Barton police did—to find out if a guy named Weaver really came from here and what made him tick. And it was damn lucky for you that I already knew, from Callahan and Ellie Grant, what your interest in the deal was, so I was able to tell them you were all right; you were just writing up the murder for a magazine. And Barton phoned Tucson and the Tucson cops let you out of the cooler."

"Sheriff, I owe you a lot of thanks for that."

"Save them. I got to wondering, right after that call, how you'd found out that Jenny Ames—Jenny Albright—came from Barton. You couldn't have guessed it, and that meant you'd found evidence you weren't turning over to me—as you should have if it was anything new. So I came out here and looked around—legally, you understand; I had a warrant. I found that stuff wrapped in the canvas out in your shed; I looked around outdoors till I found out where you'd dug it up. That was smart of you, Weaver—I got to give you that much— to find that stuff he'd buried. But you ought to have come to me with it—especially that letter. I took it along, if you've

missed it. You shouldn't have gone off on your own like that
and tried to pull a fancy one."

"I suppose I shouldn't have." Weaver said. "I—well, it
doesn't matter now. Nelson's dead, so the case is closed. Did
you find that part of it out?"

"Sure, we had the same lead to Tucson you had; we followed it up the same way, only a bit later. Nelson's dead, all
right."

He looked at Weaver, "Why'd you say a thing like that to
Jenny's mother?"

Weaver dropped his eyes to his glass. "I'm not proud of
that, Sheriff. I was a little drunk and—well, she needled me
into it by telling me she didn't care what had happened to her
daughter. Made me so mad I threw that at her without thinking."

He looked up. "And, Sheriff, I should have turned that
stuff over to you, I admit; I guess it was just for my own ego
that I wanted to follow through on it on my own. I'd have
given you the dope before the article hit print, and full credit.
I wasn't trying to chisel."

He thought, what the hell am I crawling for? This guy did
me a favor by getting me out of trouble in Tucson, but I'd have
got out anyway after they questioned me. And why am I lying
about the article? I'm not going to write it.

"All right, Mr. Weaver." Grayson stood up. "But—well,
take my advice and don't write that article just yet."

Weaver stood, too; he looked at Grayson. "Okay, I'm not
in any hurry to write it. But, out of curiosity, why not? All the
facts are in, aren't *they?*"

They were; they had to be. Even the two loose ends he'd
tried to keep from thinking about—the missing letter and
what had happened to him in Tucson.

Grayson said, "Listen, Mr. Weaver, you think you're a
detective or something just because you can write stories for
magazines. You think you're smart. You think us ordinary
officers don't know our ass from a hole in the ground. But
that's where you're wrong. You haven't got sense enough to
check little things, details, and we have."

Weaver frowned. "All right, what little things didn't I check?"

"You didn't bother to get a description in Barton, of this Jenny Albright. You didn't find out she was a blonde, not a Brunette."

"You mean—" Weaver's mind reeled. "Are you kidding me, Sheriff—trying to tell me Jenny Albright wasn't Jenny Ames? My God, the letter, everything—"

"No, I don't mean that. It was Jenny Albright who came here under the name of Jenny Ames—and she'd dyed her hair along with changing her name, which is why Carlotta Evers and Pepe Sanchez saw her as a brunette. Sure, it was Jenny Ames who was here that night, the one he saw get chased out of the house into the dark. But—there's a but."

Weaver waited.

"But it wasn't, it couldn't have been Jenny Ames or Albright that was found in that shallow grave under the cottonwood. That girl, Weaver, was a real brunette, not a dye job. I checked back to the coroner's report of his examination and that's for sure. Besides, that body measured five feet five and Jenny's mother says she was five three exactly. Two inches difference is a hell of a lot. And other things."

Weaver shook his head to clear it. "All right, I'm stupid. I'm a horse's ass or anything you want to call me. But what's the score?"

"The score is that tomorrow I'm coming out here with two men. We're going over the whole area. We may find another shallow grave or two. Maybe it wasn't just one murder. Hell, the original Bluebeard didn't kill just one woman, did he? How do we know *how many* girls Nelson lured here to bring money to him, and then killed and buried out there somewhere? We know now there were two anyway, the girl that was in the grave out there, and Jenny.

"Or maybe he did kill only one, for all we're sure. Hell, for all we know Jenny Albright might have got away; she had a lead on him going out the door and maybe she outran him. Unless we find her body we don't even know she's dead. That's what I mean when I tell you to hold off on that article."

"But—but she *must* be dead, Sheriff, or she'd have gone—"

"To the police? When she thought she was wanted for embezzlement and knew that would come out if she told her story?"

The sheriff flipped a hand. "Be seeing you tomorrow." He walked toward the door and Weaver sank back in the chair. He reached for the whisky bottle and refilled his glass; some whisky slopped out on the table but he didn't even notice.

Jenny might be alive. Why couldn't she have run faster than a man who, even then, had moderately advanced tuberculosis and whose stamina must have been low?

And if she was alive he'd find her.

Sound of the motor of the sheriff's car starting. Weaver hurried to the door and out into the night, to the side of the car. "Sheriff, will you let me work with you on this? Help you from now on?"

"You didn't give us a lot of help, keeping that suitcase and the letter from us."

"I—I'm sorry about that. No more holding back, honest."

"Well—we'll see."

"I'm interested, Sheriff. Damned interested." *Jenny, if you're alive I'll find you.* "Listen, Sheriff, I want to be *sure* of one thing. The body that was found—it *couldn't* have been Jenny? I mean—"

"That much is for sure, Weaver. Even if she grew two inches and dyed her hair all over, it couldn't have been Jenny. Jenny's mother says she's got a mole on her left hip; if there'd been a mole on the body, Doc Gomez would have made a note of it. That old boy was thorough."

Weaver turned and walked blindly into the house, into the kitchen. The sheriff's car drove off but Weaver didn't hear it.

Vi had a mole on her left hip.

Vi was five feet three and blonde. He'd met Vi three months after Jenny Ames had escaped from Charles Nelson. She'd been working as a waitress in Santa Fe, only seventy miles away on the main highway. She had no relatives. She'd been twenty-two.

Vi was Jenny. Jenny was Vi.

Santa Fe, the most likely place for her to have got a lift to, after she'd found her way back to the main highway that evening. The nearest town big enough to hide in, big enough to give her work.

He tried to pour himself a drink but this time his hands were shaking so he couldn't even hit the glass. He took a drink from the bottle.

He went to the bedroom door and opened it, looked and listened. That gross, sodden, stupid, snoring—

He braced himself against the doorjamb and made himself turn and go back into the kitchen.

Jenny.

He leaned against the table and reached again for the bottle. If he could only drink himself into a stupor quickly, *quickly;* it was the only way he could possibly keep his sanity, keep himself from—

"George."

Jenny stood in the doorway. Her eyes were bleary from sleep and drink, her face blotchy, her mousy hair snarled, her voice thick.

"George, was somebody here? And then you left the bedroom door open and the light—"

She'd come into the room as she was talking, but she stopped now, between him and the outer door, looking at him in bewilderment.

"George, what—?"

There was nothing he could do except what he *had* to do, jerk open the drawer of the kitchen table and reach inside it—

Sudden terror in her eyes, Jenny backed away from the knife, her hand groping behind her for the knob of the kitchen door. She was too frightened to scream and anyway there was no one to hear, no one but the man who came toward her with the knife—and he was mad, he must be mad. Her hand found the knob of the door and . . .

THE SCREAMING MIMI

STATE LAKE

STATE LAKE

HE WALKED BY NIGHT
SAVAGE TRUTH — DEADLY KILLER

HE WALKED
BY NIGHT

THE
SCREAMING
MIMI FREDRIC BROWN

BRUIN
CRIMEWORKS

[I]

You can never tell what a drunken Irishman will do. You can make a flying guess; you can make a lot of flying guesses.

You can list them in the order of their probability. The likely ones are easy: He might go after another drink, start a fight, make a speech, take a train . . . You can work down the list of possibilities; he might buy some green paint, chop down a maple tree, do a fan dance, sing "God Save the King," steal an oboe . . . You can work on down and down to things that get less and less likely, and eventually you might hit the rock bottom of improbability: He might make a resolution and stick to it.

I know that that's incredible, but it happened. A guy named Sweeney did it, once, in Chicago. He made a resolution, and he had to wade through blood and black coffee to keep it, but he kept it. Maybe, by most people's standards, it wasn't it good resolution, but that's aside from the point. The point is that it really happened.

Now we'll have to hedge a bit, for truth is an elusive thing. It never quite fits a pattern. Like—well, "a drunken Irishman named Sweeney"; that's a pattern, if anything is. But truth is seldom that simple.

His name really was Sweeney, but he was only five-eighths Irish and he was only three-quarters drunk. But that's about as near as truth ever approximates a pattern, and if you won't settle for that, you'd better quit reading. If you don't, maybe you'll be sorry, for it isn't a nice story. It's got murder in it, and women and liquor and gambling and even prevarication. There's murder before the story proper starts, and murder after it ends; the actual story begins with a naked woman and ends with one, which is a good opening and a good ending, but everything between isn't nice. Don't say I didn't warn you. But if you're still with me, let's get back to Sweeney.

Sweeney sat on a park bench, that summer night, next to God. Sweeney rather liked God, although not many people did. God was a tallish, scrawny old man with a short but tangled beard, stained with nicotine. His full name was Godfrey; I say his full name advisedly, for no one, not even Sweeney, knew whether it was his first name or his last. He was a little cracked, but not much. No more, perhaps, than the average for his age of the bums who live on the near north side of Chicago and hang out, when the weather is good, in Bughouse Square. Bughouse Square has another name, but the other name is much less appropriate. It is between Clark and Dearborn Streets, just south of the Newberry Library; that's its horizontal location. Vertically speaking, it's quite a bit nearer hell than heaven. I mean, it's bright with lights, but dark with the shadows of the defeated men who sit on the benches, all night long.

Two o'clock of a summer night, and Bughouse Square had quieted down. The soapbox speakers were gone, and the summer night crowds of strollers who were not habitués of the square were long in bed. On the grass and on the benches, men slept. Their shoelaces were tied in hard knots so their shoes would not be stolen in the night. The theft of money from their pockets was the least of their worries; there was no money there to steal. That was why they slept.

"God," said Sweeney, "I wish I had another drink." He shoved his disreputable hat an inch farther back upon his disreputable head.

"And I," said God. "But not bad enough."

"*That* stuff again," Sweeney said.

God grinned a little. He said, "It's true, Sweeney. You know it is." He pulled a crumpled package of cigarettes from his pocket, gave one to Sweeney, and lighted one himself.

Sweeney dragged deeply at the fag. He stared at the

sleeping figure on the bench across from him, then lifted his eyes a little to the lights of Clark Street beyond. His eyes were a bit blurry from the drink; the lights looked haloed, but he knew they weren't. There wasn't a breath of breeze. He felt hot and sweaty, like the park, like the city. He took his hat off and fanned himself with it. Then some three-quarter drunken impulse made him hold the hat still and stare at it. It had been a new hat three weeks ago; he'd bought it while he was still working at the *Blade*. Now it looked like nothing on earth; it had been run over by an auto, it had rolled in a muddy gutter, it had been sat on and stepped on. It looked like Sweeney felt.

He said, "God," and he wasn't talking to Godfrey. Neither, for that matter, was he talking to anyone else. He put the hat back on his head.

He said, "I wish I could sleep." He stood up. "Going to walk a few blocks. Come along?"

"And lose the bench?" God wanted to know. "Naw. I guess I'll go to sleep, Sweeney. See you around." God eased himself over sidewise onto the bench, resting his head in the curve of his arm.

Sweeney grunted and walked out the path to Clark Street. He swayed a little, but not much. He walked across the night, south on Clark Street, past Chicago Avenue. He passed taverns, and wished he had the price of a drink. A cop, coming toward him said, "Hi, Sweeney," and Sweeney said, "Hi, Pete," but kept on walking. And he thought about one of Godfrey's pet theories and he thought, the old bastard's right; you can get anything you want if you want it badly enough. He could easily have hit Pete for half a check or even a buck— if he'd wanted a drink that bad. Maybe tomorrow he'd want one that bad.

Not yet, although he felt like a violin's E-string that was tuned too tight. Damn it, why *hadn't* he stopped Pete? He needed a drink; he needed about six more shots, or say half a pint, and that would put him over the hump and he could sleep. When had he slept last? He tried to think back, but things were foggy. It had been in an areaway on Huron over near the El, and it had been night, but had it been last night or the night before or the night before that? What had he done yesterday?

He passed Huron, Erie. He thought maybe if he walked on down to the Loop, some of the boys from the *Blade* would be hanging out in the place on Randolph and he could borrow something there. Had he been there yet this time, this drunk? Damn the fog in his brain. And how far gone was he now? Did he still look all right to go into the place on Randolph?

He watched along the windows for a mirrored one and found it. He looked at himself and decided he didn't look too bad, too far gone. His hat was out of shape and he didn't have a necktie and his suit was baggy, naturally, but— Then he stepped closer and wished he hadn't because that was too close and he really saw himself. Bleary red eyes, a beard that must be at least three days, maybe four, and the horrible dirtiness of his shirt collar. It had been a white shirt a week ago. And he saw the stains on his suit.

He looked away and started walking again. He knew now he couldn't look up any if the boys from the paper, not at this stage. Earlier on a drunk, yes, when he still looked all right. Or maybe later, when he didn't care how he looked. And, with the realization that he inevitably *would* do just that a few days from now, he started swearing to himself as he walked, hating himself, hating everything and everybody because he hated himself.

He walked across Ontario Street, across the night. He was swearing aloud as he walked, but didn't know he was doing it. He thought, The Great Sweeney Walking Across the Night, and tried to throw his thoughts out of perspective, but they wouldn't throw. Looking into the mirror had been bad. But, worse than that, now that he was thinking about himself, he could smell himself—the stale sweat of his body. He hadn't been out of the clothes he was wearing since—how long ago was it his landlady had refused to give him the key to his room? Ohio Street. Damn it, he'd better quit walking south or he would find himself in the Loop, so he turned east. Where *was* he going? What did it matter? Maybe if he walked long enough he'd get so damned tired he could sleep. Only he'd better stay within easy distance of the square so he'd have a place to flop if he felt ready.

Hell, he'd do anything for a drink—except, the way he looked and felt tonight, look up anybody he knew.

Someone was coming toward him on the sidewalk. A pretty boy in a bright checked sport jacket. Sweeney's fists clenched. What would be his chances if he slugged the fairy, grabbed his wallet and ran into the alley? But he hadn't ever done that before and his reactions were too slow. Much too slow. The fairy, edging to the outside of the sidewalk, was past him before Sweeney could make up his mind.

A sedan went by, slowly, and Sweeney saw that it was a squad car with two big coppers in it, and he went a little weak at the narrowness of his escape. He concentrated on walking straight and looking sober and realized that he was still swearing to himself and stopped. It would be hell on wheels to be pinched right now and face a drinkless tomorrow. The squad car cruised on without slowing down.

He hesitated at the corner of Dearborn and decided to walk back north on State Street, so he went another block east. A streetcar rolled by on flat wheels, sounding like the end of the world. An empty taxi cruised by, heading south, and for a minute Sweeney considered hailing it and going down to Randolph, telling the driver to wait until he went inside and got some money. But, hell, the taxi probably wouldn't stop for him if he hailed it, the way he looked. And anyway it was past now.

He turned north on State Street. Past Erie, Huron. He was feeling a little better now. Not much, but a little. Superior Street. Superior Sweeney, he thought. Sweeney Walking Across the Night, Across Time—

And then, quite suddenly, he was aware of the crowd standing around the entrance door of the apartment building a quarter of a block ahead of him.

It wasn't much of a crowd. Just a dozen or so queerly assorted people—the odd random dozen that would collect first on North State Street at two-thirty in the morning, standing there looking through the glass doors into the hallway of the building. And there seemed to be a funny noise that Sweeney couldn't quite place. It sounded almost like an animal growling.

Sweeney didn't hasten his steps. Probably, he realized, just a drunk that had had a fall or been sapped, lying unconscious—or dead—in there until the ambulance came and collected him. Probably lying in a pool of blood; not as many as a dozen people would be standing there looking at him if he was just out cold. Common drunks are all too common in that part of Chicago. And the thought of blood didn't fascinate Sweeney. In his days as a legman, he'd seen enough blood to last him. Like the time he was right after the cops going into the pool hall on Townsend Street where the four reefered-up jigs had had the razor party—

He started out around the people standing there without even turning to look over their shoulders. He almost got past, before three things stopped him; two of them were sounds and the third was a silence.

The silence was the silence of the crowd—if you can call a dozen people a crowd, and I guess you can if they're pressed two deep around a six-foot-wide double doorway. One of the sounds was the siren of an approaching police car, less than a block away, just slowing down on Chicago Avenue to the north, getting ready to swing the corner into State Street. Maybe, Sweeney realized, what was in the hallway of the building was a *corpus delicti*. And if it was, with the cops coming, it wasn't smart to be seen heading *away* from the scene of a crime. The cops grabbed you to ask questions. If you were standing there gawking instead they'd shove you away and tell you to move on, and then you could move on. The other sound was a repetition of the one he'd heard first and he heard it clearly now, over the silence of the crowd and under the wail of the siren; it *was* the growling of an animal.

Add up all those reasons, and you can't blame him, can you? Not even after everything it led to. Sweeney turned and looked.

He couldn't see anything, of course, except the backs of a dozen miscellaneous people. He couldn't hear anything except the growling of an animal in front of him and the wail of a police siren behind him. The car was swinging in to the curb.

Maybe it was the sound of the car, maybe it was the sound of the animal, but some of the people in the middle of the group started backing away from the glass double door of the apartment building. And Sweeney saw the glass doors, and—through them. Not very clearly, because there wasn't any light on inside the hallway. Just the light that came in from the street lamps illuminated the scene within.

He saw the dog first, because the dog was nearest the glass, looking out through it. Dog? It *must* be a dog, here in Chicago; if you'd seen it out in the woods, you'd have taken it for a wolf, and a particularly large and menacing wolf at that. It was standing stiff-legged about four feet back from the glass doors; the hairs on the back of its neck were raised and its lips were drawn back in a tight snarl that showed teeth that looked an inch long. Its eyes glowed yellow.

Sweeney shivered a little as his eyes met those yellow ones. And they *did* seem to meet Sweeney's; naked yellow savagery boring into red, bleary weariness.

It almost sobered him, and it made him look away, uneasily, at what lay on the floor of the hallway beside, and slightly behind, the dog. It was the figure of a woman, lying face down on the carpeting.

The word *figure* is not lightly used. Her white shoulders gleamed, even in that dim light, above a strapless white silk evening gown that molded every beautiful contour of her body—at least those contours visible when a woman is lying face downward—and Sweeney caught his alcoholic breath at the sight of her.

He couldn't see her face, for the top of her page-boy-bobbed blonde head was toward him, but he knew that her face would be beautiful. It would *have* to be; women don't come with bodies as beautiful as that without faces to match.

He thought she moved a little. The dog growled again, a low-pitched sound under the high-pitched squeal of brakes as the police car stopped at the curb. Without turning to look behind him, Sweeney heard the doors of the car open, and the heavy sound of footsteps. A hand on Sweeney's shoulder pushed him aside, not too gently, and a voice that meant business asked, "What's wrong? Who phoned?" But the voice wasn't talking to Sweeney particularly, and he didn't answer it, nor turn.

Nobody answered.

Sweeney teetered a little from the push, and then recovered his balance. He could still see into the hallway.

There was a flashlight in the hand of the blue-serged man beside him, and with a click it shot a beam of bright white light into the dim hallway beyond the glass doors. It caught the yellow glow of the dog's savage eyes and the yellow glow of the bobbed blonde hair of the woman; it caught the white gleam of her shoulders and the white gleam of her dress.

The man holding the flashlight pulled in his breath in a soft little whistle and didn't ask any more questions. He took a step forward and reached for the knob of the door.

The dog quit growling and crouched to spring. The silence was worse than the growl. The man in blue serge took his hand off the knob as though he'd found it red hot.

"The hell," he said. He put a hand inside the left lapel of his coat, but didn't draw the gun. Instead, he addressed the little knot of people again. "What goes on here? Who phoned? Is the dame in there sick or drunk or what?"

Nobody answered. He asked, "Is that *her* dog?"

Nobody answered. A man in a gray suit was beside the man in blue serge. He said, "Take it easy, Dave. We don't want to shoot the pooch if we don't have to."

"Okay," said Blue Serge. "So you open the door, and pet the dog while I take care of the dame. That ain't no dog anyway; it's a wolf or a devil."

"Well—" Gray Suit reached a hand for the door, and pulled it back as the dog crouched again and bared its fangs.

Blue Serge snickered. He asked, "What *was* the call? You took it."

"Just said a woman lying passed out in the hallway. Didn't mention the dog. Guy put in the call from tavern on the corner north; gave his name."

"Gave *a* name," said Blue Serge, cynically. "Look, if I was sure the dame was just passed—out drunk, we could phone the humane society to pull off the pooch. They could handle it. I *like* dogs; I don't want to shoot that one. Probably belongs to the dame and thinks he's protecting her."

"Thinks hell," said Gray Suit. "He damn well is. I like dogs, too. But I wouldn't swear that thing's a dog. Well—"

Gray Suit started peeling off his suit coat. He said, "So okay, I'll wrap this around my arm and you open the door and when the dog jumps me, I'll clip him with the butt of—"

"Lookit—the dame's moving!"

The dame *was* moving. She was lifting her head. She pushed up a little with her hands—Sweeney noticed now that she wore long white cloth gloves that came halfway to her elbows, and lifted her head so her eyes stared full into the bright spotlight of the flashlight's beam.

Her face *was* beautiful. Her eyes looked dazed, unseeing.

"Drunk as hell," Blue Serge said. "Look, Harry, you might kill the dog, even if you clip it with the butt of your gun, and somebody'd raise hell. The dame would raise hell when she sobers up. I'll wait here and keep watch and you get the station on the two-way and tell 'em to send the humane guys here with a net or whatever they use and—"

There was a gasp from several throats that shut Blue Serge up as suddenly as though a hand had been clapped across his mouth.

Somebody said "Blood," almost inaudibly.

Weakly, as in a daze, the woman was trying to get up. She got her knees under her body and had pushed herself up until her arms were straight. The dog beside her moved quickly, and Blue Serge swore and yanked at his shoulder-holstered gun as the dog's muzzle went toward the woman's face. But before the gun was out, the dog had licked the woman's face once with a long red tongue, whimpering.

And then, as both detectives made a quick move toward the door, the dog crouched again and growled.

But the woman was still getting up. Everyone could see

the blood now, an oblong stain of it on the front of her white
evening dress, over the abdomen. And—in the bright spotlight that made the thing seem like an act on a stage or something seen in the glass screen of a televised horror show—they
could see the five-inch-long cut in the white cloth in the
center of the oblong stain.

Gray Suit said, *"Jesus, a shiv. The Ripper."*

Sweeney got shoved farther to one side as the two detectives pushed closer. He stepped around behind them, watching over their shoulders; he'd forgotten all about his idea of
getting away as soon as he could. He could have walked away
now and nobody would have noticed. But he didn't.

Gray Suit was standing with his coat half on and half off,
frozen in the act of removing it. He jerked it back on now, and
his shoulder jarred Sweeney's chin.

He barked, "Phone on the two-way for an ambulance and
homicide, Dave. I'll try to crease the dog."

His shoulder hit Sweeney's chin again as he, too, pulled
a gun from his shoulder holster. His voice got calm suddenly,
as the gun was in his hand. He said, "Reach for the knob,
Dave. The dog'll freeze to jump you and I'll have a clear shot.
I think I can crease him."

But he didn't raise the gun, and Dave didn't move to
reach for the knob. For the incredible thing was happening,
the thing that Sweeney wasn't ever going to forget—and that,
probably, no one of the fifteen or twenty people who, by now,
were in front of the doorway was ever going to forget.

The woman in the hallway had one hand on the wall now,
beside the row of mailboxes and buzzer buttons. She was
struggling to a standing position now, her body erect, but still
resting on one knee. The bright white light of the flash framed
her like a spotlight on a stage, the whiteness of her dress and
gloves and skin and the redness of that oblong patch of blood.
Her eyes were still dazed. It must have been shock, Sweeney
realized, for that knife wound couldn't have been deep or
serious or it would have bled much, much more. She closed
her eyes now as, swaying a little, she got up off the other knee
and stood straight.

And the incredible thing happened.

The dog padded back and reared up behind her, on his hind feet but without pushing his forepaws against her. His teeth went to the back of the white dress, the strapless evening gown, caught something, and pulled out and down. And the something—they found out later—was a white silk tab attached to a long zipper.

Gently the dress fell off and became a white silken circle around her feet. She had worn nothing under the dress, nothing at all.

For what seemed like minutes, but was probably about ten seconds, nobody moved, nothing moved. Nothing happened, except that the flashlight shook just a little in Blue Serge's hand.

Then the woman's knees began to bend under her and she went down slowly—not falling, just sinking down like someone who is too weary to stand any longer—on top of the white circle of silk in which she had stood.

Then a lot of things happened at once. Sweeney breathed again, for one thing. And Blue Serge sighted his gun very carefully toward the dog and pulled the trigger. The dog fell and lay in the hallway and Blue Serge went through the door and called back over his shoulder to Gray Suit, "Get the ambulance, Harry. Then tie that damn dog's legs; I don't think I killed him. I just creased him."

And Sweeney backed away and nobody paid any attention to him as he walked north to Delaware and then turned west to Bughouse Square.

Godfrey wasn't on the bench, but he couldn't have been gone long, for the bench was still empty and benches don't stay empty long on a summer night. Sweeney sat down and waited till the old man came back.

"Hi, Sweeney," God said. He sat down beside Sweeney. "Got a pint," he said. "Want a slug?"

It had been a silly question and Sweeney didn't bother to answer it; he held out his hand. And God hadn't expected an answer; he was holding out the bottle. Sweeney took a long pull.

"Thanks," he said. "Listen, she was beautiful, God. She was the most beautiful dame—" He took another, shorter pull at the bottle and handed it back. He said, "I'd give my right arm."

"Who?" God asked.

"The dame. I was walking north on State Street and—" He stopped, realizing he couldn't tell about it. He said, "Skip it. How'd you get the likker?"

"Stemmed a couple blocks." God sighed. "I told you I could get a drink if I wanted it bad enough; I just didn't want it bad enough before. A guy can get anything he wants, if he wants it bad enough."

"Nuts," Sweeney said automatically. Then, suddenly, he laughed. "Anything?"

"Anything you want," said God, dogmatically. "It's the easiest thing in the world, Sweeney. Take rich men. Easiest thing in the world; anybody can get rich. All you got to do is want money so bad it means more to you than anything else. Concentrate on money and you get it. If you want other things worse, you don't."

Sweeney chuckled. He was feeling swell now; that long drink had been just what he needed. He'd kid the old man by getting him to argue his favorite subject.

"How about women?" he said.

"What do you mean, how about women?" God's eyes looked a little foggy; he was getting drunker. And a touch of Bostonian broad *a* was coming back into his speech, as it always did when he was really drunk. "You mean could you get any particular woman you wanted?"

"Yeah," said Sweeney. "Suppose there's a particular dame, for instance, I'd like to spend a night with. Could I do that?"

"If you wanted to bad enough, of course you could, Sweeney. If you concentrated all your efforts, direct and indirect, to that one objective, sure. Why not?"

Sweeney laughed again.

He leaned his head back, looking up into the dark green leaves of the trees. The laugh subsided to a chuckle and he took off his hat and fanned himself with it. Then he stared at the hat as though he had never seen it before, and began to dust it off carefully with the sleeve of his coat and to reshape it so it looked more like a hat. He worked with the absorbed concentration of a child threading a needle.

God had to ask him a second time before he heard the question. Not that it hadn't been a foolish question to begin with; God hadn't expected an answer, verbally. He was holding out the bottle.

Sweeney didn't take it. He put his hat back on and stood up. He winked at God and said, "No thanks, pal. I got a date."

[2]

Dawn was different. Dawn's always different.

Sweeney opened his eyes and it was dawn, a hot, gray, still dawn. Leaves hung listlessly on the trees over his head and the ground was hard under him. All his body ached. His mouth felt and tasted as though the inside of it was caked with something unmentionable—unmentionable here, that is, not to Sweeney. He mentioned it to himself and ran his tongue across his lips to moisten them. He swallowed a few times and got the inside of his mouth moist.

He rubbed his eyes with the hairy backs of dirty hands and swore at a bird that was making a hell of a racket in a nearby tree. He sat up and leaned forward, his face in his hands, the bristle of his beard coarse against the palms of them. A streetcar went by on Clark Street and it didn't sound any louder than an earthquake or the crack of doom. Not much louder, anyway.

Awakening is never a good thing; sometimes it can be a horrible thing. With the cumulative hangover of two weeks of drinking, it *is* a horrible thing.

But the thing to do, Sweeney knew, is to get moving, not to sit there and suffer, not to lie back down on the hard ground and try to go back to sleep, because you can't ever go back to sleep when it's like that. It's hell on wheels, till you orient yourself; get wide awake and oriented and it's merely hell, one dull aching hell until you get a few drinks under your belt. Then it's all right. Or is it?

Sweeney pushed the ground away from him and stood up. His legs worked. They carried him off the grass to the cement and along the walk to the bench where Godfrey lay still asleep and snoring gently. On the bench next to him lay the bottle, empty.

Sweeney pushed God's feet back and sat down gingerly on the edge of the bench. He put his rough chin in his filthy hands and rested his elbows on his knees, but he didn't close his eyes. He kept them open.

Had he finally gone over the edge, he wondered. The dame and the dog. He'd never hallucinated before.

The dame and the dog.

He didn't believe it. It was one of the few things that couldn't have happened. So it hadn't happened. That was logic.

He held his hand out in front of him and it was shaking, plenty, but no worse than it had before at times like this. He put it back down on the bench and used it and his other hand to push himself up. His legs still worked. They carried him across the square to Dearborn and south on Dearborn—a walking ache rather than a man—to Chicago Avenue. Brakes squealed as a taxi swerved to avoid hitting him as he crossed Chicago Avenue diagonally, without looking to either side. The taxi driver yelled something at him. Sweeney walked along the south side of Chicago Avenue to State Street and turned south.

He walked three-quarters of a block and there was the Door. He stopped and stared at it, and after a while he went close to it and looked through the glass. It was dim inside, but he could see through the hallway to the door at the back.

A newsboy came along, a bag of papers slung over his shoulder. He stopped beside Sweeney. He said, "Jeez, that's where it happened, ain't it?"

"Yeah," said Sweeney.

"I know the broad," said the newsboy. "I leave her a paper." He reached past Sweeney for the knob of the door. "Gotta get in to leave some papers." Sweeney stepped aside to let him past.

When the newsboy came out, Sweeney went in. He walked back a few steps beside the mailboxes. This, where he was standing, was where she'd fallen. He looked down, then stooped to look closer; there were a few little dark dots on the floor.

Sweeney stood up again and walked to the back. He opened the door there and looked through it. There was a cement walk that led back to the alley. That was all. He closed the door and flicked the light switch to the left of it, at the foot of the stairs leading upward. Two bulbs went on, one overhead at the foot of the stairs, the other overhead up front, by the mailboxes. The yellow light was sickly in the gray morning. He flicked it off again, then—as he noticed something on the wooden panel of the door—back on again. There were long closely-spaced vertical scratches on the wood. They looked fresh, and they looked like the claw-marks of a dog. They looked as though a dog had lunged against that door and then tried to claw his way through it.

Sweeney turned off the light again and went out, taking with him one of the papers the newsboy had left in clips under several of the mailboxes. He walked past the next corner before he sat down on a step and unfolded the paper.

It was a three-column splash, with two pix, one of the girl and one of the dog. The heading was:

RIPPER ATTACKS DANCER; SAVED BY HER FAITHFUL DOG

Fiend Makes Escape;
"Can't Identify," Victim Says

Sweeney studied the two pictures, read the article through, and studied the pictures again. Both were posed, obviously publicity stills. "Devil" was the caption under the picture of the dog, and he looked it. In a newspaper pic, you couldn't see that yellow balefulness in his eyes, but he still didn't look like anything you'd want to meet in an alley. He still looked, Sweeney thought, more like a wolf than a dog, and a bad wolf at that.

But his eyes went back to the woman's picture. The caption, "Yolanda Lang," made Sweeney wonder what her real name was. But—looking at that picture of her—you wouldn't care what her name was. The picture, unfortunately, didn't show as much of her as Sweeney had seen last night. It was a waist-up shot, and Yolanda Lang wore a strapless evening gown molded to show off her outstanding features—which Sweeney well knew to be genuine and not padding—and her soft blonde hair tumbled to her softer white shoulders. Her face was beautiful, too. Sweeney hadn't much noticed her face last night. You couldn't blame him for that.

But it was worth noticing, now that there was less distraction to keep his eyes away from it. It was a face that was sweetly grave and gravely sweet. Except something about the eyes. But on an eighty-line screen newsprint picture you couldn't be sure about that.

Sweeney carefully folded the newspaper and put it down on the step beside him. There was a crooked grin on his face.

He got up and trudged back to Bughouse Square.

God was still snoring on the bench. Sweeney shook him and God opened his eyes. He stared up blearily at Sweeney and said, "Go away."

Sweeney said, "I am. That's what I came to tell you. Look, I meant it."

"Meant what?"

"What I said last night," Sweeney said.

"You're crazy," God said.

That lopsided grin came back to Sweeney's face. He said, "You didn't see her. You weren't there. So long."

He cut across the grass to Clark Street and stood there a

minute. He had a dull headache now, and he wanted a drink damned bad. He held out his hand and watched it shake, and then put it in his pocket so he wouldn't have to think about it. He started walking south on Clark. The sun was up now, slanting down the east-west streets. The traffic was getting heavy, and noisy.

He thought, *Sweeney Walking Across the Day.*

He was sweating, and it wasn't only from the heat. He smelled, too, and he knew it. His feet hurt. He was a hell of a mess, an aching mess, top and bottom and inside and out. Sweeney Walking Across the Day.

And across the Loop, and on south to Roosevelt Road. He didn't dare stop. He turned the corner east on Roosevelt Road, kept on going a block and a half, and turned into the entrance of an apartment building.

He rang a buzzer and stood waiting till the latch on the door clicked. He opened it and trudged upstairs to the third floor. A door at the front was ajar and a bald head stuck through it. The face under the bald head looked at Sweeney, approaching, and a disgusted look came over it.

The door slammed.

Sweeney put a dirty hand on the wall to steady himself and kept on coming. He started to knock on the door, loudly. He knocked a full minute and then put a hand to his forehead to hold it a while, maybe half a minute. He leaned against the wall.

He straightened up and started knocking again, louder.

He heard footsteps shuffle to the door. "Get the hell away or I'll call copper."

Sweeney knocked again. He said, "Call copper then, pally. We'll both go down to the jug and explain."

"What the hell do you want?"

Sweeney said, "Open up." He started knocking again, louder. A door down the hall opened and a woman's frightened face looked out.

Sweeney knocked some more. The voice inside said, "All right, *all right.* Just a second." The footsteps shuffled away and back again and the key turned.

The door opened and the bald man stepped back from it. He wore a shapeless bathrobe and scuffed slippers, and apparently nothing else. He was a little smaller than Sweeney, but he had his right hand in the pocket of the bathrobe and the pocket bulged.

Sweeney walked on in and kicked the door shut beside him. He walked to the middle of the cluttered room. He turned around and said, "Hi, Goetz," mildly.

The bald man was still beside the door.

He said, "What the hell do you want?"

"A double saw," Sweeney said. "You know what for. Or shall I tell you in words of one syllable?"

"Like hell I'll give you a double saw. If you're still harping back to that Goddam horse, I told you I didn't shove the bet. I gave you your fin back. You took it."

"I took it on account," Sweeney said. "I didn't need the money bad enough then to get tough about it. Now I do. So okay, let's review the bidding. You touted me on that oat-burner. It was *your* idea. So I gave you a fin to bet, and the horse came in at five for one, and you tell me you didn't get the bet down for me."

"God damn it, I didn't. The heat was on. Mike's was closed and—"

"You didn't even try Mike's. You just held the bet. If the horse had lost—like you expected—you'd have kept my fin. So whether you got the bet down or not you owe me twenty."

"The hell I do. Get out."

The bald man took his hand out of the bathrobe pocket and there was a little twenty-five caliber automatic in it.

Sweeney shook his head sadly. He said, "If it was twenty grand, I'd be afraid of that thing—maybe. For twenty bucks you wouldn't put a shooting on your record. For a lousy double saw you wouldn't have the cops up here snooping around. Anyway, I don't think you would. I'll gamble on it."

He looked around the room until he saw a pair of pants hanging over the back of a chair. He started for the pants.

The bald man snicked the safety off the little automatic. He said, "You son of a bitch—"

Sweeney picked up the pants by the cuffs and started shaking them. Keys and change hit the carpet and he kept on shaking. He said, "Someday, Goetz, you'll call a man a son of a bitch who is a son of a bitch, and he'll take you apart."

A wallet from the hip pocket of the trousers hit the carpet, and Sweeney picked it up. He flipped it open, and grunted. There was only a ten and a five in the wallet.

He took the ten out and put it in his own pocket and tossed the wallet toward the dresser. He said, "What's the matter with the pool ticket racket, Goetz? *That* bad?"

The bald man's face wasn't pretty. He said, "I told you; the heat's on. You got your money. Now get out."

"I got ten," Sweeney said. "I wouldn't take a man's last fin, pally. I'll take the other ten in trade. A bath and a shave and a shirt and socks."

Sweeney peeled off his coat and stepped out of his trousers. He sat down on the edge of the mussed-up bed and took off his shoes. He went into the bathroom and turned on the water to run in the tub.

He came out stark naked, holding a wadded-up ball that had been his shirt, socks and underwear and put it in the wastebasket.

The bald man was still standing by the door, but he'd put the little automatic back into the pocket of the bathrobe.

Sweeney grinned at him. Over the roar of water running into the tub, he said, "Don't call copper now, Goetz. With me dressed this way, they might get the wrong idea."

He went into the bathroom and shut the door.

He soaked a long time in the tub, and then shaved leisurely with Goetz's razor—providentially an electric one. Sweeney's hands were still shaking.

When he came out, the bald man was back in bed, his back to the room.

"Asleep, darling?" Sweeney asked.

There wasn't any answer.

Sweeney opened a drawer of the dresser and chose a white sport shirt with a soft collar. It was tight across the shoulders and the collar wouldn't button, but it was a shirt and it was clean and white. A pair of Goetz's socks proved a bit small, but they went on.

He eyed his own shoes and suit with disgust, but they'd have to do. Goetz's wouldn't fit. Sweeney did the best he could with a shoe brush and a clothes brush. He made sure the ten dollar bill was still in the pocket of his trousers when he put them on.

He brushed his hat and put that on, and then stopped at the door.

He said, "Nighty-night, pally, and thanks for everything. We're even now." He closed the door quietly and went downstairs and outside into the hot sunlight. He walked north on Dearborn, past the Dearborn Station. In a little restaurant opposite the front of it, he had three cups of black coffee and managed to eat one doughnut of two he ordered. It tasted like library paste, but he got it down.

Under the shadow of the El, two blocks north, he got his shoes shined and then waited, shaking a little, in a tiny cubbyhole in the back of the shop while his suit was sponged and pressed. It needed more than sponging, but it didn't look too bad when he put it back on.

He took a look at himself in the long mirror and decided he looked fair enough by now. There were circles under his eyes and the eyes themselves—well he wasn't a thing of beauty and a joy forever, and he had to remember to keep his hands in his pockets until he got over the trembling, but he looked human.

He spread the collar of the white sport shirt on the outside of the collar of his coat, and that looked better, too.

He kept to the shady side of the street, walking north across the Loop. He was starting to sweat again, and felt dirty already. He had a hunch he'd feel dirty for a long time, no matter how many baths he took. Why did anyone in his right mind live in Chicago in a summer heat wave? Why did anyone live in Chicago at all? Why, for that matter, did anyone live?

Sweeney's headache had quit being dull, now. It was a rhythmic, persistent throbbing in his forehead and behind his eyeballs. And the palms of his hands were wet and felt clammy, despite how hot the rest of him was; and no matter how often he wiped them on the sides of his trousers, they were wet and clammy again immediately.

Sweeney Walking Across the Loop. At Lake Street under the El again, he stopped in at a drugstore for a double bromo and another cup of coffee. He felt like a coiled spring that was tied down too tightly; he felt like a claustrophobic locked in a tiny room; he felt lousy. The coffee seemed to be swishing around in his guts like bilgewater inside a leaky ship—tepid, brackish bilgewater filled with little green algae, if algae are green. Sweeney's were, and they wriggled, too.

He crossed Wacker Drive, hoping that a car would hit him, but none did; he walked across the bridge in the bright hot glare of sunshine and he lifted one foot and put it down and lifted the other and put that down, for six blocks to Erie Street; he walked east past Rush and then—not daring to stop —he put his clammy hands into his pockets and went into the areaway between two buildings and through an open door-way.

This was home, if it still was. This was the biggest hurdle, for today. He took his right hand out of a pocket and rapped gently on a door off the downstairs hallway. He put his hand back quickly.

Heavy footsteps came slowly, and the door opened.

Sweeney said, "Hello, Mrs. Randall. Uh—"

Her sniff cut off whatever he'd been going to say. She said, "No, Mr. Sweeney."

"Uh—you mean you've rented my room?"

"I mean—no, you can't get in it to get something to hock to keep on drinking. I told you that last week, twice."

"Did you?" asked Sweeney vaguely. He didn't remember, or did he? Now that she spoke of it, one of the two times came back to him dimly. "Guess I was pretty drunk." He took a deep breath. "But it's over now. I'm sober."

She sniffed again. "How about the three weeks you owe me? Thirty-six dollars."

Sweeney fumbled out the bills in his pockets, a five and three singles. "All I've got," he said. "I can give you eight dollars on account."

The landlady looked from the bills up to Sweeney's face. She said, "I guess you're on the level, Sweeney, about sobering up. If you've got money, you aren't after stuff to hock. You could do a lot of drinking on eight dollars."

"Yes," Sweeney said.

She stepped back from the door. "Come on in." And, after he had followed her in: "Sit down. Put your money back in your pocket. You'll need it worse than I do, till you get started again. How long'll that be?"

Sweeney sat down. "A few days," he said. "I can raise some money, when I'm okay again."

He put his hands, and the bills, back in his pocket. "Uh— I'm afraid I lost my key. Do you have—"

"You didn't lose it. I took it away from you a week ago Friday. You were trying to carry out your phonograph to hock it."

Sweeney dropped his head into his hands. "Lord, did I?"

"You didn't. I made you take it back. And I made you give me the key. Your clothes are all there, too, except your topcoat and overcoat. You must have taken them before that. And your typewriter. And your watch—unless you got it on."

Sweeney shook his head slowly. "Nope. It's gone. But thanks for saving the other stuff."

"You look like hell. Want a cup of coffee? I got some on."

"It's running out of my ears," Sweeney told her. "But— yes, I'll have another cup. Black."

He studied her as she got up and waddled over to the stove. There ought to be more landladies like Mrs. Randall, he thought. Tough as nails on the outside (they had to be to run a rooming house) and soft as butter inside. Most of them were tough all the way through.

She came back with the coffee and he drank it. He got his key and went up the stairs. He got inside and got the door closed before he started to shake, and he stood there, it was over. Then he made it to the washbasin and was sick at his stomach, and that helped, although the sound of the water running made his head hurt worse.

When that was over, he wanted to lie down and sleep, but instead he stripped off his clothes, put on a bathrobe, and went down the hall to the bathroom. He drew himself a hot tub and soaked in it for a long time before he went back to his room.

Before he dressed again, he rolled up the spotted and worn suit he'd been wearing and the too-small shirt and socks he'd taken from the man named Goetz and put them into the wastebasket. He put on all clean clothes, including his best summer-weight suit. He put on a silk tie that had cost him five bucks and his best pair of shoes.

He straightened up the room carefully, even meticulously. He turned on the radio side of his radio-phono combination until he got a time announcement between programs and set the clock on his dresser and wound it. It was half-past eleven.

Then he got his Panama hat out of the closet and went out.

Mrs. Randall's door opened as he started down the stairs. She called out, "Mr. Sweeney?" and he leaned over the railing to look toward her. "Yes?"

"Forgot to tell you there was a phone call for you this morning, early, about eight o' clock. A Walter Krieg, from the paper you work for—or used to work for. Which is it?"

"Used to work for, I guess," Sweeney said. "What'd he say? What'd you say?"

"He asked for you and I said you weren't in. He said if you came back before nine to have you call him. You didn't— not that I was expecting you to—so I kinda forgot it. That's all that was said."

Sweeney thanked her and went on out. At the corner drugstore he bought a half pint of whiskey and put it in his hip pocket. Then he went into the phone booth, dialed the *Blade*, and asked for the managing editor by name.

"Krieg?" he said. "This is Sweeney. Just got home. Got your message. Sober. What you want?"

"Nothing now. It's too late, Sweeney. Sorry."

"All right, it's too late and you're sorry. But what did you want?"

"Eyewitness story, if you're sober enough to remember what you saw last night. A beat copper said you were around when the lid came off that Yolanda Lang business. Remember it?"

"More than the lid came off, and I damn well remember it. Why's it too late? You got one edition on the streets but the main one coming up and two others. The home edition's not in, is it?"

"Going in in fifteen minutes. Take you longer'n that to—"

"Quit wasting time," Sweeney said. "Put a rewrite man on the phone, now. I can give him half a column in five minutes. Gimme Joe Carey; he can take it fast."

"Okay, Sweeney. Hang on."

Sweeney hung on, getting his thoughts organized, until he heard Joe's voice. Then he started talking, fast.

When he was through, he put the receiver back on the hook and leaned weakly against the wall of the phone booth. He hadn't asked to have Walter Krieg put back on the line; that could wait. He'd do better going in and seeing Walter personally.

But not yet, not just yet.

He went back to his room and put the little half pint bottle of whiskey on the arm of the comfortable Morris chair and a shot glass beside it. He hung up his suit coat and Panama, and loosened his collar and tie.

Then he went over to the phonograph and squatted down on his haunches in front of the shelf of albums. He studied the titles. Not that it mattered; he knew which one he was going to hear: the *Mozart 40*.

No, you wouldn't have thought it to look at him, maybe, but that was Sweeney's favorite—the *Symphony No. 40, in G Minor, K. 550*. He stacked the three records on the phonograph, flicked the switch to start the first one, and went over to the Morris chair to sit and listen.

The first movement, *allegro molto*.

Why should I tell you anything about Sweeney? If you know the *Mozart 40*, the dark restlessness of it, the macabre drive behind its graceful counterpoint, then you know Sweeney. And if the *Mozart 40* sounds to you like a gay but slightly boring minuet, background for a conversation, then to you Sweeney is just another damn reporter who happens, too, to be a periodic drunk.

But let it pass; what you think and what I think have no bearing on this; on Sweeney unscrewing the top of the half pint bottle and pouring himself a drink. Drinking it.

There are strange things and there are stranger ones. And one of the strangest? A wooden box containing oddments of copper wire and metal plates, a half-dozen spaces of the nothingness called a vacuum, and a black wire which plugs into a hole in the wall from whence cometh our help, whence flows a thing which we call electricity because we do not know what it is. But it flows and inorganic matter lives; a table is prepared before you and revolves, bearing a disk; a needle scrapes in a groove.

A needle dances in a groove and a diaphragm vibrates, and the air about you vibrates. And the thoughts of a man a century and a half dead press upon you; you sit in light and the shadow of the soul of a man long dead. You share the troubled thoughts of a dapper little court musician in a horrible financial mess, perhaps feeling the end of his life was near and working at prodigious speed, turning out in a few weeks the greatest symphony he ever wrote.

Yes, there are strange things. And there was Sweeney, pouring his second drink as the third disk dropped and the second movement started, the lighter *andante*.

He drank them neat, the third side of the album and the second drink. He sighed and pushed himself up out of the chair; the pain in his head was still there and the pain in his soul, but the shaking of his hands was gone.

He rinsed out the glass and put away the little half pint bottle, still more than half full. He turned over the three records on the phonograph, started it again and sat back down to listen to the rest of the *40*.

He closed his eyes and just listened as the second movement ended and the dark-bright minuetto-and-trio of the

third movement lived all too briefly and died and gave birth
to what he had been waiting for: the bitter final movement,
the *allegro assai*, the power and the melancholy glory.

And then Sweeney sat listening to the silence, and after
a while he began to chuckle almost inaudibly to himself.

He was *out* of it now, off the binge, sober. Until the next
time, which might be months, might be a couple of years.
However long until enough hell accumulated inside him that
he'd have to soak it out; until then he could be normal and
drink normally. Yes, I know, alcoholics can't do that, but
Sweeney wasn't an alcoholic; he could and did drink regularly
and normally and only once in a while dive off the deep end
into a protracted drunk. There's that type of drinker, too,
although of late the alcoholics have been getting most of the
ink.

But Sweeney was out of it now, shaken but not shaking,
sober. He could even get his job back, he felt sure, if he ate a
little crow. He could climb out of debt in a few weeks and be
back where he was, wherever *that* was.

Or—

Yes, he *was* sober. But that utterly absurd decision or
resolution or whatever it had been—

What if? Why not? *Anything you want.* Didn't God have
something there: anything you want if you want it badly
enough to concentrate on getting it. Any little thing like a
million dollars or any big thing like spending a night with—
what was her name?—Yolanda Lang.

He chuckled again, and he closed his eyes and thought
back and remembered and saw again that incredible scene
behind glass in the State Street hallway.

After a few seconds he quit chuckling. He told himself:
*Sweeney, you're asking for trouble. You'll need money, for
one thing. A dime-a-dozen reporter couldn't make the grade
with that babe. And for an in, you'll have to hunt a ripper.
And you might find him.*

And that would be bad, Sweeney knew, because Sweeney
had a horror—almost a phobia—of cold steel, cold sharp steel.
Razor-edged steel in the hands of a madman, a homicidal

maniac. A razor-like knife that can slash across your abdomen and spill your guts out on the sidewalk where they won't be a bit of use to you, Sweeney.

Sure, he told himself: *You're a God damned fool, Sweeney.*

But he'd known that for a long time.

[3]

Sweeney headed for the *Blade.*

There's a nice pun in that, if you don't mind your puns obvious. *The Blade.* If you saw that pun yourself, forgive me for pointing it out. You got it, yes, but somebody else would have missed it. It takes all kinds of people to read a book.

Some people, for instance, see with their eyes; they want descriptions. So, if it interests you (it doesn't interest me) William Sweeney was five feet eleven inches tall and weighed a hundred and sixty-three pounds. He had sandy hair that was receding at the front and getting a little thin on top, but was mostly still there. He had a long thin face, vaguely horse-like but not, on the whole, unpleasing to the uncritical eye. He looked to be about forty-three, which is not strange because that is how old he really was. He wore glasses with light-colored shell rims for reading and working; he could see all right without them for any distance over four or five feet. For that matter, he could work without them if he had to, although he'd get headaches if he did it too long. But it was well that he could do without them for a while, because he was going to have to. They'd been in his pocket two weeks ago when he'd started his serious drinking and only God (I don't mean Godfrey) knew where they were now.

He threaded his way across the city room and into the office of the managing editor. He sat down on the arm of the chair across the desk from Krieg. He said, "Hi, Walter."

Krieg looked up and grunted, then finished the letter in

his hand and put it down. He opened his mouth and closed it again.

Sweeney said, "I'll say it for you, Walter. First, I'm a son of a bitch to have let you down and gone on a binge without giving you notice. I'm through. You can't mess with guys like me. I'm an anachronism. The days of the drunken reporter are over and a modern newspaper is a business institution run on business lines and not a *Front Page* out of Hecht by MacArthur. You want men you can count on. Right?"

"Yes, you son of—"

"Hold it, Walter. I said it for you, all of it. And anyway, I wouldn't work on your damn paper unless you hired me to. How was the eyewitness story?"

"It was good, Sweeney, damn good. That was a break in a million, your being there."

"You say a cop mentioned I was there. I didn't see one I recognized. Who was it?"

"You'll have to ask Carey; he handled the story. Look, Sweeney, how often do you go on a bat like that? Or are you going to tell me that was the last one?"

"It probably wasn't. It'll happen again; I don't know when. Maybe not for a couple of years. Maybe in six months. So you wouldn't want me to work for you. All right. But since I'm not working for you, I got a little check coming for that eyewitness account. I'll let you do me one last favor, Walter. You can give me a voucher to get it now instead of putting it through the channels. That story was worth fifty bucks, if Carey wrote it like I told it to him. Will you settle for twenty-five?"

Krieg glared at him. "Not a damn cent, Sweeney."

"No? And why the hell not? Since when have you been *that* much of a lousy—"

"Shut up!" The managing editor almost roared it. "God damn it, Sweeney, you're the toughest guy to do a favor for I ever saw. You won't even give me the satisfaction of bawling you out; you take the words out of my mouth so I can't say 'em. Who told you you were fired? You did. The reason you don't get paid for that piddling little story you gave over the phone is that you're still on the payroll. You've lost two days' pay, that's all."

"I don't get it," Sweeney said. "Why two days? I been gone two weeks. What's two days got to do with it?"

"This is a Thursday, Sweeney. You started your drunk two weeks ago tonight and didn't come in Friday morning. Or Saturday. But you had two weeks' vacation coming. Maybe you forgot; you were on the list for September. I gave you a break by switching your dates so you started your vacation a week ago last Monday. You're still on your vacation right now and you're not due back for a few more days yet. Monday, to be exact. Here." Krieg yanked open a drawer of his desk and pulled out three checks. He held them across to Sweeney. "You probably don't remember but you came in to try to get your last check, only we didn't give it to you. It's there, two days short, and two full vacation week checks."

Sweeney took them wonderingly.

Krieg said, "Now get the hell out of here until Monday morning and report for work then."

"The hell," said Sweeney. "I don't believe it."

"Don't then. But—no bull, Sweeney—if it happens again before your next vacation, next year, you're through for good."

Sweeney nodded slowly. He stood up.

"Listen, Walter, I—"

"Shut up. Beat it."

Sweeney grinned weakly, and beat it.

He stopped at Joe Carey's desk and said "Hi," and Joe looked up and said, "Hi, yourself. What gives?"

"Want to talk to you, Joe. Had lunch yet?"

"No. Going in—" He looked at his wrist watch. "—in twenty minutes. But listen, Sweeney, if it's a bite you've got in mind, I'm broke as hell. Wife just had another kid last week and you know how that is."

"No," said Sweeney. "Thank God I don't know how that is. Congratulations, though. I presume it's a boy or a girl."

"Yeah."

"Good. Nope, it isn't a bite. Miraculously, I'm solvent. There is a God. In fact, do I owe you anything?"

"Five. Two weeks ago last Wednesday. Remember?"

"Vaguely, now that you mention it. So let's eat at Kirby's; I can cash a check there and pay you. I'll wander on down and meet you there."

Sweeney cashed the smallest of the three checks at the bar in Kirby's and then went over to a table to wait for Joe Carey. The thought of food still nauseated him; eating anything at all was going to be so bad he'd rather get it over with before Joe came in. Watching Joe eat was going to be bad enough.

Sweeney ordered a bowl of soup as the least of evils. It tasted like hot dishwater to him, but he managed to get most of it down and shoved the bowl aside as Joe came in and sat down across the table.

He said, "Here's your five, Joe, and thanks. Say, before I forget, who was it saw me over on State Street last night? I thought I didn't know either of the coppers I saw there."

"Harness bull by the name of Fleming. Pete Fleming."

"Oh," Sweeney said. "I remember now; I met him on Clark Street before that. Let's see—I was walking south on Clark so he must have been going north. I walked south a few more blocks, cut over east and walked north on State. But I didn't see him."

"Probably got there about as you were leaving. The car that answered the call—the cops in it were named Kravich and Guerney—cut in their siren on the way. Wherever Fleming was on his beat, he followed the siren and got there after they did. Thanks for the fin, Sweeney."

The waiter came up and Sweeney ordered coffee along with Carey's order.

Then he leaned across the table. He said, "Joe, what gives with this Ripper business? That's what I want to pump you about. I could dig up some of the dope from the morgue files, but you'll know more than they will. First, how long has it been going on?"

"You haven't read the papers for the last ten days?"

Sweeney shook his head. "Except for what was in one morning paper today, about the Yolanda Lang business last night. There were references to other killings. How many?"

"Besides Yolanda Lang, two—or it could be three. I mean, there was a slashing on the south side two months ago that might or might not be the same guy. Broad by the name of Lola Brent. There were similarities between her case and the three recent ones that make the police think maybe it ties in, but they aren't sure. There are differences, too."

"She die?"

"Sure. So did the two other dames besides this Lang woman. She's the only one who didn't get killed. Pooch saved her. But you know about that."

"What's the last word on Yolanda Lang?" Sweeney asked. "She still in the hospital?"

"Supposed to be released this evening. She wasn't hurt much. Point of the shiv just barely went through the skin. She had a spot of shock; that's all."

"So did some other people," said Sweeney. "Including me."

Joe Carey licked his lips. "You didn't exaggerate that story any, Sweeney?"

Sweeney chuckled. "I underplayed it. You should have been there, Joe."

"I'm a married man. Anyway, the cops are going to keep a guard on the Lang femme."

"A *guard*? Why?"

"They figure the killer might be inclined to go back after her because he might think she could put the finger on him. Matter of fact, she can't, or says she can't. A man, tallish, in dark clothes is the best she can do."

"The light was off in the hallway," Sweeney said.

"The Ripper's waiting by the back door, at the foot of the stairs, probably standing outside it, holding it a little ajar. He hears her footsteps clicking along the hallway, steps inside and slashes. Only the pooch jumps past her after the guy and he jerks back through the door, almost missing the woman completely with the shiv and just barely gets away from the dog."

"It adds up," Sweeney said. "He'd be able to see her silhouetted against the light from outside through the front door, but he'd just be a shadow to her. The point is, was he after Yolanda Lang or was he just waiting for whoever came along?"

Carey shrugged. "Could be either way. I mean, she lived there and he could have been waiting for her because she was coming home after her last show. On the other hand, if he knew much about her, he knew the pooch would be along and it looks like he didn't figure on that. He could have, though. Known, I mean, the dog would walk behind her in the hallway and figure he could slash and get back out the door before the dog got him. But, if that was it, he missed his timing."

"She get home that time every night?"

"Every week night. She's on last at one-thirty week nights. They have shows later on Saturday and Sunday nights. She doesn't always go right home after the last show, though, she said. Sometimes stays around El Madhouse—that's the night club she's playing—know it?"

Sweeney nodded.

"—sometimes stays around for drinks or what not till they close at three. Or sometimes has dates and goes out after the show. A dame like that wouldn't be lonesome except when she wanted to be."

"Who's handling it—outside, I mean."

"Horlick, only he starts vacation Monday. I don't know who Wally will put on after that."

Sweeney grinned. "Listen, Joe, do me a hell of a big favor, will you? I *want* to work on it. I can't very well suggest it to Krieg, but you can, next time you talk to him. Suggest I got an inside start with that eyewitness business and since Horlick's leaving Monday and I'm coming back then, why not let me do the leg work. He'll fall for it if you suggest it. If I ask him— well, he might not let me, just to be cussed."

"Sure, I can do that, Sweeney. But—you'll have to bone up on the details on the other cases, and get in with the cops. They got a special Ripper detail, by the way, working on nothing else. Cap Bline of Homicide's running it and got men under him. And the crime lab's analyzing everything they can get their hands on, only there hasn't been much to analyze."

"I'll be up on it," Sweeney said. "Between now and Monday I'll study those files and get in with the cops."

"Why? On your own time, I mean. You got an angle, Sweeney?"

"Sure," Sweeney lied. "Got the assignment from a fact detective mag to write up the case, once it's solved. They don't handle unsolved cases, but it's promised to me once the case is cracked. Ought to get a few hundred out of it. Joe, if you talk Krieg into giving me the case, so I'll have all the facts ready to write once they get the guy, I'll cut you in for ten percent. Ought to get you somewhere between twenty and fifty."

"What have I got to lose? Sure, I was going to do it for nothing."

"But now you'll be convincing," Sweeney said. "For a start, what are the names of the other dames who were slashed, the ones who died? You said the one on the south side a couple months ago was Lola Brent?"

"Check. Ten days ago, Stella Gaylord. Five days ago, Dorothy Lee."

"Any of the others strip teasers or show girls?"

"First one, this Lola Brent, was an ex-chorine. Living with a short-con man named Sammy Cole. Cops figured he killed her, but they couldn't prove it and they couldn't crack him. So they threw the book at him on some fraud charges that came out, and he's still in clink. So if he did kill Lola, he didn't kill the others or make the try for Yolanda."

"What were the other two gals?"

"Stella Gaylord was a B-girl on West Madison Street. The Lee girl was a private secretary."

"How private? Kind that has to watch her periods as well as her commas?"

"I wouldn't know," Carey said. "That didn't come out. She worked for some executive with the Reiss Corporation. Don't remember his name. Anyway, he was in New York on a buying trip."

Joe Carey glanced up at the clock; he'd finished eating.

He said, "Look, Sweeney, those are the main points. I haven't got time to give you any more; I got to get back."

"Okay," Sweeney said. "What hospital is the Lang dame in?"

"Michael Reese, but you can't get in to see her. They got cops six deep in that corridor. Horlick tried to get in and couldn't."

"You don't know when she'll be back at El Madhouse?"

"Nope. Her manager could tell you. Guy by the name of Doc Greene."

"What's the dope on him?"

"Listen, Sweeney, I got to get back. Ask him what the dope on him is."

Carey stood up. Sweeney reached for his check and got it. "I'm paying this. But tell me where I can locate this Greene character. What's his first name?"

"Dunno. Everybody calls him Doc. But wait—he's in the Goodman Block. Greene with a final e. You can find him from that. Or through the El Madhouse proprietor. He books all their acts, I think. So long."

Sweeney took a sip of his coffee, which he'd forgotten to drink, and it was cold. He shuddered with revulsion at the taste of it, and got out of Kirby's quick.

He stood in front a moment, hesitating which way to go, then headed back for the *Blade*. He didn't go to the editorial offices this time, though. He cashed his two other pay checks at the cashier's window and then went to the stack room. He looked through papers of about two months before until he found the one that broke the story on the murder of Lola Brent. He bought that one and all the finals for a week following, and he bought finals for each of the past ten days.

It made quite a stack of papers, even when he'd thrown the stuffing out of the Sunday ones. He caught a cab to take them home.

On the way in, he knocked on Mrs. Randall's door; he paid her the thirty-six dollars he owed her, and paid for two weeks in advance.

Upstairs in his room, he put the pile of papers on his bed,

and then, outside in the hall, he looked up Greenes until he found one in the Goodman Block. J. J. Greene, *thtrcl.agt*. He called the number and, after brief argument with a secretary, got J. J. Greene.

"Sweeney, of the *Blade*," he said. "Could you tell me when your client is being released from Michael Reese?"

"Sorry, Mr. Sweeney, the police have asked me not to give out any information. You'll have to get it from them. Say, are you the reporter who wrote that eyewitness story in today's *Blade*?"

"Yes."

"Nice story. And swell publicity for Yolanda. Too bad she's on the dotted line for three more weeks at El Madhouse, or I could get her on for bigger dough."

"She'll be back dancing in less than three weeks, then?"

"Off the record, nearer three days. It was just a nick."

"Could I drop around and talk to you, Mr. Greene? At your office."

"What about? The police told me not to talk to reporters."

"Not even pass the time of day if you met one on the street? I never saw an agent yet that wouldn't talk to reporters. Maybe I even want to give some of your other clients public-city, and what could the cops find wrong with that? Or have they got something on you?"

Greene chuckled. "I wouldn't invite you here if the cops say no. But I'm leaving the office in about twenty minutes and I generally have a drink at one of the places I book. I have an idea that today I might stop in El Madhouse on my way north. In that case I'd be there in a little over half an hour. If you should happen to drop in—"

"I might just happen to," Sweeney said. "Thanks. Off the record, I take it Miss Lang still is at Michael Reese?"

"Yes. But you won't be able to see her there."

"Won't try it then," Sweeney said. "So long."

He hung up the receiver and wiped the sweat off his forehead with a handkerchief. He went back into his room and sat very quietly for five minutes or so. When he thought he could make it, he pushed himself up out of the chair and left.

The sun was very hot and he walked slowly. On State Street, he stopped in a florist's shop and ordered two dozen American Beauties sent to Yolanda Lang at the hospital. After that, he kept plodding steadily through the bright heat until he reached El Madhouse; on Clark near Grand.

There wasn't a uniformed doorman, with a persuasive voice, in front at this hour of the late afternoon; there wouldn't be until mid-evening, when the periodic floor shows were about to start. There were the posters though:

6 Acts 6
Yolanda Lang and Devil !
in
the Famous
Beauty and the Beast
Dance !

And, of course, there were photographs. Sweeney didn't stop to look at them. He walked from the blazing heat into the cool dimness of the outer bar, separated from the room with tables and the stage, where a cover charge topped higher prices.

He stopped inside, barely able at first to see, blinded by the transition from sunlight glare to neoned dimness. He blinked, and looked along the bar. Only three persons sat there. At the far end, a badly intoxicated man drooled over a too-sober blowzy blonde. Half a dozen stools away, a man sat alone, staring at his reflection in the dim blue mirror back of the bar, a bottle of beer and a glass in front of him. He sat there as though he was carved of stone. Sweeney felt pretty sure he wasn't Doc Greene.

Sweeney slid onto a stool at the end of the bar. The bartender came over.

"Greene been in?" Sweeney asked. "Doc Greene?"

"Not yet today." The bartender rubbed the clean bar with a dirty towel. "Sometimes comes in around this time, but today I dunno. With Yo in the hospital—"

"Yo," said Sweeney meditatively. "I like that. Gives everybody a southern accent. People turn to her at the bar and ask 'And what's Yo having to drink,' huh?"

"A good question," said the bartender. "What *is* yo having to drink?"

"Well," said Sweeney, and thought it over. He had to get some nourishment into him somehow, a little at a time, until his appetite came back and he could look at a full meal without flinching. "Beer with an egg in it, I guess."

The bartender moved away to get it, and Sweeney heard the door behind him open. He looked around.

A moon-faced man stood just inside the doorway. A wide but meaningless smile was on his face as he looked along the bar; starting at the far end. His eyes, through round thick-lensed glasses came to rest on Sweeney and the wide smile widened. His eyes, through the lenses, looked enormous.

Somehow, too, they managed to look both vacant and deadly. They looked like a reptile's eyes, magnified a hundredfold, and you expected a nictitating membrane to close across them.

Sweeney—the outside of Sweeney—didn't move, but something shuddered inside him. For almost the first time in his life he was hating a man at first sight. And fearing him a little, too. It was a strange combination of strange ingredients, for hatred—except in an abstract sort of way—was almost completely foreign to William Sweeney. Nor is fear a commonplace to one who seldom gives enough of a damn about anybody or anything to be afraid of him or it.

"Mr. Sweeney?" said the moon-faced man, more as a statement than a question.

Sweeney said, "Sit down, Doc."

He put his hands in his pockets, quickly, because he had a hunch the shakes were going to come back.

[4]

The moon-faced man slid onto the stool around the turn of the bar from Sweeney, so the two of them faced one another. He said, "That was an excellent story you wrote about—what happened last night, Mr. Sweeney."

Sweeney said, "I'm glad you liked it."

"I didn't say that I liked it," Greene said. "I said it was an excellent story. That is something else again."

"But definitely," said Sweeney. "In this particular case, wherein lies the difference?"

Doc Greene leaned his elbows on the bar and laced pudgy fingers together. He said, judiciously, "A man, Mr. Sweeney, might enjoy a bit of voluptuous description of a woman; in other cases he might not enjoy reading it. For example, if the woman was his wife."

"Is Yolanda Lang your wife?"

"No," said the moon-faced man. "I was merely, you will recall, giving that as an example. You've ordered something?"

Sweeney nodded, and Greene looked at the bartender and held up one finger. The man came with Sweeney's beer-and-egg and put a shot glass in front of Greene.

While the shot glass was being filled, Sweeney cautiously took a hand out of his pocket and rested the tips of his fingers against the front of the bar. Carefully, so the shaking wouldn't show, he began to walk his fingers up the front of the bar, over the edge, and toward the glass in front of him.

His eyes watched the ones that looked so huge through the thick spectacles. Greene's smile had gone away; now it came back, and he lifted his shot glass. "To your bad health, Mr. Sweeney."

Sweeney's fingers had closed around his own glass. He said, "To yours, Doc," and his hand was steady as he lifted the glass and took a sip. He put it back down and took his other hand out of his pocket. The shakes were gone.

He said, carefully, "Perhaps you would like to cause my health to deteriorate, Doc. If you want to try, it would be a pleasure to oblige."

The moon-faced man's smile got wider. "Of course not, Mr. Sweeney. When I became a man, I put away childish things, as the great bard says."

"The Bible," said Sweeney. "Not Shakespeare."

"Thank you, Mr. Sweeney. You are, as I feared when I read that story under your by-line, an intelligent man. And, as I guessed from your name, a stubborn Irishman. If I told you to—let us descend to the vernacular—if I told you to layoff Yolanda, it would just make you that much more stubborn."

He held up a finger for a refill of the shot glass. He said, "A threat of any sort would be silly. It would be equally useless to point out to you the futility of your trying to make my—ah—client. As you may have—indeed as you did—notice, Yolanda is not unattractive. It has been tried by experts."

"You flatter yourself, Doc."

"Perhaps. Perhaps not. We aren't discussing my relations with Yolanda."

Sweeney took another sip of his drink. He said, "It occurs to me to wonder. Just what are we discussing? I take it that you didn't meet me here to discuss publicity for any of your other—ah—clients. And you say yourself that threats would be as futile as pointing out to me the futility of what you seem convinced I have in mind. So why did you come here?"

"To meet you, Mr. Sweeney. The moment I read that story of yours I knew—I am something of a psychiatrist—that you were going to be a thorn in my side. There was an ineffable *something* about that story— So might Dante have written of Beatrice, so might Abelard have written of Heloise."

"And so," said Sweeney, "might Casanova have written of Guinevere, had they lived in the same century and had he ever seen her with her panties off." He grinned. "You know, Doc, I hate you so damn much I'm beginning to like you."

"Thank you," said Greene. "I feel the same about you;

each of us admires the other's capabilities, let us say. Or you will admire mine when you get to know me better."

"Already," said Sweeney, "I admire your line of patter. Immensely. The only thing I hate about you is your guts."

"And may the Ripper never expose them to the public gaze," Greene said. "Not that that seems likely, for thus far he has seemed to specialize in tenderer morsels." He smiled broadly. "Isn't civilization a marvelous thing, Mr. Sweeney? That two men can sit like this and insult one another, amicably but sincerely, and enjoy the conversation? If we followed the customs of a century or two ago, one of us would have struck the other across the face with the back of a hand before now, and one of us would be fated to die before the sun rises very far above tomorrow's horizon."

"A beautiful thought, Doc," Sweeney said. "I'd love it. But the authorities are fussy about such things. But back to Yolanda. Suppose you read correctly between the lines of my story. What are you going to do about it? Anything?"

"Of course. For one thing, I shall put every possible pitfall in your path. I shall warn Yolanda against you—not obviously, of course, but subtly. I'll make her think you're a fool. You are, you know."

"Yes," said Sweeney. "But she may discount the information, since it comes from a bastard. You are one, you know."

"Your intuition surprises me, Mr. Sweeney. As it happens, I really am, in the literal sense of the word. Quite possibly in the figurative sense also, but that is irrelevant. Or perhaps I should say that there is a strong probability that I was born of unwed parents; all I actually know is that I was brought up in an orphan asylum. I, myself, made me what I am today."

"Only you could have done it," Sweeney said.

"You gratify me. I didn't expect a compliment. But that was a digression. In addition to putting pitfalls in your path, I am going to help you."

Sweeney said, "Now you have me really worried."

The moon-faced man tented his fingers into a steeple. He said, "You intend to find the Ripper. It's natural that you'll try, first because you're a reporter, but second and more important—to you—you think it will give you an in with Yolanda. Trying will automatically bring you in contact with her—not as close a contact as you have in mind, maybe, but it will give you an excuse to meet her and talk to her. Also you think that if you do find the Ripper, you'll be a conquering hero and she'll fall into your arms in gratitude. Am I correct?"

"Keep talking," Sweeney said. "As if I need to suggest it."

"So. You've got two reasons for finding him. I've got two reasons for helping you. One—" He held up a fat finger. "—if you do find him, he might stick a knife in you. I think I'd like that. I hate your guts, too, Mr. Sweeney."

"Thank you kindly."

"Two—" Another finger joined the first. "—the police just might have something in thinking the killer will come back to finish the job on Yolanda. Despite the fact, and the newspapers' reporting of the fact, that Yo can't recognize him on a bet, he may decide to take a chance and play safe by killing her. That I would *not* like."

"That I can understand," Sweeney said. "Also I like it better than your first reason."

"And I don't think, Mr. Sweeney, that finding him will get you to first base with Yolanda. At least, I'll take a chance on that."

"Fine, Doc. One little thing, though. The police force of Chicago outnumbers me, considerably. Just out of curiosity, what makes you think that I, with my little slingshot, might do more than the whole blue army?"

"Because you're a crazy damn Irishman. Because you're a little fey; I suspected that from a sentence or two in your story, and I know it now. Because God loves fools and drunkards, and you're both.

"Also because, under the sodden surface, you've got a hell of a keen brain, Mr. Sweeney; another thing I suspected before and know now. And you've got a crazy warped streak in you that might take you places where the police wouldn't think to go. Like the simpleton who found the horse by thinking he was a horse and going where he'd go if he really were a horse. Not that I would compare you to a horse, Mr. Sweeney. At least not to all of a horse."

"Thank you. I am a horse's ass with a hell of a keen brain. Tell me more, he said eagerly."

"I think I could. I really *am* a psychiatrist, Mr. Sweeney, although not a practicing one. An unfortunate occurrence in what would have been my last year of internship got me kicked out on my ear. It occurred to me that satyriasis might be a logical prescription for nymphomania. We had a patient who was quite an advanced satyr, Mr. Sweeney, and I took the liberty of introducing him into the room of an enthusiastic nympholept and leaving them together for an extended period. My superiors were quite stuffy about it."

"I can understand that," Sweeney said.

"Ah, had they only known some of the other experiments I tried, which were *not* found out. But we digress."

"We do indeed," said Sweeney. "So you're going to help me find the Ripper. So go ahead and help."

Greene spread his hands. "It isn't much. I didn't mean that I have the killer's name and address in my notebook, ready to turn over to you. I merely meant that I'll gladly work with you, Mr. Sweeney; I'll give you such facts and data as I have. And, since you'll want to talk to Yolanda, I'll see that you do. You might have trouble doing even that, with the police on guard around her, as they will be."

He looked at his wrist watch. "Unfortunately, I haven't more time now. A business appointment. One must eat. Could you, Mr. Sweeney, meet me here tomorrow afternoon, about this same time?"

Sweeney frowned. He said, "I don't know. Maybe you're just wasting my time. Have you really got anything?"

"I've got Yolanda," Greene said. "She'll be released from the hospital by then. I'll bring her here with me. You'll be here, of course?"

"I'll be here, of course," said Sweeney.

"Good. We may be seeing quite a bit of one another. Let us, then, dispense with the amenities. Let us not say hypocritical good-byes. My two drinks were on you. Thank you for them, and the hell with you."

He walked out.

Sweeney took a deep breath. He let it out slowly.

The bartender strolled over. He said, "That'll be a dollar and a quarter. Don't you want your beer?"

"No. Pour it down the drain. But bring me a bromo and a shot."

"Sure. Mixed?"

"Not mixed."

He put two dollar bills on the bar. When the bartender came back, Sweeney said, "Quite a character, that Doc Greene."

"Yeah. Quite a character."

"What puzzles me about him is this," Sweeney said. "Those seemed to be his own teeth he was wearing; they weren't regular enough for false ones. How the hell could a guy like that keep his own teeth that long?"

The bartender chuckled. "Maybe it's them eyes of his. Like a hypnotist. I think a guy'd have to be pretty brave to take a poke at Doc. I'd rather not tangle with him. Funny, though, the way women go for him. You wouldn't think it."

"Including Yo?" Sweeney asked.

"I wouldn't know about Yo. She's a funny dame to figure out." He took Sweeney's bills and rang up a dollar eighty, putting two dimes on the bar.

Sweeney added a quarter to it and said, "Have one with me."

"Sure. Thanks."

"Skoal," said Sweeney. "Say, who's running El Madhouse now? Is it still Harry Yahn's?"

"Yahn owns it, or most of it, but he isn't running it. He's got another place over on Randolph."

"Sucker joint, like El Madhouse?"

The bartender smiled faintly. "Not this kind of sucker joint."

"Oh," said Sweeney. "It'd be a little bar with a big back room and if you know a guy named Joe at the door, you can leave your shirt in the back room."

The blowzy blonde at the far end of the bar was tapping the bottom of her glass on the wood impatiently. The bartender said, "The guy at the door is named Willie." He went down to mix a drink for the blonde.

Sweeney poured the bromo back and forth between the two glasses and drank it.

Then he got up and went out into gathering dusk on Clark Street. He walked south, toward the Loop. He walked slowly, aimlessly, trying to think and not quite succeeding. This stage of recovery he knew well. His mind was fuzzy, his thoughts were ghosts that walked in thick fog. But his physical senses were almost blindingly vivid; the honk of auto horns and the clangor of trolley bells were terribly loud; everything he saw was seen vividly and in sharp focus; odors ordinarily not noticed were nauseatingly strong.

He had to eat, and soon, to get his strength back. Only solid food in him would get rid of the fog, free him of the sensation of light-headedness and dissipate the physical weariness that was beginning to penetrate, it seemed, to the very marrow of his bones.

All that, and the throbbing headache, still with him.

He thought how very nice it would be to die, quietly and painlessly, without even knowing it was going to happen; just to go to sleep and never wake up. Sleep, too, could be good, but you always woke up to confusion and complication and the thousand little unpleasantnesses that periodically mount up to one vast unpleasantness from which only immersion in alcohol could bring surcease.

Only now, today, there wasn't that. The one drink he'd taken back at El Madhouse bar hadn't brought any desire for another one to keep it company. It hadn't either his mind or fogged it further. It hadn't even tasted good, or bad.

The bridge, when he reached it, was better. There was a cool breeze across it; he stood looking out over the river and letting the breeze blow into his face.

When he turned back, an empty taxi was coming. Sweeney hailed it, and gave his home address.

In his room, he slid the bottom newspaper out from under the stack on the bed and sat down in the Morris chair. He found the story of the first murder—the murder of the ex-chorine, Lola Brent. Six inches on page two, not much in the way of detail.

There hadn't been a Ripper, then. It was just a story of a woman—a not very important woman, at that—who had been found, dead, in the areaway between two buildings on Thirty-Eighth Street. A knife or a razor had been the weapon used. The crime had occurred in daylight, between four and five o'clock in the afternoon. There had been no witnesses. A child returning home from a playground had discovered the body. Police were seeking a man with whom Lola Brent was alleged to have been living.

Sweeney took up the next paper. The story had a little better play in that one, and there were two pictures. One was of Lola Brent. She was blonde, and beautiful. She didn't look the thirty-five years the story said she was; you'd have taken her for early twenties.

The other picture was that of the man the police had arrested, Sammy Cole. He had black, curly hair and a face that was handsome in the ruggedly honest way that is a conman's stock in trade. He denied killing Lola Brent, and was being held on an open charge.

The following day's story was a brief rehash; the only new angle was that Sammy Cole had confessed to several counts of operating a confidence game. The following several papers brought out nothing additional.

The Lola Brent crime had then, it appeared, faded into limbo, unsolved. There was nothing at all concerning it in the last two papers of the week's series starting two months before. There wouldn't, Sweeney knew, have been any mention of it—of importance—in the five and a half weeks' papers that he didn't have, the gap in between his first series and the series starting ten days ago.

He picked up the paper of ten days before and skimmed rapidly through the story of the murder of Stella Gaylord, the B-girl from Madison Street. He didn't try to memorize details here; he was going to concentrate on one crime at a time. He

was looking, now, only for further mention of the killing of
Lola Brent. He found it on the second day after the Stella
Gaylord murder; it was then first suggested that the crime
might be a psychopathic one, perpetrated by the same killer
who had slashed Lola Brent six and a half weeks before.

The next day's lead was a build-up of that idea, with a
comparative description of the wounds inflicted upon the two
women. Each had been killed by a horizontal slash across the
abdomen, but the weapon had not been the same one. The
knife that had killed Lola Brent had been no sharper than
average, but the blade that had slashed Stella Gaylord had
been razor keen.

Sweeney skimmed through the rest of the papers, looking, this time, only for additional details about the Lola Brent
case; one at a time was all his mind would handle and absorb
in its currently fuzzy condition. Apparently, no further dis-
coveries of importance had been made on the Brent case. The
police were still not too sure that the killer of Lola Brent was
the same homicidal maniac who had killed Stella Gaylord and
five days later, Dorothy Lee. But there wasn't any doubt about
the latter two having been killed by the same hand.

Sweeney put down the last—the most recent—of the
papers and tried to think. He now knew everything that had
been given out to the papers on the Brent murder, but none
of it seemed helpful. For that matter, what could be helpful-
short of a lucky guess—when you were hunting a killer who
killed without motive? Without motive, that is, applicable to
the particular victim and not to any woman who was blonde
and beautiful. Yes, there was that in common. The three who
had been killed, as well as Yolanda Lang, had all been blonde
and beautiful.

Sweeney went to the phone in the hall and dialed a number. When he got the man he wanted, he asked, "Sammy Cole,
the guy that Lola Brent was living with, still in the jug here in
Chicago?"

"Yeah," said the man to whom Sweeney was talking. I
won't mention his name because he's still holding down the
same job and doing right well at it, and this would get him in

trouble. Sweeney, you see, had something on him, and reporters aren't supposed to have anything on important public officials. They often do.

He said, "Yeah, we're still holding him. We could have salted him away before this, but returns are still coming in. Every once in a while we tie him in to a fraud charge and get it off the books."

"I'd like to talk to him," Sweeney said. "Tonight."

"Tonight? Look, Sweeney, can't you wait till regular hours tomorrow? It's after seven o'clock and—"

"You can fix it," Sweeney said. "I'll grab a taxi and be there quick."

That is how, within half an hour, Sweeney was sitting on the warden's desk and Sammy Cole sat on a straight chair a few feet away from him. They were alone in the office. Sammy Cole was recognizable from the newspaper picture of him Sweeney had seen shortly before, but barely recognizable. He still had black hair but it was cut too short to be curly. His face was ruggedly sullen instead of ruggedly honest.

"I told 'em," Sammy Cole said. "I told 'em every Goddam thing. I spilled my guts because *I'd* like to see whoever bumped Lola take the hot squat. There was the off chance it did tie in with something she'd been doing, see? So I spilled my guts and what does it get me? Enough raps so when I get out, *if* I get out, I'll be peddling pencils."

"Tough," Sweeney said. An envelope and a pencil came out of his pockets and he wrote "Want a drink?" on the back of the envelope and showed it to Sammy Cole.

"Jesus," said Sammy Cole, not at all irreverently. It would have been ambiguous to anyone listening in on a bug, but Sweeney took the half pint bottle, still two-thirds full that he'd bought earlier at the drugstore out of his hip pocket and handed it to Sammy Cole. Sammy Cole handed it back empty and wiped his lips with the back of his hand. He said, "What you want to know?"

"I don't know," Sweeney told him. "That's the trouble; I don't know. But I got to start somewhere. When'd you see Lola last?"

"That morning—almost noon, I guess—when she went to work."

"To work? Were you that far down, Sammy?"

"Well—yeah and no. I was working on something that would have come through big. I was tired of hand-to-mouthing on the short-con stuff. What I was doing would have got us Florida for the winter, and a real stake. Laugh it off, but I was going to turn straight. For Lola. She didn't like the grifts. So she was keeping us eating while my deal came through."

"Was she tied in on the big deal?"

"No. That was strictly me. But we worked out a little racket for her that brought in peanuts. A hundred or so a week for a few days' work. That's what she was on that day."

"Where? What was it?"

Sammy Cole wiped his lips again and bent sidewise to look questioningly in the direction of Sweeney's hip pocket. Sweeney shook his head and spread his hands.

Sammy Cole sighed. He said, "A gift shop on Division Street. Raoul's Gift Shop. That was her first day there, so I dunno much about it except what she told me, from applying for the job the day before, and what little I saw when I dropped in at six. That was part of the racket. This Raoul is a faggot."

"How would that tie in with a racket for Lola, Sammy? Unless you came in later?"

"Naw, nothing like that. I just mentioned it. All there was to the racket was Lola'd get a job selling stuff somewhere, preferably a place where she'd make a few big sales, not dime store stuff. Small store, usually, where she'd be alone when the boss went out to eat or something and left her alone a little. She'd drag down on some sales—ten bucks, fifty bucks, whatever the traffic would bear. We played extra safe because she wasn't on the blotter and I wanted to keep her off. I'd drop in later at a time we'd set and she'd slip me the moolah. She never had it on her for more'n a few minutes; she'd stash it somewhere after she dragged it down and get it just a minute before I was due to come in. It was safe as houses. Soon as she saw a mooch beginning to look suspicious at her, she'd do a fadeout; never worked anywhere longer'n a few days. Then she'd layoff a while and—well, you got the picture."

Sweeney nodded. "And she got the job at Raoul's the day before. How?"

"Newspaper ad. We had good references for her; that was my department. Job was in the morning papers. She got it in the afternoon and was to start at noon the next day. They're open till nine in the evening and she was to work noon to nine, lunch hour four to five."

"How come you didn't just arrange to meet her outside, during lunch hour?"

Sammy Cole looked at Sweeney contemptuously. "Lookit the angles," he said. "First, she'd have to walk out with the moolah on her, and that's taking a chance. Second, if he sends her out four to five, then the pansy's taking off at five, probably. Her best time to do a little business, on her own, would be from five to six, and I get there at six. If the pansy's still gone, good; if he's there she can still slip it to me. I buy something for two bits and she slips the dough in the paper bag with it. It's safe as houses."

"And you got there at six?"

"Sure. She wasn't there, and I figured something was on the off beat. I phoned the flat and a cop answered so I hung up quick and stayed away. Not that I guessed what had happened—whatever the hell *did* happen. But I figured she'd got caught on a larceny rap and I'd be better off on the outside, to try to get her out of it. Hell, I was nuts about the dame. I'd have raised some moolah somehow to get her a shyster and bail her out. I'd've knocked a guy over if I had to, to get her out. And they still think maybe I killed her. Jesus."

"When'd you find out what really happened?"

"Morning papers. I'd holed in a hotel. I near went nuts. All I could think about was getting the son of a bitch that did it and chopping him up into hamburger, slow. But I didn't know how to go looking for him without walking into cops, and I wasn't going to be able to do a Goddam thing if I did that. So all I could figure was to keep under cover till the heat was off. But I guess I was too upset to be careful enough. They got me, and by the time I get outta here, the guy'll be dead of old age.

"So, Jesus God how I hate a cop, but just the same I did all I could for 'em. I spilled my guts to 'em, just on the off chance something we'd been doing would give 'em a lead."

Sammy Cole slumped tiredly down in the chair and sighed. He looked up and asked, "Got a fag?"

Sweeney handed him a package of cigarettes and a book of matches and said, "Keep them. Look, Sammy, if you hadn't been picked up, what would you have done when the heat was off? Where'd you have started?"

"With the faggot. Raoul. Maybe he had something to do with it and maybe he didn't, but I'd have picked his petals off one at a time till I was sure."

"What happened at the gift shop? Did he catch her dragging down on a sale, or what? He must have fired her if she went home, and she was found in the areaway outside your flat."

Sammy Cole said, "That I wouldn't know. The cops ask me questions; they don't tell me. All I know is what's in the papers and they don't give me any papers. You can get papers —and stuff—in stir, if you got money. But I'm broke flat."

Sweeney nodded and took a ten-dollar bill out of his wallet and handed it across. He said, "You get no dough out of me, pal, if you were hinting. Say, would Lola maybe have put the bite on some merchandise? Rings or something? Some gifts shops have lots of small stuff that's valuable."

Sammy Cole shook his head definitely. He said, "That I'll guarantee; she didn't. I drummed that into her. Too many angles, too easy to get caught, too easy to have stuff traced back to you, and too hard to get more'n a twentieth of what the stuff's worth anyway. Not even a ring or a pair of earrings for herself; I drummed that into her."

"What was the long-con you were working on? Could that have tied in?"

"Nope, it couldn't. I didn't spill that because I was working with a guy, and I wouldn't rat on him. The cops couldn't rubber-hose it out of me because I'm no stoolie. And anyway, it *couldn't* have tied in with what happened to Lola because neither the guy I was working with or the guy we were working on knew her or knew she was alive and she didn't know them or much about them. I mean, I'd told her what the game was, but not the details or the names. See?"

"Okay, Sammy. Thanks," Sweeney said. "I can't do you any good, I guess, but I'll keep you posted. So long."

He surprised the conman by shaking hands with him and went out of the warden's office, nodding to the turnkey who'd been standing outside the door.

A clock in the outer corridor told him it was eight-fifteen, and he stood in front of the Jail, watching both ways, until a cab came along and he hailed it.

"Division Street," he said. "We'll have to look up the address on the way north; I forgot to get it. It's a gift shop named Raoul's."

The taxi driver laughed. He said "I know the joint. The guy tried to make me once. He's a queer. Say, you ain't—" he looked around at Sweeney.

He said, "No, you ain't," and turned back to the wheel.

[5]

Sweeney stood looking into the window of Raoul's gift shop. Presumably he was staring at the array of merchandise in the display; mostly he was watching over the low partition at the back of the window. Two customers, both women, were within. With Raoul, the proprietor, that made the feminine complement of the shop one hundred percent. No one would ever have to wonder about Raoul.

Sweeney studied the window and saw that it was not, in the fashion of many gift shops, cluttered with junky bric-a-brac and cheap miscellany. The items displayed were few, and good. There were foo dogs from China, thunderbirds from

Mexico, costume jewelry that was in good taste if a bit blatant, a pair of brass candlesticks of exquisitely simple design; there wasn't a single thing in the window that Sweeney could have taken exception to—except possibly the prices, and they weren't shown. His opinion of Raoul went up several notches.

One of the women inside made a purchase and came out. The other was obviously browsing and Raoul, after apparently offering to help her, relaxed gracefully against the counter.

Sweeney went inside. The proprietor, smiling a proprietary smile, came forward to meet him. The smile turned to a slight frown when Sweeney said, "From the *Blade*. Like to talk to you about Lola Brent," but he walked with Sweeney to the back of the shop, out of earshot of the remaining customer.

Sweeney asked, "She got the job when? The day before?"

"Yes. Several came in answer to an advertisement I put in the paper. Your paper, the Blade. She had excellent references from a gift shop in New York; I didn't guess they were fraudulent. She was well dressed, had a pleasing personality. And she was free, ready to start work at once. I told her to come in the next day."

"And she did, at noon?"

"Yes."

"And what happened? You caught her dragging down on a sale and fired her?"

"Not exactly. I explained it all to the police."

Sweeney said, "I could get it direct from them, but I'd rather not. If you don't mind too much."

Raoul sighed. He said, "From twelve until a little after three we were both in the store. There weren't many customers and I spent most of the time acquainting her with the stock, the prices, telling her things she should know about the business. At about a quarter after three I had to leave for a short while, on a personal matter. I was gone a little over half an hour. When I returned I asked what business she'd done while I was gone and she told me that only one customer had been in the store and that he had bought a pair of six-dollar bookends. That was the only amount that had been rung up on the register. But then I noticed that something else was missing."

"What was it?"

"A figurine, a statuette, which had been priced at twenty-four dollars. It had stood on the shelf over there." Raoul pointed. "It just happened that that particular statuette had been standing a bit askew and I had straightened it shortly before I had left on my errand. Shortly after my return, I chanced to notice that it was no longer there. There had been three figures on that shelf, and now there were only two, with the two moved closer together to avert leaving a conspicuous gap between them. So I asked Miss Brent if she had moved the statuette and she denied knowledge of it."

He sighed gently. "It was embarrassing, of course. I knew she could not be telling the truth, because—just as it happened—I was certain it had been there when I left."

"It couldn't have been shoplifted?"

"Hardly possible. The figure was ten inches high and, although slender, the arms of the figure were extended forward; it would have been a difficult object to conceal under a coat, and it would not have gone into a pocket at all. It was not the sort of object that is chosen by shoplifters, I assure you. Besides, Miss Brent had told me that only one person had been in the store. There was no doubt in my mind at all, Mr.—ah—"

"Sweeney. You accused her of having sold it and kept the dough?"

"What else could I do? I told her that I had no desire to prosecute, and that if she would permit me to search her thoroughly back in the stock room, I would permit her to go, without calling the police."

"You found the money on her?"

"No. When she saw that I really meant to call the police unless she confessed and really meant to let her go if she did she admitted the theft. She had the money, a twenty-dollar bill and four ones, in the top of her stocking. A woman's repository."

"Then you didn't have to search her. Or did you?"

"Of course I did. I had missed that particular item and

she had confessed selling it, but—since she was admittedly dishonest—how did I know that that was the only item she had sold beside the bookends? I couldn't inventory the stock. She might also have made, let us say, a fifty-dollar sale of costume jewelry and concealed the money in her other stocking or in her brassiere or somewhere."

"Had she?"

"No. At least I found no money except a few dollars in her purse which I was willing to believe was her own property. She was—ah—a little sullen about being searched, but she was reasonable when she saw my reason for insisting. Also she was not sufficiently naive to think that I wished to do so for any ulterior motive, if you understand what I mean."

"I understand what you mean," said Sweeney.

"So it would have been about four o'clock when she left?"

"Yes. Not later than fifteen minutes after four. I did not notice the time exactly."

"She left alone?"

"Of course. And to anticipate your next question, I did not notice whether she met anyone outside. Naturally, knowing her to be dishonest, I kept my eyes on her as far as the door, but not beyond. I did not notice which direction she went. But of course she must have gone directly to her home, because I understand she was found dead in the areaway there at five o'clock. She would have had to transfer to get there, and go through the Loop; it would have taken at least half an hour from here, possibly longer."

Unless she took a cab or someone gave her a lift."

"Of course. The taxi is not too likely, judging from the small amount of money she had in her purse."

Sweeney nodded. "Being picked up isn't too likely either. Her man was to meet her here in the store at six but he'd hardly have been around the neighborhood as early as four-fifteen."

Raoul's eyebrows rose a little. "He was to meet her here?"

"Yeah. To pick up whatever she'd dragged down by then."

"Indeed? The police didn't tell me that."

Sweeney grinned. "The police don't go out of their way to

tell people things. That's why I wanted to talk to you about this instead of to them. Did Lola Brent, by the way, seem to recognize anybody who did come in that afternoon, while you were here?"

"No. I'm reasonably sure she didn't."

"What was the statuette? A woman's figure, I take it, but with or without clothes?"

"Without. Very definitely without, if you understand what I mean."

"I guess I do," Sweeney said. "Even some women, let alone statues, manage to be nakeder without clothes than others do. It's a gift."

Raoul raised his hands expressively. "I do not mean to imply, Mr. Sweeney, that the statuette was in any sense of the word pornographic or suggestive. It was, rather, quite virginal—in a very peculiar way."

"You intrigue me," said Sweeney. "How many ways of being virginal are there? I thought I knew everything, but—"

Raoul smiled. "There are many ways of expressing a single quality. Of, as it were, getting it across. Virginity, in this case, is expressed through fear, horror, loathing. Virginity—or perhaps I should say virginality—"

"What's the difference?" Sweeney asked, and then answered himself, "Wait, I think I get you. One is physical and the other is mental. Right?"

"Of course. They may or may not coincide. Many married women are virginal, although they are not virgins. They have never really been touched; the physical act alone— And then again, a maiden who is *virgo intactas* may be far from virginal if her thoughts—ah—you see what I mean?"

"I do," Sweeney said. "But we wander from the statuette."

"Not far. Would you care to see the statuette? Not the one Miss Brent sold, of course, but a duplicate of it. I ordered two and liked them so well that I have one in my apartment in the next block. It's closing time now and—I assure you I have no ulterior motive Mr. Sweeney"

"Thanks," said Sweeney. "But I don't believe it's necessary. The statuette itself could hardly have anything to do with the crime."

"Of course not. I merely thought it would interest you abstractly." He smiled. "It is, incidentally, known as a Screaming Mimi."

"A what?"

"A Screaming Mimi. Girl's name—M-i-m-i. A rather obvious pun, of course, on the screaming meamies, if you know what they are."

"Intimately," said Sweeney. "And, if I may, I'm going to change my mind; I would like to meet this Mimi Mr.— Is Raoul your last name?"

"Reynarde, Mr. Sweeney, Raoul Reynarde. If you'll pardon me just a moment—"

He walked over to the remaining customer to tell her it was closing time. Sweeney followed her to the door and waited there until Reynarde had turned out the lights. They walked a block and a half east on Division Street and up two flights of stairs to the apartment.

"I can't ask you to stay long, Mr. Sweeney," Reynarde said, as he flicked on the light inside the door. "I—ah—have a guest coming. But we'll have time for a drink. May I make you a highball?"

"Sure, thanks," said Sweeney "But where is Mimi?"

"On the mantel yonder."

Sweeney's gaze, which had been roaming about the beautifully furnished—if a bit feminine—apartment to rest on a ten-inch-high statuette over the fireplace. He crossed the room and stood looking at it.

He saw now what Reynarde had meant. Definitely there was a virginal quality about the slim nude figure, but that you saw afterward. "Fear, horror, loathing," Reynarde had said, and all of that was there, not only in the face but in the twisted rigidity of the body. The mouth was wide open in a soundless scream. The arms were thrust out, palms forward, to hold off some approaching horror.

"An exquisite thing," said Reynarde's voice from across the room, where he poured drinks at a little mahogany cabinet that was complete down to an ice-cube unit. It is made of a new plastic that can't be told from ebony, unless you pick it up. The dull gloss is the same as ebony's, to the eye. If that figure were what it looks to be, hand-carved ebony, and original, it would be worth a lot of money. He waved a hand around the room. "Most things you see here *are* originals. I prefer them."

Sweeney grunted. "I don't agree with you there. I'd rather any day have a Renoir print than an art school original. But that's a matter of taste. Could you get me one of these?"

Reynarde's voice came from just behind Sweeney. "Your drink, Mr. Sweeney. Yes, I can get you a Screaming Mimi, or I think I can. The company that makes them—a small concern in Louisville, Kentucky, of all places—may possibly have some left. They generally make a few hundred of an item like that. But if you really want it, I may sell you that one. Although it has been on my mantel, it is still virginal."

He laughed. "Or I can, if you think that makes it second hand return it to the store and sell it to you from there. One advantage of being a dealer, Mr. Sweeney; I need never grow tired of an art object or bit of bric-a-brac. Often I keep objects from the store here until I tire of them and then exchange them for others. I think that I am growing a little weary of the little lady by now. Your health, sir."

Sweeney drank absent-mindedly, without taking his eyes off the statuette, emptying the glass at a single draught. He said, "Before you change your mind, Mr. Reynarde—" He put his glass down on the mantel and counted twenty-four dollars out of his wallet.

"How," he asked, "did it get named? Is that your name for it, or the company's?"

Reynarde pursed his lips. "I don't believe I re— Oh, yes. The name came from the company that made it, but unofficially, as it were. The salesman told me that the catalogue code number for it is SM-1, and someone in their office with a sense of humor decided the SM stood for Screaming Mimi."

"Who did the statuette? The original, I mean."

"That I do not know. The company is the Ganslen Art Company. They make mostly bookends and chess sets, but they do some work in small statuary, often surprisingly good at the price. Shall I wrap the figure for you?"

Sweeney chuckled. "Put pants on Mimi? Never. I'll carry her naked through the streets."

"Another drink, Mr. Sweeney?"

"Thanks, no. I think Mimi and I must be going." He picked up the statuette gently.

Reynarde said, "Sit down, Mr. Sweeney," and himself sank into an overstuffed chair, although Sweeney remained standing. He said, "Something interests me, Mr. Sweeney, despite the fact that it is none of my business at all. Are you a sadist?"

"Me?"

"You. I am curious because of the appeal that statuette has for you. The thing is an orgy of masochism; it would appeal, in my opinion, only to a sadist."

Sweeney looked at him thoughtfully. He said, "No, I'm not a sadist. I can see your point about the appeal of the figure; I don't know the answer. The instant I saw it I knew I wanted to own it, but I haven't the slightest idea why."

"Its appeal as an object of art?"

"No, not that it's well done, cleverly executed, but it isn't great art."

Reynarde pursed his lips. "Perhaps some subcon-scious association?"

"It could be," Sweeney said. "At any rate, thank you and I must be going."

Reynarde walked to the door with him and bowed slightly as they parted.

As the door closed behind him, Sweeney wondered why he *had* wanted the statuette. And why, in particular, he had resented Raoul Reynarde's probing into his reason for wanting it. He looked at the statuette in his hand, and shivered a little—mentally if not physically. It was neither pretty nor sensuous. Damn it, Reynarde was right; it would appeal only to a sadist, or to someone who had *some* abnormality in him. And yet he, Sweeney, had paid over twenty-four dollars of good money to take it home with him.

Was he punch-drunk?

No, he wasn't. The fog inside his head was lifting, definitely. And through the fog, he almost had a glimpse of something that might have been the association Reynarde had suggested. Then the fog came down again.

Well, it would come back. Sweeney sighed and started for the stairway. Coming up the stairs was a plump, beautiful young man with blond curly hair. They passed in the hallway, and the young man looked curiously at the statuette Sweeney was carrying but made no comment. He rang the bell of Reynarde's apartment.

Sweeney went on down the stairs.

Outside, and the dark night was bright with lights, the air hot and humid. Sweeney walked west on Division Street and then south on Dearborn.

He wondered how long he could keep going like this; how long he would *have* to keep going before he could eat and then sleep. The nausea was back with him now. Food was a disgusting thought, but it was a hurdle to be taken a hurdle that *had* to be taken.

Eventually.

At Chicago Avenue he turned half a block west and went into a small clean restaurant and sat down at the counter. A man in a white apron that made Sweeney think of a surgeon came up on the other side of the counter and stood there. He stood there staring at the black statuette Sweeney had placed on the counter in front of him.

"Mimi," Sweeney said, "meet Joe. Joe, meet Mimi. Or *is* your name Joe, Joe?"

The counterman grinned uncertainly. He said, "It's close. Jack. What's wrong with the little lady?"

"She is screaming," Sweeney said. He felt as though he wanted to himself. "Jack, could you get me a very special dinner?"

"Such as what? If we got what it takes, we can make it."

"Bread," said Sweeney. Two slices of white bread plain, without butter. Not too fresh, but not really stale. With the crusts left on. On a white plate. I think maybe I could eat that.

The bread, I mean not the plate. Can you do it?"

"I'll ask the cook. Coffee, too?"

"Black," said Sweeney. "In a cup."

He closed his eyes and tried to concentrate on something to keep from thinking about the smells of the restaurant but all he succeeded in doing was concentrating on the smells. When plate and cup rattled on the counter in front of him, he opened his eyes.

He took a sip of the scalding coffee and then began to nibble on one of the slices of bread. It was all right; it would go down and stay down.

He was almost through with the second slice when the waiter came back. He stood leaning against the ledge, looking at the statuette. He said, "That thing sort of gets you, when you look at it. It gives you the willies. Where'd you get it?"

"From a fairy," Sweeney said. "How much do I owe you?"

"About fifteen cents. Say, know what that statue makes me think of? The Ripper."

Sweeney almost dropped his cup of coffee; he put it down carefully.

The waiter hadn't noticed. He said, "I mean, a woman being attacked by the Ripper. No dame is that afraid of being raped or something. But a crazy guy with a knife in his hand coming after her—and she's backed in a corner maybe—"

Sweeney got up slowly. He fumbled a five-dollar bill out of his wallet and put it down on the counter. He said, "Keep the change, Jack." He grabbed Mimi firmly about the waist and went out.

Again an automobile almost ran him down as he cut diagonally across Chicago Avenue.

The fog was gone. He knew now what his hunch had been and why he'd wanted the Screaming Mimi. He should have got it when Reynarde had said the figure would appeal to a sadist; he *would* have got it then if his mind had been clear.

But it was clear as gin now. An hour or two before she'd been killed, Lola Brent had sold a Screaming Mimi. The fact that she'd dragged down on the sale had nothing to do with her death, but the fact that she'd *made* that sale had. The purchaser had been an insane sadist who had waited outside and followed her home. It had been a break for him that she'd been fired and had gone straight home, where he could close up on her in the seclusion of the area-way. Would he have tried to kill her anyway, during her lunch hour, if she'd stayed on the job?

His mind was clear now, but his body felt like hell. He walked faster. He could sleep now, and he *had* to sleep. He had to get home before he fell down.

[6]

In the morning, it was Friday. It was almost Friday noon. Sweeney awoke and lay a while in bed, and then swung his feet out onto the floor and sat there a while. His head didn't ache. Outside of that he couldn't have found much to say for himself. The room seemed to be filled with an invisible fog. But he got his eyes focused on the clock and saw that it was eleven-forty. He'd slept about twelve hours.

On top of the radio-phono, on the half that didn't lift up, stood a little ten-inch-high black statuette. It was the figure of a naked girl, her arms thrust out to ward off a ripper, her mouth open in a silent, eternal scream. Her body, which would have been beautiful relaxed, was subtly distorted, rigid with terror. Only a sadist could have liked it. Sweeney wasn't one; he shuddered a little and averted his eyes.

But it woke him up, seeing the Screaming Mimi. It woke him up to nightmare.

It made him want a drink; it made him think nostalgically of the sodden state of nonthinking in which he'd been only two days ago—a day and a half ago. It made him wish he was back there again.

And why not? He had plenty of money. Why not go out, right now, and have a drink and another?

Heat in waves came in at the open window. His body was

wet with sweat. He was breathing hard.

He stood up, making an unconscious gesture of pushing back the heat and the fog, and got a bathrobe out of the closet. He went down the hall to the bathroom and sat on the edge of the tub while it filled with cool water. Almost cold water.

Getting into it woke him. He took a deep breath and sank down into it, clear to his neck, letting the coldness of it draw the heat from his body and feeling the mist clear from his mind.

Warmth, he thought, is what man wants, what he lives for, what he works for, until he gets too much of it—and then coldness is a wonderful and refreshing thing. The thought of lying in an ever-cold grave, for instance, is a horrible thing in winter; in summer—

But that was maudlin. Like thinking of Lola Brent, the ex-chorine who had loved a con-man so much she'd taken to the grift herself, to help him. And she'd sold a small black statuette to a man who'd looked from it to her—

Sweeney swore. What did it matter, to him, that a fading ex-pony was six feet under, now? She'd have been there sooner or later anyway; five years from now, fifty years. Death is an incurable disease that men and women are born with; it gets them sooner or later. A murderer never really kills; he but anticipates. Always he kills one who is already dying, already doomed.

Actually, he never hurts the one he kills. The hurt is to whoever loved him or her, and has to keep on living. The man who'd killed Lola Brent had hurt Sammy Cole more than he'd hurt Lola.

If he, Sweeney, really came to hate Doc Greene and wanted to hurt him badly—

He sat up in the tub. What if—?

But no, that was silly. Sure, someone could have hated Doc Greene enough to want to get at him by killing Yolanda— but that left the other murders out of it; Lola Brent, Stella Gaylord, Dorothy Lee. A human being (a *sane* human being; but then, what is sanity?) couldn't conceivably hate four men enough to kill the women they loved.

And besides, it left out sadism and Mimi, and the Screaming Mimi was the key.

He didn't put his shoulders back down into the water; he got out of the tub instead and toweled himself off.

As he finished, he watched the last of the water gurgle out of the tub, and he wondered—had he just committed a murder? Isn't a tub of water, once drawn, an entity? A thing-in-itself that has existence, if not life? But then life, in a human body, may be analogous to water in a tub; through the sewerage of veins and arteries may it not flow back into some Lake Michigan, eventually into some ocean, when the plug is pulled? Yet even so, it is murder; that particular tub of water will never exist again, though the water itself will.

He removed the evidence of the crime by rinsing out the tub, and went back to his room. He put on a pair of shorts and a pair of socks. That would be enough until he was ready to go out, in that heat.

What was next? Stella Gaylord, B-girl on Madison Street. He might as well take it chronologically. The murder of Lola Brent had been two months ago; the second murder, that of Stella Gaylord, had been ten days ago.

He put the stack of old newspapers on the chair, where he could reach it from the bed, and propped the pillow up against the footboard.

Why not music? he thought. It always helped him concentrate; he could, for some strange reason, better remember what he read if he read it against a background of music. It was more vivid that way. The use of music was one thing the movie makers had discovered.

He studied the shelf of albums, wondering what would go well with the murder of a B-girl. Something vast and mysterious, perhaps. His hand hesitated at *Sacre du Printemps* and moved on. Strauss' *Death and Transfiguration*? The *Pathetique*? No, very beautiful but too corny. His hand went back to *Death and Transfiguration*. He put the records on and started the machine, then lay down on the bed and picked up the first paper, the one of ten days ago, that broke the Gaylord murder story.

It was on page one, but in the bottom right comer, six inches of type under a one-column head:

BODY OF GIRL
SLAIN WITH KNIFE
IS FOUND IN ALLEY

Sweeney read the six inches of type and decided that, as far as really important details were concerned, they might as well have let the headline stand alone.

Oh, there was the woman's name and address—on West Madison Street—and the place where the murder had occurred—the mouth of an alley off Huron Street between State and Dearborn. The body had been discovered at three-thirty in the morning and, according to the physician who had examined the body, the woman had been dead less than an hour.

Apparently there had been no robbery committed and— to Sweeney's amazed amusement—the story stated that the victim had not been attacked.

Police suspected that a homicidal maniac was at large, although the Lola Brent murder had apparently been forgotten; it was not mentioned.

The following day's paper had a picture of Stella Gaylord; it was a poor picture, apparently blown up from a snapshot, and you could tell that she was pretty but that was about all. There was more about Stella, too, including the address of the West Madison Street bar where she'd been working on percentage. She had been last seen alive when she'd left there, alone, at two o'clock, an hour and a half before the discovery of her body.

And for the first time, the murder of Stella Gaylord was tied in with the murder of Lola Brent, with the suggestion that possibly the same psychopathic killer had killed both of them.

The following day's paper had a few added details, but no new developments.

Sweeney got up to shut off the photograph. The sight of the black statuette on top of it reminded him of something he had to do. He slipped on a bathrobe and went out into the hall, to the telephone.

He got a long distance operator and put in a call to the Ganslen Art Company at Louisville. A few minutes later he had the general manager, a Ralph Burke, on the line.

"This is the Chicago *Blade*," Sweeney said. "Something about one of your statuettes has come up in connection with a murder investigation. It's an SM-1. Remember it, offhand?"

"I'm afraid I'd have to look it up."

"Maybe this will help. It's a figure of a terrified girl; somebody at your place called it a Screaming Mimi.

"Oh yes, certainly. I remember it now. What do you want to know about it?"

"Could you tell me how many of them you sold—and particularly how many of them you sold in Chicago?"

"We didn't sell many, I know. It didn't turn out be a popular number at all. In fact, we never got around to listing it in our catalogue. We made a trial lot of one gross and we've got most of them left. We gave each salesman a sample six months ago and some of them sold a few. If you want to hold the line a minute I can look up how many were sold in Chicago. Or shall I call you back?"

"I'll hold the line," Sweeney said.

It was scarcely a minute before the manager's voice was back. He said, "I've got it all here—luckily we keep a separate record on each number. There were—uh—two sold in Chicago. Only two, and both to a place called Raoul's Gift Shop. Altogether we sold about forty of them—mostly on the East and West Coasts. Want the exact figures?"

"Thanks, no," Sweeney said. "What does the SM-1 designation mean, if anything?"

"The SM part doesn't; it's just our serial number, picked in rotation. Our number before that was SL and the one after it was SN. The figure one is the size and finish. If we'd put it out in other sizes and materials, they'd have been SM-2, SM-3, and so on. But we won't, in this case. Unless, the first time our salesmen carry it, they take orders for several gross, we drop the number from our line and don't even catalogue it. It wouldn't pay. And we make only the very popular things in various sizes and styles."

"What will you do with the hundred-odd Mimi's you have left?"

"We'll get rid of them next year, in with mixed lots. If a customer orders, say, a dozen mixed figures, our choice, he gets them about half the usual list price; we get rid of our odd lots and remainders that way. At a loss, of course, to us—but it's better than throwing them away."

"Of course," Sweeney said. "Do you recall who nick-named SM-1 the Screaming Mimi?"

"Our bookkeeper; it's a hobby of his to try to think up names that match the figures and the letter designations—says it helps him remember which is which." The manager chuckled. "He hits well once in a while. I remember our number SF. He called it Some Fanny, and it was."

"I'm tempted to order one," said Sweeney. "But back to Mimi. Who designed her, or sculptured her, or molded her?"

"Fellow by the name of Chapman Wilson. Artist and sculptor, lives in Brampton, Wisconsin. He modeled it in clay."

"And sent it to you?"

"No, I bought it from him there, in Brampton. I do the buying myself, make trips several times a year. We've got quite a few artists we buy from and it's much more practical to go to their studios to look over what they have than to have a lot of stuff shipped here and have to' ship most of it back. I bought SM-1 from him about a year ago, and two other numbers. I guessed right on the others; they're selling okay."

"This Chapman Wilson—did he model Mimi from life, or what?"

"Don't know; didn't ask him. The original was in clay, same size as our copies, about ten inches. I took a chance on it because it was unusual. Something unusual may go over really big, or it may not sell at all. That's a chance we take."

"Know anything about Chapman Wilson personally?"

"Not much. He's rather an eccentric, but then a lot of artists are."

"Married?"

"No. At least, I don't think so. Didn't ask him, but I didn't see a woman around, or any sign of one."

"You say he's eccentric. Could you go as far as psycho-pathic, maybe?"

"I don't think so. He's a little screwy, but that's all. Most of his stuff is pretty routine—and sells fairly well."

"Thanks a lot," Sweeney said. "Guess that's all I need to know. Good-bye."

He checked the charges on the call so he could settle with Mrs. Randall and went back to his room.

He sat down on the edge of the bed and stared at the black statuette. His luck had been better than he had hoped—only two Mimis had come to Chicago. He was looking at one of them. And the other— Maybe the Ripper was looking at it now.

The luck of the Irish, Sweeney thought. He'd been work-ing on the case a day and had a lead the cops would give their eye teeth for.

And besides that, he felt pretty good for the shape he was in. He was even getting mildly hungry; he'd be able to put away a meal today.

He got up and hung his bathrobe on the hook, stretched luxuriously.

He felt swell. He grinned at Mimi. He thought, we're a jump ahead of the cops, Baby, you and I; all we got to do is find your sister.

The little black statuette screamed soundlessly, and Sweeney's grin faded. Somewhere in Chicago another Mimi was screaming like that—and with better cause. A madman with a knife owned her. Someone with a twisted mind and a straight razor.

Someone who wouldn't *want* to be found by Sweeney.

He shook himself a little, mentally, to get rid of that thought, and turned to the mirror over the washbowl. He rubbed a hand over his face. Yes, he'd better shave; he'd be meeting Yolanda late in the afternoon, if Doc Greene was as good as his word. And he had a hunch the agent would be.

He held out his hand and looked at it; yes, it was steady enough that he could use his straight razor without cutting himself. He picked up the shaving mug from the shelf above the washbowl and ran hot water into it, working up a lather with the brush. He lathered his face carefully and then looked, and reached, for the razor. It wasn't there, where it should have been lying.

His hand stayed that way, a few inches above the shelf, frozen like Mimi's scream, until he made a conscious effort to pull it back.

He bent forward and looked, very carefully and disbelievingly, at the mark in the thin layer of dust, the mark that was just the shape of the razor.

Carefully he wiped the lather off his face with a wetted towel, and dressed.

He went downstairs. Mrs. Randall's door was ajar and she said, "Come on in, Mr. Sweeney."

He stood in the doorway. "When did you dust in my room last, Mrs. Randall?"

"Why—yesterday morning."

"Do you remember if—" He was going to ask if she remembered seeing the razor and then realized he didn't have to ask that. Whether she remembered or not, that fresh spot in the dust was proof that the razor had been there after the dusting. He changed his question. "Was anybody in my room yesterday evening, or yesterday afternoon after I left?"

"Why, no. Not that I know of, anyway. I wasn't here yesterday evening; I went to a movie. Is something missing?"

"Not anything valuable," Sweeney said. "I guess I must have taken it while I was drunk, the last time I was here. Uh— you haven't been in my room at all since yesterday morning?"

"No I haven't. Are you going out this afternoon? I'll want to make your bed, and if you're going to be around anyway, I might as well do it now."

"I'll be leaving in a few minutes. Thanks."

He went back up to his room and closed the door. He struck a match and examined the mark in the dust minutely. Yes, there was some dust in the bare patch that was the shape of the closed razor, about half as much as in the surrounding area. Then the razor had been there for a while after the dusting. It must have been taken late yesterday afternoon or yesterday evening.

He sat down in the Morris chair and tried to remember whether he'd seen the razor at all, either last night when he'd come home with Mimi or earlier in the day when he'd been in his room to change clothes. He couldn't remember seeing it. He hadn't looked for it, of course; he'd shaved at Goetz's room, with Goetz's electric razor.

Was anything else missing? He went over to the dresser and opened the top drawer in which he kept small miscellaneous items. The contents looked intact until he remembered that there'd been a two-bladed penknife in the drawer.

It wasn't there now.

Nothing else was missing. There was a pair of gold cufflinks in the drawer, in plain sight, that was worth three or four times what the penknife was worth. And a stickpin with a zircon in it that a thief or burglar could not have been sure wasn't a diamond. But only a knife had been taken from the drawer. And only a razor from elsewhere in the room.

He looked at Mimi, and he knew how she felt.

[7]

The shining razor hovered above Sweeney's throat. It descended under his chin and scraped gently upward, taking away lather and stubble, leaving a clean, smooth swath. It rose again.

"Take this Ripper business," said the barber. He got the razor on a piece of tissue and poised it again. "It's got the whole damn town jittery. It got me pinched last night."

Sweeney grunted interrogatively.

"Carrying a razor. I keep my good hone—I got a Swatty— at home because somebody'd walk off with it around this joint. So every once in a while I take a razor home never thought anything of it. Put it in the breast pocket of my suit coat and the top of it shows and damn if a harness bull didn't stop me right on the street and get tough. I was lucky to be able to show identification. I was a barber or he'd have run me in. Pretty near did anyway. Said for all anybody knew, the Ripper's a barber, too. But he ain't."

The razor scraped. "How do you know?" Sweeney asked.

"Throats. A barber that went nuts would cut throats with it. All day long people lay stretched out in front of him with their throats bare and their chins thrown back and he just can't help thinking how easy it'd be and how—uh—you know what mean."

Sweeney said, "You got something there. You don't feel like cutting one today, I hope."

"Nope, not today." The barber grinned. "But once in a while—well, your mind does screwy things."

"So does yours," Sweeney said.

The razor scraped.

"One of the three dames he killed," said the barber, "used to work a block from here. Tavern down on the next corner."

"I know," Sweeney said. "I'm on my way there. Did you know the girl?"

"I seen her in there, enough to place her when I saw her picture in the paper. But I don't go in B-joints very often, not with the money I make. You get taken before you know it for five or ten bucks in percentage drinks, and what have you got. Not that I won't put out five or ten bucks if I get something for my money besides a little conversation. Me, I get enough conversation all day long. The whacks that sit in that chair!"

He put a steaming towel over Sweeney's face and patted it down. He said, "Anyway, I figure the Ripper uses a knife instead of a razor. You *could* use a razor like that, sure, but I figure it'd be too awkward to hold for a long hard slash across the guts like he uses. You'd have to tape the handle to get a good grip on it, and then it'd be awkward to carry, taped open. And it'd be a dead giveaway if anybody saw it. I figure he'd use a pocket knife, one small enough he could carry it legally.

A pre-war imported one with real steel in it, so he could have one of the blades honed down to a razor edge. Haircut?"

"No," said Sweeney.

"What do you figure he uses? A knife or a razor?"

"Yes," said Sweeney, getting up out of the chair. "What do I owe you?"

He paid, and went out into the hot August sunlight. He walked a block west to the address that had been given in the newspaper.

The place had a flashy front. Neon tubes, writhing red in the sun's glare, proclaimed that this was Susie's Cue. Hexagonal windows were curtained off to block the view within, but held chaste photographs of unchaste morsels of femininity. You could see in, if you tried, through a diamond-shaped glass in the door.

But Sweeney didn't try; he pushed the door open and went in.

It was cool and dim inside. It was empty of customers. A bartender lounged behind the bar and two girls, one in a bright red dress and the other in white with gold sequins, sat on stools together at the far end of the bar. There were no drinks in front of them. All three looked toward Sweeney as he entered.

He picked a stool in about the middle of the row and put a five dollar bill on the mahogany. The bartender came over and one of the girls—the one in red—was getting off her stool. The bartender beat her there and Sweeney had time to ask for a rye and seltzer before the girl, now on the stool beside him, said "Hello."

"Hello," Sweeney said. "Lonesome?"

"That's *my* line; I'm supposed to ask that. You'll buy me a drink, won't you?"

Sweeney nodded. The bartender was already pouring it. He moved away to give them privacy. The girl in the red dress smiled brightly at Sweeney. She said, "I'm awfully glad you came in. It's been dead as a doornail in this joint ever since I got here an hour ago. Anyway you don't look like a jerk like most of the guys come in here. How'd you like to sit over in one of the booths? My name's Tess, so now we're introduced. Let's move over to one of the booths, huh, and Joe'll bring us—"

"Did you know Stella Gaylord?"

Stopped in mid-sentence, she stared at him. She asked, "You aren't another shamus, are you? This place was lousy with 'em right after what happened to Stella."

"You did know her, then," said Sweeny. "Good, I'm not a shamus. I'm a newspaperman."

"Oh. One of *those*. May I have another drink, please?"

Sweeney nodded, and the bartender, who hadn't gone far, came up to pour it.

"Tell me about Stella."

"Tell you what?"

"Everything you know. Pretend I never heard of her. For all practical purposes, I haven't. I didn't work on the case. I was on vacation when it happened."

"Oh. But you're working on it now?"

Sweeney sighed. He'd have to satisfy her curiosity before he could satisfy his own. He said, "Not for the paper. I'm going to write it up for a fact detective magazine. Not just Stella Gaylord, but the whole Ripper business. As soon as the case is cracked, that is. The true detective mags don't buy unsolved cases. But I'll have to be ready to write it up quick, once the thing breaks."

"Oh. They pay pretty well for something like that, don't they? What's in it for me?"

"A drink," said Sweeney, motioning to the bartender. "Listen, sister, I'll be talking to about fifty people who knew Stella Gaylord and Dorothy Lee and Lola Brent, and to coppers who worked on it, and to other reporters wouldn't I be in a beautiful spot if I gave everybody a slice of it? Even if the case does break and I do sell the story, I'd come out behind, see?"

She grinned. "It never hurts to try."

"That it doesn't. And, incidentally, I *will* split with you if you can crack the case so I can sell it. You don't happen to know who killed her, do you?"

Her face hardened. "Mister, if I knew that, the cops would know It. Stella was a good kid."

"Tell me about her. Anything. How old she was, where she came from, what she wanted, what she looked like—anything."

"I don't know how old she was. Somewhere around thirty I guess. She came from Des Moines, about five years ago, I think she told me once. I knew her only about a month"

"Was that when you started here, or when she did?"

"When I did. She'd been here a couple of months already. I was over on Halsted before that. It was a worse joint than this one, for looks, but I made better dough. There was always trouble there, though, and God how I hate trouble. I get along with people, if they get along with me. I never start—"

"About Stella" said Sweeney. "What did she look like? I saw the newspaper picture, but it wasn't very good."

"I know I saw it. Stella was kind of pretty. She had a beautiful figure, anyway; she tried to get into modeling once, but you got to have contacts. She was about thirty; her hair was kind of a darkish blonde. She ought to've hennaed it, but she wouldn't. Blue eyes. About five-five or so."

"What *was* she, inside?" Sweeney asked. "What was she trying to do?"

The red dress shrugged. "What are any of us trying to do? Get along, I guess. How'd I know? That's a funny question for you to ask. How's about another drink?"

"Okay," said Sweeney. "Were you working here with her the night she was killed?"

"Yeah. I told the cops what I knew about that."

"Tell me, too."

"She made an after-date. After two, that is; we closed at two. It was with a guy that was in around ten or eleven o'clock and talked to her for half an hour or so. I never saw him before, and he hasn't seen me since."

"Did he pick her up at two?"

"She was going to meet him somewhere. His hotel, I guess." She turned and looked at Sweeney. We don't do that with anybody. But sometimes, if we like a guy—well, why not?"

"Why not?" Sweeney said. "And you girls don't make much at this percentage racket, do you?"

"Not enough to dress the way we got to dress. And everything. This ain't a nice racket, but there are worse ones. At least we can pick which men we want to go out with, and we get ten or twenty propositions a day." She grinned at him impudently. "Not often this early, though. Yours will be the first today, when you get around to it."

"*If* I get around to it," Sweeney said. "What do you remember about the guy she was going to meet?"

"Practically nothing because I didn't notice him. After he went out, Stella. came back to me—I was sitting alone just then for a few minutes—and mentioned she was meeting him after two and what did I think of the guy. Well, I'd just glanced at him sitting there with her before and all I remembered was that he was pretty ordinary looking. I think he had on a gray suit. He wasn't specially old or young, or tall or short or fat or anything or I'd probably have remembered. I don't think I'd know him again if I saw him."

"He didn't have a round face and wear thick glasses, did he?"

"Not that I remember. I wouldn't swear he didn't. And I'll save you one thing; nobody else around here noticed him or has any better idea. That's one thing the coppers dogged everybody about. No use asking George, behind the bar, or Emmy—that's the girl in the white dress. They were both here that night, but they didn't remember as much about it as I did."

"Did Stella have any enemies?"

"No. She was a nice kid. Even us girls who worked with her liked her, and mister, that's something. And to beat your next question, no, she didn't have any serious men friends and she didn't live with anybody. I didn't mean she never packed an overnight bag, but I mean *living* with anybody, serious."

"She have a family, back in Des Moines?"

"Her parents were dead, she said once. If she had any

other relatives anywhere she never talked about them. I don't guess she had any she was close to."

"The address on West Madison where she lived. That would be about three blocks from here, wouldn't it? What is it a hotel or rooming house?"

"A hotel, the Claremore. It's a dive. Can I have another drink?"

Sweeney crooked a finger at the bartender. He said, "Mine, too, this time."

He shoved his Panama back on his head. "Look, Tess, you've told me what she looked like, what she did. But what *was* she? What made her tick? What did she *want?*"

The girl in the red dress picked up her glass and stared into it. She looked at Sweeney, then, squarely for the first time. She said, "You're a funny kind of guy. I think I could like you."

"That's swell," said Sweeney.

"I even like the way you said that. Sarcastic as hell, but— I don't know what I mean. You meet all kinds of guys in a business like this, and—" She laughed a little and emptied her glass. She said, "I suppose if *I* got myself killed by a ripper, you'd be interested in finding out what made *me* tick, what *I* really wanted. You'd— Oh, hell."

"You're a big girl now," Sweeney said. "Don't let it get you down. I *do* like you."

"Sure. Sure. I know what I am. So let's skip it. I'll tell you what Stella wanted. A beauty shop. In a little town some-where, a long way from Chicago. Go ahead and laugh. But that's what she was saving up her money for. That's what she wanted. She saved her money, working as a waitress, and then got sick and it went. She didn't like this racket any more than the rest of us, but she'd been at it a year and in another year she'd've had enough saved up to make a break for herself."

"She had money saved up then. Who gets it?"

The girl shrugged. "Nobody, I guess, unless some relative shows up. Say, I just remembered something. Stella had a girl friend who's a waitress near where she was killed. An all-night restaurant on State just north of Chicago Avenue. And she nearly always had something to eat after she got off at two. I told the cops maybe she went from here to that restaurant for a sandwich before she kept her date with the mooch. Or maybe she met him at the restaurant instead of at his hotel room or whatever."

"You don't know the waitress' name, do you?"

Tess shook her head. "But I know the restaurant. It's the third or fourth door north of Chicago Avenue on the west side of State."

Sweeney said "Thanks, Tess. I'd better push along." He glanced at the money on the bar, three singles and some change left out of the ten he'd put there. "Put it under the mattress. Be seeing you."

She put a hand on his arm. "Wait. Do you mean it? Will you come back?"

"Maybe."

Tess sighed, and dropped her hand. "All right, then, you won't. I know. The nice guys never do."

When Sweeney stepped out to the sidewalk, the impact of the heat was almost like a blow. He hesitated a moment and then walked west.

The Claremore hotel, from the street, was just a sign and an uninviting stairway. Sweeney trudged up the steps to a tiny lobby on the second floor.

A swarthy, stocky man who hadn't shaved for at least two days was sorting mail behind a short counter. He glanced at Sweeney and said "Filled up." He looked down at the mail again.

Sweeney leaned against the counter and waited. Finally the stocky man looked up again.

"Stella Gaylord lived here," Sweeney said.

"Jesus God, another cop or a reporter. Yeah, she lived here. So what?"

"So nothing" said Sweeney.

He turned and looked down the dim corridor of doors with peeling paint, at the uncarpeted stairs leading to the floor above. He sniffed the musty air. Stella Gaylord, he thought, must have wanted that beauty shop pretty bad to have lived in a hole like this.

He looked back at the stocky man to ask a question and then decided, to hell with it.

He turned and walked down the stairs to the street.

The clock in the window of a cheap jewelry store next door told him he still had over an hour before his appointment with Greene and Yolanda Lang at El Madhouse.

It also reminded him that he still didn't have a watch, and he went in and bought one.

Putting change back in his wallet, he asked the Jeweler, "Did you know Stella Gaylord?"

"Who?"

"Such is fame," Sweeney said. "Skip it."

Outside he flagged a cab and rode to State and Chicago. The waitress who had been Stella's friend wouldn't be on duty now, but maybe he could get her address, and maybe he could learn something anyway.

The restaurant was called the Dinner Gong. Two waitresses were working behind the counter and a man in shirt sleeves, who looked as though he might be the proprietor, was behind the cash register on the cigar counter.

Sweeney bought cigarettes. He said, "I'm from the *Blade*. You have a waitress here who was a friend of Stella Gaylord. Is she still on the night shift?"

"You mean Thelma Smith. She quit over a week ago. Scared stiff to work in this neighborhood, after what happened to the Gaylord girl."

"You have her address? Thelma's, I mean."

"No. She was going out of town; that's all I know. She'd been talking about going to New York, so maybe that's where."

Sweeney said, "Stella was in here that night, wasn't she?"

"Sure. I wasn't on then, but I was here while the police were talking to Thelma. She said Stella came here a little after two o'clock and had a sandwich and coffee and then left."

"She didn't say anything to Thelma about where she was going?"

The proprietor shook his head. "But it was probably

somewhere near here, or she wouldn't have come way up here from Madison for a sandwich. She was a chippie; the cops figure it she had a hotel-room date somewhere around here after she got through at the bar she worked at."

Sweeney thanked him and went out. He was pretty sure it wouldn't pay to try to trace Thelma Smith; the police had already talked to her. And if there'd been anything suspicious about her leaving town, they'd be doing the tracing.

While he was waiting for a chance to get across the traffic on Chicago Avenue, he remembered something he'd forgotten to ask Tess. When he got across the street he phoned Susie's Cue from the corner drugstore and asked for her.

"This is the guy you were talking to half an hour ago, Tess," he told her. "Just remembered something. Did Stella ever say anything about a statuette—a little black statuette of a woman, about ten inches high."

"No. Where are you?"

"I'm lost in a fog," Sweeney said. "Were you ever up to Stella's room?"

"Yes once just a few days before she—before she died.

"She didn't have a statuette like that?"

"No. She had a little white statuette on her dresser, though. A Madonna. She'd had it a long time, I remember her saying. Why? What gives about a statuette?"

"Probably nothing. Tess, does Screaming Mimi mean anything to you?"

"I've had 'em. What is this, a gag?"

"No, but I can't tell you about it. Thanks, anyway. I'll be seeing you sometime."

"I'll bet."

When he left the drugstore he walked west to Clark Street and south to El Madhouse.

[8]

She looked just like the picture of her that had been in Sweeney's mind, except, of course, that she wore clothes. Sweeney smiled at her and she smiled back and Doc Greene said, "You'll remember her, Sweeney. You've been staring ever since you sat down."

Yolanda said, "Pay no attention to him, Mr. Sweeney. His bark is worse than his bite."

Greene chuckled. "Don't give Sweeney an opening like that, my sweet. He already suspects that I have canine ancestry." He stared at Sweeney through the thick glasses. He spoke softly: "I *do* bite."

"At least," said Sweeney to Yolanda, "he nips at my heels. I don't like him."

"Doc's all right, Mr. Sweeney. He grows on you."

"He'd better not try to grow on *me*. Doc, do you shave with a straight-edge razor?"

"As it happens, yes."

"Your own, or do you borrow other people's?"

Behind the heavy lenses, Doc Greene's eyes narrowed slightly. "Someone has borrowed yours?"

Sweeney nodded. "Again your perspicacity mystifies me. Yes, someone has borrowed mine. And a small knife as well. The only two keen-edged tools in the place."

"Not counting your brain, Sweeney. He left you that. Or was it there at the time of the theft?"

"I doubt it seriously. It must have been in the evening while I was out rather than while I was sleeping. I deduce that from the fact that, when I looked in the mirror this morning, there was no fine red line across my throat."

Greene shook his head slowly. "You looked in the wrong place, Sweeney. Our friend the Ripper has a strong predilection for abdomens. Did you look there?"

"Not specifically, Doc. But I think I would have noticed when I took a shower."

Yolanda Lang shuddered a little and pushed her chair back. "I'm afraid I must run along, Mr. Sweeney. I've got to talk to the maestro about a new number. You'll come to see me dance tonight? The first number is at ten."

She held out her hand and smiled at him. Sweeney took the hand and returned the smile. He said, "Wild horses and so forth, Yo. Or may I call you Yolanda?"

She laughed. "I think I prefer it. You say it as though you meant it."

She walked toward the archway leading from the tavern to the night club at the rear. The dog, which, had been lying beside her chair, followed her. So did the two detectives who had been sitting at the next table.

"Makes quite a parade," Doc Greene said.

Sweeney sat down again and made circles on the table with the bottom of his glass. After a minute he looked up. He said, "Hello, Doc. I didn't know you were here."

"Getting anywhere, Sweeney? Got a lead?"

"No."

Greene sighed deeply. "My bosom enemy, I'm afraid you don't trust me."

"Should I?"

"To an extent. And to what extent? To the extent that I tell you you can. That means as far as finding the Ripper is concerned." He leaned forward, elbows on the table. "As concerns Yolanda, no. As concerns yourself, no. As concerns money, no—although that shall have no reason to arise between us. But as concerns the Ripper, yes. I shall worry about Yolanda until he is caught. I would even prefer that he is killed rather than caught, because he presumed to touch her."

"With a cold blade," said Sweeney. "Not with a hot hand."

"With anything. But that is past. It's the future that worries me. Right now there are two detectives guarding Yo all the time; three eight-hour shifts of them. But the police won't do that forever. Find me the Ripper Sweeney."

"And after that?"

"After that, the hell with you."

"Thank you, Doc. The only trouble is that you're so completely honest that I distrust you."

Greene sighed again. "Sweeney," he said. "I don't want you to waste time suspecting me. The police got that little idea yesterday because I couldn't account for where I was when the Ripper attacked Yolanda. I don't know where I was either, except that it was on the South Side. I was with a client—a singer at the Club Cairo—until midnight and I got pretty stinking. I got home but I can't prove when, and I don't even know when."

"That happens," Sweeney said. "But why should I believe it?"

"For the same reason the police did, you should. Because it happens I have solid alibis on two of the other three attacks. I checked back, and the police checked back on what I told them.

"Not on the Lola Brent one, two months ago; that's too far back and I couldn't, figure out where I was. But they told me the second one— What was her name?"

"Stella Gaylord."

"—was the night of July 27th, and I was in New York on business. I was there, from the 25th through the 30th and on the night of the 27th I was—luckily—with some damned respectable people from dinner time until three in the morning. Don't waste time or distract me by asking what I was doing with respectable people. That's irrelevant. The police have checked it. Ask Captain Bline.

"And on the first of August, last week, at the moment this secretary, Dorothy Lee, was killed, I was here in Chicago, but it just happens I was in court testifying on a breach of contract suit against a theater manager. Judge Goerring and the bailiff and the court clerk and three lawyers—one of them mine and two of them the theater's—are all the alibi I've got on that one.

"Now if you want to believe I'm half a Ripper, working the first and fourth cases and with a stand-in filling in for the second and third, you're welcome. But you aren't that much of a damn fool."

"You've got something there," Sweeney admitted. He took a folded piece of blank copy paper and a pencil from his pockets. "I'll even settle for *one* alibi, if it's the real McCoy. Judge Goerring's court, you say? When to when?"

"Case was called at three o'clock and ran till a little after four. Before it was called, I was in conference with all three lawyers for a good half-hour in an anteroom of the court. According to the newspapers, the Lee girl left her office alive at a quarter of three to go home. She was found dead in her apartment at five and they thought she'd been dead an hour. Hell, Sweeney, I couldn't have *planned* a better alibi. She was killed right while I was on the witness stand, two miles away. Will you buy it?"

"I'll buy it," Sweeney said. "What were the lawyers' names?"

"You're a hard man, Sweeney. Why suspect me, anyway, any more than Joe Blow up there at the bar, or the guy next to him?"

"Because my room was entered last night. Only a razor and a knife were taken, and razors and knives tie up with the Ripper. Up to last night damn few people knew I had any interest in the Ripper. You're one of them."

Greene laughed. "And how did I find out? By reading that eyewitness story you wrote for the *Blade*. What's the circulation of the *Blade?* Half a million?"

Sweeney said, "Excuse me for living. I'll buy you a drink on that, Doc."

"Bourbon straight. Now, have you got a lead to the Ripper yet?"

Sweeney signaled the waiter and ordered, then answered. "Not a lead," he said. "What were the names of the lawyers, Doc?" He poised the pencil over the copy paper.

"I thought you were mostly Airedale, Sweeney, but you're half bulldog. My lawyer's Hymie Fieman, in the Central Building. The opposition was Raenough, Dane & Howell. Dane—Carl Dane, I think it is—and a young neophyte named Brady, who works for them but isn't a member of the firm yet, were the two who were in conference and present at the hearing. And the judge was Goerring, G-o-e-r-r-i-n-g. He's a Republican, so he wouldn't alibi a Ripper."

Sweeney nodded moodily. He said, "Wish I could snap out of this hangover and think straight. I'm as nervous as a cat."

He unfolded the sheet of copy paper and smoothed it flat. Then he held out his right hand, back up and fingers spread wide, and put the piece of paper on it. The slight trembling, magnified, vibrated the edges of the paper.

"Not as bad as I thought," he said. "Bet you can't do any better." He looked at Greene. "In fact, five bucks you can't." Greene said, "I should never bet a man at his own game, and I've never tried that, but you're on. You're a wreck, and I've got nerves like a rock."

Greene picked up the paper and balanced it flat on the back of his hand. The edges vibrated slightly, but noticeably less than they had on Sweeney's hand.

Sweeney watched the paper very closely. He asked, "Doc, did you ever hear of the Screaming Mimi?"

The rate of vibration of the edges of the paper didn't change at all. Watching them, Greene said, "Guess I win, Sweeney. Concede the bet?"

There'd been no reaction, but Sweeney cussed himself silently. The man who'd bought that statuette wouldn't have known the company's nickname for it; Lola Brent, as a new employee, wouldn't have known it to tell him.

Sweeney said, "A small black statuette of a woman screaming."

Doc Greene looked up from the paper, but the vibration of the edges—Sweeney's eyes stayed on the paper—didn't change. Greene lowered his hand to the table. He said, "What is this? A gag?"

"It was, Doc. But you win the bet." Sweeney handed over the fin. "It's worth it. You answered my questions so I can believe you—for sure."

"You mean the Screaming Mimi and the black statuette? No, I never heard of either, Sweeney. A statuette of a woman screaming? One and the same thing? The statuette is called Screaming Mimi? M-i-m-i?"

"Right. And you never heard of either. I don't necessarily believe your saying so, Doc, but I do believe the edges of that piece of paper."

"Clever, Sweeney. A homemade lie detec— No, not that; a reaction indicator. I'll keep your five, but I'll buy you a drink out of it. Same?"

Sweeney nodded. Doc signaled.

Doc put his elbows on the table. He said, "Then you were lying. You have got a lead. Tell Papa. Papa might help."

"Baby doesn't want help, from Papa. Papa is too anxious to get Baby cut up with a sharp shiv."

"You underrate me, Sweeney. I think I can get it without your help. And I'm curious, now. I will if I have to."

"Prove it."

"All right." Doc Greene's eyes looked enormous, hypnotic, through the lenses of his glasses. "A small black statuette called the Screaming Mimi. Most statuettes are sold in art and gift shops. One of the girls attacked worked, for one day—the day of her murder—in an art and gift shop. I forget where, but the newspapers would tell me. If I look up the proprietor and ask him if he ever heard of Screaming Mimi, would it get me anywhere?"

Sweeney lifted his glass. "I did underrate you, Doc."

"And I you, Sweeney, when I almost believed you that you didn't have a lead. To your bad health."

"And yours."

They drank and then Greene asked, "So do I go to the proprietor of the art store and start from there, or do you break down and tell me?"

"I might as well. Lola Brent sold a small black statuette of a screaming, terrified nude just before she was killed. There's pretty good reason to believe the Ripper was her customer, followed her home and killed her. Likely the figure set him off; it's something that would appeal only to a psycho."

"Do you like it?"

"I dislike it, but I find it fascinating. It's rather well done, incidentally. And I followed up on it. Only two were sent to Chicago. I've got one. The Ripper's got the other."

"Do the police know that?"

"No. I'm pretty sure they don't."

"I told you so, Sweeney. The luck of the Irish. By the way, are you crowding your luck too far, or are you going heeled?"

"Heeled?"

"Packing a rod, toting a gun. In a word, armed. If the Ripper—or anyone else—had called on me and removed my small armament of knife and razor, I'd bring up the artillery. If the Ripper knew where *my* room was, I'd sleep with a sawed-off shotgun across my chest. *Or does he know, Sweeney?*"

"You mean?"

"Yes."

Sweeney grinned. "You want my alibis? Well, I don't know anything about two months ago. I doubt if I could check back. As for the next two murders, well, I was on a two-week drunk. Only God knows where I was and what I was doing, and I wasn't with God all the time. As for night before last, when Yolanda was attacked, I was at the scene of the crime at approximately the time of the crime. How's that for a set of alibis?"

Doc Greene grunted. He said, "I've heard better. I can't remember when I've heard worse. Sweeney, as a practical psychiatrist, I don't think you're the Ripper type, but I've been wrong. *Are* you?"

Sweeney stood up. He said, "I'm damned if I'll tell you, Doc. In the little duel of pleasantries between us, it's the one big edge I've got on you. I'm going to let you wonder. And if I am, thanks for warning me about the sawed-off shotgun."

He went outside and it was dusk. His headache was gone and he felt almost human again.

He walked south on Clark Street without thinking about where he was going, without, in fact, thinking at all.

He let his mind alone and his mind let him alone, and they got along fine together. He heard himself humming and listened to himself long enough to find out what it was; it

turned out to be the melody of a Brahms Hungarian dance, so
he quit listening.

He watched, instead, the movies that were going on inside his head, and very nice movies they were. Yolanda sitting
across the table from him, even as she had sat only minutes
before; Devil, the dog, as well trained as any Seeing-Eye dog,
curled up at her feet with a small but incongruous bandage
on top of his head, result of a very skillful job of creasing by
the detective who'd shot through the glass at him. Sweeney
admired the marksmanship of that cop almost as much—but
not in the same way—as he admired the next sequence in his
mental movie: the beautiful body of Yolanda, seen in the spot
of the other detective's flashlight. He sighed, and then
grinned. It had never occurred to him that a woman could be
that beautiful. He still didn't quite believe it. He'd half expected disillusionment when he'd gone to El Madhouse to meet
Doc Greene and Yolanda. He had, after all, been pretty drunk
when he'd seen—what he'd seen some (How long was it?)
forty hours ago. It would have disappointed him, but not surprised him too much, had she turned out not to look like that
at all. Or if she had been beautiful but had talked with a
Brooklyn accent.

But, instead, she had been *more* beautiful than he had
remembered. Her face had, anyway. And, even more, there
had been that intriguing air of mystery about her which, forty
hours ago, he had thought was entirely subjective, due to the
strange circumstances of the affair in the hallway. It hadn't
been; it was really there. Yolanda Lang *had* something besides the most beautiful body he had ever seen.

He thought: Godfrey, you'd better be right. And then he
grinned, because he knew damned well that Godfrey was
right. If you wanted something badly enough you could get it.

And he was going to get it.

If he'd wondered that before he'd met and tangled with
Doc Greene, he'd quit wondering after. If Yolanda were fat
and forty—and she wasn't either—he'd have to carry through
out of cussedness just because he and Greene hated one
another so completely. Almost literally, the man made his

flesh crawl.

If only he could prove that Greene was the Ripper—

But there were the two alibis. The police had accepted them. Anyway, Greene had *said* the police had become interested in him and then had accepted the alibis. But that was something he could check. That was something he *would* check.

Furthermore, he could at least start to check on it right now.

He was crossing Lake Street into the Loop and he kept on going to Randolph and turned west to the tavern, between Clark and LaSalle, where a lot of the boys from the *Blade* hung out.

None of them seemed to be hanging out there at the moment, so he ordered a shot and mixed it with soda so he could work on it a while to see if any of them were coming in.

He asked Burt Meaghan, who ran the place and who was alone behind the bar at the moment, "Think any of the boys will come around for pinochle after work this evening?"

"Be an unusual evening if they don't. Where you been keeping yourself, Sweeney?"

"Around and about. I've been on a bender, if you don't know. Doesn't anybody tell you these things, Burt?"

"Yeah, I'd heard. In fact, you were in here a few times the first week of it. Haven't seen you for over a week, though."

"You didn't miss much. Burt, do you know Harry Yahn?"

"Know of him. Not personally I don't know him. I don't move in such high circles. He's got a place a couple blocks west of here that he runs himself. And an interest in a few others."

"I've been out of touch," Sweeney said. "What's the name of the place he runs himself?"

"Name on front of the tavern is the Tit-Tat-Toe; that's just the front, of course. Want an in?"

"Wouldn't need it. I know Harry from way back when. I just lost track of where he was operating."

"He ain't been there long. Month or so. 'Scuse me, Sweeney."

He went down to the other end of the bar to wait on another customer. Sweeney drew wet rings on the bar with the bottom of his glass and wondered if he'd have to see Harry Yahn. He hoped not, because monkeying with Harry Yahn was as healthy as trimming your fingernails on a buzz saw. But he was going to need money from somewhere before this thing was over. He still had about a hundred and fifty dollars left out of the three checks Wally had given him, but that wasn't going to go very far on all he had in mind.

There was a hand on his shoulder and he turned. It was Wayne Horlick. Sweeney said, "The very guy I wanted to see most. Talk about the luck of the Irish."

Horlick grinned at him. "Costs you ten bucks to be that lucky, Sweeney. I'm glad to see you too. Ten bucks' worth."

Sweeney sighed. "From when?"

"Ten days ago. In here. Don't you remember?"

"Sure," Sweeney lied. He paid up. "And a drink for interest?"

"Why not? Rye."

Sweeney downed the last sip of the drink he'd been working on and ordered two. He said, "Why I wanted to see you, if you're curious, is that you've been working on the Ripper case."

"Yeah. The recent parts of it, anyway. I don't know who did the Lola Brent part, couple of months ago. But I got put on the second one, the Stella Gaylord murder and been at it ever since."

"Any leads?"

"Nary a lead, Sweeney. And if I did get one I'd turn it over to the cops quick-like and cheerful-like. The Ripper's one boy I wouldn't care to meet. Except through bars after Bline gets him. Did you know they've got a special Ripper detail working on nothing else, with Cap Bline in charge?"

"Carey told me. Think they'll get him?"

"Sure they'll get him—if he keeps on slicing dames. But not on any clues he's left with the ones he's already cut. Say, have you talked to this Yolanda Lang dame?"

"Yes, just an hour or so ago. Why?"

Horlick laughed. "Figured you'd try—after I read that eyewitness account of yours. Nice writing there, pal. Made everybody's mouth water. Mine included. Been trying for an interview with the dame ever since, but can't get it. I figured you would."

"Why?" Sweeney asked curiously. "I don't mean why would I try, but why, did you figure I'd get one if you couldn't?"

"That *story* you wrote. Far be it from me to praise anybody else's writing, Sweeney, but that was a minor classic of journalism. And what's more to the point, it's ten thousand dollars' worth of free publicity for the dame—above and beyond the publicity from getting picked on by the Ripper, and being the first one to survive a Ripper attack. Doc Greene must love you like a brother."

Sweeney laughed. "Sure. Like Cain loved Abel. Say Horlick, anything come out about any of the cases that didn't get in the papers? I've read up on—uh—Lola Brent and Stella Gaylord; haven't got around to the third dame yet, Dorothy Lee."

Horlick thought and then shook his head. "Nothing I can think of, nothing worth mentioning. Why? You really interested? Beyond getting that interview with the strip-teaser? You don't need to explain that."

Sweeney decided to stick to the lie he'd told Joe Carey. "Had in mind to write it up for a fact detective mag. Way to do that is have all the dope ready so the minute the case is cracked, I can beat the others to the punch."

"Good idea, *if* they ever crack the case. And they will, of course, if the guy keeps on ripping. He can't be lucky forever. I hope Wally puts you on it instead of me; I don't like the job. Want me to put in a word for you?"

"Carey's going to, so you'd better not. Wally might get suspicious if we laid it on too thick. What do you know about Doc Greene?"

"Why? Going to try to pin it on him?"

"I'd love to. I love him like a brother, too. He tells me the cops got the same idea and that he was alibied on two of the jobs and they took his alibis. Know anything about it?"

Horlick shook his head. "That would have been since the Ripper tried for Yolanda, of course; in the last couple of days. No, Bline didn't tell me about investigating Greene. But then I guess they have investigated just about everyone who's ever been closely connected with any of the four dames."

"What's your impression of Greene, Horlick?"

"He gives me the creeps. Is that what you mean?"

"That," said Sweeney, "is exactly what I mean. For that, I'll buy you another drink. Rye?"

"Rye."

"Hey, Burt, a rye for Horlick. I'll pass this one."

And he really did pass it, and wouldn't let Horlick buy back. Half an hour later, he left and went home.

Mrs. Randall heard him come in and opened her door.

"Mr. Sweeney, there's a man to see you. He wanted to wait so I let him wait in my sitting room. Shall I tell him—"

A big man stepped around from behind her. He said, "William Sweeney? My name is Bline, Captain Bline."

[9]

Sweeney stuck out a paw and the detective took it, but not enthusiastically. But Sweeney pretended not to notice. He said, "I've been wanting to meet you, Cap, since I heard you were on the case. Some things I want to ask you. Come on up to my room."

Bline followed him up the stairs and into the room. He sat down in the chair Sweeney pointed out to him, the over-stuffed one with the creaky springs; it groaned under his weight.

Sweeney sat on the edge of the bed. He glanced at the phonograph and said, "Want some music while we talk, Cap?"

"Hell no. We're gonna talk, not sing duets. And it's me that's going to ask the questions, Sweeney."

"What about?"

"You're asking 'em already. Look, I don't suppose you remember where you were on the afternoon of June 8th, do you?"

"No, I don't. Unless I was working that afternoon. Even then, I wouldn't know offhand if I was in the office doing rewrite, or if I was out on a job. Unless—maybe if I checked the late editions for that day and the early ones for the next, I could spot and remember which stories I worked on."

"You didn't work on any. You didn't work that day; you were off. I checked at the *Blade*.

"Then all I can tell you is what I probably did, which wouldn't mean much. I probably slept till about noon, spent most of the afternoon here reading or listening to music, probably went out in the evening to play some cards and have a few drinks. Or maybe a show or a concert. That part I might possibly be able to check on, but not the afternoon, and I judge that's what you're interested in."

"Right. And how about July 27th?"

"As hopeless as the next one you're going to ask about, Cap. August 1st, I mean. God knows where I was either time, except that I'm pretty sure it was in Chicago. Haven't been out of town in the last two weeks that I know of."

Bline grunted.

Sweeney grinned. He said, "Only I'm not the Ripper. Granted that I don't even know where I was or what I was doing when Stella Gaylord and Dorothy Lee were killed, I know I didn't kill Lola Brent—because I wasn't that drunk, I mean drunk enough not to remember something I did, any time in June. And I know I didn't make the pass at Yolanda Lang because I do remember Wednesday night; I was beginning to come out of it then, and feeling like hell. Ask God."

"Huh?"

Sweeney opened his mouth and then closed it again. No use getting poor old Godfrey grilled at headquarters, and Godfrey couldn't alibi him anyway, not for the exact time the attack had been made on Yolanda. He said, "A manner of speaking, Cap. Only God could prove what I was doing Wednesday night. But cheer up, if the Ripper keeps on ripping, maybe I'll have an alibi for the next one."

"That will be a big help."

"Meanwhile, Cap, and seriously, what made you come here to ask me about alibis? Did a little bird tell you? A Greene one?"

"Sweeney, you know damn well why I'm here. Because you were there in front of that door on State Street Wednesday night. The Ripper was probably in front of that door. Way we figure it, he was standing at the back door of that hallway and reached in and slashed as the dame came toward him. Only he was a couple of inches short and just nicked her, and the dog ran around her and jumped and he had to duck back and slam the door without having a chance for a second try. And then what would he do?"

"You asked it," Sweeney said. "You answer it."

He might have got the hell out of there, of course. But if he followed the pattern of most psycho killers, he came out of the alley and walked around to the front and was in that knot of people looking through the door when the squad car came."

"Also maybe," Sweeney said, "having put in the call for the police from the tavern on the corner."

Bline shook his head. He said, "No, we found out who put in that call. Guy that had been standing at the bar there with two other guys, talking, for hours. He left there a little before two-thirty and he was back in a few minutes. Told the guys he'd been talking to and the bartender that there was something going on in a hallway down the street. That a dame was on the floor and a big dog wouldn't let anybody open the door and go in to see what was wrong with the dame, so maybe he better phone the cops. So he did, and then he and the other two guys—all three of them this time—went together to the place and were there when the squad car came. I've talked to all three of them—the bartender knew one and I found the others through him. They say there were about a dozen people in front of the doorway. That what you'd say?"

"Pretty close. Not over fifteen at the most."

And the squad car coppers—even after they saw it was a

Ripper job—didn't have sense enough to hold every one of them. We've located five out of the twelve or fifteen if only we had *all* of 'em—"

"Who is the fifth?" Sweeney asked. "The three who were together and I made four; who else?"

"Guy who lived in the building. Guess he was the first one to see the woman and the dog. Came home and couldn't get in because the dog started to jump him every time he started to open the door. Other passers-by saw something was happening and stopped to look in too. When the guy from the tavern—the one who made the phone call—got there, there were six or eight people. When he got back with his two friends, there were nine or ten besides them.

"I was probably the next arrival," Sweeney said. I got there just a minute before the squad car came. And to answer your next question, no, I didn't notice anybody else in the crowd. Couldn't identify a one of them. All I noticed was what was going on inside and what the squad car coppers did. Probably couldn't identify even them."

Bline said dryly, "We don't need them identified. I'd give a lot, though, to have everyone of that crowd in front. Instead of five—and four of those five cleared.

"Not counting me?"

"Not counting you."

"What clears the man who lived in the building? The one who, according to his own story, was the first one there?"

"He's reasonably clear. Works a night shift of the *Journal of Commerce* on Grand Avenue; he's a printer. Didn't punch out on the time clock till one forty-five and it'd have taken him that long to get there; he wouldn't have had time to go in the alley way, wait a while, and then go around to the front. Besides he has solid alibis for all three other rippings; we checked them."

He frowned at Sweeney. "So of the five men we have located who were in that crowd in front of the door, you're the only one without an alibi for anything at all. By the way, here's your cutlery; the lab couldn't get anything on it."

He took an envelope from his pocket and handed it to

Sweeney. Without opening it, Sweeney could feel that it contained his penknife and straight razor.

He said, "You might have asked me for them. Did you have a search warrant?"

Bline chuckled. "We didn't want you in our hair while we were casing the joint. As for a warrant, does it matter now?"

Sweeney opened his mouth and then closed it again. He was mad enough to start something; those things being gone had given him some bad moments. On the other hand, it was going to be helpful if not necessary to have Bline friendly to him; there were things the police could do that he couldn't.

So he said, mildly, "You might have left a note. When I missed those, I thought maybe the Ripper thought I was the Ripper. Say, Cap, what do you know about this guy Greene, Doc Greene?"

"Why?"

"I kind of like to think of him as the Ripper, that's all. He tells me he's got alibis and that you've checked them. That right?"

"More or less. No alibi for Lola Brent, and the one for Dorothy Lee isn't perfect."

"Not perfect? I thought that was the one where he was testifying in court under Judge Goerring."

"The times don't fit perfectly. His alibi takes him up to about ten minutes after four. Dorothy Lee wasn't found dead until about five o'clock—maybe a few minutes after. The coroner said she'd been dead at least an hour when he saw her at five-thirty, but that means she could have been killed at four-thirty, twenty minutes after Greene's alibi ends. He could have made it, in a taxi, from the court to her place in that time."

"Then it's no alibi at all."

Bline said, "Not an iron-clad one, no. But there are angles. She left work at two forty-five to go home because she was sick; ordinarily she worked till five. Even if Greene knew her—and there's no proof he did—he wouldn't have known he'd find her home if he rushed there right from court. Only someone who worked with her would have known that."

"Or anyone who dropped in her office or phoned for her."

"True, but Greene didn't drop in. He would barely have had time to phone, and still get to her place by four-thirty."

Bline frowned. "You're stretching probabilities."

"Am I? Suppose Greene knew her—well. He could have had a date to pick her up at her apartment after five. But he gets through in court a little after four and goes there to wait for her. Maybe he even has a key, and lets himself in to wait, not knowing she came home sick and is already there."

"Oh, it's *possible*, Sweeney. I told you it wasn't a perfect alibi. But you've got to admit it isn't likely. The Ripper probably followed her home, seeing her on the street for the first time after she left work. Like he probably followed Lola Brent home from the gift shop. He couldn't have been waiting for Lola Brent at her place for two reasons—first, he couldn't have known she was going to be fired and come home early; second, she was living with a man, Sammy Cole; he couldn't have known Sammy wouldn't walk in on him."

"And anyway," Sweeney said, "Lola wasn't killed in her apartment but in the areaway outside the buildings. Sure, she was probably followed. And so was Stella Gaylord—followed as far as the mouth of the alley. But the Ripper doesn't always use the following technique. He didn't follow Yolanda Lang home; he was waiting for her outside that door at the back of the hallway in her building."

"You've really studied this case haven't you Sweeney?"

"Why not?" Sweeney asked. "It's my job."

"As I get it, you haven't been assigned to it yet. Or am I wrong?"

Sweeney considered whether to give Bline the song-and-dance about the fact detective magazine and decided not to; Bline might ask which magazine, and then check up on him.

He said, "Not exactly, Cap. But I was assigned on at least one angle of it when Wally Krieg told me to write that eyewitness account. And I figured because of that in I had on the case, he'd probably ask me to do more when I go back to work Monday, so I read up on the case what's already been in the papers, and asked a few questions."

"On your own time?"

"Why not? I got interested in it. You'd still follow the case if you got taken off it, wouldn't you?"

"Guess I would," Bline admitted.

"How about Greene's other alibi, the New York one? How well did you check on that one?"

Bline grinned. "You're hell-bent to fit Greene into this huh, Sweeney?"

"Have you met him, Cap?"

"Sure."

"That's why. I've known him a day and a half now, and I think the fact that he's still alive is pretty good proof I'm not the Ripper. If I was, he wouldn't be."

Bline laughed. "That ought to work both ways, Sweeney. He seems to like you almost as much as you like him. And you're still alive. But about the New York alibi; we gave it to the New York police and they checked the hotel he was staying at, the Algonquin. He was registered there from the 25th through the 30th."

Sweeney leaned forward. "That's as far as you checked? The Gaylord murder was on the 27th, and it's only four hours by plane from New York to Chicago. He could have left there in the evening and been back the next morning."

Bline shrugged. "We'd have checked further if there'd been any reason for it. Be honest, Sweeney; what have you got against him except that he rubs you the wrong way? And me too, I admit it. But aside from that, he knows *one* of the four dames who were attacked. To my mind, that's damn near an alibi in itself."

"How the hell do you figure that?"

Bline said, "When we get the Ripper, I'll bet you we find he knew *all* of the four women or none of them. Murderers—even psychopathic ones—follow that pattern, Sweeney. He wouldn't have picked three strangers and one friend; take my word for it."

"And you've checked—?"

"Hell yes, we've checked. We've made up lists as complete as we could of everybody who knew each of the four women, and then we've compared the lists. There's been only one name that appeared on even two of the four lists, and that much is allowable to coincidence."

"Who is it?"

"Raoul Reynarde, the guy who runs the gift shop that Lola Brent got fired from the day she was killed. Turns out he also had a slight acquaintance with Stella Gaylord, the B-girl."

"Good God, what for?"

Bline grinned. "I see you've met him. But why not? Lots of faggots have friends who are women. You have male friends, don't you? Anyway, it was just a slight acquaintance, both according to Reynarde and to the other friends of Stella Gaylord that we checked with."

But he could have known the other two then. It's hard to prove that he hadn't met—"

"In one case, no; we can't ask Dorothy Lee. We could only ask her other friends and none of them knew Reynarde. But we could and did ask the strip-tease dame And Yolanda Lang doesn't know him from either name or photograph."

"You checked him for alibis?"

"Fairly good ones on two of the cases. Especially on the Lola Brent one. He couldn't have followed her home after he fired her without closing the store and there's fairly good evidence—negative evidence, anyway—that he didn't close it."

Sweeney sighed. "Wash him out, then. I still like Doc Greene."

"Sweeney, you're nuts. All you mean is that you *don't* like him. Not a thing to point to him otherwise. We've got a hell of a lot better suspect than Greene."

"You mean me?"

"You're damn right I mean you. Look, not even a shadow of an alibi for *any* murder. Your extreme interest m the case. The fact that you are psychically unbalanced—or you wouldn't be an alcoholic. And that, in one case out of the four, we can put you right at the scene of the crime at the time of the crime. I'm not saying that's enough evidence to hang a dog on, but it is more than we've got on anybody else. If you weren't—"

"If I weren't what?"

"Skip it."

Sweeney said, "Wait, I get it. You mean if I wasn't a reporter, you'd probably drag me in and sweat me down a bit on the off chance. But you figure I'll be writing on the case and that you couldn't hold me long and once I got out the *Blade's* stories would play merry hell with the captain in charge of the Ripper detail."

Bline's laugh was a little embarrassed. He said, "I guess that isn't too far off, Sweeney. But damn it, man, can't you give me something that'll let me write you off, so I won't have to waste so much time on you? There ought to be some way you could check where you were at the time of at least one of the murders."

Sweeney shook his head. "I wish there was, Cap." He glanced at his wrist watch. "Tell you what, though. I'll do the next best thing; I'll buy you a drink. At El Madhouse. First show goes on at ten; that's in a few minutes now. You know she's dancing again tonight already."

"I know everything. Except who the Ripper is. Sure, Sweeney, I was thinking of dropping in there tonight anyway. Let's go."

At the door, before he reached back to tum out the light, Sweeney looked at the black statuette on the radio, the slim, naked girl, arms outraised to ward off ineffable evil a silent scream eternally frozen on her lips. He grinned at her and tossed her a kiss before he flicked off the light and followed Bline down the stairs.

They hailed a cab at Rush Street. Sweeney said "El Madhouse" to the driver and then leaned back and lighted a cigarette. He looked at Bline, sitting back, relaxed, his eyes closed. He said, "You don't really think I might be the Ripper, Cap. Or you wouldn't relax like that."

"Like what?" Bline's voice was soft. "I was watching your hands and letting you think my eyes were all the way closed. And there's a gun in my right coat pocket, the side away from you, with my hand on it. I could use it quicker than you could pull a knife, if you started to."

Sweeney laughed.

And then he wondered what was funny about it.

[10]

El Madhouse was crowded. It seemed strange to Sweeney that he hadn't thought of that. With all the publicity Yolanda Lang had received—the best of it at Sweeney's own hands—he realized that he should have realized that the joint would be jammed. As they went in the door he could see the husky waiter stationed at the inner doorway turning people away. Over the waiter's shoulder he could see that more tables than usual had been crowded into the big back room, and that every table was crowded.

A three-piece orchestra—not good but not bad—was playing back there now, and a woman with gravel in her throat was singing a torch song, probably the first number of the floor show. But from the outer room the barroom, you couldn't see the stage—or floor or platform, whichever it would be.

He grunted disgustedly, but Bline took him by the arm and started with him toward a table from which a couple was just rising. They got the seats and Bline said "We don't want to go back there yet. Show's just starting and Yolanda won't come on for forty minutes or so."

"We'll play hell getting back there at all. Unless—Yolanda told me to come around and catch the show; maybe she had more sense than I did and made a reservation for me. I'll check; you hold this seat for—" He started to get up again.

"Sit down and relax," Bline told him. "You got a police escort. Any time we want, we'll go back there, if they have to put chairs on top of tables for us. Don't think they'll have to, though; I told one of the boys to save me a place at his table, and we can crowd an extra chair in if there's room for one."

He caught a rushing waiter by the arm and said, "Send Nick over right away, will you?"

The waiter tried to pull loose. "Nick's busy. We're all going nuts tonight. You'll have to wait your—"

Bline's free hand pulled back his lapel for a brief flash of silver plate. He said. "Send Nick over."

"Who's Nick?" Sweeney asked, when the waiter had vanished into the crowd.

"Nick runs the place, nights, for Harry Yahn." He grinned. "I don't really want to see him, but it's the only way we'll get drinks right away. What you having?"

"Whiskey highball. Maybe I'll have to buy one of those badges. It's a system, if it works."

"It works," Bline said. He looked up as a dapper, stocky man came up to the table. "Hi, Nick. Everything under control?"

The stocky man grunted. "If there weren't so many deadheads in the house, we'd be doing better. Four coppers back there already taking up room, and now you come."

"And Sweeney, Nick. This is Sweeney, of the *Blade*. He comes, too. You can crowd in an extra chair for him, can't you?"

"Cash customer?"

"Cash customer," Sweeney said.

Nick smiled, and from the smile Sweeney expected him to rub his hands together, too. But instead he stuck one out to Sweeney. "I was kidding, Mr. Sweeney. It's on the house for you. I read that story you wrote. But it cost us money, too."

"The hell" said Sweeney. "How?"

"Greene. He's holding us up, and we got to pay it to cash in." He turned around and grabbed a flying waiter, the same one Bline had grabbed. "What you gentlemen having?"

"Whiskey and soda for both of us," Bline told him.

"Make it three, Charlie, and make it next," Nick told the waiter. Then he said, "Just a minute; I get a chair." He brought one from somewhere and sat down at the table with them just as the drinks came.

"Bumps," Sweeney said. "And how come Greene could hold you up; isn't Yolanda under contract?"

"Sure she is. For four more weeks. But—"

Sweeney cut in; "Doc Greene told me for three."

"Greene wouldn't tell the truth on a bet even where it don't matter, Mr. Sweeney. If it'd been three weeks he'd've told you four. Sure, she's under contract through September 5th, but the contract's got a clause."

"Most contracts have," Sweeney said.

"Yeah. Well, this clause says she don't have to work if she's sick or hurt. And Greene got one of the docs at the hospital to write a paper that says that because of shock she shouldn't ought to work for a week or even two weeks."

"But would she get paid for that time if she didn't?"

"Sure she wouldn't. But look what we can cash in on her if she does. Lookit the crowd tonight, and they're spending money, too. But because Doc had us by the nuts we had to offer a one-grand bonus if she'd forget she was shocked. A bonus—that's what Doc calls a bribe."

"But is she okay to dance this soon?" Sweeney asked. "She really was suffering from shock. I saw her face when she stood up in that hallway."

"You didn't mention her face."

"Sure, I did. Before the dog pulled the zipper. Say, Nick, how come she wasn't wearing a net bra and a G-string under that dress? I never thought to ask, but unless the police rules here have changed, she'd have been wearing them for the show."

"Wasn't she? They don't show much. I thought you was just exaggerating to make it a better story."

"So help me God," said Sweeney.

"Well, it could be. We got a pretty good dressing room with a shower here, and Wednesday was a hot night. Probably she took a shower after the last show and didn't bother to put on anything under a dress to run home in if she expected to go right to sleep. Or something."

"If it had been something, she wouldn't have been alone" Sweeney pointed out. "But we got off the track. Isn't it a bit soon for her to start dancing again?"

"Naw. If she got shocked, she was over it by the time she had a night's sleep. And the scratch was just a scratch. She'll be wearing a strip of adhesive tape six inches long, but that's what the customers are paying to see. Well, not all they're paying to see." He pushed back his chair and stood up. "Well, I got to do things. Want to go back now? Yo won't be on for half an hour yet, but the rest of the show don't stink too much."

The voice of an emcee telling jokes came from the back room and both Sweeney and Bline shook their heads. Bline said, "We'll look you up when we want to move back."

"Sure. I'll send you two more drinks here, then."

He went away, taking his chair back to wherever it had come from.

Sweeney asked Bline, "Yolanda just do one number?"

"Right now, yes. Before the excitement, she was on twice. A straight strip tease for the third number on the show, and then the specialty with the dog for the last number. But Nick told me this afternoon that to get her to go back on right away, they agreed to let her do just the one number, the specialty, on each show. Not that that matters; they'll get as big crowds here to see her do one number a show as two."

Their drinks came. Bline looked down into his for a moment and then squarely at Sweeney. He said, "Maybe I was a little rough on you tonight, Sweeney. In the cab, I mean."

Sweeney said, "I'm glad you were."

"Why? So you can pan me in the *Blade* with a clear conscience?"

"Not that. As far as I know to date, you don't deserve any panning. Not for the way you've handled the case. But now I can hold out on you with a clear conscience."

Bline frowned. "You can't hold back any evidence, Sweeney. Not and get away with it. What is it you're holding back?" He leaned forward, suddenly intent. "Did you notice anything there on State Street Wednesday night that you didn't tell about in the write-up? Recognize anybody, maybe, or notice anybody acting suspiciously? If you did—"

"I didn't. You've got the whole truth and nothing but the truth on that. I mean, if in playing around with the case and doing my own investigating and question-asking, I come on anything that you missed, it's my own business. I mean, until I get enough of it to beat you out on cracking the case."

Bline said, "Let's take it as of now. Right here and now. Will you give me your word of honor on the answer to one question?"

"If I answer it at all, I'll answer it straight. It isn't, by any chance, whether I'm the Ripper, is it?"

"No; if you *are*, I wouldn't expect a straight answer. So I'm asking this on the assumption that you're not. But by God, Sweeney, if you won't answer this *Blade* or no *Blade* I'm going to take you in and work on you. And the same goes if you do answer it and I ever find out it wasn't straight.

"Do you know, or even think you might know, who the Ripper is? Either by sight or by name, do you even suspect anybody?"

"No, definitely not. Unless it's Doc Greene, and I haven't a damn bit of reason for that except that I'd *like* him to be."

Bline sat back. He said, "Okay, then. I've got a lot of men under me on this, and besides that we've got the whole police force keeping an eye out. If you, all by yourself, get anything we miss, it's your baby. It'd probably get you a knife in the belly, but that's your business."

Sweeney said, "Fair enough, Cap. And for those kind words—especially about the knife, I'll even forgive you for taking my razor and penknife without telling me, and scaring the pants off me when I found them gone. Why didn't you leave a note?"

"Wanted to see how you'd react. If you'd been the Ripper, and found them gone, you'd have probably been even worse scared; you'd like as not have taken it on the lam and we'd have picked you up. You know, Sweeney, I've just about decided you're not the Ripper."

"Awfully sweet of you, Cap. But I'll bet you tell that to all the boys. By the way, have I been tailed while you thought I was it?"

"Today, yes. Hadn't got around to you yet yesterday. But I'll pull the guy off of you now, I guess. Especially now that you know about it."

"I might suggest you put him on Doc Greene. Say, was it Doc's salesmanship that made you suspect me to begin with?"

Bline grinned. "You two really do love one another. Is that enough of an answer to your question? Well, what do you say we go in out of the rain? She'll be on in ten minutes."

They found Nick and he took them past the big waiter who guarded the portal. The gravel-voiced torch singer was at it again as they threaded their way through barely navigable aisles among the close-packed, crowded tables. No tête-à-tête tables tonight, Sweeney noticed; at least four people were at every table and five or even six were at some of them. Two hundred people, more or less, were jammed in a room whose normal complement wasn't much over half that number.

They had barely started across the room when Sweeney felt his arm gripped from behind and turned. Bline was leaning his head close. He had to yell to make himself heard above the music and the noise, but pitched his voice so it wouldn't carry past Sweeney. "Forgot to tell you Sweeney. Keep your eyes open in here. Watch the faces and see if you see anybody you remember being by that door on State Street. Get me?"

Sweeney nodded. He turned and started following Nick again, but this time kept watching as many faces along the route as he could. He didn't think he'd remember anybody who'd shared Wednesday night's spectacle with him; all he'd really seen outside the door had been the backs of heads. But it didn't hurt to try, and Bline's idea that the Ripper might have come around to the front and joined the crowd seemed quite reasonable. Also, he agreed with the thought that the Ripper might have come here tonight.

Nick led them to a table where three men sat one chair was empty, tilted against the table's edge. He said, "I'll send over a waiter with another chair; they can crowd you in here. Same to drink, both of you?"

Bline nodded, then said, "Sit down, Sweeney. Want to talk to an outpost or two before I squat."

Sweeney took the chair and glanced at his three companions, all of whom were watching the singer and paying no attention to him. One of them looked familiar; the others were strangers to him. He watched the singer. She wasn't bad to watch, but he wished he didn't have to listen to her, too.

The chair arrived, as did the drinks, before Bline came back. Sweeney moved over to make more room, and Bline said, "Sweeney-Ross, Guerney, Swann. Anything doing, boys?"

The one called Swann said, "Guy over at the corner table acts a little screwy; I been keeping an eye on him. The one with the carnation in his buttonhole. Maybe he's just a little drunk."

Bline watched that way a while. He said, "Don't think so. The Ripper wouldn't call attention to himself dressing up like that and wearing a flower, would he? And I don't think the Ripper'd get drunk."

"Thanks for that last thought," Sweeney said.

Bline turned to him. "See anybody might have been there that night?"

"Only the guy across from me there, the one you introduced as Guerney. Isn't he one of the boys from the squad car?"

Guerney had turned back at the sound of his name. He said, "Yeah. It was me that creased the dog."

"Nice shooting."

Bline said, "Guerney's one of the best shots in the department. His partner's here, too. Kravich. He's at the bar out there, watching 'em as they come and go."

"Didn't notice him."

"He noticed you. I saw him start toward you when you came in the door; then he saw I was with you and turned back. Sure you haven't seen anybody else that—"

"No," said Sweeney. "*Shhhh.*"

The emcee was on stage—it had turned out to be actually a stage, although a small one, about eight feet deep and twelve feet wide—and was building up an introduction to Yolanda Lang and her world-famous Beauty and the Beast dance. Sweeney wanted to hear.

Not that it was worth hearing. The emcee had dropped his corny humor and was being cornier by far. It was pathetically bathetic, Sweeney thought. He tried now *not* to listen about the brave courage of the courageous little woman who had risen from a bed of pain to answer the call of her art and the demand of her public, to do for them the most wonderful, the most sensational dance in the world, with the aid of the most wonderful trained dog in the world and the most courageous, who had courageously saved his mistress's life at the risk of his own and who had also been injured but courageously had—

Sweeney couldn't take any more of it. He said to Bline, "Who does the bastard think he's introducing—Joan of Arc?"

Bline said, *"Shhhh."* Sweeney listened to forty-five seconds more of it and then, mercifully, it ended; nothing can last forever, not even an emcee with an unprecedented opportunity to go dramatic.

The lights dimmed, and the room was quiet. As miraculously quiet as though two hundred people were holding their breath. You could hear the click of the switch as a spotlight went on, from somewhere in the back of the room, throwing a bright circle of yellow light on the left side of the stage. Everyone watched the yellow circle of light. A drum began to throb and the tone and pitch of it pulled Sweeney's eyes away from the stage and toward the three-piece orchestra; the three-piece orchestra wasn't there. Rather, two-thirds of it wasn't there; the pianist and the sax-player had left the platform. The trap-drummer had left his traps and sat before a single kettledrum, a big one, tuned low. His only weapons were two drumsticks with big well-padded heads.

Smart, thought Sweeney, and he wondered if Yolanda or her manager deserved the credit for that idea. Resonant rhythm without music. And not even the lousiest drummer can corn up a kettledrum with padded sticks, set out of reach of his cymbals, blocks and bells.

The drum throbbed a slow crescendo and the spotlight dimmed; you caught a flash of movement in the dimness, then as the yellow circle blazed bright again, she stood there full in its center, stood poised, unmoving.

And she *was* beautiful; there was no doubt of that. The picture Sweeney had been carrying in his mind had not been exaggeration, not in the slightest. He thought, now, that she was the most beautiful woman he had ever seen. And by the collective catch of breath of the audience, he knew that he was not alone in thinking so. What, he wondered, was she doing in a dive like this, on Clark Street in Chicago? Even if she couldn't dance—

She wore a gown exactly like the one she had worn for the scene in the hallway, except this one was black and that had been white. This one was better, Sweeney thought. Contrast of black and white. It was strapless, molded to every curve of her body.

She was barefoot; the black gown her only visible garment. No ribbon, no gloves, no bolero; this wasn't to be a gradual strip tease like other strip teases; it would be one blinding flash from black to white, from cloth to flesh.

The drum throbbed.

You thought she was a statue there, and then—so gradually that you weren't sure at first—she moved. Merely to turn her head.

And when it was turned your eyes followed hers. You saw, as she saw, what crouched in semi-darkness on the other side of the stage. It was Devil, the dog; only he wasn't a dog at all now. He was all devil. He crouched there, his jaws slightly parted in a silent snarl of bared white teeth, his yellow eyes luminous in the dimness.

The drumbeat died down to almost-inaudibility. And in the almost-silence, the dog snarled loudly. It was the same sound, exactly the same sound, that Sweeney had heard before, two nights ago. It had put a cold chill down his spine then, and it put a cold chill down his spine now.

Still half-crouched, the dog took a stiff-legged step toward the woman. He snarled again and crouched to spring.

There was a sudden quick movement across the table from him that pulled Sweeney's eyes from the tense drama on the stage. And at the same instant that Sweeney saw the movement, Bline's big hand reached across the table and grabbed Guerney's arm.

There was a gun in Guerney's hand.

Bline whispered hoarsely, "You Goddam fool, it's part of the act. He's trained to do that; he's not going to hurt her."

Guerney whispered back, "Just in case. In case he *does* jump her. I could get him before he got her throat."

"Put back that gun, you Goddam sap, or I'll break you."

The gun went slowly back into the shoulder holster, but Sweeney saw, out of the corner of his eye, that Guerney's hand stayed on the butt of the gun.

Bline said, "Don't get trigger-happy. The dog jumps her; it's part of the act, Goddam it."

Guerney's hand came out from under his coat, but stayed near his lapel. Sweeney's eyes jerked back to the stage as a sudden intake of breath from the audience backgrounded a yip from a woman at a table near the stage, a yip like a suddenly stopped scream.

The dog was leaping.

But the woman moved, too, one step aside and the dog flew past her and down, alighted and turned in a flash of brownness, crouched again, and now she was in the middle of the stage as he leaped. Again she was not there when he landed.

And Sweeney wondered if that was going to go on indefinitely, but it didn't. That was the last time. The dog—as though convinced that leaping was futile—crouched now in the center of the stage, turning as she danced around him.

And she *could* dance; well, if not superlatively; gracefully, if not significantly. The dog, now no longer snarling, pivoted, his yellow eyes following every move she made.

Then alongside the now-tamed dog, the Beast, Beauty sank to her knees and put her hand upon the dog's head, and he snarled, but tolerated the caress.

The drum throbbed, the beat accelerated.

And then as Yolanda gracefully rose to her feet, facing the audience from the center of the yellow circle of light that already, but very gradually, was starting to fade, the dog padded behind her. It reared up, as tall as she, and then as it started downward its teeth caught the tab sewed to the tag of the zipper and pulled.

And the black dress, as had the white one, fell suddenly into a circle about her feet.

She was incredibly beautiful despite—Sweeney thought —the fact that she was overdressed. Overdressed in a narrow, transparent bra of wide-mesh net, diaphanous as dew and confining as air, that seemed to accentuate rather than conceal the beauty of her voluptuous breasts; and in a G-string which, in the slowly fading light, might not have been there at all, which needed to be taken on faith in the integrity of Chicago's vice squad; and one more garment: a six-inch strip of black adhesive tape, slightly slanting, across her white belly just below the navel. And somehow the contrast of that black on white made her seem even more naked than she had seemed when—two nights ago—Sweeney had seen her actually so.

The drumbeat faded slowly. Yolanda raised her arms— her breasts lifting with them—and spread her bare feet apart; the dog, from behind her, walked between her legs, halfway, and stood there with her astride him; his head raised to look out over the audience as though daring any man to approach that which he now guarded.

"Cerberus guarding the portals of Heaven" Sweeney whispered to Bline.

Bline said, "Huh?"

The drumbeat faded, and the light faded and then went out and the stage was dark. When the lights went on, the stage was empty.

And the lights went on brightly all over the room, and the floor show was over. People applauded madly, but Yolanda Lang did not return, even to take a single bow.

Over the noise, Bline asked Sweeney, "How'd you like it?"

"It, or her?"

"It. The dance."

"Probably symbolic as hell, but symbolic of what I don't

know. I don't think the choreographer did, either. If there *was* a choreographer. My idea is that Doc Greene figured it out. It's just crazy enough—and just smart enough—for his fine Italian hand."

Bline said, "Greene's not Italian. I think he's mostly German."

Sweeney was spared answering because Guerney had turned around and Bline was looking at him balefully. He said, "You Goddam fool, for a plugged nickel I'd make you turn in your gun and go without one."

Guerney flushed and looked foolish. "I wasn't gonna shoot, Captain, unless—"

"Unless the dog jumped at her. And he did, twice. Good God, but that would have been a stink for the department."

Sweeney felt sorry for the squad-car copper. He said, "If you *had* shot that dog, Guerney, I'd have stuck up for you."

Bline said, "And a lot of good that would have done him, unless you could have got him a paper route carrying the *Blade*."

Nick saved Guerney further embarrassment by appearing at their table. He said, "Another round of drinks is coming, gentlemen. How'd you like the show? Sure is a well-trained pooch she's got, ain't it?"

Sweeney said, "He showed more self-control, under the circumstances, than I would have."

"Me either," Guerney said. He started to grin, but caught Bline's eye and found he was still in disgrace. He said, "Gotta see a man about a—I mean, I gotta go to the can. Excuse me."

He threaded his way off between the tables. Nick slid into the vacated chair and said, "I'll stay a minute till he gets back. Did you notice anything during the show, Captain?"

Sweeney said, "Everything the G-string didn't cover. You know, sometime I'd like to see her without *anything* on."

Nick stared at him. "Huh? I thought, according to your story in the paper—"

Sweeney shook his head gloomily. "Gloves," he said. "She wore long, white gloves."

Bline snorted. He said, "This guy has a one-track mind,

Nick. What did you mean, did I notice anything during the show?"

Nick leaned forward. "Only this; that part where she's posed there, still, facing the audience and front-stage-center with the light fading out. Look, I shouldn't take a chance changing my own show—not that it matters; we could get a crowd here to listen to her sing Annie Laurie in a diving suit—but I been worried about that. I don't want her killed either, and if the Ripper should show here, that'd be his chance."

"Maybe, but how?"

"The audience is in the dark, almost dark anyway. And if he decided to throw that shiv of his, it'd be hard to tell just where it come from."

Bline looked thoughtful and then shook his head. "Sounds pretty remote, Nick. Unless he's already a knife-thrower, and it's a million to one against, it'd take him months of practice to learn. And I don't think he'd use a gun—guys like that stick to one weapon and one style of using it—and I don't think he'd try to kill her in a crowd anyway. I think the big danger point is on her way to and from here, or at her place at night. And we're taking care of that."

"For how long?"

"Until the Ripper's caught, Nick. At least as long as she'll be playing here, so *you* don't need to worry."

"You have someone go through her flat before she goes in when she goes home?"

Bline frowned. "Look, Nick, I'm not telling anybody *exactly* what precautions we're taking or not taking. Especially with a reporter sitting here who'd put it in the paper so the Ripper would be sure to know."

"Thanks," said Sweeney, "for demoting me from suspect to reporter. But that suggestion of going through her flat before she goes into it is good, if you aren't already doing it. If I were the Ripper and wanted to get her, I wouldn't try it on the street again; I'd be under her bed waiting for her. Say, does Devil sleep in the same room with her?"

Bline looked at him sharply. "That's not for publication. But yes."

"About that knife-throwing," Nick said. "What about if he can throw them?"

Sweeney said, "Here he comes. Ask him if he can."

[11]

Doc Greene was coming toward them, worming his way through the people who were leaving after the first floor show, a wide, satisfied grin on the bland, round face that Sweeney would have loved to slug.

Bline looked to see who was coming and then looked at Sweeney disgustedly. He said, "You and that damn hunch."

Maybe you feel disgusted with him too, and if so I hold no brief for him. It was just a hunch, and you know what a stubborn fool an Irishman with a hunch can be; if you didn't know when you started reading, you should know by now. Once a hunch gets into him, you almost have to blast to get it out; there wasn't much chance of blasting happening in the case of Sweeney. There was, of course, a much better chance, an excellent chance, of his finding out whether his hunch could leak out—along with other things—through the slit a knife or a razor could make across his abdomen. Yes, there was an excellent chance of that happening, and it almost did happen; but not just then. Doc Greene was carrying a foul, fat cigar, but no knife.

Nick stood up and said, "Hi, doc. Well, I got to go. So long."

Doc nodded to him, and asked Bline how he liked the show.

Bline said, "Great. Sit down, Greene."

Guerney, coming back, hesitated as he saw his chair being taken. Bline motioned to him and then told him to take a break and get some fresh air outside. Guerney left.

Doc Greene grinned at Sweeney. Not a nice grin. He said, "Do I have to ask how you liked it?"

"No," Sweeney told him. "I hear you held Nick—or rather, Harry Yahn—up. For a thousand bucks."

"I wouldn't call it a holdup. Yolanda shouldn't be dancing so soon after what happened. It's taking a chance with her health. Naturally, she deserves something extra for that, if she does."

"Does she get it?"

"Naturally. Of course, as her manager, I get my cut."

"What percent is that?"

"That's my business."

"And business is good," Sweeney said. "You know, Doc, there's something I'd like to ask you."

"I might even answer it."

"How come Yolanda is playing a place like this? It's peanuts to the bookings you could get her."

"You're telling me. But we're under contract here; I told you that. Yahn won't let us break the contract. Know what we're getting here? A lousy two hundred a week. I could get her a thousand a week damn easy, and we have to be tied down here for another month. And by that time—"

"You don't get me," Sweeney said. "What I mean is why *was* she working for a lousy two hundred a week? Even without the publicity, she ought to have been nearer to the big time than Clark Street."

Greene spread his hands. "Maybe you could do better for her. It's easy to say, Sweeney. Only you won't get a chance to try; I got her signed up under contract."

"For how long?"

"Again, my business."

Sweeney said, "I suggest you haven't wanted to get her better bookings, for reasons of your own."

"You're very suggestive. Would you like me to make a suggestion?"

"I could guess it in advance. But I can make another one." Sweeney glanced quickly to see that Bline was listening. He said, "How's this for a suggestion? Maybe the Ripper never attacked Yolanda at all. Maybe it was a publicity stunt. Nobody *saw* the Ripper slash at her. Maybe you cooked it up;

she could have given herself that little cut with, say, a safety razor blade, and then she could have lain down on the floor till someone saw her through the glass."

"Having swallowed the razor blade?"

"Having, possibly, dropped it in her mailbox slot. She was standing right by the mailboxes."

Bline said, "No, Sweeney. The hallway was searched, including the mailboxes. No weapon. And it wasn't in a shoe or in her dress, either. She was searched at the hospital. Don't think we didn't think of the possibility of it being a hoax."

Sweeney said stubbornly, "Doc could have been there and gone off with the blade, as easily as the Ripper could have been there and gone off with his weapon."

Greene bowed ironically. "Thank you, Sweeney. For implying for the first time that I'm not the Ripper."

"Don't mention it. And then, Cap, there's still another possibility. Maybe you've already thought of it. But that wound was pretty slight; not enough to incapacitate her. How do you know she got it in the hallway at all?

"I mean, she could have come home, gone up to her apartment, made that slit with a razor and washed the razor or whatever and put it away, then she could go back downstairs and lie in the hallway till somebody saw her."

Bline said, "We thought of that. Several little things against it, and one big one. Little things like the scratch marks on the back door. They could have been put there, sure, for the purpose of being found. And the fact that it would take a lot of nerve to give yourself a cut like that. *Could* be done, sure. Another little thing; it couldn't have been sure—unless you were in on it, Sweeney—that you'd be there to give it that write-up. Were you in on it?"

Sweeney grinned. "Sure. That's why I'm suggesting it now. Doc won't give me my cut, so I'm turning him in. But what's the one big thing that proves it wasn't a put-up job?"

"The shock, Sweeney. She got over it within twelve hours, yes, but she was really suffering from shock when she got to the hospital. Bad. And genuine. I talked to the doctors who treated her, and they're positive it couldn't have been acting—

nor drugs, either, for that matter. It was bona fide shock and you can't fake it."

Sweeney said, "Okay. It was an idea while it lasted. I'm glad it was wrong. It would have made a prize sucker out of me for the story I wrote."

Greene said blandly, "I'll tell Yo what you thought and that you suggested it to the police. She'll like you better for it, no doubt."

Sweeney glared at him.

Greene smiled and leaned across the table. He said, "The thing I like about you, Sweeney, is that your reactions are so completely predictable, so primitive, so utterly lacking in subtlety. You should know that I would do no such foolish thing as to inform Yolanda of your base insinuation."

"And why not?"

"Because I *am* subtle, and civilized. The last thing I would do is to make Yolanda angry at you, lest anger react. Women are subtle, too, whether civilized or not. But you wouldn't understand that. Even you, however, should have realized that if I were actually going to snitch to Yolanda, the last thing I would have done is to forewarn you that I would."

Bline was grinning at Sweeney. He said, "I'm liking this. It's your turn."

Sweeney said, "I'd rather discuss this outside."

"The animal plane," Greene said. "The three things for which the Irish are famous: drinking, fighting, and—well, the third, in Sweeney's case, is reduced to *voyeurism.*"

He leaned still farther across the table and he no longer smiled. "And even for that, Sweeney, I hate your very guts."

"The mask slipped then," Sweeney said. "You really are a psychiatrist, Doc?"

"I really am."

"And you honestly do not recognize that you yourself are not sane? Look, I don't know your relations with Yolanda—and don't bother trying to tell me, because I wouldn't be able to believe you, either way. But, whichever, your attitude toward her is not sane and normal. As her manager, you let her get up in front of a crowd of creeps in a honky-tonk, strip for

them, and get their tongues hanging out, and you tolerate it.
Maybe you even like it; maybe you've got a case of inverted
voyeurism. Or something. I wouldn't know what, but you
ought to, if you're a psychiatrist."

Bline was looking from one to the other of them, chuckling. He said, "At it, boys; I'll referee. The first one to lose his
temper to the extent of taking a poke at the other loses—and
maybe goes to the hoosegow."

Neither Greene nor Sweeney even glanced at him.

Sweeney said, "Thousands of men must have wanted her
and tried to get her. You couldn't have reacted to all of them
as you've reacted to me; your adrenals wouldn't have stood
the strain. So there's something different in my case. Know
what it is, Doc?"

Greene was wary, his eyes hooded. You could have counted to ten, slowly, before he answered, and then it was only to
say, "No, I don't." He sounded honestly puzzled.

"Then I'll tell you. It's because these other guys have only
wanted, and tried. You know I'm going to succeed."

Bline must have been watching Greene's face, because he
was on his feet and leaning over the table even as Greene
started across it. Greene's chair went over backward but he
stopped as Bline caught his arms, although he paid no attention to Bline. He said softly, "I'm going to kill you, Sweeney."

Then he jerked loose from Bline's grip, turned and
walked away.

Nick was suddenly there. "Anything wrong, gentlemen?"
he asked.

"Everything is lovely," Sweeney told him.

Nick looked uncertainly from one to the other of them.
He said "Shall I send another drink?" Sweeney said, "Thanks,
no, not for me," and Bline said, "I'll pass this one, too, Nick."

"There's not going to be any trouble?"

"No, Nick," Bline said. "But—yeah, I'll have a drink at
that, if I can."

Nick nodded and left them. Bline relaxed in the chair and
turned to Sweeney. "Just wanted to get rid of him. Sweeney,
you'd better be careful."

"I guess maybe you're right, Cap. I honestly don't think he's completely sane. That's why I goaded him; I wanted to show you."

"Of course he didn't mean what he said about killing you; he wouldn't have said that in front of me if he really meant it. He was just trying to throw a scare into you; that's all."

Sweeney said, "I wish I was sure of that. If he's sane, yes. But—Ripper or no Ripper—I wouldn't bet on his being sane."

"How about yourself?"

Sweeney grinned. "I may be crazy, but I'm not insane." He stood up. "Maybe that's enough excitement for one evening. Guess I'll hit for home."

"Your door got a good lock?"

Sweeney frowned at him. "You should know," he said. "Unless I left it unlocked the other night when you borrowed my razor."

Bline stood up too. He said, "I'll walk with you a block or two; I can use some fresh air."

When they were outside, walking north on Clark, he said, "If your razor being missing really scared you, Sweeney, I'm sorry about it. Happened this way; I sent two of the boys around to bring you in for questioning Thursday night and told 'em to bring your arsenal too. I didn't tell them to bring the arsenal if you *weren't* there, and they overstepped a little. One of them—I won't say who—is pretty good on locks and loves a chance to show off how he can open them."

"I know who that would be. You needn't tell me."

"Don't be foolish, Sweeney. Lots of guys on the force are good at locks."

"But only one of them has been to my room before, and anybody else would have had to ask Mrs. Randall instead of going straight up. And with her there they couldn't have gone on in. So that makes it the guy I'm thinking about. And I thought he was a friend of mine."

"Forget it, Sweeney. God damn it, man, friendship doesn't count when you're looking for a killer. And I'd told him you were under strong suspicion. Sweeney, we've *got* to get that guy before he butchers any more dames."

"For the dames' sake, or so you don't lose your job?"

"Both, I guess, but it's not all on account of my job. I wasn't on the Lola Brent one two months ago, but they dumped it in my lap after the second case, when it began to look like there was a psycho loose. I looked at the B-girl, Gaylord, at the morgue for a starter, and I saw the steno, Dorothy Lee, before they moved her. They weren't nice to look at. Christ."

He turned to look at Sweeney. "You saw a job of his work—a botched one. It wouldn't be so funny to you if you'd seen the real McCoy."

"I don't think it's funny."

"Then I wish you and Doc Greene would layoff that Punch-and-Judy show of yours and quit messing things up trying to make each other out to be the Ripper. Yeah, he fooled me, Sweeney. It was after a talk with him Thursday evening that I sent the boys around for you and your cutlery. I didn't know then that he was using me as a cat's-paw because he hated you for personal reasons."

"And if I try to get you to suspect him, I guess you think it's for personal reasons, too."

"Isn't it? Mostly?"

Sweeney sighed. "That and a hunch."

"Well, play your hunch if you want to. But don't expect me to. Greene's couple of alibis may not be perfect, but they're good enough for me—especially because, like I told you, I figure that the killer either knew *all* the dames or none of them. One kind of nut might kill the woman he's crazy about, but it's another kind that follows strangers home and kills them. For my money—not that I'm a psychiatrist—the same kind of nut doesn't do both."

They were nearing the corner of Erie and Bline slowed down. He said, "You turn east here. Guess I'll go back to the madhouse. And look, stay away from Greene. I don't want to have to jug you both for mayhem, and it's going to be that or worse if you keep tangling."

He stuck out a hand. "Friends, Sweeney?"

"I'm not the Ripper? You're sure?"

"Reasonably sure."

Sweeney took his hand, and grinned. "And I'm getting to be reasonably sure you're not a son of a bitch, Cap. I sure had you pegged as one for a while."

"Can't say I blame you. Well, so long."

Sweeney stood for a moment on the corner. He saw Bline look around and then cut diagonally across the street, which took him out of his way if he was returning to El Madhouse. He understood when, a hundred yards down, Bline stopped to talk to a man who had been looking into the window of a hockshop, and then Bline and the man walked south together.

That meant—unless there'd been two of them, which he doubted—that Bline had pulled Sweeney's tail off the job. To make sure, he pretended to turn south at Erie and State and then waited in the doorway of a store next to the corner one to see if anyone would turn into State Street after him. No one did.

He whistled a little as he went back to Erie and on east to his room. There was no Ripper waiting for him. But there was Mimi.

Number SM-1 of the Ganslen Art Company of Louisville, Kentucky. Screaming Mimi.

He picked her up and held her gently, and she screamed at him, pushing toward him with tiny, fending hands; again that little chill went down his spine.

Somewhere in Chicago there was another Mimi just like this one, and *she* had something to scream about. The Ripper had her.

Call her Mimi number one. What if the Ripper knew that he, Sweeney, had Mimi number two?

But the Ripper couldn't know that. At least, not unless the Ripper was Raoul Reynarde, who'd sold him Mimi number two, after Lola Brent had sold Mimi number one to the Ripper and had tried to drag down the money on the sale. And if Raoul was the Ripper, then Raoul wouldn't have had any reason to tell him about Mimi and— Hell, if Raoul was the Ripper then the whole story about Lola having sold a Mimi might have been out of the whole cloth, to distract attention from himself. But then Raoul would have told the police about it. Well, of course, Raoul had told the police the same story, but the police hadn't happened to follow through by looking at a duplicate of the statuette on which Lola had dragged down, and so they'd missed the point—the point that the man who'd bought the statuette had been the Ripper. Raoul himself had missed it. He, Sweeney, might have missed it except for the hunch that made him buy Mimi from Raoul—and then the remark of the counterman in the lunchroom.

He put Mimi down, very gently. He wished she'd stop screaming, but she never would. A silent scream can never be silenced.

No, definitely the police didn't know about Mimi; otherwise Bline would never have sat here in the same room with her without noticing or mentioning her. He'd looked right at her at least once.

And, of course, he'd mentioned Mimi to Doc Greene and Doc hadn't reacted. But—although he couldn't believe it—Doc might have been able to control his nerves enough not to let that sheet of paper move when "small black statuette" had been sprung on him. No, if Greene really was despite alibis, despite everything—the Ripper, then maybe the whole Mimi lead was a blind alley; maybe the Ripper hadn't made that purchase from Lola Brent at the gift shop.

Sweeney, he told himself, you can't have your cake and eat it too; if Mimi is a legitimate lead to the Ripper, then Greene can't be the Ripper—as you damn well would like to have him be.

He sighed.

Then he sat down on the bed and started the job he'd come home to do—reading up on the third murder, the Dorothy Lee one. He felt that he knew Stella Gaylord and Lola Brent pretty well by now.

He picked up the *Blade* of August 1st.

That story, of course, he didn't have to look for; it was the third Ripper job, and it splashed page one banners the day it broke, in the biggest type size the *Blade* used short of a declaration of war or an armistice.

RIPPER SLAYS ANOTHER WOMAN

There was a three-column picture of Dorothy Lee, and Sweeney studied it. She was blonde—like Lola, like Stella, like Yolanda—and definitely pretty, if not beautiful. It was a good portrait photograph and—if it was taken recently—she was probably in her early twenties. Details were not too clear, as though it had been blown up from a small picture or—more likely, since it was a portrait—they'd had to make the halftone from a toned sepia print instead of a glossy. At any rate, Dorothy Lee had been at least attractive; she might have been beautiful.

The story said she was beautiful, but the story would have said that in any case, provided only that she was under forty and didn't have buck teeth or crossed eyes.

The story said that she was Dorothy Lee, 25, beautiful blonde private secretary of J. P. Andrews, sales manager of the Reiss Corporation at an address on Division Street that Sweeney recognized as being near Dearborn. Her home address, he noticed with surprise, was on East Erie Street, only a block from his own. Only a block from where he sat right now reading about it. Good Lord, he thought, why hadn't Bline mentioned that? Of course—Bline thought he already knew it, since he was working on the case.

And maybe that was another reason why Bline had suspected him.

Before reading on, he pictured mentally a map of Chicago and mentally marked the scenes of the four forays of the Ripper. Three had been quite near, on the Near North Side. One, the attempt on Yolanda, five blocks away; another, the murder of the B-girl, in the mouth of the alley off Huron between State and Dearborn, had been about four blocks; Dorothy Lee's murder, one block.

True, the very first murder, that of Lola Brent, had been on the South Side, miles away, but it had probably started on the Near North Side—when the killer had trailed her home from the gift shop on Division Street, only a dozen blocks north. As he might possibly have trailed Dorothy Lee home from the Reiss Corporation on that same street.

He fixed those imaginary x's on the imaginary map in his mind and then went back to the newspaper.

The body had been found a few minutes after five o'clock by Mrs. Rae Haley, divorcee, who lived in the apartment next to Miss Lee's. Returning home after an afternoon at the movies, Mrs. Haley noticed what seemed to be a stream of blood—and which, it later turned out, really was blood—coming from under the doorway of Dorothy Lee's apartment.

Of course it might have been that Dorothy—with whom Mrs. Haley was acquainted—had dropped and broken a jar of tomato juice or a bottle of ketchup. Nevertheless, this was the third Ripper case, and Mrs. Haley, along with most of the rest of Chicago, was Ripper-conscious. She had *not* knocked on Dorothy's door, perhaps to have it opened by someone she had no desire to meet. She had dashed into her own apartment and locked and chained the door; then she had phoned down to the janitor telling him what she had seen.

David Wheeler, the janitor, had put an old service revolver in his pocket and climbed from the basement to the third floor—which contained five small apartments, including those of Miss Lee and Mrs. Haley. With the gun ready in his hand, he had tried the doorbell first and then the door, which was locked. He then bent down to examine the little red rivulet and decided that it was quite probably blood; David Wheeler had once been a hospital orderly and knew what blood looked like.

He had rung the bell of Mrs. Haley's apartment and, when she opened it on the chain, told her that the police had better be sent for. Mrs. Haley had phoned them herself, being too frightened by that time to open her door wider than the length of the chain, even to admit Wheeler. Wheeler had stood guard in the hallway until the police arrived. They had broken down the door of the apartment and had found Dorothy Lee lying on the floor about three feet back from the locked door.

They had found that the chain of the door had not been fastened and that the lock was a snap type which would have locked automatically after the killer when he had closed the door after him. There seemed little reason to doubt that he had left by the door. Both of the windows of Dorothy Lee's apartment were open, but neither led to a fire escape and there was no way, short of dropping twenty feet to a concrete areaway, that he could have left by a window.

The police believed, from the position of the body, that the killer had barely entered the apartment. Miss Lee still wore her hat (it had been a hot day and she had worn no coat) and had obviously just returned to her room. Police believed the killer had followed her home and had rung the doorbell almost as soon as Miss Lee had closed the door.

When she had opened the door, he had stepped through and used his knife. Perhaps she had not had time to scream; if she had, no one had heard her. Police were still canvassing tenants of the building to see which, if any, had been in their apartments at the time.

Having made the fatal cut, police reasoned, the Ripper had immediately backed out of the door, closing it and letting it lock after him. Aside from the body there was no sign of his presence in the apartment, which was neat and in perfect order. Miss Lee's purse was on a small table near the door; it contained about fourteen dollars in bills and change. Neither her wrist watch nor an opal ring had been taken from the body.

She had left work at two forty-five, complaining of a toothache; the office manager had suggested that she visit a dentist and take the rest of the afternoon off. Her movements from that time on, until her death, had not yet been traced but police were canvassing dentists on the Near North Side and in the Loop to ascertain which one she had seen and when. The coroner's physician who examined the body found evidence that she had really visited a dentist; there was a temporary packing in a tooth that appeared to be abscessed.

If the temporary packing hadn't stopped her toothache,

the Ripper had. According to the physician who had examined the body at five-thirty, she had at that time been dead between one and two hours—between half-past three and half-past four. She had, then, probably been dead at least a half hour when Mrs. Haley, at five o'clock, had seen the blood which led to the discovery of the crime.

The story ended with statements by the Chief of Police and by Captain Bline, in charge of the special detail attempting to find the Ripper.

Sweeney took up the next paper and looked for further details.

The dentist had been found, a Dr. Krimmer, who had his office on Dearborn Street, a little over three blocks south of Division Street. Recognizing her picture in the *Blade,* he had come forward before the police canvass reached him.

Dorothy Lee had come to him at about three o'clock, suffering from a toothache. She had no appointment and was a new patient, but because she was obviously in distress, he had taken her out of turn, as soon as he finished work on the patient then in his chair. That would have been, he estimated, about ten minutes after three.

She had been in his chair only ten or fifteen minutes, he had been able to give her only a temporary treatment to relieve the pain. He had suggested an appointment for further work the next morning. She had asked if he could take her in the afternoon instead, explaining that she worked Saturday morning but was off in the afternoon and, with an afternoon appointment, she would not have to lose more time from work.

He had given her an appointment at four o'clock, his first free time after noon, but told her that if the tooth became seriously painful earlier in the day she should come to him then and he would manage to take her out of turn to relieve the pain.

He had no record of the exact time she had left his office, but he thought it would hardly have been earlier than twenty minutes after three nor later than half-past.

Sweeney thought that through and saw that it did not

change the situation concerning the time of the crime. She could have reached home as early as three-thirty if she had taken a taxi. Sweeney looked at his mental map again and estimated distances. If she had walked over to State from Dearborn and taken a State Street car south to Erie, then walked from State and Erie, she would have reached home about a quarter of four. Had she walked all the way—a total distance of about a dozen blocks—she would have reached home by four o'clock or a few minutes sooner. Assuming, of course, that she had not stopped over anywhere enroute.

He skimmed through the few succeeding issues of the paper and found no new developments of importance.

He went back to the first one and studied the picture of Dorothy Lee again. It looked vaguely familiar—which wasn't strange if she lived only a block away. Damn it, he'd probably passed her on the street half a dozen times. He looked at the picture again and wished that he had known her. Of course, if he had known her, he'd have found her just another uninteresting stenographer, stupid, vain and self-centered, who preferred Berlin to Bach and *Romantic Confessions* to Aldous Huxley. But now violent death had transfigured her and those things didn't seem to matter. Maybe, really, they didn't matter.

He jerked his mind back from the edge of maudlinness to the problem at hand.

The Ripper.

Bline had been right, then, about Doc Greene's alibi; it wasn't perfect, but it was good. If his alibi covered him—with the word of attorneys and a judge—until ten minutes after four, miles away, he *could* have taxied to the Near North Side in time to pick up the trail of Dorothy Lee if, and only if, she had stopped over somewhere between the dentist's office and her home. But it didn't seem likely. To rush from court—

Damn Greene, he thought. If only he could positively eliminate Greene, maybe he could get some constructive thoughts in other directions.

He got up and began to pace back and forth, trying to think.

He glanced at his watch and saw that it wasn't yet quite midnight and the evening was a pup.

Maybe he could eliminate Greene, tonight. Maybe—better, if possible—he could implicate him, tonight.

A spot of burglary, suitably chaperoned, might accomplish either.

He grabbed for his suit coat and Panama.

[12]

He locked the door on Mimi, leaving her alone and screaming in the dark. He stopped at the phone in the hallway and dialed the number of an inexpensive hotel on downtown Clark Street. He gave a room number; it was rung, and an annoyed voice answered.

Sweeney said, "Ehlers? This is Sweeney."

"The hell, Bill; I was just going to turn in. Tired. But since when you call me Ehlers instead of Jay?"

"Since last night."

"Huh?"

Sweeney said, very distinctly, "Since yesterday evening when you entered my room without a warrant."

"Huh? Listen, Sweeney, it was orders. And what was Bline's idea in telling you it was me?"

"Bline didn't tell me. And it wasn't orders."

Ehlers said, "Oh—hell. All right, what you want me to do, get down on my knees and say I'm sorry?"

"No," Sweeney said. "Something harder than that—and more practical. Keep your clothes on till I get there. In about ten minutes; I'll take a cab."

He put the receiver back on the hook. Fifteen minutes later he knocked on the door of Jay Ehlers' room.

Ehlers opened it and said, "Come in, Sweeney." He looked faintly embarrassed and faintly belligerent. His coat and tie were off, but he hadn't undressed any farther than that.

Sweeney sat down on the bed, lighted a cigarette, and looked at Ehlers.

He said, "So you thought I might be the Ripper."

"That wasn't *my* idea, Sweeney. It was the captain's."

"Sure, and it was all right for him. Bline didn't know me; he hadn't been a friend of mine for ten years or more. And he sent you and your pal around to bring *me* in—and any cutlery you found around. I wasn't home and it was your bright idea to show how smart you are with locks and burgle my room. You didn't follow orders; you exceeded them. And how many drinks have we had together m ten or twelve years, how many games of cards, how much money have we borrowed from one another? And how about the time I— Hell, I won't remind you of that."

Ehler's face was reddening. He said, "I remember the time you saved my job; you don't have to remind me. All right, so I should have thought twice. But is this leading to something or did you just come up here to get a bawling-out off your chest?"

"It's leading to something. I'm going to give you a chance to wash it out. I'm going to let you open a door for me, a door to a man's office."

"You crazy, Sweeney? Whose?"

"Doc Greene's."

"Can't do it, Sweeney. You're crazy"

"Were you crazy when you opened the door of my place? You did that on your own hook, without a warrant and without orders."

"That's different, Sweeney. At least I had orders to exceed. I was told to get your razor and any knives you had, for the lab. What are you looking for in Greene's office?"

"The same thing. Only I won't bother them unless they're bloodstained, and if we get anything on him you can have the credit."

"You don't think Greene really *is* the Ripper, do you?"

"I hope to find out, one way or the other."

"What if we get caught?"

"Then we get caught. We try to talk our way out of it."

Ehlers stared at Sweeney and then shook his head. He said, "I can't, Sweeney, I'd lose my job no matter how much talking we did. And I got a chance to put in for lieutenant within a few months."

"To put in for it, but not to make it."

"What do you mean?"

Sweeney said. "It means we're not friends any more, Ehlers. It means you start off on the *Blade's* s.o.b. list, and go on from there. It means I'm going to spread the good word about you to every reporter I know. It means you wouldn't get your name in ink if you stopped a bank robbery single-handed, but we'll drown you in ink if you spit on the sidewalk. It means this is your choice to make up for the dirty trick you pulled on me and if you don't take it, by God, I'll pull every string I can get hold of—in the department itself as well as in print—to break you."

"Yeah? Goddam it, you can't—"

"I can try. I start off tomorrow morning by bringing suit against the police department for entering my room without a warrant, through a locked door, and for petty larceny."

Ehlers tried to laugh. "You couldn't make it stick."

"Of course I couldn't. But don't you think the commissioners would start their own little investigation to see what it was really all about? They'd jump on Bline and Bline would tell them the truth. And they'd back you to save the department from paying damages, and let you lie out of it and no, I couldn't prove my point and collect. But you'd sure rate highly with the commissioners after that. Lieutenancy hell; you'll be back in harness, pounding pavement so far out there wouldn't be any pavement."

"You wouldn't do that, Sweeney."

Sweeney said, "I thought you wouldn't burgle my room, and I was wrong. You think I wouldn't do that, and you're wrong."

"Where *is* Greene's office?" Ehlers was perspiring slightly; it may have been the heat.

"Goodman Block, not far from here. A few blocks, in fact.

And I know the building and there won't be any trouble or any danger. I won't take over fifteen minutes inside."

He saw he'd won his point, and grinned. He said, "And I'll buy you a drink first. Dutch courage, if you're more afraid of Greene than you were of me."

"That was different, Sweeney."

"Sure it was different; I was a friend of yours. Greene isn't. Come on."

They caught a cab on Clark Street after Ehlers had turned down the Dutch courage in favor of a drink afterwards, and that was okay by Sweeney. They took the taxi only to within half a block.

The Goodman Block was an old ten-story office building, tenanted mostly by not-too-prosperous lawyers, agents, brokers and (Sweeney happened to know) headquarters of several bookies and at least one small numbers ring.

Sweeney had figured it would be the type of building that would be open twenty-four hours a day for those of its tenants who wanted to burn midnight oil, and saw that he was right. He and Ehlers walked past on the opposite side of the street and saw that lights still burned in several of the offices. And, through the entrance, they could see that an elevator man was on duty, reading a newspaper while he sat on a chair beside the open elevator door.

They kept on walking and Ehlers asked, "Going to take a chance on having him take us up? We can give him a song-and-dance, but even so, he'll remember us."

They crossed over. Sweeney said, "We'll try not to use him. We'll wait—a little while, anyway—outside the entrance and out of his sight; we'll be able to hear the bell ring and the elevator start if he gets a call from upstairs, and we can get through the lobby without his seeing us."

Ehlers nodded agreement, and they waited quietly outside until, luckily only ten minutes later, they heard the buzzer of the elevator and the clang of its door closing.

Sweeney picked Greene's room number, 411, off the building directory as they went through the outer hall; they were on the stairway between the second and third floors when the elevator passed on its way down from whatever upper floor it had serviced.

They tiptoed quietly the rest of the way to the fourth floor and found 411. Fortunately no other office on that floor seemed to be occupied; Ehlers did not have to use particular caution in applying his picklocks. He got the door open in seven minutes.

Inside, they turned on the lights and closed the door. It was a little cubbyhole of an office. One desk, one cabinet, one file, one table, three chairs.

Sweeney shoved his hat back on his head as he looked around. He said, "This won't take long, Jay. Sit down and relax; you've done your share, unless I run across a locked drawer; there isn't any lock on that file."

The bottom drawer of the three-drawer file contained a pair of overshoes, a half-full bottle of whiskey and two dusty glasses. The middle drawer was empty.

The top drawer contained correspondence—all incoming correspondence; apparently Greene didn't make carbons of his own letters. It disgusted Sweeney to find that the correspondence was filed only in approximately chronological order; that there was no separate section or folder for Yolanda; he'd hoped for some clue to what he thought was Doc's rather unusual way of handling her. But he didn't want to spend too much time on the file and glanced only at sample letters pulled out at random and put back when he'd looked at them. All he learned was that Greene really did business as a booking agent and did have other clients and get bookings for them. Not, as far as he could tell, on any big-time circuits or top clubs.

He left the file and tried the cabinet. Stationery supplies on the shelf, an old raincoat hanging on one of the hooks, and a portable typewriter case standing on the bottom. He looked in the raincoat's pockets and found nothing but a dirty handkerchief and a pair of month-old theater stubs. He opened the portable typewriter case to make sure that it contained a typewriter, and it did.

It looked pretty much like the one he himself had owned

—up to the point on his recent bender when he'd taken it out to sell. It was the same make and model but when he looked at it closely he saw it wasn't the same typewriter, which would have been a fascinating discovery.

The drawer of the table contained nothing more fascinating than an old hectograph, two of the three chairs were empty and the third chair contained only Jay Ehlers, who was staring at him with a saturnine expression.

Jay asked, "Well, find anything?"

Sweeney grunted an answerless answer and turned to the desk. On top of it was a blotter pad, a pen set and a telephone. He looked under the blotter pad; there was nothing there. He tried the drawers. Only the left-hand top one was locked. He said, "Hey, pal. Your department."

That was the drawer that interested him. He went through the others hastily while Jay opened the locked one. There wasn't anything in any of the other drawers of particular interest to Sweeney, except, possibly, one full bottle of whiskey. And right now he wasn't interested in that.

Jay opened the drawer and glanced at his watch. He said, "Snap it up, Bill. You said fifteen minutes and we've been here twenty-three already."

Inside the locked drawer was a ledger and a thick brown envelope marked "Current Contracts."

Sweeney looked at the ledger first, but it turned out to be a journal rather than a ledger, not indexed, and listing receipts and expenditures in chronological order. He thumbed through it rapidly but saw that he wasn't going to get anything from it—aside from the fact, which he didn't doubt anyway, that Greene had a legitimate business as a booking agent. Probably the figures wouldn't be too straight anyway, but were kept for income tax purposes.

He took up and opened the envelope marked "Current Contracts."

There were a dozen of them there, but only one interested Sweeney; that was the contract between El Madhouse, Nick Helmos signing, and Yolanda Lang. The contract called for two hundred dollars a week for the joint services of Yolanda Lang and Devil. But neither Yolanda nor the dog had signed it; the signature was Richard M. Greene.

Sweeney upped an eyebrow. He asked, "Can't she write?"

"Can't who write?"

Sweeney said, "I can understand why the dog didn't sign it."

"Look, I thought you were looking for a razor or a shiv."

Sweeney sighed. What he'd really been looking for most was a small back statuette. But if Doc had that, it was at his flat or hotel or wherever he lived, not at his office. And—even if he could find out, at this late hour, where Doc lived—he couldn't crowd his luck by burglarizing it tonight.

And anyway, why couldn't he get Doc Greene off his mind so he could concentrate on other angles? A trip to Brampton, Wisconsin, for instance, to talk to the sculptor—what was his name? Chapman Wilson—who had made Mimi. There was a chance, an off chance, that might lead somewhere. He didn't see where or how. And maybe, getting back to Greene, damn him, a trip to New York to see whether Greene's alibi—his only solid one—was really one hundred percent solid. The police there might or might not have dug under the surface fact that he was registered at a hotel. Sweeney doubted that they had.

Or, if he had a lot of money, he might save himself that trip by having a New York private detective do the job for him. But that would have to be on Sweeney; the *Blade* would never cover it.

Damn money! He still had a hundred dollars or so out of the checks Wally Krieg had given him, but at the rate it was vanishing, he'd barely get by for the ten days before another check would be coming from the *Blade*. Let alone spending any money on the Ripper or on Yolanda.

He heard Jay Ehlers move restlessly, and looked back at the contract in his hand. He said, "Just a minute, Jay."

He read the contract through and frowned. He read one paragraph again to make sure it really said what he thought it said, and it did. He put the contract back in the envelope with the others, put the envelope in the drawer, and told Jay to relock it.

Jay said, "Well, find what you were looking for?"

"No. Yes. I don't know what I was looking for, but I found something."

"What?"

"I'm damned if I know," Sweeney said. But he thought he did; he'd found some money if he was willing to take a chance.

Jay grunted as the lock clicked. He said, "Come on, then. Let's clear out of here. We'll argue about it over a drink."

Sweeney turned out the lights and waited in the hallway while Jay relocked the door of Room 411.

They walked very quietly down to the second floor and there Sweeney put his finger to his lips and then pressed the button of the elevator signal. As soon as they heard the door clang shut a floor below them, they started down the stairs and were on the first floor by the time the operator opened the door on the second. They were out of the building and two doors away by the time the elevator got back down to the first floor.

Ehlers said, "He'll know somebody pulled a fast one to get out of the building without being seen."

Sweeney said, "Sure he will, but he didn't see us. And he won't chase us."

He didn't.

They waited until they were out of sight around the corner before they flagged a cab. Sweeney asked Jay where he wanted the drink and Jay suggested Burt Meaghan's; it was only two blocks from his hotel and he could walk back from there.

In Burt's place, Sweeney started toward the bar but Ehlers took Sweeney's arm and pulled him toward a table instead. He said, "We got a minute's talking, Bill, in private."

At the table, he glowered at Sweeney until their drinks had come and the waiter had gone. Then he said, "Okay, Bill. I burgled your room and I shouldn't have. But I burgled another place for you to make up, so we're even. Right?"

"Right."

"We're friends?"

"Friends. All is forgiven."

Jay said, "All right, then, we start from there. We're friends now, but we're not going to keep on being friends if you hold out on me. I want the pitch; I want to know why you wanted into Greene's office and what you got there, and didn't get. I'm a cop, Sweeney, and I'm working on the Ripper case. Just as a flunky under Bline, sure, but I'm still working on it. I want to know what the score is. I can't *make* you tell me, because you got me by the short hairs. I can't tell Bline or anyone else you were in Greene's office because I'd lose my job for my part in it. You're safe as hell, but by God, I write *you* off *my* books if you don't tell me."

Sweeney nodded. "Fair enough, Jay. So okay, I've had a strong suspicion that Greene is the Ripper. No reason for it at all; just a dumb hunch, because I hate the guy so much. Well, a little more than that: I think he fits the role. Psychiatrist or not, I think he's psychopathic. A couple of hours ago at El Madhouse, I got through his guard and he threatened to kill me. Out loud and in front of the police. To be specific, in front of Cap Bline. And another copper—hell, *two* coppers, guys named Ross and Swann, sitting right at the table. I got his goat on purpose to try him out."

"The hell. But what's that got to do with his office?"

Sweeney said, "I hoped I could find something there that would help me make up my mind, pro or can, about Greene. But—word of honor, Jay, I didn't. I didn't find a damn thing to indicate Greene might be the Ripper. I didn't find a damn thing to indicate he isn't, except the proof that he really is what he says he is, an agent and manager for night club talent."

"Keep on. What did you find?"

"Something that interested me personally, Jay. I found the contract for Yolanda and Devil versus El Madhouse. And there's something in it I think I can use. But illegally; you wouldn't want to know about it."

"Illegally how?"

"To pick up a piece of change that I need."

"Who from?"

"The guy who owns El Madhouse."

"You mean Nick Helmos or Harry Yahn?"

"Yahn. Nick's just a figurehead."

Jay Ehlers pursed his lips and stared into his glass for a moment. He said, "Careful, Bill. Harry Yahn's a tough mug."

"I know it. But I'm going to bite him. I'm going to make the bite small enough that it won't pay him to use his torpedoes on me. He's tough, but he's smart. He won't take a chance for peanuts."

"Me, I'd rather buck the Ripper, Bill."

Sweeney grinned. "Me too. But I'm going to buck Yahn for the dough to buck the Ripper with."

"You're crazy, Bill."

"I know it. Another drink?"

Ehlers said he'd better turn in, and left. Sweeney wandered over to the pinochle game and watched the play for a few minutes, then went to the bar for one more drink.

The few he'd had at El Madhouse had worn off completely and the one he'd had just now wasn't enough to feel. One more drink, even two, wouldn't hurt him.

He had two, and they didn't hurt him.

[13]

The two drinks didn't hurt him, but they didn't do him any good, either. He was cold sober when he went out of Meaghan's Bar into the night. The lonely, teeming night.

The warm, chilling night. The bright, dark night. He was afraid, and it annoyed him that he should be afraid. He didn't mind being afraid of the Ripper; that was the Unknown, the Mysterious. But he didn't like being afraid of Harry Yahn. Harry Yahn was a mug. There wasn't anything mysterious about Harry Yahn; and the things that were unknown about him were strongly suspected by the police, whether they could be proved or not.

Harry Yahn was a plenty tough mug, but still just a mug. Sweeney told himself that and told himself that he wasn't afraid, because the bite he was going to put on Yahn wasn't big enough to bother a man with an income like Yahn's.

The funny thing was that he'd had Yahn in mind as a possible source of revenue even before the trip to Greene's office tonight; there were some things that Sweeney knew about some things that Yahn had done, several years ago, that would have been worth money—to anyone desperate enough to try to collect it. But this new angle was better, and safer—a little safer, but a lot better.

It wasn't blackmail, exactly.

The neon sign said redly, "Tit-Tat-Toe Club." Sweeney took a deep breath and went in. It was an ordinary bar, only moderately swank, and not as large as Meaghan's place. It was populated at the moment by one bartender and half a dozen customers. It looked like the type of bar that might be a front for something else. It was.

Sweeney went to the bar and decorated it with a bill. The bartender lumbered over and Sweeney said, "Shot. Water chaser." And then before the bartender could turn away, "Is Harry here?"

"Harry who?"

"The name is Sweeney, Bill Sweeney. He knows me."

The bartender turned to the backbar for glass and bottle. As he poured the shot he said, "Knock on the back door there, around the corner from the john. If Willie knows you, you get in."

"Willie doesn't. But Harry does."

"Tell that to Willie. He can talk; he can ask Harry. If Harry's here."

"Okay," Sweeney said. "Have one with me."

"Sure."

"And wish me luck."

"Sure," said the bartender. "Luck."

"Thanks."

"For what?"

Sweeney laughed, and felt better. He went back around

the corner from the john and knocked on a heavy door. It opened a few inches and a face looked out, the eyes—and they weren't nice eyes—well above the level of Sweeney's head.

Under the eyes was a broken nose, and under the nose was a pair of thick lips that said "Yeah?" and showed broken teeth between them.

Sweeney said, "Willie Harris. I didn't know the Willie on the door was Willie Harris."

"Yeah. What you want?"

"The hell, Willie. Don't you remember me? I covered three of your fights when I was doing Sports. Bill Sweeney. I was on the *Trib* then."

The door opened wider, eight inches instead of six. Willie said, "Yeah?"

Punchy, Sweeney thought. He said, "Okay, you don't remember all the reporters ever talked to you. Listen, Willie, I want to talk to Harry Yahn. On business. Not the games. He knows me. Tell him Bill Sweeney wants to talk to him. Bill Sweeney."

Short sentences like that, Willie would get. He said, "Sweeney. I'll see."

"Bill Sweeney. Hang on to it, Willie. Bill Sweeney."

The door closed.

Sweeney leaned against the wall and lighted a cigarette. When an inch was gone from the length of the cigarette, the door opened again, wider.

Willie looked out to be sure nobody but Sweeney was there and said, "Okay. He'll talk to yah."

He led Sweeney along a short stretch of hallway and pointed to a door. "In there. Go ahead."

Sweeney went in. He said, "Hello, Harry," and Yahn said, "Hi, Sweeney. Sit down."

Harry Yahn, seated at a battered desk that looked as though it had been bought second hand for about ten dollars, looked like Santa Claus without his whiskers. He was fat and smiling; he looked both complacent and complaisant. Sweeney wasn't fooled. But he was glad, at least, that they were alone.

"Haven't seen you for a long time, Sweeney. Still on the *Blade?*"

Sweeney nodded. "Read that story about Yolanda?"

"Which one?"

"The eyewitness one, the scene in the hallway. In the *Blade.*"

"The hell; did you write that? I skimmed it, but I didn't happen to notice the by-line."

Sweeney didn't call him a liar. He merely said, "Yeah, I wrote it. And a damn fine job, if I say so myself—and why shouldn't I, since everybody else does?"

"Y'know, Sweeney, that story hasn't hurt business at El Madhouse a bit. Where you staying? I'm going to tell the boys to send a case of whiskey over for you."

"Thanks," Sweeney said, "but I'm on the wagon. Almost. And I've got a better idea, Harry. How about letting me handle the publicity for you for the next four weeks—while Yolanda's playing there?"

Yahn pursed his lips and stared at Sweeney. He said, "That would have been a better idea before all this happened. We don't need it now. El Madhouse is turning them away Nick tells me, and what'd we do with more suckers? Hang 'em from the rafters? And we've got Yolanda under contract for only four more weeks, like you say, and it'll hold up that long."

He laughed. "You gave it away, Sweeney. Sure, I'd have paid you to get that story you wrote into print, but it *was* in print; it's a dead horse now. And look—there was plenty publicity outside of that. Just getting jumped by the Ripper, that's enough to pull them in to see Yolanda. Your eyewitness story just tied it up in cellophane. Nope, Sweeney, we got all the publicity we can make use of."

Sweeney shrugged. He said, "It was just an idea. I'll work on it from the other end, then."

"The other end?"

"Doc's end. A little more publicity—and I think I could swing it—and he could book Yolanda for real money in anyone of several places with twenty times the take of El Madhouse. He could get two, maybe three thousand a week instead of two hundred. Or instead of four hundred and fifty if you prorate over four weeks the thousand buck bonus she's getting for going back to work right away."

Harry Yahn's eyes were half closed, as though he was bored. He said, "It's an idea. If you can keep the publicity hot for four weeks more, she might still pull down that kind of money, or almost that kind."

Sweeney said, "She's worth it right now. I caught your first show at El Madhouse tonight, Harry, and did a little figuring. You ought to have capacity crowds for four weeks. Capacity's two hundred each show, three shows, six hundred a night. Let's be conservative as hell and say each mooch pays five bucks and that one buck out of that is clear profit. Six hundred bucks a night profit for a week is four thousand, two hundred; times four weeks, sixteen thousand, eight hundred dollars."

Yahn said dryly, "We did some business before we had Yolanda."

"Sure, about half as much as you'll be doing for the next four weeks. And with half as much, the overhead is higher. Let's say having Yolanda for the next four weeks will bring in about ten thousand dollars profit that you wouldn't have otherwise. Fair enough?"

"Too high. But what are you leading up to?"

"All right, it's too high. Let's say it's worth seven thousand dollars. Is seven thousand conservative enough?"

Yahn's eyes were almost closed and he was smiling faintly; he looked now more like a sleeping Buddha than like Santa Claus. Sweeney wasn't fooled; Harry Yahn was neither sleeping nor contemplating nirvana. Not when money, in the thousands, was the subject of conversation.

Yahn said, "I hope you're leading somewhere."

Sweeney stalled deliberately by taking out a cigarette and lighting it. Then he said, "If I do publicity for Greene and Yolanda instead of for El Madhouse, I would advise my friend Doc to book Yolanda elsewhere right away instead of waiting four weeks. But that would cost you seven thousand dollars, Harry, and I wouldn't like to do that, because I've always considered you a friend of mine."

"Yolanda is under contract for four more weeks."

Sweeney smiled. He asked, "Have you read the contract?"

Yahn's eyes opened fully halfway and he looked at Sweeney.

He asked, "Are you representing Greene on this? Did he send you to shake me down?"

"No. And nobody is trying to shake you down, Harry."

Harry Yahn said a nasty word. He said, "It doesn't wash, Sweeney. If there was a hole in that contract that would let Greene book Yolanda elsewhere, he'd be in there pitching. For himself. Why would he tell you about it?"

Sweeney leaned back comfortably in his chair. He said, "He didn't tell me about it. He doesn't know about it, yet. He and I had a little bet about how much Yolanda and Devil were getting at El Madhouse and he showed me his copy of the contract—with Nick's signature—to win his bet. And he won the bet. But while I had the contract in my hand I happened to read it. Have you?"

"What's the gimmick?"

"Sweet and simple. It must have been an El Madhouse contract, a standard one you give your talent there, because it's full of escape clauses for the party of the first part, which is El Madhouse. But there's also an escape clause for the party of the second part, only it's one that wouldn't be worth a damn in any ordinary case. But this isn't an ordinary case."

"And what is the clause?"

"One that wouldn't be worth the paper it's written on to anybody else, Harry. It provides that the contract may be canceled by the party of the second part by payment of the face amount of the contract—by refunding all moneys received under the contract and paying an amount equal to the balance still to be received under the contract.

"Yolanda's contract is for seven weeks, three down and four to go, at two hundred a week. Doc could buy her out of that for seven times two hundred—fourteen hundred dollars. And if he could book her elsewhere for two thousand a week for the next four weeks, he and Yolanda would be ahead six and a half thousand dollars. Maybe more; I think right now he could get more than two grand a week from her current publicity, even if I don't add to it."

Sweeney leaned forward and stubbed out his cigarette in the ash tray on Yahn's desk. He said, "The only bad thing about it is that Greene's gain would be your loss."

"Greene doesn't know that's in the contract?"

"Obviously not. He probably read the contract when it was signed, but a clause like that wouldn't have meant any-thing then. Only in case a performer's value suddenly in-creases ten times overnight would a clause like that really *be* an escape clause. And the odds are a thousand to one against his happening to reread the contract. He thinks he knows what's in it."

Sweeney stood up. He said, "Well, so long, Harry. Sorry we couldn't see eye to eye on my doing a little publicity for your club."

"Sit down, Sweeney."

Yahn jabbed a button on his desk and it seemed he had hardly lifted his finger off it before Willie Harris was in the doorway. He said, "Yeah, Boss?"

"Come in and close the door, Willie. And just stick around."

"Want me to take this guy apart for you?"

Yahn said, "Not yet, Willie. Not if he sits down."

Sweeney sat down. Willie stood, ready. If you looked at Willie's face you might have got the idea that Willie hadn't taken anybody apart for a long time and had been missing it badly. Anyway, that's the idea Sweeney got. He quit looking at Willie's face and got out another cigarette and lighted it, moving very slowly and carefully so as not to startle Willie. He wished that he felt as casual as he hoped he was acting.

Yahn picked up the phone on his desk and dialed a number. He asked for Nick. He said, "Harry, Nick. You got the contract for Yolanda Lang in the safe there. Get it out and put it in your pocket and then call me back. Right away, and privately. Use that phone in the back office and be sure nobody's in hearing distance, see? And don't let anybody notice what you're taking out of the safe . . . Okay."

He put the phone back on the hook and looked at Sweeney. Sweeney didn't say anything. Nobody said anything. In three minutes the phone rang.

Sweeney said, "Tell him the sixth paragraph, Harry. That'll save time."

Yahn talked briefly and then listened. He said, "Okay, Nick. Put it back. And don't mention this . . . Yeah, that's why I had you read it to me. We'll talk it over tomorrow. How's business?" He listened a moment and then said "Okay," and hung up.

Sweeney asked, "How *is* business?"

Yahn didn't look at him for a moment. Then he did look at him. He said, "Well, what do you want?"

Sweeney said, "I figure handling publicity for you for the month in question ought to be worth nine hundred bucks."

Harry Yahn didn't look like either Santa Claus or Buddha. He asked, "And if Greene finds out anyway? Happens to reread that contract?"

Sweeney shrugged. "It could happen. There won't be any reason why he would."

Harry Yahn laced his fingers over his stomach and stared a moment at his knuckles. Without looking up, he said, "Willie, go tell Haywood to give you nine hundred. Bring it here." Willie went.

Harry Yahn asked, "How come nine hundred? How'd you hit on that odd amount?"

Sweeney grinned. Inside, the grin was a little shaky and he hoped the outside of it looked better. He said, "I figure you for a four-figure man, Harry. I cut just under. If I'd asked for a thousand—I might have got something else."

Harry laughed; he looked like Santa Claus again. He said, "You're a smart son of a bitch, Sweeney." He got up and slapped Sweeney on the back. Willie came in with money in his hand. He handed it to Yahn and Yahn handed it to Sweeney without counting it. Sweeney didn't count it either; he put it in his pocket.

Yahn said, "Show him out, Willie. And let him in again

any time he comes." Willie opened the door and Sweeney went out to the hall; Willie started after and Yahn called him back for a moment. Then Willie came out and opened the door to the outer hallway.

As Sweeney started through it, Willie's hand, as big as both of Sweeney's put together would have been, grabbed his shoulder and spun him around. Willie's other hand, doubled into a fist the size of a football but harder and heavier, slammed into Sweeney's stomach. Willie let go of his shoulder and Sweeney fell, doubled up. He wasn't out, but he couldn't get his breath and he was sick at his stomach. And the pain was so great that he wished the blow *had* knocked him out, especially if there was more coming.

There wasn't.

Willie stepped back. He said, "Harry said to give you that, too." He added, as though explaining why Sweeney had got by so luckily, "He said just one, and easy." It was very obvious that Willie Harris would have preferred it to be more and harder.

He closed the door.

Within a minute Sweeney was able to get to his feet and, a bit doubled over, make it as far as the john. He was sick and after that he was able to stand almost straight. He bent over the wash bowl and rubbed cold water into his face, which the mirror showed him to be almost as white as the porcelain bowl.

But he was breathing almost regularly by now. His abdomen was almost too sore to touch and, very gingerly, he let his belt out two notches to take pressure off it.

He leaned back against the wall and took the money out of his pocket and counted it. It was nine hundred all right, and it was real. He'd got all he'd asked for, and only one thing more. He'd been lucky, plenty lucky.

He put the money into his wallet and, walking as though on eggs, he went out through the bar of the Tit-Tat-Toe Club. He didn't look at the bartender or at anyone else on his way through.

He stood outside breathing the cool night air. Not in

deep breaths; that would have been unbearably painful. He didn't look around to see if anyone came out after him; he knew no one would.

He'd been unbelievably lucky. Even that poke in the stomach was a good sign, in a way. Harry wouldn't have told Willie to do that if he'd intended to send some of the boys to work him over seriously, or to shoot him. He hadn't really thought there was much danger of being shot—not for nine hundred dollars. But a working-over had been a real possibility, a working-over that might have put him in the hospital for a week or a month and would have played hell with all his plans. Now he felt reasonably confident that he'd been paid in full, both ways. He was going to be plenty sore for a few days, and he was going to have to sleep on his back—and very gingerly at that. But there wasn't any permanent harm done. Worse things had happened to him—and for less.

A cab came cruising by and he hailed it. He walked to it as an old man walks and it hurt him to pull the door open.

He said, "Drive over to the lake and north along it for a while. A little sick; I can use some fresh air."

He got in. Closing the door jarred him.

The cabby peered back at him. He asked, "How sick, Mac? Not going to mess up my cab, are you?"

"Not sick that way. And I'm sober."

"Want me to take you to a sawbones?"

Sweeney said, "I had a poke in the guts, that's all."

The cabby said, "Oh," and started the cab. He drove east to Michigan Boulevard and north until they were on Lake Shore Drive. Sweeney leaned back in the cab and began to feel better, especially after they were on the Drive and a cool breeze off the lake came in the open windows.

The cab didn't jar him; the gentle motion seemed to help.

He felt pretty good with nine hundred bucks in his pocket and no worse price for it than this. A prizefighter took a hell of a lot worse and, except for the top few, for a hell of a lot less.

He wasn't angry at Willie. Willie was punchy to begin with, and had been carrying out orders—even though he'd enjoyed doing it and would have more enjoyed doing more. But too many punches had addled Willie's brains, what few he had ever had.

He didn't blame Harry Yahn either. After all, it *had* been blackmail; Harry had let him off easy.

He saw they were passing Diversey Parkway and said, "Guess this is far enough; you can head back now."

"Okay, Mac. Feeling better?"

"Practically okay."

"Should I have seen the other guy?"

Sweeney said, "Yeah, you should have seen the other guy. He's about six feet three and weighs about two-twenty."

"The hell you say. Must have been Willie Harris. I picked you up in front of the Tit-Tat-Toe."

"Forget I said it," Sweeney told him. "I was kidding you."

"Okay, Mac. Where'll I drop you off?"

"Bughouse Square."

"Bughouse Square at this hour? What the hell you want to do there?"

Sweeney said, "I wish to commune with God."

The cabby didn't answer that. In fact, he didn't say another word until he announced the fare at Sweeney's destination.

[14]

Bughouse Square stirred restlessly in the warm night as Sweeney walked into it. The benches were lined with human cargo; there were men sleeping on the grass, too. Shut off from the lake breeze by the buildings on Dearborn, the leaves of the trees hung dead still, the blades of grass did not ripple; the stirring was the restless moving of men who slept or tried to sleep because they had nothing else to do.

The fourth bench on the right on the northeast diagonal walk, that's where God would be if he was there. He was there, looking older and more disreputable than when Sweeney had last seen him. But maybe that was partly contrast; Sweeney's own looks and dress were different tonight from what they were when he had last seen Godfrey. Unconsciously, one judges others by comparison with oneself; and two people both of whom have eaten onions cannot smell each other's breath.

But Sweeney didn't try to smell God's breath; he shook God's shoulder, gently and then harder, and God blinked and looked up. He said, "Whattahell?"

Sweeney grinned at him. He said, "Don't you know me?"

"No, I don't know you. Beat it before I call a cop."

"Want a drink, God? Badly enough?"

"Badly enough to what?"

Sweeney said, "To reach in your right-hand coat pocket."

Godfrey's hand reached into his pocket, clutched something, and stayed there. His voice was a little hoarse. He said, "Thanks, Sweeney. Haven't had a drink since afternoon; it'd have been a hell of a morning. What time is it?"

"About half past three."

God swung his feet off the bench. He said, "Good. How's it coming with you, Sweeney?"

"Good."

God pushed himself up off the bench. Sweeney said, "Look at the figure on the corner of that bill before you hand it over."

God pulled his fist out of his pocket and looked at a corner of the crumpled bill. He glared at Sweeney. He said "A Goddam capitalist. Showing off."

He thrust his fist back into his pocket and got up off the bench. He walked away without looking back.

Sweeney, grinning, watched him until he'd reached the street—mostly to be sure that nobody had heard or seen and would follow. No one followed. Sweeney went the opposite direction and caught a cab on Chicago Avenue. It was almost four o'clock when he got home, and he was tired. But before he went to his room he called the Northwestern Station from the phone in the hall.

Yes, they told him, Brampton, Wisconsin, was on the Northwestern Road; the next train that would take him there left at six o'clock, in a little over two hours. The train after that? None that went through Brampton before evening. What time did the 6:00 A.M. train get in? One-fifteen in the afternoon.

Sweeney said thanks and put the receiver back on the hook.

In his room he looked longingly at his bed, but he knew that if he lay down to try to get an hour's sleep before he started for the train, he'd never be able to get up when the alarm clock went off.

And if he waited until the evening train, he'd be losing a day's time right when it mattered most. This was Saturday already and Monday morning he had to be back at the *Blade* ready for work and—even if Wally came through and assigned him to the Ripper case—Wally would never sanction a trip to Brampton on the paper's time. Let alone sanction a trip to New York to check on Greene's alibi there. Well, unless something came up that would save him from having to do that, he could fly there and back next week end on his own time. And his own money; that was no longer a worry.

An hour ago, with his own hundred, he'd had a thousand dollars. Now, after tithing with God, he still had nine hundred.

If he had any sense, he realized, he'd do something with part of it; he wouldn't carry that much money with him.

But he didn't have that much sense.

He looked again at the clock and sighed. He looked at Mimi and swore at her for being so important that he was losing sleep to trace down her origin and talk to her creator, little as that was likely to get him.

He went over and turned her around on top of the radio so her back was toward him and he couldn't hear her scream. But, even from the back, every line of her body showed terror.

He felt for her so strongly that, for a moment, he contemplated euthanasia. But even if he did break her there would be a gross minus one of her still screaming somewhere.

Wearily—and very gingerly because of his tender abdomen—he undressed. He bathed, shaved and put on clean clothes, decided he wouldn't have to take anything with him, and left for the station. He would be too early but he wanted to allow time for a couple of drinks. Not *as* drinks, but because with them he ought to be able to sleep on the train; otherwise he'd probably be too tired, after six, to sleep in a coach or chair car. He'd have paid double price for a Pullman but knew he couldn't get one; railroads have the strange idea that people should ride horizontally only at night.

He had to walk to State Street, through the gray still dawn, before he caught a cab. He took it to a place on West Madison within a block of the station which he knew would be open even at the late or early hour of five. He had his two drinks—and a third for the road. He considered, before he remembered that he was on the wagon, buying a bottle to take along on the train; but he remembered in time and didn't buy it. Besides, too much to drink would get him wide awake again.

He got to the station at a quarter to six, hoping that the train would be loading by then, and it was. Luckily there was a chair car on the train and the ticket agent sold him a ticket for it and said that he wouldn't need a reservation, that the chair car wouldn't be crowded.

It wasn't. He picked the most comfortable-looking seat in the car, sat down carefully, and put his ticket in the band of his hat so the conductor wouldn't have to wake him. He sprawled out his legs and put his hat, ticket side up, over the bruised portion of his anatomy. It was a lightweight Panama so it didn't hurt too much.

Or if it did, he didn't know it; he was asleep almost the minute he closed his eyes. He opened them briefly a couple of hours later and found the train pulling out of a station. It was Milwaukee, and it was raining. When he opened his eyes again it was a few minutes after noon, the train was in Rhinelander, and the sun was shining. And he was as hungry as a horse.

He found the diner and ate the biggest meal he'd eaten in weeks. And finished his second cup of coffee just in time to get off at Brampton.

He went into the station and looked in the phone book; no Chapman Wilson was listed. Sweeney frowned and walked over to the ticket window. He asked, "You happen to know where in town Chapman Wilson lives?"

"Chapman Wilson?"

"Yes."

"Never heard of him."

"Thanks."

Sweeney left the station on the side opposite the tracks and took a look at Brampton. About five thousand population, he estimated. In a town that size, it shouldn't be too hard to locate someone, even if they didn't have a phone.

He was already, he found, on the main street; the business distinct, about four blocks long, started immediately to his left. He went into the first store he came to and asked about Chapman Wilson. He drew a blank. And in the second, the third, and the fourth. Not to mention the fifth and sixth.

The seventh place was a tavern and he ordered a drink before he asked his question. When the drink came he asked. The drink was good but the answer wasn't.

Sweeney swore to himself as the bartender moved off. Could he have misunderstood the man he'd talked to at the Ganslen Art Company? No, he'd said it clearly enough: "Fellow by the name of Chapman Wilson, lives in Brampton, Wisconsin. He modeled it in clay."

At least he was sure of the Chapman Wilson. Could he have misunderstood the Brampton part?

He motioned the bartender over. He asked, "Is there any other town in Wisconsin that has a name that sounds like Brampton?"

"Huh? Oh, I see what you mean. Let's see. There's Boylston, up near Duluth."

"Not close enough."

"Stoughton? Burlington? Appleton? And there's a Milton, but the full name is Milton Junction."

Sweeney shook his head sadly. He said, "You forgot Wisconsin Rapids and Stevens Point."

"They don't sound like Brampton."

"That's what I meant," Sweeney said. "Have a drink."

"Sure, thanks."

"But you've never heard of a Chapman Wilson?"

"No."

Sweeney took a meditative sip from his glass. He wondered if he could raise anyone by phone at the Ganslen Art Company in Louisville. Probably not, on a Saturday afternoon. He might possibly manage to locate the man he'd talked to there—Burke? Yes, Burke was the name. But it wasn't too good a chance.

Sweeney, the rest of his life, was never proud of it, but it was the bartender who saved the day. He asked, "What's this Chapman Wilson do?"

"Sculptor. Artist and sculptor."

For seconds nothing happened. Then the bartender said, "I'll be damned. You must mean *Charlie* Wilson."

Sweeney stared at him. He said, "Don't stop there, Esmeralda. Go on."

"Go on where?"

"To pour us another drink. And then tell me about Charlie Wilson. Does he model little statuettes?"

The bartender laughed. "That's the guy. Crazy Charlie."

Sweeney gripped the edge of the bar. He said, "What do you mean, Crazy Charlie? Crazy, as in *razor?*"

"Huh? Razor? Oh, you mean what *started* him. It was a knife, not a razor."

"A blonde," said Sweeney. "A beautiful blonde?"

"You mean the dame? Yeah, mister, she was both of those. Purtiest thing in town. Until she got attacked with that knife."

Sweeney closed his eyes and counted up to two slowly. It was too good to be true, and he had been about to leave town and go back to Chicago.

It had to be too good to be true; things didn't happen like this. He said, "You mean *attacked,* as in Ripper?"

"Yeah. Like that Chicago business on the radio."

"You are not referring, by any chance, to a small black statuette? You mean a real woman was attacked up here?"

"Sure. A blonde, like the radio said all the dames in Chicago were."

"When?"

"Three years ago. While I was sheriff."

"While you were sheriff?"

"Yeah. I was sheriff up to two years ago. Bought this place then and couldn't keep up both, so two years ago I didn't run."

"And you handled the Ripper case?"

"Yeah."

Sweeney said, "I am proud to meet you. My name is Bill Sweeney."

The bartender stuck a big paw across the bar. "Glad to know you. My name's Henderson."

Sweeney shook the hand. "Sweeney, he said, "of the Chicago *Blade*. You're just the man I was looking for, Sheriff."

"Ex-sheriff. "

"Look, Sheriff, is there any way we can talk privately for a little while without you having to interrupt yourself?"

"Well—I don't know. Saturday afternoon and all that."

"I'll buy a bottle of the most expensive champagne you got, and we'll split it while we talk."

"Well—I guess I can get the frau to take over for ten or fifteen minutes. We live upstairs. Only let's split a pint of Haig and Haig instead; the champagne I got isn't very good and anyway it'd take time to ice it."

"Haig and Haig it is." Sweeney put a bill on the bar.

Henderson rang up money and gave Sweeney a little back. He took a bottle from the backbar, put it in his hip pocket, and said, "Come on; I'll get Ma."

He led the way to a door at the back that opened to a flight of stairs. He called up them, "Hey, Ma! Can you come down a few minutes?"

A voice called out, "Okay, Jake," and a few seconds later a tall, thin woman came down the stairs. Henderson said, "This is Mr. Sweeney, Ma, from Chicago. We want to talk a while, upstairs. Can you take over?"

"All right, Jake. But don't you get started drinking. This

is Saturday, with Saturday night coming up."

"Won't touch a drop, Ma."

He led Sweeney up the stairs and into a kitchen. He said, "Guess we can talk best here, and glasses and everything are handy. Want anything to mix it with?"

"Haig and Haig? Don't be silly, Sheriff."

Henderson grinned. "Sit down. I'll get glasses and open this."

He came back with glasses and the opened bottle and poured a generous shot for each of them. Sweeney lifted his. "To crime."

"To crime," Henderson said. "How're things in Chicago?"

"Ripping," Sweeney said. "But let's get to Brampton. First, let's make sure this Chapman Wilson I'm talking about and your Crazy Charlie are one and the same person. Tell me something about him."

"His name is Charlie Wilson. He's an artist and a sculptor; guess what money he makes out of it is mostly from the stuff he models. He sells them to some companies that make statuettes and stuff. Arty little things. Guess he doesn't sell many paintings."

"That's the guy," Sweeney said. "Probably uses Chapman as a professional first name; Chapman Wilson sounds better than Charlie Wilson. But how crazy is he?"

"Not really. When he's sober, he's just—what you call it? —eccentric. He's pretty much of a lush, though, and when he gets tanked up—well, I've had to kick him out of my place half a dozen times. Mostly for trying to pick fights." Henderson grinned. "And he's about five feet two and weighs about a hundred and ten pounds soaking wet. Anybody take a real poke at him, they'd probably kill him, and yet he's always wanting to start a fight when he gets tanked. A real screwball."

"Does he make a good thing out of his work?"

"Hell, no. Doubt if he makes five hundred bucks in a year. He lives in a little shack out at the edge of town that nobody else'd live in; gets it for a few bucks a month. And proud as all hell; thinks he's a great artist."

"Maybe he is."

"Then why doesn't he make some money out of it?"

Sweeney opened his mouth to mention Van Gogh and Modigliani and a few others who'd been great artists and had made less than five hundred bucks a year out of it; then he remembered his audience and that time was flying.

He asked, instead, "And Charlie Wilson is now running around loose? In Brampton?"

"Sure. Why not? He's harmless."

"Well, this Ripper business. How does Charlie Wilson tie in with that?"

"He shot him."

"You mean Charlie shot the Ripper or the Ripper shot Charlie?"

"Charlie shot the Ripper."

Sweeney took a deep breath. "But the Ripper got away?"

"Hell, no. Killed him dead as hell. Charlie got him with a shotgun from about two yards away. Blew a hole through him you could stick your head through. Only good thing Charlie ever did in his life. He was kind of a hero around town for a while."

"Oh," said Sweeney. He felt disappointed. A dead ripper wasn't going to be much help to him. He took another sip of the Scotch. "Let's start it from the other end. Who was the Ripper?"

"His name was Pell, Howard Pell. A homicidal maniac who broke out of the county insane asylum—that's about twenty miles from here. Let's see, it was four years ago; I told you wrong when I said three because it was in the first year of my second two-year term and that would've been at least four years ago, maybe a few months more than that even. Yeah, a few months more because it was in spring, I remember, and it's August now. Think it was in May."

"And what happened?"

"Well, this Pell broke out of the asylum. Killed two guards with his bare hands; he was a big guy, built like an ox. Bigger than I am. Outside, the siren hadn't gone off yet and he flagged a car and the damn fool driver stopped to pick him up. Guy named Rogers. Pell got in the car and killed Rogers. Strangled him."

"Didn't he use a knife at all?"

"Didn't have one yet. But he got one all right, then and there. This Rogers was a canvasser selling a line of aluminum kitchenware. But he had some sidelines and one of them was a carving set. The knife in it was a beauty, ten inches long and an inch wide, sharp as hell. Don't know exactly what he was searching the car for, but he found that. And liked it. He tried it out on Rogers, even though Rogers was already dead. Want the details on that?"

"Not right now," Sweeney said. "But I could use another drink. A short one."

"Sorry." Henderson poured it. "Well, he operated on Rogers and threw his body out of the car into the ditch. Not all at once, y'understand."

Sweeney shuddered slightly and took a quick sip of the Scotch. He said, "I'd just as soon not understand too thoroughly. Go on."

"Well, this was about eight o'clock in the evening just after dark. Anyway, that's when they found the two guards dead and Pell gone from the asylum. They called me quick— along with sheriffs of other counties around and local police officers and everybody and meanwhile what guards they could spare fanned outward from the asylum in cars to start the search.

"Well, right off they found what was left of this guy Rogers, and the car tracks showed 'em what'd happened so they knew Pell had a car. They cut back to the asylum and phoned me and everybody that Pell would be in a car and to set up roadblocks and get him.

"We got the roadblocks up quick, but he fooled us. He did head toward Brampton all right, but a little outside of town he turned the car into a side road and left it there. And he came in across the fields on foot so he got through us. Even though between us, me and the police chief here in Brampton, we had every road guarded by that time. Within fifteen minutes of the time we got the call from the asylum."

"Fast work," Sweeney said, approvingly.

"Goddam tooting it was fast work, but it didn't do any good, because he got through us on foot. The next day we could trace back exactly the way he went from the car because he had so much blood on him. Y'see he cut up Rogers right in the driver's seat of the car and then had to get there himself to drive the car, and he was kind of covered with blood all over. God, he even had it in his hair and on his face and his shoes were soaked with it. And looking like that, and with the bloody knife in his hand, was how he come across Bessie taking a shower."

"Who is Bessie?"

"Who *was* Bessie. Bessie Wilson, Charlie's younger sister. She was about eighteen, then, maybe nineteen. She was staying with him then because she was sick. She didn't live in Brampton; she had a job in St. Louis, hatcheck girl in a night club or something, but she got sick and broke and came back to stay with Charlie; their parents had been dead ten years or so.

"Guess she didn't know, when she came back, how broke he was or she wouldn't've come, but she probably, through the letters he'd written her, thought he was doing pretty good. Anyway she was sick and needed help, and what happened to her here in Brampton didn't help her any, I guess. Maybe it'd been better if she'd been killed right out."

"This Pell attacked her?"

"Well, yeah and no. He didn't actually lay a hand on her, but it drove her nuts and she died later. It was this way. That shack of Charlie's is just one fair-sized room that he uses to live in and work in both and that's where they lived. But there's another littler shack, sort of like a tool shed, out in back of it on the lot. The can's in there, and Charlie fixed up a shower in there, too. In one corner, just a makeshift kind of shower.

"Anyway, this would've been about half-past eight, the kid sister, Bessie, decides to take a shower and goes out of the shack and along the path to the shed, in a bathrobe and slippers, see? And that must've been just about the time Pell is, coming to their yard, cutting into town and keeping off the streets and the road, so he sees her go into the shed.

"And with the carving knife in his hand, he goes up and yanks the shed door open."

"Wouldn't there be a catch on it?"

"I told you he was big as an ox; he just yanks it open so hard the hook pulls off. And Bessie is standing there naked under the shower getting ready to reach up and turn it on. And he takes a step inside toward her, waving the knife. How's about another drink?"

"An inspiration," said Sweeney.

Henderson poured two.

He said, "You can't blame her for going nuts, can you? Sick to begin with, and seeing *that*. Guy over six feet, two-twenty pounds, in a nuthouse uniform that started out being gray but that ended up being red, with blood in his hair and on his face, and coming at her with a ten-inch carving knife. God"

Sweeney could picture it. He'd seen Mimi.

He took a sip of scotch. He asked, "What happened?"

[15]

Henderson said, "Well, I was two blocks away and I heard her scream and keep on screaming. It was maybe five minutes before I got there—and of course it was all over long before that—but she was still screaming then.

"What happened was that the first scream she let out, Charlie grabbed for his shotgun—he's got one because he does a lot of hunting, not so much for fun like most of us but because he gets some of his eating that way. And he ran out the back door of the shack and saw the guy with the knife in the doorway of the shed and past him he could see Bessie back in the corner under the shower that wasn't turned on yet, screaming her head off.

"So he runs toward the door; it's only about ten feet from the shack to the shed, and runs a little to one side so he can shoot Pell without shooting Bessie too, and from right outside the door he lets go with the shotgun and, like I said, puts a hole through Pell that you could stick your head through."

"But *must* I?" Sweeney asked. At the blank look on the ex-sheriff's face, he changed his question. "And Bessie Wilson went crazy?"

"Yeah, and died about six-seven months later. Crazy as a bedbug. No, not in the asylum near here; that's for incurables. And for a while they thought they could cure Bessie. It was in some little private sanitarium downstate near Beloit. There was a lot of publicity on the case and one of the doctors down there got interested. He had a new treatment and thought he could cure Bessie and took her on as a charity case. But it didn't work; she died six-seven months later."

Sweeney asked, "And Charlie? Did he go off the beam, or was he crazy before that?"

"Like I told you, he isn't really crazy. But he was off the beam before that, and I guess that didn't make him any worse. He's an artist. That's crazy to begin with, isn't it?"

Sweeney said, "I guess it is. Where is this shack of his?"

"On Cuyahoga Street; that's eight blocks west of here, almost at the edge of town in that direction. I dunno the number, if there is a number on it, but it's a block and a half north of Main Street—that's the street you're on now—and there are only a few houses in that block and his is the only one-room shack and it's painted green; you can't miss it. Another drink? There's still a couple left in here."

Sweeney said, "Why not?"

There didn't seem to be any reason why not, so Henderson poured them and they killed the bottle.

Sweeney stared moodily into his. This had looked so good, less than half an hour ago. He'd found the Ripper. Only the Ripper was dead, four and a quarter years dead, with a hole in him Sweeney could stick his head through if he wanted to, only he didn't want to, especially with the Ripper four and a quarter years dead.

Sweeney took a sip of his drink and glared at Henderson as though it was Henderson's fault.

Then he thought of a new angle. It didn't seem likely. He asked, "This Charlie Wilson. He ever out of town?"

"Charlie? Not that I know of. Why?"

"Just wondering if he ever got to Chicago."

"Naw, he couldn't afford train fare to Chicago. And besides, he didn't."

"Didn't what?"

"Didn't commit your three Ripper murders. Our new sheriff—Lanny Pedersen—was talking about them the other night downstairs. Naturally, we thought of the coincidence of our having had a Ripper here, even if he was dead, and I asked Lanny what about Charlie, if maybe Charlie could have—uh—sort of got the idea from what he saw, or something, and he said he'd thought of that and that he hadn't thought so or anything but that he'd checked with Charlie's next-door neighbors out on Cuyahoga Street, and Charlie hadn't been out of town at all. They see him every day and most of the day because he does most of his painting or sculpting outdoors in his yard."

Sweeney took another sip. "And this Pell," he asked. "There's no doubt but that it was Pell that Charlie shot? I mean, the shotgun didn't mess him up so he couldn't be recognized or anything."

"Nope, didn't touch his face. No doubt about identification at all, even if he didn't have the bloody uniform on and everything. Shotgun blast hit him in the chest; guess he must have heard Charlie at the door and turned around. Blew a hole in his chest that you could put your head through."

Sweeney said, "Thanks just the same," and stood up. "I guess it was a bust, Sheriff. I had an idea I could tie your Ripper case up with ours, but it doesn't look like it can be done with Charlie alibied and everybody else concerned dead. And anyway, you thought of it before I did. Well, thanks anyway."

He waited while Henderson washed out the glasses they'd used and hid the empty bottle at the bottom of the garbage pail, and then went downstairs with him and Henderson relieved his wife at the bar. She glared at him before she went back upstairs and he had a feeling that Henderson's precautions with the glasses and the bottle had been futile. Even if she didn't find the bottle, she'd know that there had been one.

There were only four customers in the bar and Sweeney unhappily set up a drink around for them before he went out. He had only a short beer for himself.

He trudged back to the railroad station and asked what time the next train left for Chicago.

"Eleven-fifteen," the agent told him.

Sweeney glanced up at the clock and saw it was only half past four. He asked, "Is there an airport around where I can get a plane for Chi?"

"A plane for Chicago? Guess the nearest place is Rhinelander. You can get one there."

"How do I get to Rhinelander?"

"By train," the agent said. "The eleven-fifteen. That's the next train headed that way."

Sweeney swore. He bought a ticket for Chicago on the eleven-fifteen and had the agent wire to reserve him a lower berth. Anyway, he'd get to Chicago early Sunday morning with a good night's sleep under his belt.

He sat down on a bench in the station and wondered how he'd ever manage to kill over seven and a half hours without drinking too damn much if he drank at all. And if he did that, he'd probably miss the eleven-fifteen and that would ruin tomorrow, which was his last day on his own before he had to go back to the *Blade*.

He sighed, and decided that he might as well see this this Charlie-Chapman Wilson while he was here anyway and had to do something to kill the time.

But he'd lost all enthusiasm for it now. It had sounded so beautiful when the ex-sheriff had opened up about a crazy Charlie named Wilson and a blonde being attacked by a Ripper. It had sounded so good that the anti-climax made him wish he'd never heard of Brampton, Wisconsin.

Well, he still had Mimi as a lead but he'd have to trace her the other way, forward instead of backward, and find the Ripper who had a copy of her. Tracing her back here had lead only to a coincidence—but a coincidence that was a beautiful confirmation of the idea that Mimi would appeal strongly to a Ripper; she'd been born, in a sense, through contact with a Ripper. Only, alas, not the one who was now operating in Chicago.

Well, he'd still talk to this Chapman Wilson. And if Wilson was a lush, a bottle would be the best way to get him to talk. He bought a bottle, a fifth this time, at a liquor store on his way down Main Street to Cuyahoga. He found Cuyahoga and the small green shack with a shed behind it. But there wasn't any answer to his knock at the door.

He tried the door of the shed, but there wasn't any answer there either. The door of the shed was unlocked; it was fixed to lock only from the inside. Sweeney pushed it open and looked in. Inside, one corner had been partitioned off with beaverboard and was obviously a toilet. In the opposite back corner, sans curtains or partition, was the crude shower the ex-sheriff had described.

A string hanging beside the door operated to turn on the light, a bare bulb in the middle of the ceiling. Sweeney turned it on, and he could see in the far wall, between the shower and the toilet, the place where the charge of the shotgun must have hit, and gone through; there was a square of beaverboard nailed over it now.

He looked back at the shower corner and shivered a little, picturing a full-scale model of his Screaming Mimi—only in soft white instead of hard glossy black—standing there screaming, her slender, rounded arms thrust out in ineffable terror, warding off—Sweeney turned out the light and pulled the door shut. He didn't like his mental picture of *what* she had been warding off. No wonder the poor girl had gone fatally mad.

He went back to the front of the shack and knocked again. Then he went to the house next door and knocked. A man with handlebar mustaches answered the door and Sweeney asked if he knew whether Charlie Wilson was gone for the day or would be home soon.

"Oughta be home soon, I guess. Saw him walk toward town couple hours ago. He always gets home time to fix his own supper; he wouldn't be eatin' downtown."

Sweeney thanked him and went back to the front of the shack. It was five o'clock and already beginning to be dusk; he might just as well wait here as do anything else he could think of.

He sat down on the wooden step and put his package—the bottle—down on the grass beside the step, resisting an impulse to open it before Charlie came home.

It was six o'clock, and twilight, when he saw Charlie coming. He recognized him easily from Henderson's description—five foot two, a hundred ten pounds dripping wet. He looked even lighter than that, possibly because he wasn't dripping wet, not on the outside, anyway. From the way he walked, he was not suffering from an internal drought.

He could have been, Sweeney decided as he turned in the gate and came closer, anywhere between twenty-five and forty-five. He had straw-colored, uncombed hair and wore no hat; his clothes were rumpled and he hadn't shaved for at least two days. His eyes were glassy.

Sweeney stood up. "Mr. Wilson?"

"Yeh." The top of his head was just level with Sweeney's chin.

Sweeney stuck out a hand. He said, "Sweeney. Like to talk to you about a certain statuette you made. Ganslen's number SM-1, a girl screaming—"

Charlie Wilson's hand came out, too, but it passed Sweeney's instead of shaking it. And the hand was doubled up into a fist that landed in Sweeney's sore stomach. Sweeney's stomach screamed silently and tried to crawl through his backbone.

Sweeney himself said something inarticulate and bent almost double, which put his chin in handy reach for an opponent Charlie Wilson's height. Charlie's fist hit his chin and knocked him off balance, but didn't straighten him up.

Nothing would have persuaded Sweeney to straighten up, just then. Nothing at all. He'd didn't really feel the poke on his chin at all because the pain in his stomach was too intense. You don't feel a mosquito bite when you've got your leg in a bear-trap.

Sweeney staggered back, still doubled up, and sat down on the doorstep again, his hands protectively clapped over his stomach. He didn't care if Charlie Wilson kicked him in the face, as long as he didn't touch his stomach again. He didn't care about anything in the world except protecting his stomach. Still with his hands over it, he leaned sideways and started to retch.

When he recovered sufficient interest to look up, Charlie Wilson, arms akimbo, was staring down at him with an utterly amazed expression on his face. His voice matched his expression. He said, "I'll be damned. I licked you."

Sweeney groaned. "Thanks," he said.

"Didn't really hurt you, did I?"

Sweeney said, "It feels lovely. Everything's wonderful." He retched again.

"Didn't mean to hurt you, really. But hell, I always get licked whenever I take a poke at anybody, so I try to take as good a poke or two as I can get in before it happens. Hey want a drink? I've got some gin inside. Inside the hovel, I mean; not inside me. That's whiskey."

"What's whiskey?"

"Inside me. Want a shot of gin?"

Sweeney picked up the wrapped fifth of whiskey beside the step. "If you can open that—"

Wilson got it open by using the rough edge of a key on the celluloid and turning the cap with his teeth. He handed the bottle to Sweeney and Sweeney took a long drink. Sweeney handed back the bottle. "You might as well have one too. To the start of a beautiful friendship. And just what *did* start it?"

"I hate reporters."

"Oh," said Sweeney. He thought back. "And just what gave you the idea I'm a reporter?"

"You're the third in a week. And who else would—?" He broke off, a puzzled look coming into his eyes.

Sweeney said, "Who else indeed? But let's start over again, and differently. You're Chapman Wilson?"

"Yes."

"My name is Sweeney. Mortimer Sweeney. I'm with the Ganslen Art Company. Of Louisville."

Charlie Wilson put a hand to his forehead. He said, "Oh, my God."

"You may well say it."

"I'm sorry as hell. Look, can you stand up yet? So I can get the door open. Don't; I've got a better idea. I'll go around back and open it from inside and then I can help you in."

He went around the side of the shack, looking considerably more sober than when he'd first come up the walk. Sweeney heard a back door being opened and then the front door. It nudged his back.

Wilson's voice said, "Sorry, I forgot it opens out. You'll have to stand up anyway to let me get it open. Can you?"

Sweeney stood up. Not all the way up, but far enough for him to move to one side and then go in when the door opened. He made it to the nearest seat, which was a camp stool without a back; that didn't matter because he didn't feel inclined to lean back anyway.

The light was on, a single overhead bulb as in the shed back of the shack. Wilson was washing two glasses at the sink in one corner. The sink was piled high with dishes but there weren't any on the shelves above the sink; obviously Wilson washed dishes when and as he needed them for use rather than the more orthodox system of washing them and putting them away each time after they'd been used.

He poured a generous slug from Sweeney's bottle into each of the glasses and came over with one of them for Sweeney.

Sweeney took a sip and looked around him. The walls, every available inch of them, were hung with unframed canvases. There were landscapes vaguely in the manner of Cezanne that Sweeney rather liked, and there were abstractions that looked interesting; Sweeney wasn't enough of an expert to know how good they were, but he could tell that they weren't bad. There didn't seem to be any portraits or figure work.

At one side of the room a sculptor's stand held a partially finished twelve-inch statuette of what appeared to be a gladiator.

Wilson had followed Sweeney's gaze. He said, "Don't look at that. It isn't finished, and it's horrible anyway."

He walked across the room and threw a cloth across the clay figure, then sat down on the edge of the cot across from Sweeney.

Sweeney had begun to feel better. He said, "It's not bad—the gladiator, I mean. But I'd say oil is your real medium and that the statuettes are pot-boilers. Right?"

"Not exactly, Mr. Sweeney. Of course if you weren't from Ganslen I'd say you were exactly right. By the way, what is your job there?"

Sweeney had been thinking about that. He didn't know anything about the set-up of the Louisville art firm and, more important, he didn't know how much Wilson knew; Wilson might even have visited there and be pretty familiar with the officers. Besides, he didn't want to do any buying or rejecting. He said, "I'm just a salesman for them. But when the boss heard I was passing through Brampton on this trip, he told me to stop off and see you"

"I'm sorry as hell, Mr. Sweeney, that I—uh—"

"That's all right," Sweeney lied. "But first, what's this business about two other reporters—I mean, two reporters having been here to see you? From what papers, and why?"

"From St. Paul papers. Or maybe one was from Minneapolis. It was about that statuette you mentioned, your SM-1. That's why I thought you were another reporter I guess. What was it *you* wanted to' ask about that?"

Sweeney said, "Let's get it straight first about what these oth—these reporters wanted to know about SM-1."

Wilson frowned. "On account of these Ripper murders in Chicago they wanted to do a rehash of my shooting of the maniac I had to shoot here about four or five years ago. Both of them knew about the statuette I made of Bessie so I guess they must have talked to Sheriff Pedersen before they came out here."

Sweeney took a thoughtful sip of whiskey. "Had either of them seen it, or a photo of it?"

"I guess not. What they wanted to know mostly was what company I'd sold it to. If they'd seen one, they could have found what company made it. They stamp their name under the base."

"Then the sheriff here knew you'd made such a statuette but didn't know what company you sold to?"

"That's right. And he never saw it. I got a crying jag about it one night when he jugged me for disorderly conduct."

Sweeney nodded and felt relieved. Then the St. Paul-Minneapolis papers didn't have the important part of the story about Screaming Mimi. They had the inconsequential part—the part he'd learned today from the ex-sheriff—but they didn't know the important, the *all*-important, fact that Chicago's Ripper had a copy. And they didn't have even a photo of the statuette. All they had was a rehash of an old local story; it would make their own papers but wouldn't go out on the AP and UP wires to spoil Sweeney's angle.

Wilson leaned back against the wall behind the cot he was sitting on and crossed his legs. He said, "But what is it Ganslen sent you to talk to me about, Mr. Sweeney?"

"Something that I'm afraid won't work, if you don't like the idea of publicity for the statuette and how it originated. You see, we're taking a loss on that particular number, as things stand. We made a gross of them to try them out—and we'd have lost money if the whole gross had sold, but it sold too slowly to justify our making it in quantity. But it's even worse than that. We're stuck with about a hundred out of the original gross; it just turned out not to have any general ap-peal at all."

Wilson nodded. "I told Mr. Burke that when he took it. It's one of those things; you like it a lot or else you don't like it at all."

"How did you feel about it, as an artist? How did it strike you?"

"I—I don't know, Mr. Sweeney. I should never have done it, and I should never have sold it. It's too—personal. Jesus God, the way Bessie looked standing there screaming, the way I saw her through the doorway past that— Well, the picture just stuck in my mind until I finally had to do it to get it *off* my mind. It was haunting me up to last year. I had to either paint it or model it and I'm not good at figure work with the brush so I modeled it. And once I did that, I should have destroyed it.

"But I'd just finished it when Mr. Burke stopped in on one of his buying trips, and he liked it. I didn't want to sell it to him, but he insisted, and I needed the money so badly I couldn't turn it down. Hell, it was like selling my own sister; it *was* in a way. I felt so lousy about it I stayed drunk a week, so the money didn't do me any good anyway."

Sweeney said, "I can see how you must have felt about it."

"But I told Mr. Burke then I didn't want any publicity about it and he promised he wouldn't give the story of it to anybody to try to sell more of them. So why does he send you now to open the subject again?"

Sweeney cleared his throat. "Well—he thought that, under new circumstances, you might change your mind. But, I can see you still feel pretty strongly about it, so I won't even try to persuade you."

"Thanks, Mr. Sweeney. But what new circumstances do you mean?"

"The same thing those St. Paul reporters meant. You see, right now, there's a Ripper actively operating in Chicago, and it's a big story—not just local, but a coast-to-coast big crime story, about the biggest thing since Dillinger. Right now, while the iron's hot, we could sell a flock of them if we could cash in on *that* publicity, advertising them—and honestly—as a statuette of a woman being attacked by a Ripper, and from life. From the memory of a sculptor, who'd actually seen the attack—and prevented it. But we'd have to release the whole story to do that."

"I see what you mean. And it would mean a little extra, I guess, in royalties to me. But—no, I guess not. As I said, I'm sorry I sold it at all and to drag poor Bessie before the public again— How's about another drink? It's your whiskey."

"Ours," said Sweeney. "You know, Charlie, I like you. Not that I thought I would after the way you greeted me."

Wilson poured refills. He said, "I'm really sorry as hell about that. Honestly. I thought you were another of those Goddam reporters like the first two, and I'd made up my mind I wasn't going to *take* another one of them."

He sat down again, glass in hand. "What I like about you best is your not trying to talk me into letting Ganslen release publicity on it. I might weaken if you did. God knows I need money—and God knows it wouldn't do me any good if I got it that way.

"Even with the God-awful prices you get for your statuettes, you might sell thousands of them with a story like that back of them. And with that much money—"

Sweeney asked curiously, "How much money? I mean, Burke didn't happen to mention exactly what the arrangements with you were on the deal."

"The usual. Usual for me, anyway; I don't know what kind of a contract they give their other sculptors, but on all the statuettes they buy from me, it's a hundred bucks down and that covers all they sell up to a thousand copies—that's the point, Burke says, where they start to break even on a number and over that they show a profit. Is that right?"

"Close enough," Sweeney said.

"So if they would sell two or three thousand copies, I'd have one or two thousand coming in royalties—and that hasn't happened yet. And God help me if it did—in this case. I told you I stayed drunk for a week on the hundred bucks I got out of selling that figure of Bessie the first time. Well, if I cashed in a thousand or two out of the story of it getting dragged through the papers again—after she's dead, at that— well, I'd go on such a *God*damn drunk I probably wouldn't live through it. Even if I did, the money wouldn't. I'd be broke and broken, and hate myself the rest of my life."

Sweeney found he could stand up, not too certainly. He stuck his hand across the space between them. He said, "Shake, Charlie. I like you."

"Thanks. I like you, Sweeney. Another drink? Of your whiskey?"

"*Our* whiskey. Sure, Charlie. Say, which *is* your first name, Charlie or Chapman?"

"Charlie. Chapman Wilson was Bessie's idea. Thought it sounded more like an artist. She was a swell gal, Sweeney. A little screwy sometimes."

"Aren't we all?"

"I guess I am. They call me Crazy Charlie around here."

"Around Chicago they probably call me Crazy Sweeney." He picked up his glass. "Shall we drink to craziness?"

Charlie looked at him somberly for a moment. He said, "Make it to our kind of craziness, Sweeney."

"What oth— Oh. To our kind of craziness, Charlie."

They touched glasses and drank, and Sweeney sat back down.

Charlie stared into his empty glass. He said, "*Real* craziness is something horrible, Sweeney. That homicidal maniac, covered with blood and the carving knife in his hand. I still get nightmares about his face as he turned away from Bessie and looked at me as he heard me coming.

"And Bessie—she was such a swell girl. And to see her go to pieces—well, you can hardly call it going to pieces; that implies something gradual. And she went wild-crazy all at once from that horrible experience. Why, we had to hold her down to get clothes on her; she was stark naked when— But you know that, of course; you've seen that statuette. I—I think it's a good thing that she died, Sweeney. *I'd* rather be dead than insane, really insane. Like she was."

He dropped his head into his hands.

Sweeney said, "Tough. And she was only nineteen."

"Twenty, then. She was twenty-one when she died in the asylum almost four years ago. And she was swell. Oh, she wasn't any angel. She was kind of wild. Our parents died ten years ago when I was twenty-four and Bessie was fifteen. An aunt of ours tried to take her but she ran off to St. Louis. But she kept in touch with me.

"And when she got in trouble five years later, it was me that she came to. She was— Well, that business with the maniac gave her a miscarriage and took care of that." He looked up. "Well, maybe she's better off— Life can be a hell of a mess."

Sweeney got up and patted Charlie on the shoulder. He said, "Quit thinking about it, kid." He poured them each a drink and put Charlie's glass into Charlie's hand.

And once he was up he wandered around the room looking at the canvases on the wall, studying them more closely. They weren't bad; they weren't bad at all.

Charlie said, "We were really close, a hell of a lot closer than brother and sister usually are. We never lied to each other about anything. She told me everything she did in St. Louis, every man she'd had anything to do with. She was a waitress first, and then a pony in a chorus line in a cheap burlesque; that's what she was doing when she found she was pregnant and came here. And then that escaped loonie—"

"Quit talking about it," Sweeney ordered gruffly.

"He died too quickly. If I'd've shot his legs off instead of shooting at his chest, I could have taken that carving knife and— Oh, hell, I wouldn't have, anyway." He shook his head slowly.

"Anyway, at that range," he said, "it put a hell of a big hole in him. Big enough you could stick your head through it."

Sweeney sighed and sat down. He said, "Look, Charlie, forget it. Let's talk about painting."

Charlie nodded slowly. They talked about painting, got off onto music, got back to painting again. Sweeney's bottle emptied itself and they started on Charlie's gin. It was pretty horrible gin. After a while Sweeney found difficulty focusing his eyes on paintings they were discussing but his mind stayed clear. Clear enough anyway to know that he was enjoying the evening and having some of the best conversation he'd had in a long time. He wasn't sorry any more that he'd come to Brampton. He liked Charlie; Charlie was his own breed of cat.

And Charlie could hold his liquor, too, remarkably well. His tongue got thickish, but he talked sense.

So, for that matter, did Sweeney. And he had sense enough to keep an eye on his watch. When it was ten-fifteen, an hour before his train time, he told Charlie he'd better leave.

"Driving?"

"No. Got a reservation on the eleven-fifteen. But it's quite a hike to the station. I've had a swell evening."

"You won't have to hike. There's a bus runs back and forth the length of Main Street. You can catch it on the corner a block and a half down. I'll walk down with you."

The cool night air felt good and began to sober him up.

He liked Charlie and wanted to do something for him. More than that, he suddenly saw *how* he could do something for him. He said, "Charlie, I got an idea how I can get you those royalties on the Scream—on SM-1, without that public-city you don't want. It'll be publicity for the statuette itself, but it won't have to bring either you or your sister into the picture at all."

"Well, if you can do that—"

They were at the corner and Charlie was waiting with him until the bus came along.

"Sure, I can do it. Just on the Chicago angle. Look, Charlie, I know something nobody else knows—and it'll give you a flock of publicity for that statuette in its own right, apart from the way it was conceived and executed. Your name or your sister's won't have to come it at all."

"If you can keep Bessie out of it—"

"Sure, easy. That isn't even the real story, as far as the story I'm going to break is concerned. It's frosting, but we can leave it off the cake. And for your sake I'll send Ganslen a telegram and tell them to start making more SM-1's right away to cash in on the boom. And listen, Charlie, do you ever get to Chicago?"

"Haven't for a couple of years. Why?"

"Well look when you get some of these royalties, drop down and we'll have an evening together; I'll show you the town. We'll hang one on. If you get in town in the daytime, phone me at the *Blade,* city room. If you get in after dark, phone—"

"City room? *Blade?* You a reporter?"

Sweeney said despairingly, "Oh, Lord." He shouldn't have; he should have put his hands over his stomach right away, quick. But he didn't.

Charlie's fist went in it, up to Charlie's wrist, and Sweeney folded like a jackknife, just in time for Charlie's other fist to meet his chin coming down. But, as before, he didn't even feel the punch on his chin.

He heard Charlie say, "You lousy, double-crossing son of a bitch. I wish you'd get up and fight."

Nothing was farther from Sweeney's mind, or rather, from what was left of Sweeney's mind. He couldn't even talk. If he'd opened his mouth something might have come out, but it wouldn't have been words.

He heard Charlie walk away.

[16]

There's no need to describe how Sweeney felt; that was the third time he'd been hit in the stomach and it didn't feel any different, except in degree, from the first two times. To go into detail would be sadistic, not to say redundant. And it's bad enough that *he* had to go through it a third time; you and I do not.

After a few minutes he managed to get to the curb and sit there doubled up until, after about ten more minutes, he heard and saw the bus coming and managed to get to his feet, if not quite erect, and boarded it.

He sat doubled up in the bus, he sat doubled up in the station, and then on the train he lay doubled up in his lower berth. He didn't get to sleep, soundly, until early dawn, just as the train got into Chicago.

By the time he got to his room, though, the worst was

over, and he slept. It was well into the afternoon—thirteen minutes after two, if you wish exactitude—when he awoke. But by then the worst was over and he could walk without being bent over.

And it was Sunday and the last day of his vacation, and three o'clock by the time he was bathed and dressed.

He went outside and looked east and west along Erie Street with a jaundiced eye and finally made up his mind to go east and see if he could find any angle on the Dorothy Lee murder that the police had missed. He didn't think he would. He didn't.

Luck was with him in finding both the janitor and Mrs. Rae Haley, the woman who had phoned the police, in. But luck was against him in finding out from either of them anything significant that he didn't already know. He ran out of questions to ask after fifteen minutes with the janitor, who had not known Miss Lee personally at all. It took him an hour and a half to listen to everything Mrs. Haley thought of to tell him, and at the end of that hour and a half he knew a lot more than he had known about Dorothy Lee—nearly all of it favorable—but none of it in the slightest degree helpful, unless negatively.

Rae Haley, a buxom wench with hennaed hair and just a touch too much make-up for a Sunday afternoon at home, turned out to be an ad-taker for a rival newspaper, but seemed nonetheless eager to talk to the *Blade*—or to Sweeney.

She had known Dorothy Lee fairly well and had liked her; Dorothy was "nice and quiet." Yes, she'd been in Dorothy's apartment often. They had eaten together frequently, taking turns, each in her own apartment, in doing the cooking, and that way avoiding each having to cook a separate meal. Not all the time, of course, but several times a week. So she knew Dorothy's apartment pretty thoroughly and, as he had suspected, Sweeney found that "small black statuette" drew a blank. The apartment was rented furnished and Dorothy hadn't gone in for buying pictures or bric-a-brac of her own. She did, though, have a nice table-top phonograph and some nice records, mostly "sweet swing." Sweeney concealed a shudder.

Yes, Dorothy had had boyfriends; at one time or another she'd gone out with four or five of them, but none had been "serious." Mrs. Haley had met each of them and knew their names; she'd given the names of all of them to the police. Not because there was any possibility that any of them had been concerned in the horrible thing that had happened to Dorothy, but because the police had asked for the names and had insisted. But apparently the police had found all of them to be all right, because if they had arrested one of them it would have been in the papers, wouldn't it? Sweeney assured her that it would have been. She said that they were all nice boys, very nice boys, and when one of them had brought her home he'd always said goodnight at the door and hadn't come in. Dorothy had been a nice girl.

The walls of these apartments were almost paper-thin and she, Mrs. Haley, would have known if. She carried the sentence only that far and stopped delicately.

The poor kid, Sweeney thought, and wondered if she had died a virgin. He hoped that she hadn't, but not aloud. It's fine, he mused while Mrs. Haley talked on, for a girl to save herself for Mr. Right, but it's damn tough on her if Mr. Wrong comes along with a carving knife first. Even the prototype of Screaming Mimi, poor Bessie Wilson, hadn't been handed that tough a break.

Sweeney thought, for no particular reason, that he would have liked Bessie Wilson; he rather wished that he had known her. And damn it, he liked Charlie Wilson in spite of what Charlie had done to him. A cocky little guy but quite likable when, he wasn't punching one in the stomach.

He decided that he'd keep his promise to Charlie anyway and send that telegram to the general manager of Ganslen. He was planning how to word it when he remembered where he was and realized that Mrs. Haley was still talking and that he hadn't been listening at all. He listened for long enough to find out that he hadn't been missing a thing, and made his getaway, turning down an invitation to stay for dinner.

He walked downtown to the Loop and found a Western

Union office open. He sat down with a pencil and pad of blanks and tore up two tries before he evolved a telegram that came even close. Then he read that one over again, saw several things missing in it, and gave up. He tore that one up too and walked to a telephone exchange where he asked to see, and was given, a Louisville telephone directory. Luckily Sweeney had a good memory for names and he recalled, from his previous call to Ganslen Art Company, the first name as well as the last name of the general manager. He found a home telephone listed.

He got a handful of change and went into a booth. A few minutes later he was talking to the general manager and buyer of Ganslen.

He said, "This is Sweeney of the Chicago *Blade,* Mr. Burke. I talked to you a few days ago about one of your statuettes, the SM-1. You were kind enough to tell me who modeled it."

"Yes, I remember."

"To return the favor, I want to tip you off to something that will make some money for you and for Chapman Wilson. Only I'm going to ask you to keep this confidential until the *Blade* breaks the story tomorrow. You'll agree to that?"

"Uh—exactly what am I agreeing to, Mr. Sweeney?"

"Merely that you don't tell anyone at all what I'm going to tell you now until after tomorrow noon. You can go ahead meanwhile and act on the information; you can start getting ready to cash in."

"That sounds fair enough."

"Okay here's the dope. You sold two SM-1's in Chicago. Well, I've got one of them and the Ripper's got the other one. You've heard of our Ripper murders, haven't you?"

"Of course. Good Lord! You mean—"

"Yeah. Tomorrow the *Blade* will print a picture of Screaming Mimi—about four columns wide on page one, if I judge rightly—and break the story. Probably the Ripper will be caught. A friend or his landlady or someone will have seen it in his room and phone the police. He can hardly have had it for two months without *someone* having seen it.

"But whether he's caught through it or not, it's a nation-wide big story. You're likely to be swamped for weeks with orders for Mimi. I'd suggest you put her in production immediately—work a night shift tonight if you can get anybody down to your factory or workshop or whatever it is. And if I were you I wouldn't sell those hundred-odd copies you have; I'd get them to dealers quickly to use as samples to take orders. Get them to Chicago dealers, in particular, as fast as you can. Start one of your salesmen up this way tonight with a trunk full of them."

"Thank you, Mr. Sweeney. I can't say how much I appreciate your giving me this much notice on—"

"Wait," said Sweeney. "I'm not through yet. One thing I want you to do. Put a special mark somewhere on each one you sell from now on, so it can be told from the one the Ripper's got. Keep the mark secret so he can't duplicate it, and let the police know what the mark is when they come to you—as they will after that story breaks. Otherwise, they'll be on my neck for tipping you off to flood the Chicago market with them, see? But they'll see that, in the long run, we're doing them a favor. If there are more Mimis coming, the Ripper may keep his, whereas if he knows his is going to keep on being the only other one in Chicago, he'll get rid of it quick. And he won't know about the secret mark all the others will have. Listen, make the secret mark a tiny chip out of the bottom of the base in the right front corner—so it'll look accidental if anyone looks at just *one* of them."

"Fine. That will be simple."

"I'll do it on mine. And you've got a record, I hope, of just where the forty or so that you actually sold throughout the country went, haven't you?"

"Our books would show that."

"Good, then if an unmarked Mimi shows up, it can be traced back to prove it's not the one the Ripper bought. And one more thing—"

"Yes?"

"I'm not going to drag in the origin of Mimi. Charlie-Chapman Wilson's pretty sensitive about what happened to his sister, and this is a big enough story without using that. After all, that's past history and our Ripper is very much current. He said you promised not to use that for publicity—so stick to your promise to him."

"Of course, Mr. Sweeney. And thanks again, tremendously."

After he hung up, Sweeney dropped another nickel but Yolanda's phone wasn't answered so he got it back. It was too early for her to be at the night club; she was probably out eating somewhere. Well, maybe he'd better skip trying to talk to her until after tomorrow when he'd broken the Screaming Mimi story in the *Blade*. And maybe by then the Ripper would be caught and she wouldn't have an escort of cops everywhere she moved.

Of course he could watch her dance tonight. Or could he? He looked up the number of the Tit-Tat-Toe Club and called it. A bit of argument and the use of his name got him Harry Yahn. Harry's voice boomed cheerfully over the phone. "Hello, Sweeney. How're things?"

"Going fine, Harry. I'm going to break a big story on the Ripper tomorrow. Extra publicity for Yolanda."

"That's great. Does it—uh—concern anyone I know?"

"Not unless you know the Ripper. Do you?"

"Not by that name. Well, what about it? You don't want any more money, I hope."

"My God, no," said Sweeney. "Look, Harry, that's a dead issue. What I want to know is, are we still friends?"

"Why, sure, Sweeney. Did you have any reason for thinking we weren't?"

"Yes," said Sweeney. "But did that wash it out? Specifically, am I going to be *persona non gra*— I mean, if I show up at El Madhouse or the Tit-Tat-Toe, do I get in and out again safely? Or do I wear a suit of armor?"

Harry Yahn laughed. "You're welcome any time, Sweeney. Seriously. As you said, it's a dead issue."

"Swell," said Sweeney. "I just wanted to be sure."

"Uh—did Willie use discretion?"

"For Willie, I imagine it was. I just wanted to be sure you

hadn't passed the good word on to Nick. I'll probably, otherwise, go around to El Madhouse tonight."

"Fine. Nick's due to phone me soon and I'll tell him to hold a chair for you, and not to take your money. No kidding, Sweeney, I like you. No hard feelings?"

"Very tender feelings," Sweeney said. "And the worst of it is, they've been worked on twice since then. That's just why I wanted to be sure before I went to El Madhouse tonight. Since it's okay, thanks for everything."

"Don't mention it, Sweeney. Take care of yourself."

After he'd hung up, Sweeney took a deep breath and although it hurt his stomach a little—he felt better.

He went back for another handful of change, an even bigger handful this time. A nickel of it got him the long distance operator again. He let the New York operator do the looking up this time for he felt pretty sure Ray Land would have a home telephone in his own name. Ray Land had been a Chicago homicide cop once; now he was running a small agency of his own in New York.

Ray was home.

Sweeney said, "This is Sweeney. Remember me?"

"Sure. So?"

"Want you to investigate an alibi for me. In New York." He gave the details, Greene's name and hotel and the exact date. "I know he was registered at the hotel on that day and the day before and the day after. The police checked that. What I want to find out—for sure, not a probability—is whether he was really there that night, the 27th."

"Can try. It's almost two weeks ago. How far do you want me to go?"

"As far as you can. Talk to everybody at the hotel who might have seen him come in or go out, the maid who'd have made up his room in the morning, everything like that. Listen, the crucial time is 3 o'clock in the morning. If you can definitely locate him six hours or less either side of that, I'll settle."

"Twelve hours isn't so bad. Maybe I can do it. How much you want me to spend?"

"Spend all you want provided you do it right away. With-in reason, that is. I'll wire you a hundred cash for a retainer. If you go a little over it, even double it, okay."

"That ought to cover it, Sweeney. It'll cover two days' time and since it's right on Manhattan there won't be any expenses to speak of. If I can't get anything in two days, I probably can't at all. Why the six hour leeway?"

"I want to convince myself that he wasn't in Chicago at 3 a.m. Counting time to and from airports on either end, get-ting a plane and everything, that's the least he could have done it in. Maybe five hours would be safer. If you can prove he was at the hotel as late as ten in the evening or as early as eight the next morning, I'll be convinced. And, just in case it could have been a ringer, someone else there using his name, here's a description." Sweeney gave it. He added, "If you can't alibi him, you might try that description at the airport. Or if it comes down to that, I'll try to get you a photo. Check with me after you've got everything you can get at the hotel. Good enough?"

"Good enough. I'll get around there this evening. It'll be the night shift I'll mostly want to talk to."

Outside the telephone exchange, Sweeney found that it was getting dark and that he was getting hungry. He remem-bered he hadn't seen a Sunday paper and might have missed something; he found copies of two of them still left on a newsstand and very early editions, still sticky with ink, of two Monday morning papers. He bought all four and took them into a restaurant with him.

Reading while he ate, he found out that nothing new had happened or transpired. All the papers were keeping the story above—it was too big a story to let an issue pass without *something*—but the somethings added up or canceled out to nothing.

He stretched the eating and the reading until it was almost ten o'clock and then left. He remembered the retainer and stopped in at the Western Union office again to send it to Ray Land.

That still left him over seven hundred dollars and he

wished there was some way he could spend some of it on Yolanda. Well, there'd be time for that after the cops quit watching her. Meanwhile, there *was* one sighting shot he could take. He found a flower shop in a hotel still open and ordered two dozen red roses sent to her at El Madhouse as soon as they could get a messenger to take them there. He tried writing on, and tore up, three cards. On the fourth, he wrote "Sweeney" and let it go at that.

He caught a taxi and directed it to El Madhouse; it would get him there just in time for Yo's first performance of the evening.

It did, and Nick was still saving a place for him.

After the floor show (you wouldn't want me to describe it again, would you?) he wandered out to the bar and managed to get a place at it. But it was ten minutes before he could get a drink.

He sipped it and brooded.

Unless breaking the story that the Ripper had bought and now presumably still owned a copy of Ganslen's SM-1 brought results, it looked as though he was stymied.

That was the only real lead he'd found: the fact that the killer of Lola Brent, two months ago, had undoubtedly been the same person who had purchased from her the statuette whose purchase price she had dragged down. Sweeney didn't doubt that for a second; it fitted too perfectly to be a coincidence. It *had* to be.

But for the rest he had nothing. The trip to Brampton had been completely a blind alley—an alley populated with little men who kept pounding on his sore stomach, before and after getting drunk with him. And almost worse than those punches had been the anticlimax of learning—after he'd heard first of a Ripper, a blonde, and a crazy artist that the Ripper and the blonde were dead long since and the crazy artist was well alibied. And even of Charlie Wilson hadn't been alibied, Sweeney couldn't picture him as the Ripper. He had a hair-trigger temper, but he wasn't the type that ran to carving knives.

Well tomorrow would tell the tale. If a four-column pic-

ture of SM-1 splashed on the front page of the *Blade* didn't
make something happen—

He sighed and took another sip of his drink.

Someone tapped him on the shoulder.

[17]

Sweeney turned and found himself staring full into the thick
glasses that magnified Greene's eyes and made them so
frightening.

Sweeney grinned and said, "Hi, doc. What'll you have?"

"I've got a drink, over at a table. And Nick's holding my
chair and another. Come on over."

Sweeney picked up his drink and followed Greene to a
corner table. Nick, standing beside it, said, "Hi, Mr. Sweeney," and then hurried off about his business. Sweeney and
Greene sat down.

"Getting anywhere?" Greene asked.

"Maybe. I don't know. I'm breaking a big story tomorrow; the biggest one to date."

"Outside of the actual murders."

"Maybe bigger," Sweeney said.

"It would be useless for me to ask what it is, I suppose."

"You've got something there, Doc. But cheer up; it'll be
on the streets in twelve hours."

"I'll watch for it. I'm still worried about something happening to Yo. So I hope you have really got something." He
took off his glasses and polished them. Sweeney, studying
him, saw that he looked quite different without them. He
looked tired, genuinely worried. Stranger, though, he looked
human. Sweeney almost wished he had back the hundred
dollars he'd just wired to New York. Almost, not quite.

Doc Greene put the glasses back on and looked at Sweeney through them, and his eyes were enormous again. Sweeney
thought the hundred dollars was well spent.

Greene said, "Meanwhile, Sweeney, take good care of yourself."

"I will. Any special reason?"

Greene chuckled. "Yes, for *my* sake. Since I lost my temper the other night and shot off my mouth, Captain Bline has had me on the carpet. Everything but a rubber hose. It seems he took my little threat seriously."

"And was he right?"

"Well—yes and no. You did, that one time, get under my skin and I think I meant it when I said it. Of course, after cool deliberation I realized I'd been silly. By saying that, I did the one thing that made you completely safe—from me. If you ever want to kill a man, Sweeney, don't make the announcement before the police and hope to get away with it."

"Then why the warning to take good care of myself?"

"As I said, for *my* sake. Bline told *me*—promised me that if anything happens to you after my threat, my silly threat, he'd arrest me and rubber-hose me to hell and back. Even if I had an alibi, he'd figure that I hired the job done. I'm going to be a dead duck, Sweeney, if anything happens to you."

Sweeney smiled. "Doc, you almost tempt me to commit suicide, without leaving a note."

"Don't, please. Not that I think you would, but you worry me talking about breaking a big story tomorrow. You might say that to someone who wouldn't want a big story to break for fear of what it might be. You see what I mean."

"I see what you mean. But you're the first person in Chicago whom I've told. The only other one is hundreds of miles from here. Of course, you could pass it on."

"Perish the thought, Sweeney. Your safety has become a matter of importance to me. I've told you why." He shook his head slowly. "I am amazed at myself for having said such a foolish thing—in such company. I, a trained psychiatrist— Have you had any psychiatric training, Sweeney? From the skillful way you maneuvered me into loss of control— Well, there's no harm done if nothing happens to you. But until this mess is over, I'll chip in half the cost if you want to hire a bodyguard. Willie, maybe? Have you met Willie Harris?"

"Willie is wonderful," Sweeney said. "But I doubt if Harry Yahn would care to part with him. No thanks, Doc, whether you're serious or not I'll take my chances without a bodyguard. Or if I should hire one, I won't tell you about it."

Greene sighed. "You still don't trust me, Sweeney. Well, I've got to run along. To see a client at another club. Take care of yourself."

Sweeney went back to the bar and had his drink replenished. He drank it very slowly and thought about how he was going to write the story for tomorrow's *Blade,* and thus managed to kill time until the second floor show went on.

He saw it; it was different in one very minor but very important detail. Yolanda Lang wore a red rose pinned to the waist of her black dress. Sweeney's roses had arrived, then, after the first show but before the second.

And she'd worn one. That was all he wanted to know. He thought, but wasn't sure, that her eyes met his in the instant after the dog had reared up behind her. But that wasn't important; she *had* worn one of the roses he'd sent.

After the show—wondering whether he was being as astute a psychiatrist as Doc Greene had credited him with being—he didn't try to see her or speak to her. There'd be cops—and Doc—around if he did. Maybe, just possibly, by tomorrow night the cops wouldn't have to be guarding Yolanda. And Doc—well, he'd worry about Greene when the time came.

At least, he didn't have anything to fear from Greene for the moment; he did believe him that far. Doc had pulled his own stinger by making that open threat on Sweeney's life.

He didn't wait for the third show. Tomorrow might turn out to be a big day, and it was after midnight already. He went home and to bed, read a while and got to sleep by two o'clock. His alarm woke him at half-past seven, and it was Monday.

It was Monday, and it was a bright, cheerful day; the sun was bright but not unduly hot for August the eleventh. No clouds in the sky, but a cooling breeze off the lake. Not bad at all.

He had a good breakfast and got to the *Blade* promptly

at nine.

He hung up his coat and hat and then, before the city editor could catch him, he headed right for Wally Krieg's office. The package containing SM-1 was under his arm.

Wally looked up as he came in. He said, "Hi, Sweeney. Reported to Crawley yet?"

"Nope. Want to show you something first." He started to unwrap the package.

"All right, but after that report to Crawley. Somebody took a jewelry salesman for his samples last night and we want to get on it quick. Over at—"

"Hush" said Sweeney. He got the package unwrapped and set Mimi on the desk, facing the managing editor.

"Mimi, meet Wally Krieg. Wally, meet Mimi. Screaming Mimi."

"Charmed. Now take that thing out of here and—"

"Hush," said Sweeney. "She's got a sister. *One* sister, in all of Chicago."

"Sweeney, what are you getting at?"

"The Ripper," said Sweeney. He's got Mimi's sister. We got Mimi—and don't think she doesn't go on the expense account for the full purchase price. That is, if you want to send her up to the photo department and run a pic of her on page one today."

"You say the Ripper's got one like her? Are you sure?"

"Reasonably sure. There were two in Chicago; the Ripper bought the other one from Lola Brent just before he followed her home and killed her. It's probably what set him off. Look at it!"

"And his is the only other one in Chicago?"

"Yes," Said Sweeney. "Well, if you're not interested I'll go stick it in my desk drawer and then look up Crawley." He picked up Mimi and started out the door. Wally said "Hey!" and he waited.

"Wally," he said, "I'm getting fed up on this Ripper business. Maybe you'd better keep me off it. Of course I could get the whole thing for the first edition today but you can have Mimi anyway, if you want her, and one of the other boys can check her pedigree—with Raoul Reynarde—and trace her back like I did, and give you the story for tomorrow or part of it for a late edition today. But I'd just as soon not—"

"Sweeney, quit blithering. Shut the door."

"Sure, Wally. From which side?"

Wally just glared at him and Sweeney decided that enough was enough and shut it from the inside. Wally was getting the city ed. on the phone. He barked that someone else should go on the jewelry case and that Sweeney was on special assignment. He jiggled the receiver and got the photo department and apparently was satisfied with whoever answered the phone for he told him to come down right away.

Then he swung on Sweeney. He said, "Put that thing down, carefully, before you drop it and break it."

Sweeney put Mimi back down on the desk. Wally stared at her. Then up at Sweeney.

He said, "What the hell you waiting for? A kiss? Go ahead and write the story. Wait a minute; don't start yet. Lots of time before first edition; sit down and tell me about it first. Maybe there are angles somebody else can be doing while you're batting it out."

Sweeney sat down and told most of it. As much, at least, as he intended to put into the story itself. There was an interruption while a photographer came in and Wally gave him Mimi with instructions—and with threats of almost unbelievable things that would happen to him if Mimi were dropped and broken before the photograph had been taken. The photographer left, walking carefully and holding Mimi as though she were made of eggshell. Sweeney resumed, and finished.

Wally said, "Good. Go ahead and write it. Only you didn't do the story any good phoning Ganslen and telling them to cash in while it's hot. The police aren't going to like that. They'll want there to be only *one* Mimi, Chicago for as long a time as possible. And I mean *one;* I'm going to order this one broken to pieces as soon as I see a good photo of it. Put that in the story. It narrows things down. Plenty. What the hell did you want to phone that art company for, to tip them off?"

Sweeney felt uncomfortable. It *had* been a boner, and he

didn't want to explain about Charlie Wilson and his real reason for the call. He said, weakly, "Thought I ought to pay 'em back for the favor they did me on the first call, Wally. Telling me only two had been sold in Chicago. Without that—"

Wally said, "Well, I'll phone them and head them off while you write the story. Look, mention that the statuette was made by Ganslen Art Company, Louisville, and they won't *have* to send any salesmen or samples to Chicago or anywhere in this area. They'll be swamped with orders by telephone, just from that information and the photo in the paper. Every dealer in the area will be calling them."

"I'll phone and tell them that. Who'd you talk to?"

"General manager. Burke."

"Okay, I'll talk to Burke and tell him to go ahead and take all the orders he wants from this area but to stall as long as he can on shipping and not to send any samples right away. And I'll make sure he's taking your suggestion on putting a special mark on each of them. Don't mention *that,* though, in the story. And bring it here when you've finished; I want to pass on it personally."

Sweeney nodded and stood up. Wally said, "And one other thing I'm going to do, and that's phone Bline. If we break this story without tipping him off first, we'll be number one on the department's s.o.b. list. I'm going to give him the story first and tell him we're breaking it today but we're giving him advance notice."

"What if he crosses you by giving it to the other papers?"

"I don't think he will. If he does, they still won't have Mimi or a pic of her. The story itself isn't worth much without the pic, and I'm going to splash that smack in the middle of the front page. Four columns by about fifteen inches."

"Shall I mention that we're running the pic in full color— black?"

"Get the hell out of here."

Sweeney got the hell out and sat down at his desk. He realized, as he pulled paper into the ancient Underwood that both of Wally's ideas had been good; it wouldn't hurt the story to give the cops a couple of hours' notice and it wouldn't hurt

Ganslen's sales (or Charlie's royalties) if they didn't fill orders from Chicago for a week or so. The story would stay good— and would turn better if it actually led to the capture of the Ripper.

He looked at his wrist watch, saw that he had an hour to go, and started typing. His phone rang and it was Wally. Wally asked, "Going to have plenty of time? Or would you rather dictate it to a fast rewrite man?"

"I can do it."

"Okay. Send it to me as it comes out of the mill, a page at a time. I'll have a boy waiting at your desk. Slug it MIMI."

Sweeney slugged it MIMI and kept typing. A minute later a copy boy was breathing down his neck, but Sweeney was used to that and it didn't bother him. He sent the last page in ten minutes before the first edition deadline. After that he lighted a cigarette and pretended to be busy so Crawley wouldn't think of anything else for him to do right away, until deadline was past and he figured Wally would be free again, and then he wandered into Wally's office again.

"How's Mimi?" he asked.

"A broken woman. Look in my wastebasket if you don't believe me."

"I'd rather not," Sweeney said.

A boy came in with papers fresh off the press and put three of them on Wally's desk. Sweeney picked one up and glanced at the page one layout. There was Mimi, all right, slightly larger than actual size. She had the banner head, two columns of story, four columns of picture. And Wally had by-lined the story for him.

Sweeney said, "Nice layout," and Wally grunted, reading.

Sweeney said, "Nice story, too. Thanks for telling me so." Wally grunted again.

Sweeney said, "How about the rest of the day off?"

This time Wally didn't grunt; he put down the paper and got ready to explode. "Are you *crazy?* You've been off two weeks, come back to work for two hours and—"

"Relax, Wally. Don't break a blood vessel. Where do you think that story came from? Out of the air? I've been working twenty hours a day on it, more or less, for three days. In my own time. I came in with that star ready to write up. And brought Mimi with me for company. And why? Because I worked till four o'clock this morning and got two hours sleep, that's why. Dragged myself out of bed half-awake to come in and write the biggest story of the year for you and then you-"

"Shut up. All right, get the hell out of here. Of all the Goddam goldbricks—"

"Thank you. Seriously, Wally, I *am* going home. I'll be in my room the rest of the day and you can reach me by phone. I'm going to rest, but I won't get undressed—and if anything breaks on this story call me quick. I'll be on it just as fast as I would if I were waiting around here. Okay?"

"Okay, Sweeney If anything breaks, you're on it. And listen, Sweeney—win, lose or draw it's a swell story"

"Thanks," Sweeney said. "And thanks to hell and back for carrying me while I was—gone."

"This makes up for it. You know, Sweeney, there are damn few real reporters left. And you're—"

"Hold it," said Sweeney. "Pretty soon we'll be crying into our beer, and we haven't got any beer to cry into. I'm going to beat it."

He beat it.

He took one of Wally's papers with him so he wouldn't have to hunt one up elsewhere or wait for one on the street, and went home. He took a cab, partly because he still had more money than he knew what to do with and partly because —temporarily—he really did feel tired as hell. It was partly the letdown, but mostly the fact that, for a while now, there was nothing intelligent to do but to wait.

Either the story of Mimi would lead to a big break in the story of the Ripper or it wouldn't. If it did, it would probably happen this afternoon or this evening. Or possibly tonight.

If it didn't—well then it didn't. He'd be back at work at nine o' clock tomorrow morning and he didn't think, now, that Wally would keep him off the Ripper case. He'd just have to forget Mimi and try to dig up another angle, somewhere. Probably by going over again, and more thoroughly, a lot of the ground he had already covered.

At home, he made himself comfortable and read the story through, leisurely and carefully. Wally had added to it splicing in some recapitulation on the stones of the other three women who had been attacked (for the Mimi story had concerned directly only Lola Brent, who had sold Mimi to the Ripper), but he had changed hardly a word of what Sweeney had written.

This time he even read the continuation on an inside page; then he folded the paper together and put it with the others that covered the various Ripper murders.

He sat down and tried to relax, but couldn't. He went over to the phonograph—it seemed naked now without the naked statuette atop it—and played the Brahms Fourth. That helped a little, although he couldn't really concentrate on it.

By two o'clock he was hungry, but he didn't want to risk missing a phone call so he went downstairs to Mrs. Randall's rooms and got her to fry some bacon for a sandwich.

By that time he'd decided he didn't give a damn if the phone rang or not. Then it rang, and he almost choked swallowing the big bite of sandwich he'd just taken and almost fell getting up the stairs to answer the phone in the second floor hallway. The call was for another roomer, who wasn't in.

He went back downstairs and finished the sandwich.

He went back upstairs to his room, put the records of a De Falla album on the phonograph and, while they played, tried to reread the short stories in a Damon Runyan collection. He didn't do too well with either the reading or listening.

The phone rang. He got there in nothing flat slamming the door of his own room to shut off part of the sound of the phonograph—which was about one second quicker than stopping to shut off the phonograph itself would have been.

It was Wally. He said, "Okay, Sweeney. Get over to State Street. You know the address."

"What's up?"

"They got the Ripper. Now listen, we got a headline and a bulletin going in the Final—it's going to press now—and we're not holding it for details. We got the main facts and the full story will have to go in tomorrow. It's an even break; we'll beat the morning papers on the bulletin and the main facts, but they'll beat us on getting a detailed story.

"So there's no rush. Get over there and get the full dope, but you can write it up when you get in tomorrow."

"Wally, what happened? Did he make another try at Yolanda Lang? Is she all right?"

"I guess so. Yeah, he made another try and this time the dog got him, like it almost did last time except that last time he slammed the door on the dog—"

"I *know* what happened last time. What happened *this* time?"

"I told you, dammit. They *got* him. He's still alive but probably won't be long. Took him to a hospital, but don't waste time; they won't let you talk to him. He went out a window. At the dame's place, I mean. Good work, Sweeney; that Mimi story of yours broke it. He not only had the statuette, but had it *with* him."

"Who? I mean, have they got his name?"

"Name? Sure we got his name. It's Greene, James J. Greene. Captain Bline says he's suspected him all along. Now quit pumping *me;* get over there and get the story."

The receiver banged in Sweeney's ear, but he stared into the black mouthpiece of the wall phone for seconds before he put his own receiver back on the hook.

[18]

It wasn't quite believable somehow. He'd thought it all along, and yet the reality was hard to swallow. For one thing, one simple thing, he couldn't think of Doc Greene as being dead. But Horlick—who was already there when Sweeney got there —was saying that he was.

"Yeah," he said. "Bline got a call from the hospital; he sent two of the boys with Greene to try to get a detailed confession and get it signed, but I guess they didn't make it, and that he couldn't have signed it anyway what with both arms broken, among other things. And he wasn't very coherent, what I heard of him. I got here before they took him away."

"How come so quick, Wayne?"

"Bull luck. I was already on my way here. For part of the follow-up tomorrow on that Mimi story you broke today, Wally sent me to interview Yolanda Lang, to ask her if she'd ever seen such a statuette. And if not, and it probably would have been not, I was to get a story anyway by asking her what her reaction was to a picture of it—whether it looked like she felt when the Ripper was coming at her in the hallway. That kind of crap. And I got here about the time the police ambulance did."

"And Yolanda isn't up there?"

"Nope, she ran out with the dog, just after it happened. Shock again, or fright. She's probably having the meamies somewhere but she'll show up. I'm going in with what I got; you go on upstairs and see if you can get more if you want to. Bline's up there."

He went his way, south on State Street, and Sweeney pushed his, way through the knot of people who were standing around the doorway of the apartment building on State just south of Chicago Avenue, the same doorway through which Sweeney had stared only a few nights ago and had seen a woman and a dog. This time the crowd was bigger, although there was nothing to be seen through the glass. Sweeney pushed through to a policeman guarding the door. His press card got him inside and he ran up the stairs to the third floor.

Yolanda Lang's apartment was the rear north one of four on the third floor. There wasn't any need checking the number on the door because the door was open and the place was full of cops. At least it looked full of cops; when Sweeney got in, he saw there were only two besides Bline.

Bline came over to him. "Sweeney, if I wasn't so happy, I'd break your neck. How long did you have that Goddam statuette?"

"Don't remember exactly, Cap."

"That's what I mean. But—well, we got the Ripper, and without another ripping, although that must've been a pretty close thing. And I'll settle for that. I'm even ready to buy you a drink. Guess I'm through here; I'll leave one of the boys to wait for the Lang dame to be sure she's all right when she comes back."

"Is there any doubt that she isn't?"

"Physically, sure: He didn't touch her with the knife at all this time; the pooch got in ahead. But she's probably in a mental tizzy, worse than last home. Hell, not that I blame her."

"Did Devil kill Greene?"

"Well he chewed him up a bit but didn't kill him; Doc must've managed to keep an arm over his throat. But he went out that window and that killed him all right. Must've backed up against it and a lunge of the dog knocked him out backwards."

Bline had gestured to a wide-open window and Sweeney went over to it and looked out. Two stories below was a small cement courtyard. It was pretty well littered with junk people had thrown out of windows.

Sweeney asked, "Where's the statuette?"

"Down there in the courtyard, most of it. We found enough pieces of it to identify it. Doc must still have had hold of it when he went out the window. Probably trying to club off the dog with it. The knife was there, too; he must've had the statuette in one hand and the knife in the other—it's a wonder the dog managed not to get hurt. But I guess Doc had to keep one arm to cover his throat and wasn't fast enough with the other. A dog like that is hell on wheels in a fight."

Sweeney looked down into the courtyard and shivered a little.

He said, "I'll take that drink, Cap. And I'll buy back. Let's get out of here."

They went to the corner of State and Chicago, the tavern from which the phone call had been made the night of the first attack on Yolanda. Bline bought.

Sweeney said, "I know everything except what happened. Can you put it in order for me?"

"The whole thing? Or just this afternoon?"

"Just this afternoon."

Bline said, "Yolanda was alone in her apartment—as of a few minutes after three o' clock. We know that because I had a guy stationed to watch the place, from across the hall. We'd sublet the flat across from hers for that purpose, and there was a man stationed there at all times, except of course when she was working at the club. He had a peephole rigged so he could watch the door to her place.

"He saw Doc Greene come up with a shoebox under his arm and knock on her door, see? Well, that was all right; Doc had called there before and I'd said it was okay to let him in. If it had been a stranger, Garry—that's the guy who was on duty—would have had his door open and a gun ready."

Sweeney asked, "Did Doc call on business? I mean, when he'd been there before?"

Bline shrugged. "Don't know and didn't care. We're not the vice squad; we were just hunting the Ripper. And I'd thought, from Greene's alibis, that he was in the clear. Well, I was wrong. Did you really suspect him, Sweeney, or did you keep needling him just because you didn't like him?"

"I don't really know, Cap. But what happened?"

"Well, Yolanda answered the door and let him in. He was in there about five minutes when things started to happen. Garry heard Yolanda scream and the dog growl and Greene yell, almost all at once, and he yanked his own door open and started across the hallway. He yanked at Yolanda's door, but it was locked—a snap lock—and he was just about to put a bullet through the lock when the door opened.

"He says Yolanda had opened it and she pushed past him into the hallway, her face as white as a sheet and looking like something pretty horrible had happened. But there wasn't any blood on her; she wasn't hurt. Garry tried to grab her with his free hand—he had his gun in the other—but the dog jumped at him and he had to let go to cover his throat. The dog took a piece out of his sleeve but didn't happen to get hold of his arm.

"By that time Yolanda was past him and starting down the stairs and the dog wheeled and followed her. So he didn't have to shoot the dog. And as long as Yolanda seemed all right, he ran into Yolanda's apartment to see what went on there. There didn't seem to be anyone in there and he wondered what had happened to Greene; then he heard a groan from the courtyard and looked out the open window—it's a pretty big one, the kind that swings but instead of raising—and there was Doc Greene lying in the courtyard.

"So he phones for me and the ambulance and we get here. Greene was still alive, but dying and not very coherent. He could just say a few words, but they were enough."

Sweeney asked, "What do you figure sent Greene around there?"

"How do you figure how a homicidal maniac reasons Sweeney? How the hell do I know? But I think it was your story about that statuette that set him off. He had it, and maybe Yolanda knew that he had it and the jig would be up as soon as she happened to see your front page. Why he took it along in a shoebox when he went to kill her I don't know.

"But he had it out of the box, in one hand, and the knife in the other hand—when the dog saved her by getting him. Chewed him up pretty bad; maybe he even jumped out of the window to get away from the dog, but I think it's more likely he got backed up against it and went out accidentally when the dog jumped for him again."

"What do you figure happened to Yolanda?"

"Shock again, of course. She's probably wandering a-round in a daze, but she's well protected. She'll snap out of it by herself, probably, and come back. If not, she can't be hard to find—a dame like that with a dog like that. Well, I got to get in and report. So long, Sweeney."

Bline left and Sweeney ordered another drink. And another and then one more. It was getting dark when he left the tavern and went back to Yolanda's flat. There was still a policeman at the door. Sweeney asked him if Yolanda had come back, and she hadn't.

He strolled over to Clark Street, stopped in at Ireland's

and ordered a lobster. While it was cooking he went to the phone booth and called Ray Land, the private detective he'd hired in New York.

He said, "This is Sweeney, Ray. You can call it off."

"That's what I figured, Sweeney. Heard on the radio while I was eating dinner that your Chicago Ripper was caught and his name was familiar. So I figured you wouldn't want me to keep on. Well, I put in a day on it, so you got fifty bucks coming back. I'll send you a check."

"Get anywhere on it?"

"Hadn't yet. It was tough going, what with it being two weeks ago. Best bet I had was a maid who managed to remember that one morning his bed hadn't been slept in, but she couldn't remember which morning it was. I was going to see her again after she'd had time to think it over. Shall I send you that check care of the *Blade?*"

"Sure. And thanks, Ray."

He called Captain Bline at headquarters and asked, "Any reports on Yolanda yet?"

"Yeah, Sweeney. A funny one." Bline's voice sounded puzzled. "She turned up at El Madhouse some time ago. Just half an hour after Greene had tried to attack her. She got some money from Nick and left again. And no report on her since."

"The hell," said Sweeney. "How did she act?"

"A little funny, Nick said, but not too bad. He said she was pale and a little jittery, but he didn't think anything of it; he hadn't heard about what happened to Doc yet, and she didn't say anything about it. Just wanted some money—gave him a song-and-dance about being able to buy something she wanted for a hell of a bargain if she did it right away for cash. Nick said he figured somebody had offered her a stolen mink coat or something for a few hundred bucks and she wanted it but was a little afraid of the deal and that was why she was nervous."

"How much did he give her?"

"A week's salary. She had it coming as of tomorrow night anyway so he figured he might as well give it to her a day sooner."

"That's funny."

"Yeah, but I think I can figure it. I'd guess it that she just wanted to hide out for a day or two. It was shock, but temporary, that sent her chasing out of the building after Greene tried to attack her a second time; but she must've got over the worst of it quick if she could talk normally to Nick within a half hour. Only I'd guess she just didn't feel up to facing us and all the reporters and everything. But she'll show up in a few days when she gets her balance back. She won't miss cashing in on her contract and all the publicity and everything."

"Could be. You hunting for her?"

Bline said, "No. Why should we? We could find her easily enough, just checking hotels. But from what Nick says, she's all right, so it isn't our business. If I thought she was wandering around in a daze from shock or something—"

"She didn't go back home to get any clothes or anything?"

"No; our man's still there and he's to phone me if she shows back there. Guess that's partly what she wanted money for, so she wouldn't have to go back there and face the music."

"Okay, Cap," Sweeney said. "Thanks a lot."

He got back to his table just as the lobster arrived.

He ate it thoughtfully. He didn't know exactly what he was being thoughtful about until the lobster had been reduced to a shell.

And then, suddenly, he knew what he had been thinking and it scared hell out of him.

[19]

He didn't hurry. His coffee came and he drank it slowly, still horrifying himself by what he was thinking. And then it got worse, for he found he wasn't thinking it anymore; he *knew* it. A lot of it was guesswork, but each guess dropped into place like a piece in a jigsaw puzzle that will fit nowhere else and at no other angle.

He paid the check and walked south to El Madhouse. Nick saw him the moment he went in and came to meet him. He said, "Hi, Sweeney. I'm worried; know anything about where Yo is, or if she's coming tonight?"

Sweeney said, "I'm worried, too. Listen, Nick, did you happen to notice when Yolanda left here whether she took a taxi?"

"No. She walked north."

"How was she dressed?"

"In green, what they call a daytime dress. No coat or hat. And the dog was along, but not on a leash. Sometimes she has him on a leash, sometimes not. Say, it's hell about Doc, isn't it?"

"Yeah."

"And he threatened to kill you. You're lucky, Sweeney."

"Yeah," said Sweeney.

He went outside and wondered how lucky he was going to be. It had been about five hours ago that Yolanda had left here. It was a break that she'd walked north, away from the Loop. In the Loop, it would have been impossible to trace her.

He was lucky. A block north, and thirty questions later, he found a newsboy who'd been at his stand all afternoon, and he'd seen Yolanda Lang; sure, he knew her. By sight, he explained. She'd passed him and turned west on Ohio Street.

Sweeney turned west on Ohio Street.

It wasn't too difficult. A gorgeous blonde in bright green, with a dog that looked like a fugitive from a James Oliver Curwood story. Within two blocks he found two people who had seen them.

In the third block, without turning off Ohio Street he hit the jackpot. A tobacconist had not only seen girl and dog, he had seen them enter a building across the street—the one right there, with the sign 'Furnished Rooms.'"

Sweeney entered the building with the sign that said "Furnished Rooms."

Just inside the door was a bell and a sign that said "Ring for Landlady." Sweeney rang for landlady.

She was big and slovenly; she had a mean eye. Sweet reasonableness wasn't going to work, and she didn't look as though she'd scare. Sweeney pulled out his wallet.

He took a twenty dollar bill out of it, so she could see the figure in the corner. He said, "I'd like to talk to the girl who took a room late this afternoon. The one with the dog."

She didn't even hesitate in reaching for the bill. It disappeared into the neckline of her dress, into a bosom so redundant that Sweeney wondered if she'd be able to find the bill without searching. She said, "She took a room on the second floor—the door right opposite the head of the stairs."

Sweeney said, "Thanks." He took another bill, of the same denomination, from his wallet. She reached for that one, too, but he didn't give it to her. He said, "I'm rather curious to know the circumstances; what she told you and what she's done since she came here."

"What do you want with her? Who are you?"

Sweeney said, "Okay, it doesn't matter. I'll just go up and talk to her." He started to put the second twenty back into his wallet.

She said, very quickly, "She came here late this afternoon and wanted a room. I said we didn't take dogs and she said she'd pay extra if I did and that the dog was well behaved, so I gave her the room. She didn't have any baggage. Not even a coat or hat."

"How long did she say she'd be staying?"

"She didn't know. But she said she'd pay for a full week no matter how short a time she stayed."

"How much *did* she pay you?"

She hesitated. "Twenty dollars."

Sweeney looked at her. He thought, *you bitch. And you sell her out for another twenty.* Aloud, he asked, "And since then?"

"She went out and left the dog in her room. She came back with a lot of packages. Then she took the dog down for a walk, on a leash; she hadn't had one on him before. And she was disguised; she had on a black wig and shell-rimmed glasses and a different dress. You'd have hardly knowed her."

"Was it a wig or a dye job?"

"A dye job couldn't have dried that quick."

"Anything else you can tell me about her?"

She thought a moment, but shook her head. Sweeney held out the second bill, holding it carefully so his hand wouldn't be touched by hers. He watched its course into her capacious bosom and thought that for forty dollars he wouldn't reach down there to take his two twenties back.

Something in his expression made her take a step backwards.

And that was fine; Sweeney didn't want to have to brush against her as he went by and up the stairs. Halfway up, he heard her door slam. For forty dollars, she didn't care what he wanted with her new guest. Sweeney wished he hadn't given her any money; he could have got most of that information out of her anyway. He felt ashamed of himself for having taken the easy way.

And then he stood in front of the door on the second floor at the head of the stairs, and he quit thinking about the landlady who'd directed him there.

He tapped gently at the door.

There was a rustle of movement within, and it opened a few inches. Wide eyes stared at him through shell-rimmed glasses, under black hair. But the eyes themselves he'd seen before, and often. They'd stared at him blankly through the glass of a door on State Street on a night that seemed many years ago. They'd looked at him across a table at El Madhouse. They'd looked at him from the El Madhouse stage.

And they'd looked at him from the face of a small black statuette that screamed as silently as its model had screamed noisily.

Sweeney said, "Hello, Bessie Wilson."

Her eyes widened and she gasped. But she stepped back and Sweeney walked in.

It was a small room, and dingy. It contained a bed, a dresser and a chair, but Sweeney didn't notice them. To Sweeney, the room seemed full of dog. Even though the landlady had talked about the dog, even though he himself had been thinking about it and had traced Yolanda through it, he had somehow managed to overlook the fact that Devil would be here.

But Devil was. He crouched, ready to spring at Sweeney's throat. The sound that came from deep in Devil's chest was that ominous buzzsaw sound that Sweeney had heard once before.

Yolanda said, "Quiet, Devil. Guard him." She had closed the door.

Sweeney felt something wet on his forehead. He felt something cold crawling down his back. It came to him now that he had been so interested in solving a problem that he had completely forgotten the personal danger its solution would place him in.

He stared at Yolanda Lang—at Bessie Wilson.

Even with the black wig, with the glasses, she was incredibly beautiful. Her only visible garment was a house-coat; under it, her feet were bare. The housecoat had a long zipper down the front.

Sweeney wondered if—and then realized he didn't have time to wonder. He'd better say something, anything.

He said, "I finally figured it out, Bessie, except a few details. The doctor or psychiatrist from the sanitarium near Beloit, the one who took an interest in your case after—after what happened to you at Brampton. That must have been Doc Greene—wasn't it?"

He'd have felt better if she'd answered—even to say, uselessly, that she didn't know what he was talking about— but she didn't speak.

She took off the glasses and the wig and put them on the dresser beside the door. She shook her head and her blonde hair fell again into the pageboy bob. She regarded him gravely —but silently.

Sweeney's throat felt dry. He had to clear it before he could talk. He said, "It *must* have been Greene, whether he was using that name then or not. And he fell madly in love with you. Literally madly—so insanely that he ran out on his career to be with you. Or did he get into some trouble that made him have to leave his profession anyway?

"Did you know that he sent your brother a letter telling him that you had died? He did; Charlie thinks you're dead. But Greene must have signed papers to get you out, and then quit his job to bring you to Chicago.

"He must have thought he'd cured you as nearly as you could be cured. He must have known that you'd never be fully sane, but figured that, as a psychiatrist, he could handle you and control you. And he could and did, I guess—until something that he didn't know about set you off. He was a pretty brilliant guy, Yolanda. I'll bet he did the choreography for that dance you and the dog do. And it's good, damned good. I wondered for a while why he didn't get you better bookings— but it must have been because he didn't dare risk letting you become really famous, under the circumstances. He kept you in the small time deliberately—as deliberately as he covered his real relationship to you, as doctor and patient, by becoming a bona fide agent and getting other clients."

Sweeney cleared his throat again, hoping she'd say something.

She didn't. She just looked at him. And the dog looked at him yellowly, ready to spring at the slightest word or signal from its mistress—or at the slightest move from Sweeney.

He said, "And you were all right until that day, two months ago, when you happened to go into Raoul's gift shop and bought that statuette from Lola Brent. Did you recognize that statuette, Yolanda?"

He thought she might answer that. She didn't.

He took a deep breath and the dog began to growl because his shoulders had moved. Sweeney stood very still and the dog quit growling.

He said, "Your brother Charlie made that statuette, Bessie. You were the model for it. It expressed, pretty perfectly, what you felt when—when the thing that drove you insane happened. Whether you recognized yourself in the statuette and knew that it was Charlie's work, I don't know. But seeing that statuette undid everything Doc Greene had done for you. "Only there was a *transference*. Seeing yourself—in that statuette—as a *victim,* seeing yourself in that state from the outside, you became, in your mind, the attacker. The killer with the knife.

"And the woman from whom you bought the statuette was a beautiful blonde, and your mania fixed on her. You went out and bought a knife and waited, with it in your purse, until she left to go home. And because she was fired, it wasn't a long wait. You followed her home and killed her—as the ripper in Brampton would have killed you if Charlie hadn't shot him. So—"

There wasn't anywhere to go from the "So—" and it hung there. When it got tired of hanging there, Sweeney said, "You took the statuette home and—did you make a fetish of it, Yolanda? It must have been something like that. Did you worship it, with a ritual that involved a knife? Or what?"

No answer yet, and he thought her eyes were starting to glaze a little, staring at him. He went on talking because he was afraid of what would happen when he stopped.

"And you killed twice more. Each time, a beautiful blonde. Each had passed your place on State Street just before she was killed. I'd guess that each time was just after some mystical ritual with the statuette after which you went down to the street and followed—and killed—the first woman who went by and who was blonde and beautiful, who fitted your fixation.

"And it wasn't until after that third killing that Doc Greene suddenly found out, or suddenly realized, that it was *you* who'd been doing them. He didn't know about the statuette then, but somehow he learned or realized who the Ripper was. And it scared him stiff. He would have been in a beautiful mess if the truth came out. They'd merely put you in an institution again, but Doc—I don't know exactly what grounds they'd get him on, but they'd get him plenty; they'd throw the book at him. So he tried something pretty desperate. Did you know it was he who attacked you that night, Yolanda?"

If she'd only answer—

He said, "Doc tried a really heroic cure. Shock treatment. He thought being attacked again might reverse your fixation —at least put you back into the type of insanity you had before. And *anything* would be better than having you homicidal. He probably figured he could handle anything short of homicidal insanity.

"So he attacked you that night in the hallway. Of course he wouldn't have used an ordinary knife or razor—because he didn't want to hurt you physically. What he used would have been a piece of wood, say, with a razor blade projecting out only an eighth of an inch or less, so it would make just a surface cut. And unorthodox as his psychiatry was, it worked —up to a point. If he'd known, then, about the, statuette and had hunted it up in your apartment while you were in the hospital, you might not have gone haywire again.

"But he didn't know about the statuette until after I broke the story in today's paper. He must have had a hunch all along that I was going to crack this thing, though, because he kept in touch with me, pretending he was interested in getting the Ripper caught so you'd be safe from another attack. We had a lot of fun, Doc and I. I'm sorry he's—"

Sweeney took a deep breath. He said, "But when Doc read today's paper, he learned about the statuette and saw that it was what had set you off. So he decided to get it away from you right away. He went up to your flat this afternoon with an *empty* box that would hold it. He didn't want to be seen carrying a package *out* that he hadn't brought *in;* he didn't want anyone who might be watching your place to wonder what was in the package. He was still gambling his life to save you, and this time he lost.

"He found the statuette—in your dresser or closet or wherever you kept it—and the knife with it. He'd both of them in his hands, and the sight of him touching your fetish threw you into—well, you sicked Devil on him, and Devil killed him."

Sweeney glanced down at Devil, and wished he hadn't.

He looked back at Bessie Wilson. He said, "You didn't know for sure whether he was dead or not, down there in the courtyard and you didn't know what he'd tell the police if he wasn't, so you ran. But he didn't tell on you, Yolanda. Instead —because he knew he was dying—the damn fool took the rap for you; he said *he* was the Ripper. He must have thought, or at least hoped, that once the statuette was broken and you didn't have it any more, you'd be all right again, even without him."

He stared at her and opened his mouth to ask the Sixty-five dollar question—*Are you? Are you all right now?*

But he didn't have to ask it, because the answer was there, in her eyes.

Madness.

Her right hand fumbled for the tab of the zipper of her housecoat, found it, zipped downward. It fell down in a circle about her bare feet. Sweeney caught his breath a little, just as he had that night when he had looked through the glass into the hallway.

Reaching behind her, she opened the top left drawer of the dresser felt inside it. Her hand came out holding a knife, a brand-new eight-inch carving knife.

A nude high priestess holding the sacrificial knife.

Sweeney sweated. He started to raise his hands and the dog growled and crouched before he'd moved them an inch. He quit moving them.

He made his voice quiet and steady. "Don't, Yolanda. I'm not the one you want to kill. I'm not blonde or beautiful. I'm not a prototype of Bessie Wilson who was attacked by a maniac—"

He was watching her eyes and it came to him that she didn't understand a word he was saying by now, that the connection had broken, just when he did not know. Yet she had started a step forward when he had stopped speaking and had stood still, the knife in her hand and ready—but words, the sound of his voice, had arrested her in mid-step. Words, not what he said, but the fact that he was talking—

Her foot was moving again, the knife coming up. Again Sweeney took the mere ghost of a backward step, and again the dog growled and crouched to spring at his throat.

"Four score and seven years ago," Sweeney said, "our fathers brought forth on this continent a new nation, conceived in liberty and dedicated to the proposition that all men are created equal . . ."

Yolanda stood still again, an almost cataleptic stillness.

Sweat was running down Sweeney's sides, from his armpits. He said, "Now we are engaged in a great civil war, testing whether—uh—that nation— That's all I remember. Mary had a little lamb; its fleece was white as snow . . ."

He finished Mary and the lamb, hit high spots of the *Rubaiyat,* Hamlet's soliloquy. After a while he remembered that he could repeat himself, and after another while he found that—if he did it a sixteenth of an inch at a time—he could ease his way back toward the wall behind him and, finally, lean against it.

But he couldn't move, even a sixteenth of an inch, toward the door or toward Yolanda. He couldn't raise his hands.

And after a time—a long time—his voice was so tired he couldn't talk any more. But he kept on talking anyway. If he stopped talking for as much as ten seconds he was going to die.

Sweeney could tell from the one small window of the room, on the side opposite from the wall he leaned against that it was dark outside. Years later a clock somewhere tolled midnight. Centuries after that, the window began to get light again.

". . . Beneath a spreading chestnut tree," said Sweeney hoarsely, "the village smithy stands. The smith, a mighty man is he, beneath the spreading chestnut tree. A rose by any other name would waste its fragrance on the desert air, and all our yesterdays have lighted fools the way to dusty death. And when the pie was opened, they all began to sing . . ."

Every muscle of his body ached. He marveled, with what was left of his mind, at how Yolanda could stand there—incredibly beautiful, incredibly naked—and not move at all. Catalepsy, of course, hypnosis, whatever you called it, it was hard to believe—

". . . Alas, poor Yorick!" said Sweeney. "I knew him,

Horatio: a fellow of infinite jest, of most excellent—uh— The owl and the pussycat went to sea, in a beautiful pea green boat . . ."

It got lighter, slowly. It was nine o'clock in the morning before there was a knock at the door. An authoritative knock.

Sweeney raised his voice, with as much effort as it would have taken him to raise a piano. It was a hoarse croak. "Bline? Come in with your gun ready. The dog will jump one of us."

The dog, growling, had moved to a position where he could watch both Sweeney and the knocked-on door. But the door moved and Sweeney didn't, and the dog jumped at Bline, in the doorway. But Bline had been warned; his coat was wrapped around his forearm, and as the dog leaped and closed its jaws on the coat, the barrel of Bline's pistol tapped the dog's skull.

"'The mouse ran up the clock,'" Sweeney was saying in a voice that wasn't much above a hoarse whisper; "'the clock struck one— Thank Heaven you finally came, Cap. I knew you'd see holes in Doc's story when you had time to think it out and that you'd come looking for Yolanda and get to her the same way I did. Listen, Cap, I have to keep on talking and I can't stop. She isn't even looking at you and doesn't know what's going on except that if I stop talking— Walk up on her from that side and get the knife—"

Bline got the knife. Sweeney, still mumbling hoarsely, slid slowly down the wall.

~§~

And then it was late evening. Godfrey was there on the park bench and Sweeney sat down beside him. "Thought you were working," God said.

"I was. But I broke such a big story Wally let me talk him into getting off a while without pay. A week, two weeks, or whenever I get back."

"You sound hoarse, Sweeney. Did you spend a night with that dame you were raving about?"

"That's why I'm hoarse," said Sweeney. "Listen, God this

time I left money, quite a bit of money, with my landlady. But I held out three hundred. Do you think we can get drunk on three hundred bucks?"

God turned his shaggy head to look at Sweeney. "If we want to badly enough. If you want something badly enough, you can get anything you want, Sweeney. Like spending a night with that dame. I told you you could."

Sweeney shuddered.

He pulled two flat pint bottles out of the side pockets of his coat and handed one of them to God . . .

Bruin Asylum
Make Your Reservations Today!

The Witching Night
  C. S. Cody – Booking Now
A Garden Lost in Time
  Jonathan Aycliffe – Booking Now
The Fungus
  Harry Adam Knight – Booking Now
I Am Your Brother
  G. S. Marlowe – Booking Now
Dr. Mabuse
  Norbert Jacques – Booking Now
Walpole's Fantastic Tales, Volume I
  Hugh Walpole – Booking Now
The Magician (Expanded Edition)
  W. Somerset Maugham – early 2017